Prodigal Son

PRODIGAL SON

GREGG HURWITZ

THORNDIKE PRESS
A part of Gale, a Cengage Company

Copyright © 2020 by Gregg Hurwitz.
An Orphan X Novel.
Thorndike Press, a part of Gale, a Cengage Company.

Thorndike Press® Large Print Core.
The text of this Large Print edition is unabridged.
Other aspects of the book may vary from the original edition.
Set in 16 pt. Plantin.

LIBRARY OF CONGRESS CIP DATA ON FILE.
CATALOGUING IN PUBLICATION FOR THIS BOOK
IS AVAILABLE FROM THE LIBRARY OF CONGRESS.

ISBN-13: 978-1-4328-8542-7 (hardcover alk. paper)

Published in 2021 by arrangement with St. Martin's Publishing Group

Printed in Mexico
Print Number: 01   Print Year: 2021

For Marshall Herskovitz

*From whom I learned that the top
of the alpha dominance hierarchy
is still beneath the lowest level of
what constitutes wisdom*

Hast thou only one blessing, father?

— Esau, Genesis 27:38

This thing of darkness I acknowledge mine.

— Prospero

1
A NEW BRAND OF DANGER

A stir moves through the Pride House Group Home, and seconds later adolescent faces pig against the muggy front window. Evan, at twelve, still has not hit his growth spurt. He jockeys for position and loses, Charles Van Sciver's elbow knocking him to the rear of the pack. A tiny gap opens between Tyrell and Jamal, and Evan catches a fleeting glimpse of a slender man disappearing around the fence of the cracked basketball courts across the street. The conversation wafts back at him.

"Well? Was that the guy?"

"I dunno, Charles. *Looks* like him."

"Real helpful, shitbird."

The herd is unsupervised, which is never good. Papa Z, the sturdy Polish-American house father, has retired to the bathroom with the *Baltimore Sun*. The fact that it's a Sunday edition, paired with his chronic and oft-referenced constipation, means he could be missing for hours.

Van Sciver leads the way, naturally, as they spill out of their gone-to-hell row house in the shadow of the high-rise Lafayette Courts projects. They reach the asphalt park and spread out, only seven kids today because Danny got yanked into juvie and Andre's been missing since Friday, no doubt on another fantasy quest looking for the parents he never knew. Nothing to see but brick and concrete, sweaty in the August humidity, and the usual junkies and corner boys. Cookie-cutter row houses stare back from all sides like crooked teeth.

"I *swear* it was him again," Tyrell says.

The boys are adrenalized by the Mystery Man's reappearance. He materializes at intervals, eyeing the boys as they strut and roughhouse in the park, the sun glinting off his gold watch. Masked by black Ray-Bans, he smokes through his pack with conveyor-belt efficiency, and when he finally moves, he walks at a leisurely pace, his fingers skating along the chain-link. The theories are endless — he's a weenie-wagger; he's a real-estate tycoon from Streeterville looking to adopt; he's a cannibal who subsists on young flesh.

Van Sciver circles them up. "Get over here. Everyone over here!"

The blue bandanna is cinched around his forehead as always, his reddish blond bangs falling over the band of fabric. He's a head taller than everyone except Ramón, but Ramón's built like a skeleton so the height doesn't get him much respect. Van Sciver wears a sleeveless Washington Redskins shirt to show off his biceps, which bulge enough to have grooves in them already. His upper lip sports a few scraggly hairs and a dried smear of the protein muscle drink he downs religiously every morning, mixed powder from the canister he painstakingly saves up for each month, the canister the other kids dare not touch.

Though he's just two years older than Evan, they might as well be different species. They've tangled only twice, Van Sciver bloodying Evan's nose when Evan stood up to him for cheating at blackjack, and splitting his lip for backing Tyrell, whose sister *is* a whore but who probably doesn't need to be reminded of it as often as Van Sciver thinks he does. Van Sciver came into the home when his dad got nailed for a bank heist, which makes him royalty in this zip code. A few coveted photographs and a yellowed newspaper clipping confirm his provenance.

Evan on the other hand is without the benefit of a rousing lineage. He simply *appeared* like something mythical — Moses in a basket of pitch-darkened bulrushes, Athena springing

11

fully formed from the brow of Zeus. From various social workers, he'd gleaned only the barest facts about his origin. That his birth mother had traveled from out of state to turn him over for adoption in Maryland when he was six days old. That his first adoptive mother had been debilitated by a series of strokes she'd kept secret, right up until she and her overwhelmed husband had dropped Evan back into the system. Since Evan's birth mother had retained the right to select the adoptive family, his fate was frozen while social services tried to locate her. But young women who travel out of state to relinquish newborns don't want to be identified, let alone found. By the time the bureaucracy had unsnarled itself sufficiently to declare him "abandoned," he'd knocked around a series of homes. Even by the time he was four years old, his face had grown guarded, no longer a blank slate upon which a couple could project their dreams. He had a whiff of inferiority about him, another kid fit for the damaged-goods bin.

Papa Z's group home is the latest stop on the merry-go-round. Five to fifteen kids on perennial rotation, graduating to trade school or jail or jobs involving wrenches and name-patch coveralls. The choices are few, the outcomes predetermined, the tracks laid pointing to a dismal future. That is what is so intriguing about the Mystery Man and his gold watch, no matter how awful his intentions may be. He does not belong to this world, to these city blocks. He represents not just a new brand of danger but a new road to a new place, and any route out of East Baltimore is a good one.

Van Sciver says, "I talked to Eddie in Paco's garage who talked to his cousin who said the Mystery Man takes kids and turns them into something."

Turns them into something. But *what*? The only point of reference Evan has for this comes from the army recruiting office across from the arcade in the mall. In between rounds checking the video-game change slots for forgotten quarters, he and Tyrell watch the slouchy teenagers go through that glass door bearing the decal of the American flag. They always come out a little straighter.

They come out men.

Ramón's voice cuts through Evan's reverie. "Turns them into sex-slave dicksuckers," he says, and a few kids risk snickers.

But Van Sciver continues, undeterred. "Eddie's cousin? He said he knew a guy came up in a Westside home — New Beginnings? — and *that* guy said the Mystery Man picked another kid, the *best* kid, out of the group. The tallest. The fastest. The *strongest.* And *that* kid? One day he just *vanished.*" He draws out the pause, the boys huddling closer, still breathing audibly from their dash across the street. Now it's no longer a story but an urban legend, a campfire ghost story, and somehow that makes it *more* real. Evan senses some dark truth in the spaces between the lies. Van Sciver has let the cliffhanger linger long enough. Conspiratorially, he looks left, right, then back at the group. "Four years later he came back. For a day."

A block or two over, a car is blaring Run-DMC with the bass cranked up high. The sound fades. Tyrell's sneaker scrapes the asphalt as he leans in even closer. *"And?"*

"He was *built,*" Van Sciver says. "Muscles like this. And badass. Had a scar across his cheek. And a Porsche."

The details are delicious, tantalizing. Evan's stomach pitches with excitement, as if he's in roller-coaster free fall.

A wino shuffles by tangentially, and Van Sciver shoots him a hostile glare. "Get the fuck outta here, Horace." Back to his captive crowd. "This guy, he said he went to a house — best house ever. A *real* home. Hot meals three times a day and Nintendo and a pool. You get your *own* room. Said they trained him."

"To do what?" Evan asks.

14

Van Sciver has to look down to meet his eyes. "No one knows."

2
SERIOUS BUSINESS

Sixty-five motherfucking dollars.

That's all it costs to jar your life off track. No — not just off track. Pile-driven into the side of a mountain like a locomotive blasted off the rails.

That's why Andrew Duran was here working the midnight shift at an impound lot on the East Side, crammed into a booth not much bigger than a doghouse, breathing in the overpowering scent of Old Spice deodorant from Juan, who worked the shift before him. Minimum wage put Duran at $420 a week, but by the time federal, state, Social Security, Medicare, and wage garnishment took a bite outta him, it looked more like $300 out the back end. Which was about $500 less than what he needed to pay for child support and food and a roof over his head, but then again he could be a broke-ass beggar selling smoked-down cigarette butts in Calcutta, so he tried not to complain.

Perspective.

That's what they talked about on all them self-help podcasts. That's what they talked about in the meetings, too. *There but for the grace of God. One day at a time. Nothing's so bad a drink won't make it worse.*

Clichés, sure, but he'd lost enough already not heeding them. He'd lost everything.

He sighed and stared through the grease-smudged window, king of all he surveyed. Which at the moment was a labyrinth of smashed-to-hell impound vehicles — rusting VW Bugs, wrecked Ferraris, twisted American muscle. Some had blood spatter on the headrests. Others had claw marks scouring the paint jobs at the trunks where the drug dogs got after it. A few, missing wheels, had been hauled in here on the back of a trailer and left for dead.

Duran's job was to watch over them and sign off on a confusion of forms when cops or tow-truck drivers or beleaguered owners came to claim them.

Cerebral work, this.

How he'd gotten here from owning his own home — even a shitty-ass one-bedroom in the city of El Sereno — he'd never know. Wait, scratch that. He did know.

Sixty-five motherfucking dollars.

For a motherfucking parking ticket he got in the twenty seconds when he ran inside a liquor store to get change for the meter. He'd stopped for lunch in Bakersfield on his way to visit his homey in Kern Valley State Prison eighteen months back. Twenty seconds was all it took.

Duran couldn't pay it 'cuz he'd promised Brianna he'd hit the child-support mark that month for Sofia, who was turning eleven and needed better clothes for middle school. Which she deserved, 'cuz, shit, she drew the short straw when she got him as a daddy, so the least he could try'n do was help Bri get her some shirts from Walmart instead of the Salvation Army so the kids wouldn't make fun of her the way he got made fun of his whole damn childhood.

So he'd spent the sixty-five bucks on his daughter instead of on the Bakersfield Department of Transportation. And a few weeks later when he was pulled over for a broke taillight ($25 fine, $2 surcharge, $35 court dismissal fee, $115 parts and labor to actually fix the piece of shit), he got another surprise when the cop ran the plates. An outstanding warrant. Turned out that Johnny Mac, Duran's supervisor on the roof-inspection gig, had put on a half dozen parking tickets when he'd borrowed Duran's car for lunch runs, and he'd torn up every last one like the Irish fuck he was. On top of that shit, Duran learned he'd already missed a court date he didn't even know he had, and failure to appear was serious business, even if it was for Johnny Mac's tickets.

The cop wrote up every last late fee, every penalty assessment, every vehicle-code infraction, the accrued fines tripling and tripling till they had more zeros than the national deficit.

Duran felt himself slumping in the driver's seat, a punch-drunk boxer on a ring-corner stool. "This is some bullshit," he muttered. "I was on my way to fix it."

"You're one of those, huh?" the cop said. "Nothing's ever your fault?"

"Nope," Duran said. "I make plenty of mistakes, just like everyone else. But guys like me don't catch a break when they need it."

The cop tore off the sheaf of tickets, handed them through the window, then breathed out a breath that smelled like Tic Tacs. "Ah," he said, smiling with his shiny white teeth. "Lemme guess. I'm a racist, right?"

"No," Duran said, "I'm thinking you're enough of a asshole to do this to rich white dudes, too."

19

That didn't go over so hot.

The courtroom was packed to the gills, all body heat and working-class weariness, the judge hammering through her docket. Duran's was the seventeenth case that hour.

He had some scrawled notes he'd prepared from late-night online searches, but ever since childhood courthouses had made him nervous. His hands were sweaty enough to make the ink run, and the judge was exhausted and impatient, and he couldn't really blame her, 'cuz he was stuttering like a idiot and she had a million more cases to get through before lunch.

She'd imposed a civil judgment, the statute getting an upgrade from an infraction to a misdemeanor, and his only real option to clear the warrant was to go to jail. Turns out it was pay-to-stay up in those parts — $100 booking fee, $50 each day inside. A week to get out meant a fat hotel bill and enough missed appointments for Johnny Mac to fire his ass, and in the meantime them parking tickets kept gobbling up interest and penalties like Pac-Man snarfing him some dots.

When Duran hit the outside, he scrambled for work, took whatever he could find. They garnished his wages, but he swore he'd only let that eat into him and not Sofia. For the income he sublet his tiny little house in El Sereno to a Korean businessman who was barely ever in the country but whose checks never bounced. Then Duran sold his car for more cash and rented a not-to-code room above a Chinese kitchen. He mailed a check every month to Brianna with a note to use it well for his little girl.

Who he was too ashamed to see.

Living where he was in a place no social worker would approve for visitation. Dressing like he did. Smelling like he did, the stink of General Tso's chicken seeping up through the floorboards at all hours. He could hardly stand to look in the mirror. He couldn't imagine what he would look like to Sofia. He'd been through a lot, but he thought if his little girl looked at him with disgust — or worse, pity — it just might break him for good.

Sofia begged to see him — Bri angrily recounted every last tear for him in their monthly call. And he wanted nothing in the world more than to see her. But something stopped him. An invisible hand on his shoulder, keeping him from stepping forward. That familiar voice in his ear, whispering, *You ain't good enough.*

You don't deserve it.

Not until he paid off the last $775 he

owed in fines. Till he moved back into his house like he was his own man and fixed up a proper bed for his little girl to sleep in. Till he saved enough to show up with a properly wrapped toy and take her out for a meal and not worry about if she ordered a soda or got a appetizer, too.

Six months had turned into a year and now a year and change, and he caught himself wondering if he'd be able to face his little girl at all — if she even *was* still a little girl. Wondering if his shame and pride had already cost him everything. She couldn't know he was scraping by and washing his sheets in the sink with hand soap so he could honor his child support. She couldn't know he thought about her every waking minute of the day.

She probably felt abandoned. And rightly so.

He knew that feeling, too, knew it in his gut. It was an old song, calling to him from shore, luring him into the jagged rocks.

His stomach grumbled. A Three Musketeers bar from the cabinet cost fifty cents. He kept most of his money in a zippered pouch because fuck ATM fees. He unzipped it now, counted out the change, and left it in the dish. He knew by heart how much he had in the pouch — $147.85 minus one

Three Musketeers bar with the employee discount would leave him with $147.35.

He chewed the chocolaty nougat and thought of the smell of Sofia's head when she was a newborn. How he'd held her in the hospital first 'cuz Bri was whacked out from the C-section. Sofia had fit right in his arms, that warm tiny body snug between his elbows and wrists when he held her out before him on his lap. Looking down at her, he thought he'd finally done one right thing in this life.

All at once the security monitors on the north wall of the doghouse kiosk turned to fuzz.

They'd never gone out before. He slapped the side of the nearest monitor a few times as if that might help. Then he leaned over and checked the cord connections, but they all looked good.

He was so distracted that he didn't notice the two people who had walked up to the service window till they were standing right in front of him.

The dude had a thin manicured beard and a high-fashion suit like you wouldn't believe — some kind of not-quite-velvet with dark blue strips lining the lapels and a handkerchief to match. Duran's two-sizes-too-big security uniform, made more humiliating by the contrast, itched as he regarded the man. Homey looked like he belonged on a red carpet somewhere instead of a East Side impound lot. He was built too — not a swole prison body but like he spent plenty of time in one of them CrossFit gyms where they jump around and swing kettlebells like circus monkeys.

The woman at his side looked equally out of place here, all shiny and new. The organizing principle of her life seemed to be the color red. Red nails, a red hair scrunchie, red pumps, red lipstick, red buckle on her satchel briefcase. Fluffy blond hair like cotton candy.

Duran was so taken aback he needed a moment to find his voice. "Help you?"

"I hope so." The man's voice was slightly too high, almost feminine, and it sure as shit didn't match his alpha-dog bearing or the way he filled out that suit. "We're trying to find the man who belongs to that truck." He spoke properly, but there was a street cadence beneath the words that Duran knew all too well. It was like the guy had listened to a bunch of rich people on TV and was doing his best to imitate them.

Dude gave a nod to a Bronco at the end of the nearest row. Crumpled grille, bashed front panel, wires snarled out from the shattered mouth of the headlight.

Duran hoisted his eyebrows. Out of the corner of his eye, he could see the black-and-white dots dancing on the security monitors. "You don't look like no Marshals Service."

"I know," the woman said sympathetically. "That's the point."

She had a full face of makeup and was attractive at first glance, but Duran got the sense that she looked like a different human when that mask was wiped off.

"Jake Hargreave is his name," Mr. Slick said. "The man who belongs to that Bronco. There was a shoot-out on the 110, and he crashed and abandoned the vehicle. You can see why it's a necessity for us to talk with him."

The man produced a badge and held it out for Duran to see, but Duran didn't know what he should be looking at, so he just tugged at his chin and frowned as if this answered everything.

The woman unbuckled her briefcase and removed an envelope. "We pay our confidential informants," she said. "For tips."

She counted ten hundreds from the envelope onto the counter, fanning them like a casino cashier's cards. Duran could feel his eyes bulging. A grand meant he'd be out from under those loans. Free and clear. That he could find his way back to his house. And then to his daughter.

The woman gathered up the bills, tapped them once on the counter to align them, and slid them into the envelope again. Neat little magic trick, making all that cash disappear.

The man ran his thumb and forefinger around his mouth, smoothing down the glistening chestnut facial hair. "Owners require an appointment to claim their vehicle, is that correct?"

Duran said, "Don't know if they *require* it, but pretty much everyone calls first to make sure their car's here, yeah."

"When the man sets up his appointment to claim the car, we'd appreciate a heads-up," the woman said. She raised the envelope, gave it a shake for emphasis, and put it back in her satchel briefcase. "We can take it from there."

"Why don't you just pull the files?" Duran said. "If you're Marshals Service. Track him down your own selves?"

"We have," the man said, that thin, reedy voice unexpected each time out. "He's gone to ground. But he needs his truck." He was smiling again, like he was the most pleasant guy in the world. "And we need *him.*"

Duran realized he was sweating. Like his body knew something his mind couldn't grasp.

The man cocked his head. Not meeting Duran's gaze, but focusing lower, the just-missed eye contact unsettling. "You broke your jaw," he told Duran. "When you were a child."

Duran's hand rose reflexively, touching the spot where a punch had cracked the bone. It was just a hairline, treated with a bag of frozen peas and a paper cup to drool into, and it had left no visible imperfection. At least that's what Duran had always thought.

"A closed fracture," the man continued, his eyes lasering in. "Up by the temporo-mandibular joint. Must've hurt something awful."

Duran didn't like the look in the guy's eyes. Like he was hungry.

Duran forced a swallow, his throat suddenly dry.

The man finally broke off his gaze, jotted down a phone number on a blank slip of paper, and handed it to Duran. "Carrot or stick," he told Duran with that amicable smile. "You get to choose."

They turned and walked out of the yard.

As soon as they cleared the outer fence,

the security feeds blinked back online. Either those deputy marshals had some mage-level government tech skills or it was a helluva coincidence.

Duran looked at the monitors, showing nothing now but the empty lot and the midnight mist creeping in. It thickened up until the city lights winked off, until the cars barely peeked out like boulders on some desolate mountaintop. He chewed his lip and thought about the bizarre woman and the guy staring at his jaw with that odd expression. He thought about what the U.S. Marshals Service could do to him if he didn't cooperate. He thought about that thousand dollars.

They needed his help. No — they'd demanded it.

Okay, he thought.

Why not? he thought.

What's the worst that could happen?

3
WHITTLED DOWN TO
USELESSNESS

A week later Evan is awakened by a foot in his chest. It is nothing personal. As the smallest kid, he sleeps on the mattress between the bunk beds, and this is what happens. His eyes open to a slow-motion stampede. Andre, back from another fruitless parent search, is the only one who bothers to whisper an apology.

The others are rushing quietly to the doorway, peering around the jamb with a sort of thrilled terror. The frame itself is crosshatched with countless height markers that Papa Z notched with his pocketknife this summer, another endeavor whittled down to uselessness given the turnover rates of the boys. Evan crawls over; the only space left at the doorjamb is floor-level.

From his snail's-eye view down the long hall, he catches a partial angle of Papa Z embedded in his venerable armchair, one meaty fist clamped around a Coors tallboy. His face and neck are splotchy red; it is not the first beer of the evening.

A hushed voice emanates from the space across from him, over by the shit-brown corduroy couch with the missing cushion. "—can only take one right now. Sure it's a way out. But he needs to show an ability to perform."

"Charles has that," Papa Z confirms. He draws again from the sweating can, his tree-trunk throat glugging up and down.

Van Sciver has gone stiff in the doorway. Evan can sense him above, as tense as a dog pointing to prey.

Jamal whispers, "Is that . . . ?"

"The Mystery Man," Ramón confirms before Van Sciver hushes them viciously.

"Charles seems the most likely," the hushed voice says. "Or the other one. Andre."

Andre pulls his head back slightly.

Down the hall Papa Z wipes his lips. "What about Evan?"

They strain to make out the Mystery Man's voice. "The little one?"

"Yup."

"Too small."

"But *willful*," Papa Z says. "So willful."

"Nah," Mystery Man says. "The little one's no good."

Muted sneers rain down on Evan. Then

cease instantly as the weary floorboards of the living room creak.

Mystery Man steps into view, a facial profile over bony shoulders. Two slender fingers clamp a business card, extended to Papa Z. That gold watch glints. The Ray-Bans are on, even inside, even at night.

"Have Charles Van Sciver call," he says.

The boys creep back to bed, buzzed on adrenaline. Whispered theories and dirty jokes fly back and forth.

"I'm gonna do it," Van Sciver says. "Whatever the fuck it is, I'm gonna do it."

"How 'bout Andre?" Ramón asks. "Mystery Man got his eye on him, too."

"Oh, no, sir," Van Sciver says. "Andre's gonna move in with his mom and pop. Just as soon as he finds 'em. Ain't that right, Andre?"

"What do you say, Dr. Dre?" Tyrell says. "You find your daddy this time?"

Assorted guffaws.

Andre doesn't bother to look up from his spiral notebook, the one he draws in constantly, sketches of superheroes and soldiers and curvy girls. He hates being called Dr. Dre, almost as much as he hates being called Dre-Dre or his middle name, some crazy-ass biblical word written on his birth certificate that even he doesn't know how to pronounce. The home is a perpetual testing ground, every insecurity exposed, every vulnerability jabbed until it broke you or you broke it.

"Least my sister ain't no whore," Andre says. Tyrell's eyes widen, white against his shiny dark skin. "Least I know who my family is, bitch."

Ramón laughs, claps his hands quietly, his skinny arms so thin they look like they might snap from the impact. "Always good to know 'zactly who don't want you."

"You wait and see, fools," Andre says, his hand never slowing, the pencil scratching calmingly against paper. "Mystery Man's gonna choose me, 'cuz he got some taste. Then I'll drive a big-ass Cadillac and move to Cali. They got palm trees and shit and blond girls with juicy booties who Rollerblade in bikinis all day long."

Evan thinks about Cali and palm trees and Rollerblading blondes, Andre's fantasy weaving into his until it's one big tapestry way up out of reach.

He waits silently until the voices quiet, until the sounds of breathing turn uniform, until the room is still.

Then he creeps out of bed and down the hall toward the blaring TV. Papa Z is snoring operatically, his last Coors nestled in his crotch. Evan peers at the business card balanced on the arm of the chair next to the remote. At first he does not understand.

The card is solid black.

But then a commercial interrupts the *Doogie Howser* rerun and the changing glow casts the card in a different light. Visible only now, matte black against glossy black, are ten digits. A hidden phone number.

Leaning for a better angle, hands on his knees, Evan commits it to memory.

He swivels back toward the hall, his face nearly colliding with Van Sciver's chest.

The bigger boy stands perfectly still, arms crossed, blue bandanna perfectly in place. "Don't even *think* about it," he says. His lips move, but his teeth stay clenched, and a snakelike vein swells in the side of his neck.

Papa Z stirs. "Boys? What's the problem?"

Van Sciver offers a wide grin. "No problem at all, sir."

"Who is this?"

"Not Charles Van Sciver."

"I figured that. What do you want?"

"What do *you* want?"

"Where'd you get this number?"

"On the card you left."

"I told him not to give it to anyone else."

"He didn't. I sneaked a look."

Silence. Then, "The park around the block with the outdoor handball courts. Last one on

33

the south side. Behind the wall. Tomorrow at noon."

Click.

Evan rounds the handball wall, the weight of the shade falling across him. The Mystery Man is over at the fence, smoking, those slender fingers tangled in the chain-link. He looks up, and his face flickers with disdain. "You?"

He strolls over. Suddenly Evan is acutely aware of how isolated they are here behind the last court on the south side. They face a glass-strewn alley and a burned building, the one that went down when Jalilah's nana fell asleep smoking a blunt. The only sign of life is a black sedan parked at the edge of the asphalt plane, angled directly at them. The windows are tinted. All of them, even the windshield. Evan figures it might be the Mystery Man's car, though no one has ever seen the guy drive.

Then again, no one has ever seen the Mystery Man this close. Sallow features, wispy hair, face unshaven enough that it seems a statement, not an oversight. He flicks his cigarette butt with a practiced air as he nears Evan.

Evan feels his heartbeat tick up a notch, his rib cage *bump-bump-bumping* against his worn-thin T-shirt. In the approaching Ray-Bans, he sees his twinning reflections, small and pathetic. He clears his throat to speak.

The Mystery Man backhands him.

Not with full force, but not holding back either. The blow snaps Evan's head on the stalk of his neck, spins him down onto all fours, a cord of crimson-lined drool connecting his lower lip to the asphalt.

The voice comes from behind and over him. "Lesson one. Be ready. Now, get the fuck outta here."

The static clears from Evan's vision by degrees. He stands up, wipes his lip. "What's lesson two?"

Mystery Man swallows, surprised. He glances over at the dark sedan, and for the first time Evan senses nervousness in his body language. And Evan realizes: The car *doesn't* belong to the Mystery Man.

The Mystery Man hesitates, as if trying to read the dark windshield. Then he shakes his head with disgust. "All right. You want another shot? Tomorrow. Same time, same place."

As Evan runs home, the shame burns out of him at last, hot tracks down his face. Van Sciver is waiting in the bedroom and no one else. Word has spread. He holds his belt, looped once, the ends clenched in his wide fist.

He says, "We never finished that conversation last night."

4
NEXT-LEVEL DEEP SHIT

Two weeks later Duran had almost forgotten about the pair of deputy marshals who'd breezed in at the midnight hour and asked him to keep tabs on the owner of that banged-up Bronco. Built dude with the squeaky voice and that woman done to a turn, all long red nails and fluffy hair — it was like he dreamed them up.

But the call jogged his memory.

Jake Hargreave phoning up to ask about his truck. He had a husky voice and a shifty temperament, and Duran could understand why he had the Marshals Service on his tail. And yes, he wanted to come now, at half past two in the morning, which seemed a sketchy time for a dude to want to reclaim his ride.

Duran reviewed the paperwork. "Okay," he said. "But I don't see how you're gonna drive it outta here, condition it's in."

"Why don't you let me worry about that,"

Hargreave said, and cut the line.

Duran unzipped his pouch — $128.95 — and took out that phone number the deputy with the high-pitched voice had scrawled down. Staring at it, he chewed his bottom lip. Something felt wrong. But it felt just as wrong to *not* call.

For all Duran knew, Hargreave was a Ten Most Wanted fugitive, and contacting the authorities right now was the only way to stop him from shooting up a mall or *Silence of the Lambs*-ing some lady in a basement well.

Plus, the thousand dollars.

Which was pretty much all that was standing between him and his little girl, who was becoming less little every day his sorry ass couldn't get his shit together.

He dialed.

A woman picked up. "U.S. Marshals Service." In the background he could hear music playing, Rihanna asking some lucky fool to stand under her umbrella, ella, ella.

"Hi . . . uh. I was asked to call this number —"

Rihanna cut off abruptly. Then the woman said, "Yes, that was us."

Now he recognized the voice: Ms. Red.

It occurred to him that neither of the deputies had given him their names. Looking down at the scrap of paper, he wondered why they hadn't left an official business card.

But the conversation was already proceeding without him.

"Well?" she repeated impatiently.

"Sorry," he said. "What?"

"I said, did the owner of the Bronco call?"

Duran thought about how the security feeds had gone to static when the deputies made their appearance and then magically restored themselves after they'd exited the yard.

"Mr. Duran," she said firmly.

He felt himself sweating. He hadn't given her his name. Ms. Red had clearly done some digging in the federal databases.

"Yeah," he heard himself saying. "Yeah, he did."

"He's coming in to get it now?"

"That's right."

The line clicked off.

Perspiration cooled on the side of Duran's face. He set the phone down on the counter and stared at it. The chill of the yard crept into the kiosk, fogging the window. The November wind kicked up, howling through the hull of a burned-out Mustang.

From its spot in the nearest row, the Bronco stared back at him.

He recalled the male deputy's words: *He needs his truck. And we need him.*

Why did Jake Hargreave need his truck?

Duran got out of the kiosk, stepping onto ground crusted with broken glass. The toe of his sneaker caught a smashed bottle cap, sent it skittering across the asphalt.

Approaching the truck, he shone his flashlight through the spiderwebbed windshield. A scattering of safety glass across the dashboard. A plastic parking permit hooked over the rearview mirror, along with a bouquet of Little Tree air fresheners. A dark smudge on the black webbing of the seat belt — dried blood?

The driver's door was caved in, but the rear gave with a creak. Duran searched the backseat, the cargo area, the floorboards — nothing but a few more glass pebbles and a stray quarter. He crawled through to check the glove box. Totally empty.

Someone had been thorough.

Duran backed out and squatted, chewing his lip.

He felt out of alignment, a snow-globe storm of instincts and impressions flurrying inside him, refusing to settle. Every time he reached for a thought, it twirled away, lost to the squall.

Rising, he cracked his back and decided

to patrol the property to clear his head. He passed a motorcycle with a pancaked front wheel that had undoubtedly cost a life or two. He passed a forty of King Cobra, a crumpled paper bag slumped around the bottle's midsection like a skirt. He passed the hole in the chain-link that the possums were fond of sneaking through, pale vagabonds with marble eyes.

Behind him the motion-activated light in the kiosk clicked off, bathing the lot in semidarkness. He pulled the company Maglite from his pocket and clicked it on. Weaving through the dark outer edges of the labyrinth, he let the flashlight pick across all those vehicles. Cracked windshields fragmented the beam, sent it kaleidoscoping across the rows of battered cars. Atop the chain-link fence, security cams peered down at intervals, robots noting his progress. The whole scene felt eerie and otherworldly, an urban landscape from a dystopian future.

He wondered what kind of deputy marshal was up at 2:30 A.M. listening to Rihanna.

No business cards. The woman who'd answered the phone generically, still not giving up a name. The dude with the crazy voice and the crazier suit. Duran had seen plenty of deputy marshals, but never one who dressed like that.

He finally pinned down the suspicion fluttering beneath all the noise.

What if they weren't deputy marshals at all?

He stopped at the far edge of the lot. Clicked off his flashlight. Stood in the darkness to let the full weight of his misgivings land.

He cursed himself for not digging deeper before now. Had he not wanted to admit that something felt wrong? After all, they'd offered him a thousand reasons to deceive himself.

He took the slip of paper from where he'd crammed it in his pocket and stared at the digits. He didn't want to check. Not at all.

But he had to.

He called information, asked to be put through to the Marshals Service office downtown.

Dispatch answered, a woman with a pack-a-day voice who sounded not entirely awake.

"Yeah, hi," he said. "I was given a phone number by a deputy who . . . uh, might not have been a deputy. If I read it to you, can you tell me if . . . uh, if it's real?"

"I can't disclose any phone numbers of federal employees," she said.

"Right. I get that. I'm giving *you* a number." He rattled it off quickly, before she could cut him off. "I just need to know if it's someone impersonating one of you guys. Before I give up any classified information."

She grunted. Said nothing.

But he could hear the keyboard rattling away.

In the ensuing pause, a set of headlights swept into the lot way across the maze of wrecked cars, throwing wild shadows over the twisted metal. He couldn't see the vehicle, not directly, just the refracted beams needling through the gloom.

He felt his heartbeat kick up a notch, fluttering the side of his neck. The vehicle crept toward the heart of the yard.

"I'm sorry, sir, but that number isn't registered to the Service," the woman said. "And it's not listed in the database as a personal number for any of our —"

He hung up. Sucked in a lungful of frigid night air.

The headlights eased toward the kiosk. Halted. A dinging announced an open door.

Duran edged out from a row of cars and peered up the makeshift aisle.

A Prius was parked by the wrecked Bronco. The driver's door was open, the dome light throwing a globe of yellow. At first Duran didn't see anyone.

Then a movement brought his attention to the Bronco. A broad-shouldered guy — Hargreave? — had ducked through the passenger door of the truck and was leaning over the dashboard.

"Hey!" Duran shouted. *"Hey!"*

The guy slid out of the Bronco, took a few steps in front of the Prius, and stood backlit by the headlights' glow, a perfect black cutout. His hands were at his sides, his head cocked with either curiosity or concern.

Duran jogged a few steps toward him. "You should get out of here. These guys are after you. They fooled me — I'm sorry, but —"

The faintest hum reached his ears. About thirty yards away from Hargreave, safely back from the throw of light from the kiosk, Duran halted.

Hargreave turned, half his silhouette catching the headlights' blaze, a vertical seam splitting his body.

The hum grew louder, rising in pitch.

Hargreave twitched once, violently.

There was the briefest moment of calm.

And then a jet spurted from his neck, two feet high.

It took Duran a moment to assemble what he was seeing, to make the pieces fit.

44

Blood.

Carotid.

As if Hargreave had been jabbed by a scalpel.

Except there was no scalpel. And no hand to hold it.

Hargreave clamped a palm to the side of his neck. His fingers trisecting the jet, three streams spraying through.

His knees buckled.

He sagged to the ground.

He curled up in a loose fetal position. His knees twitched on the asphalt once, twice, and then stilled. A wet circle dilated beneath his head, as mesmerizing as an oil slick. The headlights laid a blanket of light over his hunched form.

No one had been near him.

Nothing had touched him.

There'd been no gunshot, no projectile, no pop of a mini-explosion.

It was impossible, and yet Duran had seen it with his own eyes.

He was the only person in the lot. He was the only person on the security footage. Which meant he'd be the only person to blame.

From the darkness he stared at the limp form, his flesh prickling. It was incredible how quickly a life could be extinguished.

A jerking inhale shuddered through him. His senses had revved into overdrive. His skin on fire. The breeze chilling the wetness in his eyes. Even at thirty yards, he swore he could smell blood, taste the iron in the air. He pictured the two fake deputies with their well-dressed confidence, how the security monitors had fritzed out in perfect concert, a display of tech genius or dark magic.

And now Hargreave lay emptied out on the ground thirty yards away, felled by an invisible hand.

Duran could barely hear the humming over the white-noise rush in his ears, but he sensed it clearly, a vibration in his teeth. It was still present in the air, thrown like a ventriloquist's voice, hovering over Hargreave's body, then buzzing around the kiosk. And then, inside, a faint sound amplified between the tight walls.

Searching.

Searching for him.

He took a step forward. Crumpled the piece of paper in his fist, his palm slick with sweat. The next few steps came with excruciating slowness, his wobbling legs threatening to give way. Peering out from behind a dismembered minivan, he gasped in a few breaths. The faint disturbance in the air still seemed to be moving inside the kiosk.

He sprang forward, darted to the kiosk, and slammed the door closed. Fighting the key from his pocket, he jammed it halfway into the lock, then reared back and kicked the shiny metal head. It snapped off, pinging around in the darkness.

Already he was running for the perimeter.

He braced for the sound of the hum pursuing him but heard nothing aside from his breath thundering in his ears.

Sliding into the rear fence, he skinned his palms, tore the knee of his shitty security slacks. He shoved through the hole the possums used, stray spikes of chain-link gouging his spine.

Squirming free, he shot a look over his shoulder but could make out nothing more through the diamonds of chain-link than the dark expanse of the lot.

They'd seen his face.

They knew his name.

He was in some next-level deep shit.

He careened into the nearest alley, his shoulder scraping the rough brick. His mind whirled through options and outcomes. He was starting to grasp just how utterly screwed he was. Tied to a murder. On the run.

No one to turn to.

5
A KILLING TOOL

Sweat cooling across his bare chest, Evan watched her doze off, running his fingers through her curly hair.

Lying naked, bathed in the pale blue glow, she looked like a painting. The moonlight spill through the window painted her skin a flawless gold. One leg was drawn to the side, putting her hips on a slight tilt, the tilde of her waist dipping beneath the strokes of her ribs. The sheets gathered around her swirled like cake frosting. Her shoulders bore streaks from where he'd clutched her.

From this particular angle in the uneven light, with her face turned away, she might have been someone else. For a moment Evan let his eyes feed him the lie.

Then she lifted her head and nuzzled into his touch, her features coming clear, wide-set eyes, caramel skin, broad ski-jump nose.

Not Mia Hall, the single-mother district attorney who lived in his building and occupied an outsize space in his thoughts.

But Jeanette-Marie, a woman he'd met earlier that night at the Beverly Hills Hotel's Polo Lounge. She'd been sipping Cîroc, a perfectly acceptable choice of vodka, and when he'd sat next to her and ordered Jewel of Russia Ultra, he'd caught her attention. Like him she was nicely into her thirties, and she had the poise and grace to show for it.

A grin pulled her mouth to one side. "That was . . . gymnastic." She blew a corkscrew sprig of hair out of her eye. "What's your name again?"

Evan said, "David."

"Are you gonna call me?"

He kept stroking her hair lazily, the back of her neck hot against his fingertips. "No," he said, not unkindly.

"That's fine." She stretched, catlike, content. "I'm so sick of bullshit. Thanks for being honest."

"Thank you for letting me spend time with you."

She cocked her head. "You're a funny one, David. Polite and . . . hmm, formal, I guess. I mean, don't get me wrong, I dig it." She slid up and pulled on a lace camisole, which had landed slung over her headboard. "Can I make you something to eat?"

"No thank you," he said. "I can show myself out."

"You sure? You want an espresso, something?" She caught herself. "I'm sorry. Ugh. It's just — women, we're used to making ourselves useful."

"You don't need to. You're delightful doing nothing."

He was on his feet now, hunting for his boxer briefs on the white Carrara marble floor. His RoamZone, discarded near an overturned high heel, showed a missed call.

Same number as the last three calls, starting with the country code of Argentina.

The one time he'd picked up, he hadn't liked what he'd heard.

There was a time when a missed call to 1-855-2-NOWHERE would have been cause for concern. But he'd moved on to a normal life — or at least a simulacrum of what a normal life could be. A life that allowed for the Polo Lounge, women with broad ski-jump noses, and evenings that didn't bring with them the promise of violence.

He exhaled deeply, cracked his neck, breathing in perfume and sweat. Stretching his shoulders, he took in the warmth of the decor.

The luxury bungalow floated above the

50

Hollywood Hills, the massive bed centered in the great room between two pillar candles, each the width of a tank gun's barrel. The open kitchen was modern-chic with a Moroccan-tile backsplash, sage-green cabinets, and a rough-sawn farm table. A white plastic trash bag, neatly knotted, leaned against a wood-paneled refrigerator. A substantial picture window looked down at the Sunset Strip, alive with traffic lights and tall-wall billboards displaying It Girls and Boys like larger-than-life jewels. Or perishables.

He was distracted by that missed call. The woman behind it was proving to be persistent. What the hell did she want? Who had sent her?

Jeanette-Marie studied him, her eyes glinting. "Okay. Lemme guess. You're a . . . sous-chef."

Amused, he said, "Sure."

Evan had an average build, the better to blend in. Just an ordinary guy, not too handsome. He kept his muscles toned but not pronounced. When he was dressed, it was hard to discern just how fit he was.

But he wasn't dressed now.

Jeanette-Marie had certainly seen him up close, but she scanned him once more with the benefit of greater perspective. "No —

wait." She snapped her fingers. "A trainer! Hang on, no, like a physical therapist?"

He said, "Sure."

"Okay. A sous-chef–trainer–physical therapist. We'll leave it at that." Her smile was radiant, youthful. "What do you think *I* do?"

"I think you're a painter, educated at the Royal College of Art. You prefer to work in oils, and you teach part-time at UCLA."

Her lips pressed together, her brow furrowed with incredulity. "Um. How . . . ?"

He found his boxer briefs beneath a throw pillow that had lived up to its name. "You have calluses on the side of your left middle finger near the joint from holding a thin brush. Your shirt had paint stains on the cuff. Acrylics are water-based, so they would've washed out by now. So: oil. At the Polo Lounge — after you wouldn't let me buy you a drink — you paid with a Bruin faculty credit-union card."

She pursed her lips, taking a moment to catch up to this. "Okay, fine. But the Royal College?"

"You mentioned a favorite café on Prince Consort Road in London, which is right around the corner."

She was sitting perfectly upright now on the mattress, her hands in her lap. "Wow. You actually pay attention."

He unearthed one of his boots from beneath her flung-aside jacket. "Some people are worth paying attention to."

"God," Jeanette-Marie said. "You are the opposite of my ex. You're the *un*-ex. Given how things ended with him, you're exactly who I needed for the night."

"It didn't end well?"

"Let's see. I got the house, so that's good. But he got the bank accounts. Which were numerous. He's an I-banker, Harvard asshole. You know the type. Quite different from us Royal College assholes." Her grin lightened her face once more. "Opposites attract. Until they don't."

Evan thought of the scattering of freckles across Mia's nose. That birthmark at her temple. The smell of her neck.

He said, "Right."

"But when you fall for someone, it's gonna be different, right? Every time. And then it's not. It's always not." She pulled her curls up in the back, the moonlight striking the side of her neck. Evan paused to admire her.

"I'm the common denominator, though," she continued. "So I shouldn't blame Donnie. I mean, on paper? He's really good. I think I fell in love with my *image* of him, which is even more powerful than being in love with a real person, because, man, what it takes to knock the shine off an image." She shook her head. "He's harmless enough. Just a cheater and a dick. I knew it for longer than I wanted to know it. But being alone? It gets old, right?"

Evan said, "Right."

"That's what I miss. Even more than the sex. Someone to . . . you know, cook dinner once in a while, take out the trash."

Before he could respond, he heard the metallic purr of a key sliding into the front-door lock.

"Oh, *shit,*" she said.

The dead bolt retracted loudly, and the door swung open.

A guy in a rumpled suit sauntered across the threshold. Three men at his back with flashing eyes and bad energy — simmering hostility tempered by a whiff of sheepishness. They looked well lubricated, their movements loosened with alcohol, and they stank of tequila. An inferior spirit.

"Goddamn it, Donnie," Jeanette-Marie said. "This isn't your place anymore. Get out *now.* And give me your key or I'm changing the locks."

Donnie threw his arms wide. "Well, look what we have here. *My* fucking wife in *my* fucking house with a naked fucking guy."

He spoke with the careful articulation of the very drunk.

She said, "Bad night at the strip clubs?"

He glowered at her.

"I said give me the key, Donnie. *Now.*"

Still he didn't answer. The front door was open, the wind carrying the thrum of a bass guitar from a club way down on the Strip. The smell of stale cigars came off the men's clothes, poisoning the scent of night-blooming jasmine.

She looked at Evan, and he watched the concern on her face migrate to fear. "I'm really sorry."

Evan shrugged.

"Don't you apologize to *him,*" Donnie said. "You look at me. *Look at me,* you fucking whore."

Evan grimaced. So much for evenings that didn't hold the promise of violence.

"Listen," Jeanette-Marie said to Donnie, more cautiously now. "He's just leaving. Let him go, and you and I, we'll talk in the morning."

Donnie frowned, considering. "Okay. You know what? You're right." He held up his hands, retreated to the front door. Paused. His jaw flexed a few times, the shiny, clean-shaven skin of his cheek rippling. "Fuck it," he said, and flipped the door shut.

He swung back around to face them, his mouth shifting left, right.

Jeanette-Marie appealed to the others. "Eric? Jim? Rich — c'mon. This isn't you guys. You know that. What are you gonna do? Beat up some guy you don't even know? What's that gonna accomplish?"

Evan flipped aside a corner of the duvet with a bare foot and found his jeans. He usually wore cargo pants but had upgraded to dark 501s as a concession to the Polo Lounge.

"Hey, motherfucker," Donnie said. "Hey, you. You enjoy being in my bed? You enjoy being in my wife?"

Evan picked up his jeans and sat down on the bed. "You really want me to answer that?"

Donnie's laugh turned into a sputter. He took a step forward, his friends fanning out behind him. "You're an idiot. There are four of us."

"I see that," Evan said. "Need me to wait while you get more?"

They blinked at him.

The biggest of the quartet — Rich — stripped off his suit jacket. "We'll be enough."

Evan pulled on his jeans, one leg, then the other. One more irritated glance at the

56

missed call with that 54 country code before he shoved the phone into his pocket. He finished dressing calmly, the men staring at him in disbelief. He buckled his belt and then held out his hands, palms up. "Okay," he said. "Make an example out of me."

Rich struck a boxing stance, shifting his weight from side to side. Donnie dropped his right foot back, which along with the watch on his left wrist signaled that he was right-handed. He gave a target glance at Evan's chin, telegraphing where he intended to strike. The two beta males filled out the semicircle at the edge of Evan's peripheral vision.

Jeanette-Marie's bare feet hit the floor with a thump. "Donnie, you call this off right —"

The big guy led first as Evan knew he would, a haymaker, all force, no nuance. Evan slapped the fist aside with an open-hand deflection, placed his insole behind Rich's heel, and jerked the guy's loafer sharply two feet forward. Rich went airborne, landing hard on his shoulder blades. His lungs expelled a grunt, the wind knocked clean out of him.

Already Donnie was angling for the cheap shot, but Evan stepped aside and flicked his knuckles at the looming nose, shattering it neatly, a healthy spurt painting the front of Donnie's designer shirt.

Jim came in halfhearted, his body already registering his fate, though his booze-addled brain was too slow to catch up. Evan smacked both sides of his head, boxing his ears and putting a concussive barb straight through his brain. As Jim's hands rose protectively, Evan grabbed his dress shirt in the back and raked it up, a prison-yard move that trapped his arms. Then he kicked out Jim's front leg, dumping him on the marble next to Rich, who was still sucking for oxygen.

By that time Donnie was reentering the fray, bellowing and swinging blindly. Evan grabbed his wrist in a *bong sau/lop sau* trap, sliding into an arm control. Locking Donnie's elbow, he spun him around in a half turn and slammed his forehead into the farm table, bouncing him onto the floor next to the other two.

Then he turned to face the last man standing.

Frozen in place, Eric stared at him, panting, eyes rimmed with a good show of white. Giving Evan wide berth, he eased around the others and ran out, leaving the front door swinging in the breeze. Jim untangled himself from his shirt and hustled out after

Eric in a limping run.

Rich lay on his back, as exposed as a flipped turtle. Evan offered his hand, and Rich flailed for it, missing once before Evan hauled him to his feet. Rich's face had purpled, his lips still wavering in search of air.

"Lean over," Evan said. "It's just a diaphragm spasm. Slow deep breath in through your mouth, push out your stomach. Okay. Good. Once more. Now door, please."

Evan gave the big guy a gentle prod. Bent over, he hobbled out.

Donnie gripped the table and pulled himself up, his face awash in blood and snot. He made a wheezing sound, choked with sobs. His shirt was little more than a rumpled rag, and his pants had torn at the knee, his wallet twisted inside a front pocket. He wiped at his watering eyes, holding up his other hand to fend Evan off.

Evan pulled out his Strider folding knife, snagging the shark fin atop the blade on the edge of his pocket so it snapped open with a menacing click as it emerged.

Aside from a Zippo, a Strider was the only item one hundred percent made in the United States with a lifetime guarantee. Unlike a lighter it could — with a modicum of skill and intent — turn a human being into

59

a velociraptor. One side of the handle was made of G-10, a high-strength, acid-resistant, nonconductive fiberglass and epoxy synthetic. Titanium, ridged for a better grip, constituted the other half. The blade itself was S35VN, a refined-grain metallurgy comprising a precise mixture of carbon, chromium, vanadium, molybdenum, niobium, and iron. The knife was as finely made and precise a killing tool as anything earth, man, and science had conspired to manufacture.

Donnie's mouth was open, emitting silent cries, his spine curled in submission.

Evan stepped forward and flicked the knife at his crotch.

There was a tear, a yielding of fabric.

Donnie stared down, his eyes swimmy.

An instant later his wallet and keys dropped from the slit in his pants pocket and struck the floor.

Evan crouched, picked up the key ring, and flipped it around a finger into his palm. Then he removed the most likely suspect.

Turning, he held the key up for Jeanette-Marie. "This one?"

Her mouth slightly ajar, she nodded.

He clicked it down onto the farm table.

Donnie's knees went out, and Evan caught him. "Okay, pal. Tilt your head back. Pinch here. Lean on me. There you go. Let's get you on the other side of the door."

Donnie clutched at Evan's shoulder, dragging his legs, still finding his feet.

Evan said, "You're gonna want to get some ice on that." He paused, looked back to Jeanette-Marie. "You good?"

"Sweet Jesus," she said. "Thank you. And . . . um, also? Thank you?"

He gave her a little nod. "Ma'am."

As he helped Donnie to the door, Evan reached down, grabbed the knotted white trash bag, and took it out with them.

6
A SUICIDAL GHOST

Neon rolled across the laminated armor glass of the windshield as Evan steered through the Hollywood night toward the Wilshire Corridor, one hand clamped on top of the steering wheel. He stared down at the flap of dry skin lifted from the knuckle of his trigger finger. The windows of his Ford F-150 didn't roll down due to the Kevlar armor hung inside the door panels, but cold leaked in through the vents, tightening his skin, making him feel alive. The taste of adrenaline lingered in the back of his throat, the bittersweet aftermath of the fight holding on.

A keenness always amped his senses in the wake of a confrontation.

He tried not to focus on how much he missed the sensation.

He'd placed the RoamZone with its missed call on the passenger seat as if he needed to keep an eye on it. The preposterously encrypted phone, with its hardened rubber-and-aramid case, used to be his tether to another life.

At the age of twelve, Evan had clawed his way out of poverty. He'd been given a new identity by a man named Jack Johns, his father figure and handler, the closest thing to family he'd ever known. Jack had taught him everything from Slavic languages to ancient Greek warfare. Had shown him how to top off bank accounts in nonreporting territories and how to live like a ghost. Had brought in subject-matter experts to drown-proof and interrogate him, to teach him how to zero a sniper rifle, where to nick a femoral artery with a box cutter.

Jack had turned him into Orphan X.

For years Evan operated in a black program so covert that even denizens of the Capitol Building knew it only through whispers and rumors. He required no backup, left no footprint. Every mission was illegal under U.S. and international law.

He did not exist.

There was only one complication: Jack had raised him not just to be a killer but to remain human.

At a certain point, Evan had to choose.

And just as he'd once escaped the foster-care system, he'd left the Orphan Program behind, going off the grid, hunted by the very government that had created him.

He'd turned his skills to a new venture, one more aligned with the ethics embedded in him by Jack. As the Nowhere Man, Evan remained on call 24/7 for people who were being terrorized, people who found themselves under the heel of a crushing predicament, people with nowhere left to turn. After a decade and change spent leaving a trail of dead high-value targets across six continents, he figured he owed something to the universe.

He also figured he owed something for getting out where others had not. Out of the foster system. Out of East Baltimore. Out of the Program.

But recently he'd been ready to discharge his duty as the Nowhere Man and the awful, awesome responsibilities that came with it. He'd reached a tentative truce with no less an authority than the president of the United States. She'd granted him an unofficial pardon — but made clear that it would be withdrawn the instant he conducted any extracurricular activities as the Nowhere Man. It wasn't just that what he did on behalf of his clients was illegal; it was that he was too sensitive an asset to have his operational capabilities put on display. If he didn't wish to be neutralized, he had to remain on the shelf.

So he'd agreed to leave his work as the Nowhere Man behind.

He was ready to try to lead an ordinary life, whatever that was. A life he'd never thought he could have, never thought he deserved. One without knife wounds and concussions. Without a threat around every corner, the reek of death one wrong turn away.

People would have to go about helping themselves the ways they had before he'd come along. Or the ways they hadn't.

The RoamZone should have stopped ringing with any more missions. And yet he'd received a series of calls from the same number.

The first time, he'd picked up and found a woman on the other end. She'd addressed him by name.

And claimed she was his mother.

He'd hung up immediately, figuring her for a lure designed to draw him out.

And yet — who'd sent her?

How did she know his name?

What did she want?

Her voice was unfamiliar, of course, and yet something about it had tugged the thread of a memory. No, not a memory, exactly. More like a wisp of a forgotten dream.

Evan. It's your mother.

After severing the connection, he'd stared at the phone in his hand, a box of silicon chips, amplifiers, and microprocessors that had conveyed the feminine voice across two continents.

It was an effective little ploy, sinking a hook into the soft part of his heart, jabbing a vulnerability he didn't even know he had. An uncomfortable sensation, like he'd been ensnared by a strand of a much bigger web. The feeling had proved hard to shake.

He wasn't sure why.

He'd dealt with his share of psychopaths and tyrants. This was just another variation on the theme; the woman was either delusional or conniving.

Or perhaps both.

Refocusing his thoughts, he arrived at his residential high-rise, Castle Heights, and left his truck in its spot between two concrete pillars on the subterranean parking level.

In the lobby he detoured to the bank of mailboxes and confirmed that his was empty; one of the great benefits of not existing was receiving no junk mail.

He crossed the marble floor, clearing his

throat to awaken Joaquin, who'd dozed off in his chair behind the reception console.

Joaquin snapped to, smoothing down the front of his guard uniform. "Mr. Smoak. I was just resting my eyes."

"Good technique to lure the bad guys into a false sense of security."

Joaquin smiled sheepishly and thumbed the button to summon the elevator. "Fun night, huh?"

"Took some clients out to dinner." Here at Castle Heights, Evan was known as a bland importer of industrial cleaning supplies.

"Late dinner."

"They wanted to go clubbing. What adults want to go clubbing?"

Joaquin said, "You'd be surprised."

"I was."

The elevator arrived with a ding, and Evan stepped aboard. The PENTHOUSE button was already lit, and he rode up, enjoying the silence.

His condo, seven thousand square feet of concrete and glass, was sparse and spotless. The workout stations were buffed to a high sheen, unmarred by fingerprints. The brushed-nickel kitchen appliances gave a catalog-clean sparkle, even in the semidarkness. Behind a freestanding fireplace, a spiral staircase wound its way up to a reading loft where he'd actually found time these past few weeks to lounge. There was a black suede couch he'd sat on maybe a dozen times in the years since he'd moved in, most of those times in the past month.

Several evenings ago he'd even raised the retractable flat-screen TV from its slit in the floor and watched a Buster Keaton movie.

That was him now. Mr. Ordinary.

Especially if you overlooked the bullet-resistant laminated polycarbonate thermoplastic resin composing the windows, the discreet armor sunscreens made of a rare titanium variant, the motion- and shatter-detection sensors rigged in the frames, the base-jumping parachute stowed behind the inset panel of the planter strategically positioned on the south-facing balcony.

He stood in the stillness of the gunmetal-gray plain of the great room. The penthouse was unlit and lifeless. A heavy bag dangled from its chain like a suicidal ghost. The dumbbells slumbered on their rack, turned precisely so the weight labels were aligned north. Ambient city light glowed through the lowered sunscreens, throwing a sheet of pale gold across the poured-concrete kitchen island, illuminating neither crumb nor smudge.

He stretched luxuriously, felt his spine crack at the base. Then he crossed to the open kitchen, passing between the Sub-Zero and the island to the newest addition to his penthouse. A glass-walled mini-room, the back seated against one of the floor-to-ceiling windows overlooking Century City. He tugged at the door, freezer mist swirling out as he entered. Rows of shelves, also glass, held bottles of the finest vodka the world had to offer. They were positioned equidistant from one another, three inches of clearance on either side. A small stand-alone bar in the center held accoutrements — a variety of crystal glasses, steel martini picks, a trio of shakers.

Another indulgence of retirement. The time to build, to spend, to direct his restless focus on pleasure. It struck him now that freezer rooms and late-night trysts had their limits. They helped broaden the hours but didn't add much depth to the days and nights.

The chill air put a burn in his lungs. His nightly drink was a ritual of sorts, the purest alcohol, the coldest air, a calming anesthesia to wash away the filth of his past. Did he deserve this? The wealth? The calm? A carved-out sanctuary in which he could seek to dispel his sins?

He reached for the slender bottle of Ao. Distilled from rice and clarified through bamboo filtration on Kyushu island in the shadow of an active volcano, it took its name from the Japanese word for "blue." He popped an ice sphere from its silicone mold, dropped it into an old-fashioned glass, poured two fingers of vodka, and exited into the warm embrace of the kitchen proper.

Vegetation fluttered on the living wall, a vertical drip-fed garden at the kitchen's edge. Evan plucked off a mint leaf, floated it on the clear liquid, and gave the glass a swirl. The mint would enhance the sweet undertaste of coconut and banana leaves.

Padding across the great room toward his bedroom, he took a sip, closing his eyes, letting the freezing warmth wash across his palate. The melody of flavors harmonized into the faintest note of rice pudding on the finish.

Delightful.

His bedroom was as bare as the rest of the condo.

Bureau. Nightstand. Window.

Even the bed was minimalist, a mattress resting on a floating slab of metal. The metal was at once propelled into the air by steroidally powerful neodymium rare-earth magnets and tethered to the floor by steel cables, a ceaseless push-pull that mirrored Evan's own vacillation between chaos and order.

That missed call had tipped him out of alignment.

Evan. It's your mother.

Were he inclined to sneer, he would have now.

He stripped to his boxer briefs, knocked back his vodka, and set the glass down on the nightstand.

Then he lifted it and looked at the faint condensation ring. He wiped the ring off with the hem of his shirt, then wiped the bottom of the sweating glass and set it back down. He checked again.

Another ring of moisture, albeit fainter.

Cursing physics, he wiped off the nightstand again and then set the glass on the floor just to have some peace and quiet.

He sat on the bed crossed-legged, straightening his back, making microadjustments, stacking vertebra on vertebra. He veiled his eyes, letting the lids grow heavy until the room blurred into a play of light and shadow. Focusing on the precise point that each inhalation began, he breathed until breathing was all he was doing, until it was all that he was.

A few minutes into the meditation, he became aware of his bones, his muscles and ligaments, his skin wrapping him into an embodied whole. The boundary between him and the room blurred until he felt of a part with the space around him, the air itself, until he —

The RoamZone vibrated on the bed beside him.

Aggravated, he rolled off the bed onto his bare feet and picked it up. He'd upgraded the screen recently from Gorilla Glass to an organic polyether-thiourea that was able to self-repair when cracked.

He was tempted to shatter it himself now when he saw the caller ID.

Same number. Same Argentina area code.

Glaring at the digits, he felt an uncharacteristic rise in body temperature. He argued with himself.

Looked away from the screen.

Looked back.

Clenching his jaw, he thumbed the green virtual button and answered.

7
COOKIE-CUTTER PSYOPS

Normally as the Nowhere Man, Evan would ask, *Do you need my help?*

But now he just waited.

He could hear her breathing on the other end.

"Who are you?" he said.

"I told you."

Her voice was regal and touched with age, a slight huskiness that put her in her late fifties, maybe early sixties. She spoke with no accent and enunciated well, as if she'd had training in theater.

"No," he said. "No."

"I heard you help people."

"I'm retired." Curiosity flared, a fuse burning down. "How did you hear that?"

"I know someone who needs your help."

"Who are you?"

The call, routed through fifteen encrypted virtual-private-network tunnels on both hemispheres, crackled in the silence. The pause felt dramatic. She was thinking. He was, too.

"I left you with Rusty and Joan Krauss," she finally said. "A stalwart couple. Or so I thought. Joan was medically compromised, though I didn't know it at the time."

He felt a drop of sweat trickle down his temple. "Who are you?"

"I'd driven through the night," she said. "Across the border from Lancaster, Pennsylvania."

"You could have looked any of this up," he said.

"I know your middle name."

"Well, I don't," he said. "So that doesn't help us any."

"After . . . after I left you, I got two blocks away from the Krausses' house and I pulled over. And wept."

He swallowed.

"I didn't want to leave you there, but it was a different time. It wasn't easy being an independent-minded young woman. I don't mean to imply hardship, but you take my meaning. It's just important to me . . ."

His legs felt numb, his bare feet insensate against the cold concrete. If this was a gambit, it was a superb one, playing all the right notes on the bars of his ribs, coaxing an emotional response into resonance.

74

He heard himself say, ". . . what?"

His voice sounded different than it had in decades. Smaller.

She said, "It's important you know that you were wanted."

He cut the connection, threw the phone onto the bed, and stared at it, breathing hard, his shoulders heaving.

It hadn't occurred to him to want to be wanted.

The phone gazed up blankly, the screen dark. He wasn't sure if he hoped she'd call back.

He reached for the fourth of the Ten Commandments that Jack had handed down to him: *Never make it personal.*

"It's bullshit," he told the phone, the room, himself. "Cookie-cutter psyops. Clear your head. You know better than that."

No answer save the gentle whisper of the vent overhead.

"Don't be an idiot," he said. "You're being played."

He snatched up his glass and the phone and walked into the bathroom. He nudged the shower door hanging on its barn-door track, the frosted-glass pane vanishing into the wall. Stepping inside the stall, he gripped the hot-water lever. An embedded digital sensor read the print of his palm, allowing him to twist the lever in the wrong direction. An inset door, seamlessly camouflaged by the tile pattern, swung inward, and he stepped through into a hidden space.

The Vault.

An armory, a workbench, and an L-shaped sheet-metal desk crammed into an irregular four hundred square feet of walled-off storage space. The public stairs to the roof zigzagged the ceiling overhead, an optical illusion that made the room appear to be shrinking.

He circled to the desk, sank into his chair, and flicked the mouse on its pad. The three walls horseshoeing the desk illuminated. A mosaic of heretofore invisible OLED screens, each less than three millimeters thick, awakened to cloak the rough concrete walls.

Right now the front wall displayed pirated feeds from the Castle Heights surveillance system, the same footage Joaquin would be watching at his security station downstairs right now if he were managing to stay awake. The north wall was plugged into a variety of state and federal databases, Evan's personal hijacked portal into the computing power of the agencies. And the south wall displayed the call log of his RoamZone.

He'd already captured the caller's IMEI

and pegged the location using advanced forward-link trilateration, which forced the network to automatically and continually report the woman's phone's position between cell towers. Based on the phone's movements and resting times, it seemed she was staying in the affluent Recoleta neighborhood on the northeast slant of the city. He'd been to Buenos Aires only twice, once to garrote a visiting Venezuelan dignitary on the D line of the underground, the other to sit surveillance on a cartel leader whom he'd eventually dispatched in the parking lot of El Gigante de Alberdi, a fútbol stadium in Córdoba seven hundred kilometers to the interior.

When he'd tried to backtrack the user identity on the SIM card earlier, he'd run into a dead end. It was a prepaid Movistar, available at pretty much any kiosk, supermarket, or pharmacy. This was suspicious, but not as suspicious as it might be in the U.S., especially if the woman was traveling.

He stared at the blinking GPS dot just off the Plaza Francia, watching her in real time.

He drummed his fingers, an uncharacteristic fidget. Then he looked down at the pinecone-shaped aloe vera plant resting on the desk in a glass bowl beside his mouse pad. His sole companion was named Vera

II. He'd killed her predecessor with neglect, a sad statement as she required nothing more than an ice cube dropped in her dish once a week. The edges of her serrated spikes were browning now, and she was glaring up at him from her bed of cobalt glass pebbles, clearly displeased.

"Look," he said, "I'm sorry. I've been trying to move on. It's not you. It's me."

She was unmoved.

He fished the diminished ice sphere from the old-fashioned glass and rested it atop her spikes just to shut her up. The trace of vodka wouldn't hurt either.

He sensed movement on the front wall of monitors. Mia Hall entering the building from the parking level, struggling under the weight of her nine-year-old son, Peter, who was slumped in her arms, comatose. Small for his age, he wore a Mickey Mouse–ear hat cocked to the side, his cheek smudged pink and blue from some sugary indulgence. They'd just come through a traumatic stretch, and Mia had vowed to spend more time with him, which evidently included hooky days at Disneyland.

Evan wondered what Disneyland was like. And pink-and-blue candy. He'd never indulged in either. But he'd carried Peter asleep a time or two as Mia carried him now, and Evan recalled the warmth of the boy's cheek against his shoulder, his sweat-sticky blond hair against his chin. Those few episodes when his life had stitched together with Mia's and Peter's lives represented his closest brush with what normal might feel like. If she weren't a district attorney sworn to uphold the law and he hadn't been raised an assassin sworn to break it, perhaps the road ahead might have felt like a solid pos-sibility rather than a tiptoe across land mines. Mia didn't fully know what Evan did, but she knew enough to know that he — and their affiliation — was less than safe.

Evan switched his focus back to the south wall, concentrating on the blinking GPS dot of a phone in Argentina. His supposed mother.

Vera II stared at him.

"There's no way," he told her. "It's impos-sible. She can't be."

Vera II stared at him.

"What are the odds? And how the hell would she have found me? Found *me*?"

Vera II stared at him.

He leaned back and crossed his arms. It was the longest of long shots. But still. He needed to know.

On the front wall, Mia bundled Peter across the lobby and waited for the elevator. The overheads caught her spill of wavy brown hair, highlighting gold and chestnut. Her bare arms flexed under the weight of her son. Her lips were moving. She was murmuring a lullaby.

He tore his eyes from the lobby feed, refocusing on the beacon of the prepaid cell phone.

He couldn't operate as the Nowhere Man anymore. Not without jeopardizing his informal presidential pardon. One move deemed insufficiently discreet and he'd have the full force of the United States government back on his tail. Which would mean no more leisurely evenings at the Polo Lounge. No more sipping Japanese vodka for the sheer joy of it rather than to take the edge off the operational wear and tear on his body and mind. No more nights with oil painters from the Royal College of Art. And no more hope of maybe, just maybe, having a shot at nights more meaningful than that.

Out of the corner of his eye, he noted the elevator doors open downstairs. Mia and Peter stepped inside, vanishing from view.

There was so much to recommend normalcy.

And yet.

He thought about the drive home from Jeanette-Marie's. The taste of adrenaline.

80

The sharpness of the night air. All five senses alive, and maybe even a sixth.

"I don't miss it," he told Vera II. "I really don't."

Already his hand was moving the mouse, bringing up an incognito search engine.

"I'm not breaking the agreement," he said, keying the number of one of his forged passports into the airline website. "It's not a mission. It's just a trip."

He risked another glance at Vera II, but she'd already made her position clear. She assimilated carbon dioxide disapprovingly.

He clicked *purchase*.

8
SUCKER

The next day at noon, the dark sedan is back, and so is the Mystery Man, both in the same place. Evan rounds the handball wall and stops, holds his fists up as he's seen boxers do on TV, a technique the boys mimic in street fights to questionable results. His ribs ache from Van Sciver, and beneath his shirt his back hosts a collection of scarlet abrasions from the belt that look like half-formed question marks. But he is here and he is ready. The Mystery Man throws his hands wide and does something wholly unexpected. He smiles.

"Good. That's a good stance." He starts toward Evan. "Look, kid. Sorry about yesterday. Sometimes I can be a little overzealous. I mean, what the hell was I thinking? A grown man —"

He sucker-punches Evan again. Too late, Evan realizes he's been disarmed, that he's let his arms drift south. The fist connects with his cheek, grinding flesh into bone. Not a hard punch, but perfectly placed, and again Evan goes down, and this time he stays down, crouching on one knee, trying to breathe.

The Mystery Man leans over him, hands on his thighs. The cigarette is still there, jutting from between two fingers; he didn't even bother to put it out before swinging. "Look at you," he says. "Do you honestly think you have what it takes?"

Evan forces the words through the pounding in his skull. "I'll get bigger."

"You think that's all it takes? Bigger?"

"It's all I'm missing."

At this the man laughs. "Look, I get it, kid. Grit and drive and all that. But you gotta understand — there's *nothing* you have that I want. You're not gonna surprise me. The kid I want? Charles Van Sciver? *He's* got it. We're just about done vetting him. And if he fails, next in line'll be that husky kid, Andre. You're not even on the list. Now, go home or whatever you call it and get on with your life."

Evan stands up, wipes his bloody mouth roughly. He looks at the tinted windows of the sedan, back to the Mystery Man. "I want to try again."

"There's no trying again." The man points at Evan's face with the red cherry of the cigarette. "Get the fuck out of here. Or I promise you this: You'll find out what a real punch feels like."

Jogging home this time, Evan feels the pain in his ribs anew, the reality pounded into him by Van Sciver.

It feels like defeat.

At dinner Van Sciver spoons extra mac and cheese from the pot, then flicks the wooden spoon at Evan across the table, landing a few stray noodles on his shirt and his swollen lip. "What happened to your face?"

"What happened to yours?"

It's not the wisecrack so much as the covered laughter from the others that lets Evan know he will pay for this later. Papa Z is across on his armchair, massaging his lower stomach as he does when his bowels won't cooperate.

Van Sciver points at Evan with the spoon. "Wait till you fall asleep."

But that night Evan does not fall asleep. After bed check there is a face-off, Van Sciver staring at him from his bed across the room, Evan staring back from the mattress on the floor, neither wanting to drift off first. By the time Van Sciver's eyes stop glinting through the darkness, the inside of Evan's thigh is purple where he's been pinching himself to stay awake.

84

Evan creeps across and watches the rise and fall of the bigger boy's chest, watches the blue bandanna around his head, the bandanna he wears at all times, even sleeping. Then he sneaks down the hall, finds the cordless on the kitchen counter, dials the ominous ten digits.

The Mystery Man's voice sounds tired, cracked from sleep, a human vulnerability that seems discordant with what little Evan knows of him. "Yeah? Hello? Hello?"

"Okay. I get it. I'll never be Van Sciver. I'm not what you're looking for. But I have something you need to know about him."

"What?"

"Tomorrow. Same time, same place."

Now it's Evan who hangs up.

9
THE WOMAN

Buenos Aires felt like a European city plunked down at the edge of the wrong continent. December was Argentine summer, heat leaking up through the cobblestone street through the soles of Evan's Original S.W.A.T. boots. Dusk had come on fast, the sun bleeding into the horizon through the endless blocky rise of the skyline.

Evan sat at an outdoor table sipping an arabica coffee worth its weight in rhodium. He'd been ranging around the plaza for seven hours, rotating surveillance positions among the proliferation of cafés. In the center two performers danced a tango wearing outfits straight out of a guidebook — glossy black fabric with fiery red trim. A few distracted German tourists ambled by, tossing pesos into an upended top hat resting next to the retro boom box. It was 7:53 P.M., which passed for morning in a city with a nightlife that found its feet around midnight. Three million souls rousing themselves after a long day of working and siestaing, ready to dance and drink and dine on entraña, a skirt steak capable of eliciting rapture. The residential buildings hemming in the square presented a cacophony of styles, charming and intricate. Municipal smudges of pollution shaded the stone and concrete façades.

But Evan wasn't here for the mercenary tango dancers or the celestial steak or the grimy old-country charm. He was here to confront the woman who had claimed to be his mother. The woman whose prepaid phone's GPS signal blinked steadily in the screen of his RoamZone, pinning her down inside the ornate apartment building kitty-corner from the rickety chair he currently occupied.

Her red dot blinked on his screen, an uncertain warning signal — *stop, stop, stop.*

And then — at last — it was moving.

He watched the stone face of the luxury high-rise. A doorman waited outside, anachronistic in his brass-buttoned jacket, white gloves, and impassive visage. At a movement inside, he animated, his shiny heels clicking against the pavement. He swung the door open with a flourish and a Victorian quarter bow that was promptly ignored by the emerging foursome.

Three large men, richly tailored suits, in a triangle formation around a woman.

Bodyguards.

Curious.

Despite the hour the woman wore a sleeveless black dress and an oversize black summer hat with a white satin scarf tied around it, draped across her face alluringly or strategically. She flashed into view between the bodyguards' bulky shoulders and then was lost behind a sea of navy wool gabardine as her men closed ranks. When they turned to head for Avenida Pueyrredón, he caught a glimpse of white cheek and smoky eye shadow.

She looked to be in her late fifties and exceptionally well preserved.

Evan dropped a few Eva Perón banknotes on the table and followed.

The tango music blared, accompanied by an overlay of speaker static, as the couple twisted and dipped. Evan cut through the sparse crowd at the plaza's edge, maintaining a half-block distance behind the mysterious woman and her men.

Was she of such substantial wealth as to require constant security? In witness protection? Had she crossed a local crime lord?

Or — most likely — the bodyguards were there to ensnare Evan if he answered the call.

The men gave the woman more stand-off room as they crossed the boulevard, but from Evan's perspective he could make out little more than the back of her hat and the swaying of a single toned arm.

He spooled out more line, letting them stretch to a block and then a block and a half. Having scouted the area extensively, he knew the pedestrian ebbs and flows of the neighborhood.

The Third Commandment: *Master your surroundings.*

They rimmed the border of the park, nearing the Gomero de la Recoleta, a massive rubber tree that was a planet unto itself. The centuries-old tree spread its tentacles across a distance wider than half a football field, some of the meter-thick branches swooping low to the ground. To remain aloft many of them required metal posts; one even rested across a statue of Atlas, who bore his load stoically on a welded steel shoulder. Children flitted along the branches, swinging and climbing.

The woman paused to watch them, her back to Evan, a breeze riffling the white scarf. Evan turned to face a vending machine offering oranges and apples, the fruit arrayed in neat rows behind a shiny pane, the glass providing a useful reflection of the woman behind him. He watched her through the grainy cloak of dusk.

She turned partway, her gaze seeming to hitch on him. But then she continued, strolling through the grand entrance of the cemetery, the well-heeled muscle moving in orbit around her.

He waited a few minutes and then followed, passing through neoclassical gates bookended by Doric columns. A security guard warned him that they'd be closing soon.

The Recoleta Cemetery was one of the world's great necropolises. Nearly five thousand mausoleums in various states of disrepair were crammed into fourteen acres, rising like miniature houses along miniature neighborhood blocks. Street signs denoted each tree-lined lane, lending a Disneyesque touch to the diminutive town. The tombs ranged from art nouveau to baroque, simple to opulent, single-story to three-tiered. Some rose like Greek temples, others were embellished with statues — a beatific robed elder, an eternal sentry brandishing a sword, a loyal dog long oxidized, its nose rubbed to a bronzen shine. Beyond the tall cemetery walls, sleek high-rises soared, striking a surreal contrast with the ancient stone.

As darkness overtook the tombs, the last sightseers drifted toward the entrance, stray cats flossing between their ankles. Evan's boots crunched across shards, broken bits from shattered stained-glass windows that once adorned a set of grand decorative doors.

He kept the woman barely in view — the sway of her hips rounding a corner, a stiletto-heeled foot disappearing behind the edge of a tomb. Her men branched out wisely, minding the lanes around her.

For a time they all cat-and-moused through the venerable gridiron.

Evan found a deserted pocket and paused, pretending to admire a sitting room visible through a crumbled tomb wall. On marble shelves inside, coffins lay beneath long-rotted casket veils. A rusted chain had been strung haphazardly across the gap, but the front door remained intact, dried flowers protruding from the keyhole. A perfectly symmetrical spiderweb framed the doorknob, a backplate of glistening silk.

He closed his eyes, letting the warm air press into his skin, opening himself to vibration and movement and sound. One of the bodyguards creaked the stone just behind

91

the mausoleum; another coughed, a single ragged note coming from two lanes over. Evan smelled the faintest hint of lilac riding an easterly breeze.

The woman.

The third man would no doubt be at her side, close-in protection.

Evan edged east, sourcing the tinge of perfume.

Night had come on hard, the jagged mausoleums framed in shadow and ambient light from the distant streetlights. The three monkeys of lore, rendered in gray marble, crouched at gargoyle readiness atop a slab of funereal stone, their shadows stretched grotesquely across the ground.

Listening for the two roving guards, Evan eased around a small-scale cathedral with caskets slotted into its rear wall. At the end of the lane, bent in the thickening darkness, the woman reached for a marble statue at the foot of a tomb.

As his eyes acclimated to the night, the age-old statue came into focus — a baby swathed in cloth, the newborn's likeness preserved in marble. The woman's head was angled mournfully, her face lost behind the wide brim of the hat, her hand resting on the baby's stone chest as if feeling for a heartbeat.

Evan's inhalation hitched ever so slightly in his throat. He became aware of a hike in his heart rate, the hot night air wrapping itself around his neck.

As he breathed himself back to steadiness, he admired the woman's tradecraft. A grief-steeped mother paying respect to a lost child — a clever ruse designed to turn a key inside him, to access some long-buried vulnerability.

It almost worked.

More important, it meant they suspected he was watching.

As he drifted back out of sight, he sensed movement mirroring him on either side behind the mausoleums. Sure enough, as he came to the next intersection, the two roving bodyguards stepped into view to his left and right.

10
A Dog's Breakfast

Evan faced ahead, favoring neither side, keeping both bodyguards in his peripheral vision.

"Hello, friend." The guy to his left spoke in a voice that was theatrically low, with an excess of patience that a large, dangerous man could afford. Lightly accented English — either he'd gauged Evan's gringo skin or knew who he was. "Is there some reason you're following the lady?"

Evan stared straight ahead at the darkness. Neither man reached for hip or lapel; they assumed this could be handled without firearms.

Too bad they didn't have an opportunity to acquaint themselves with the First Commandment.

Evan said, "She asked to speak with me."

"Did she, now," the man said. Not a question. "I find it unlikely that Ms. Veronica would ask anything of you. I think you

shouldn't be stalking women around ceme-
teries after hours."

"I understand your opinion on the matter," Evan said. "But it doesn't interest me."

The other spoke up. "We have encountered many men who weren't interested in
our opinions. Their broken bodies are now
at the bottom of the Río de la Plata. You
will see them soon enough."

He took a step forward. His counterpart
paralleled him on the left side.

Evan said, "This isn't a good idea."

The second man chuckled, leaned back
on his heels. They each had at least four
inches and fifty pounds on Evan. "You don't
look like much."

Evan said, "That's why this isn't a good
idea."

The man sidled forward, resting a firm
hand on Evan's shoulder. The clenched grip
was supposed to be intimidating, but it ac-
complished little more than making the
man's limb available.

Evan said, "We're really gonna do this,
then?"

"We are."

Evan said, "Okay." He grabbed the man's
hand and rolled it outward, snapping wrist
and elbow with two percussive pops. A sa-
vate piston kick staved in the guy's knee

from the side, and he grunted and sank a few inches, evening out the height differential.

Before the bodyguard to the left could react, Evan reached across the injured man's broad back, gripped him beneath the armpit, and pinwheeled him into his partner. Hurled sideways, the man hit his colleague at mid-leg, hyperextending both knees with a pleasing crackle. They tumbled into a stone edifice, the first man's head smacking the wall from the momentum of their fall, the second's after Evan clipped his chin with a well-placed jab, driving his skull into the granite.

They weren't unconscious, but they couldn't manage anything more than breathing, wet rasps and shudders. Evan looked down at them, doing his best not to consider how satisfying it felt to knock the rust off his fighting-muscle memory. It had all the dark deliciousness of giving in to a bad habit. He knew too well the costs of surrendering to it and yet couldn't shake the sense right now, with the night air keen at the back of his throat and the rush of blood in his veins, that this was in fact the thing he was meant to do.

The greater the gift, the greater the curse.

Evan patted the men down, finding on

each a Bersa Thunder .45, the predictable choice for an Argentine strongman.

The corroding door of the mausoleum had wedged halfway open, exhaling a faint waft of rot and mold. Evan rolled the men through the gap, letting the dank interior swallow them. Their pained exhalations floated out, ghostly echoes.

Evan dropped the magazines from both guns, cleared the rounds in the chambers, and tossed the pieces into a nearby trash can.

Then he started back toward the spot where the woman — Veronica? — had posed in feigned vigil over the child's tomb.

The third bodyguard stood in the middle of the next lane, perfectly backlit, the glow from the distant high-rises bleeding around his silhouette. His gun was out, aimed at Evan.

They confronted each other a few feet apart.

Evan said, "Bersa Thunder .45, huh?"

"A nicely weighted gun."

"I always found it lacking. The trigger-return spring gives out after a few hundred rounds."

The man shifted his weight. He was barrel-chested, the glow of the streetlamps limning the side of his face, highlighting muttonchop sideburns. "I hadn't noticed." His accent was thicker, with the Italian lilt that qualified the Spanish here. He kept the pistol aimed at Evan's heart. "Slide-lock issues, though." He made a clucking sound to voice his disapproval.

He took a slight step forward. His gun hand stayed steady. Not his first rodeo.

Evan eyed the frame-mounted safety at the rear of the pistol. It was off. The man's thumb was under the safety lever, not riding on top of it, a tell that he was not as experienced an operator as he projected. The .45's heavy recoil could cause the thumb to slip on the grip and accidentally engage the safety.

The man flicked his head at the darkness behind Evan. "My men?"

"They're alive."

The man sidled forward a bit more, bringing the muzzle within a few feet of Evan's chest. With its mishmashed frame angles, oversize levers, and aggressively angled trigger, it was a dog's breakfast of a pistol.

Which made it a nice match for the man's face.

He smiled, revealing beautiful square teeth inside a dense beard. "My name is Raúl. I am in charge of Ms. Veronica. I am under specific orders not to let anyone near her."

"Were those orders given by Ms. Veronica?"

"This is not your business. And you are unarmed. I understand you got past my associates, and that has given you confidence. But they are boys. You are about to find out what happens when you meet a man."

Evan nodded, chewed his lip. "Let me be clear. I'm a nice guy by choice."

Raúl grinned again. "You are a nice guy who is about to —"

Evan's hand flashed out, slapping Raúl's thumb upward, engaging the safety an instant before Raúl pulled the trigger. Raúl's eyes dropped to the Bersa, and Evan drove a wing chun *bil jee* finger jab into his larynx. Raúl clutched at his throat, releasing the pistol. As it fell, Evan caught it by the slide, his hand rising in an uppercut, the metal curled in his fist like a roll of quarters. When he struck the jawbone, he heard those beautiful teeth splinter.

Raúl went down, shoulder blades slapping concrete. His hands pressed to the bottom of his face, which was no longer the shape it had been an instant prior. Evan stepped over him carefully and turned the corner.

The woman was still before the tomb with the baby's carved likeness. But she was standing now, staring directly at him. She was poised, exceptionally so, shoulders back, swanlike neck, her hands at repose at her narrow waist like those of a ballerina in first position. Given the gloom and the eclipse of her black summer hat, he could see nothing of her features. And at this distance he was confident that she could see nothing of his.

Unsure what to expect, he started for her. Moonlight glossed the edges of the mausoleums. The air was heavy with the sweet-rot scent of dead flowers.

She didn't move as he drew near.

And then her arms straightened nervously, one hand picking at the hip of her dress. A resonance in his chest caught him off guard; it was as though she'd teleported her trepidation to him. But how did he know she was apprehensive?

And more to the point, why *was* he?

He was aware of his arms swinging heavily at his sides, the distance closing one painstaking step at a time. And then he was standing before her. Her breathing had quickened, her chest rising and falling, her collarbones and the hollow of her neck pronounced.

Trace of lilac. The faint pressure of her breath in the air. The total black of her face.

She reached tentatively for his cheek and

then seemed to lose her nerve. Her hand froze, wobbling in the air.

An exhale escaped her, putting more slack in her posture. Averting her gaze, she looked down to one side. A straw-yellow glow from a streetlight beyond the cemetery's wall caught half her face, mascara-laden lashes casting a shadow down her cheek, doubling the smoky look of her eyes.

He looked at her wide cheeks and dark shimmering eyes.

And knew it was her.

Something beneath the surface of her pale skin, something deeper than an expression or even bone structure, a physical resonance no less profound than the one that had transmitted her apprehension to him.

Ms. Veronica.

The woman who'd given birth to him.

In the pit of his gut, he felt something knot and release simultaneously. It was a yielding and a hardening, though into what and against what he did not know. His face felt hot, an uncharacteristic flush creeping north from his throat. Moments before, he'd engaged three large men without so much as an uptick in heartbeat, but now he sensed his breath moving irregularly in his throat.

She lowered her hand all the way. "Evan," she said.

He nodded.

She removed her hat, and he looked at her.

She was so much more attractive than he was, her age showing only in the textured skin of her neck and hands. She looked keenly vulnerable, almost lost, and he sensed it was not an expression she wore often.

For a moment they regarded each other.

And then the sky above exploded, a police helicopter swooping down and laying a spotlight across them. Even through the glare, Evan could make out the lettering on the side: POLICÍA DE LA PROVINCIA DE BUENOS AIRES. Rotor wash flapped the summer hat in Veronica's hand as a second helo banked into view to the east, quickly joined by a third. All around the cemetery, he heard tires squealing, sirens blooping, brakes whining.

He glanced back at Veronica. Any trace of seriousness had evaporated from her face. She looked around with cynical amusement, her mouth tugged to one side in what would have been a smirk had she bothered to put more effort behind it.

"Oh, dear," she said, her voice like a sigh. "I forgot Raúl already called for backup."

11
JUST FUCKING PERFECT

They stood for a moment in the wash from the helos overhead. Veronica had to raise her voice to be heard over the thump-thump-thump. "What happened to my men?"

"They threatened me."

"I'm sorry about that," she said, lacing her arm in his and heading calmly for the exit. "Matías is a bit excitable."

"Matías?"

"The minister of foreign relations." She seated the hat back on her head. "I'd wager that you'll meet him in a moment."

"How do you know the minister of foreign relations?"

"I'm dating him, dear. At least when I'm in this hemisphere."

Well, Evan thought, *that's just fucking perfect.*

Her arm stayed woven around his, their flesh touching. Evan pulled free, rested his

hand on her back, and steered her to the
neighboring lane to dodge the spotlight and
the wreckage of the bodyguards.

Control.

"What's your last name?" he asked.

"LeGrande."

"French?"

"Oh, honey, I'm a mutt." She cast a
sideways glance at him. "Though not as
much as you." She pressed her lips together,
smoothing the lipstick veneer. "It was an
Ellis Island botch job that my grandfather
renovated into something swankier than the
original. I'm sure it was actually Legonski
or something appalling."

A loudspeaker out front was blasting
directives in Spanish, but the crackle of
static blurred it to unintelligibility. The gate
drew into view up ahead, sets of headlights
blaring through the black iron bars, fuzzed
by the creeping mist.

He halted. She turned to face him.

"How did you get my number?" he asked.

"Years ago I tried to find you."

"How did you know where to start?"

"I'd always kept track from afar. Every
few years or so. I'd found out belatedly that
the arrangements I'd made for you with that
couple in Silver Spring had fallen apart. The
Krausses. And that you'd been moved from

placement to placement, and I used some of my relationships to . . . intervene. And get you to a more stable environment."

"The Pride House Group Home," Evan said, "was certainly a stable environment."

"One had to consider the alternatives."

He just looked at her. She looked away.

"So you knew where I was," he told her. "All those years."

"No matter how much I wanted to, I couldn't muster the nerve to see you. But two years ago I realized that I wanted to . . . I suppose I needed to meet you."

He could smell the perfume of chardonnay on her breath. She laid her hands on his shoulders, feeling his muscles, the mass of him. It was so odd to be touched that way, a sensual experience that wasn't the least bit sexual. Her face radiated a kind of maternal pride as alien to him as the red dust of Mars.

He shook himself free. She seemed neither wounded nor deterred.

"Then what?" he said.

"I started prying around the foster-care system for records. And someone caught wind of it and called me back. A man. John?"

Heat crawled beneath Evan's scalp. "Jack."

She nodded. "That's it."

His throat clutched. "When?" he said. "When was this?"

"It was Thanksgiving Day," she said. "Easy to remember."

Despite the nighttime chill, a wash of heat moved through Evan. That day was impossible for him to forget as well. The day Jack was killed. Which meant Jack had called her when he knew he was heading to his death.

Minutes left to live and he'd reached out to Veronica. Why? Was Jack — ever the father figure — trying to set things right? Was this setting things right or a colossal mistake?

Overhead the helos darted like hummingbirds, trying to pick them up again.

Veronica was talking. "He told me that you were chosen out of the boys' home. To do good. Some sort of pilot program. He said you were very successful. I was so proud. He told me you help people. I need you to help someone now."

Evan almost fed her the rote answer, that he was retired, but he stopped himself, taking a moment to find his bearings. "What else did he tell you?"

"That based on the demands of your job, you prefer to stay off the radar. I wasn't sure what that meant. Some sort of State Department analyst? A war-crimes attorney who

106

has to keep a low profile? Hostage negotiator?"

She was beaming, and he realized that this was a story she'd carried with her like a precious stone, that she'd polished in her mind's eye until it gleamed with potential. The promise of her lost boy having turned out to be something so much better than what he was.

It was a kind of discomfort he'd never experienced, a cramping at the base of his skull that reached down through him, pulling strings in his spine, his chest — and perhaps even deeper than that.

She was watching him still, that prideful shimmer in her eyes, and he felt a sudden horrible weight descend on him. He'd never had the experience of having someone else's hopes wrapped up in him. Of knowing that he'd come up short of the imagined mark. That he'd be found lacking.

Everything was moving so fast — the rattle of SWAT gear beyond the gate, the choppers veering above, the spotlights scanning the tombs, the cascade of unfamiliar sensations setting his nerves on fire.

And the awful responsibility of deflating this woman's expectations.

The loudspeaker blared again, staticky Spanish demanding that they come out, but they both ignored it.

He wanted so badly to tell her that yes, he was a cyberterrorist analyst, a prosecutor at the Hague, a hostage negotiator capable of defusing situations with a talking cure.

His mouth was dry from the wind hammering down from the rotor blades, or maybe from something else.

"No." It took a moment for him to work up the words. "I was trained to kill people."

She recoiled.

Took a halting step back.

Painful as it was, he held eye contact so she could see who he was. He watched revulsion and fear ripple beneath her features, barely visible through the cracks in her tough façade. And then she closed ranks within herself and it was like looking at any other face in the world.

The smell of dust and stone intensified. Lights strobed through the gate, muted by the thickening fog. The loudspeaker commands sharpened, telling them to exit immediately. The choppers swooped above, their beams searching the tombs all around, throwing wild shadows.

They were standing in full view, and yet no spotlight had found them. The gate clanked open, and four men entered, pistols drawn. They spread out, darting up separate lanes, one heading directly for them.

"We'd better show ourselves," Veronica said, "before someone gets shot."

She reached down and took Evan's hand. Stepping forward, she ushered them into the faint light of an antique lamppost.

Releasing his hand, she waved an arm. "Over here!"

The man zeroed in on them, melting from the mist, leading with his gun muzzle. Military bearing, pressed police uniform, requisite mustache.

Broken English. "Ms. Veronica, are you all right?"

"Of course. Matías is overreacting as usual."

The barrel swung over, aimed at Evan's center mass. It jerked upward twice. *"Manos. Manos."*

Evan showed his palms, a nice excuse to raise them into an approximation of an open-hand guard.

"This really isn't necessary," Veronica said.

The policeman's gaze shifted to her and then back to the space where Evan had just been. Evan was behind the man now. Controlling the cop's gun hand from behind, Evan palmed his left ear and knocked his head gently against the lamppost.

He crumpled.

Evan turned to Veronica. If she was shocked, she covered it well.

He'd give her this: She was quick to acclimate. It struck him that he owed some of his own disposition to her. How novel to consider that parts of him had been inherited in the twisted ladders of his DNA. The thought undressed him, peeling away a lifetime's worth of armor he hadn't known he'd been wearing.

He walked out. She scurried to keep at his side.

They exited the gates into the embrace of a semicircle of police vehicles, headlights aimed at them like cannons. The mist thickened, swirling like white dust in the beams, flowing over the shoulders of the men. The air tasted of rain.

Evan looked down the bores of countless guns.

The stakes were real once again. If he were caught, his informal presidential pardon would be voided, which meant he would spend the rest of his life consigned to a dank cell in some rendition-friendly country. Or put down in a quiet field somewhere, his flesh burned, his bones powdered and spread to the wind.

He settled himself and started forward.

One man stood apart and slightly ahead

of the phalanx, his uniform advertising him as the deputy commissioner. Leaving Veronica behind, Evan strode up to him, keeping his hands in sight. The fog swelled, cutting visibility even more. By the time Evan reached him, only the deputy commissioner and nearest two policemen were in view. All three aiming at him from close quarters.

"Look," Evan said. "I don't want to injure anyone and start an international incident. What do you say we just part ways amicably?"

The deputy commissioner's mouth twitched as if he'd tasted something and found it not to his liking. "Handcuff this man," he said. "We will deal with him in interrogation."

12
PEOPLE SKILLS

One of the cops stepped behind Evan to cuff him, and Evan allowed it. As he was steered to the nearest police car, he stumbled, brushing against the guy. He was deposited roughly into the backseat. As the door swung shut, he slung the seat belt aside, flopping it out. The vinyl strap caught in the frame when the door slammed, wedged beneath the latch.

Mist rolled across the vehicle with carwash intensity. The car might as well have been underwater.

The commotion of excited voices escalated outside, arguing in Spanish. Then a voice cut above the others. *"¿Dónde están mis pinche llaves?"*

By then Evan had used the key to unlock his cuffs. There was no inside handle, so he shouldered into the door, and it unstuck from the jammed seat belt with a soft click.

He fell outside, rolled under the car, and

flattened against the asphalt.

Then he waited.

A few seconds later, the expected outcry arose. Various department-issue shoes shuffled into view, a colorful bouquet of Spanish curse words issuing from above. Then there was running and more swearing, which quickly gave way to recriminations.

Evan relaxed, pressed one cheek to the cool ground, watched wisps of mist furl and unfurl in his slivered view. At one point the exasperated deputy commissioner passed into sight, close enough for Evan to catch a whiff of his spicy cologne. One flap of his blue uniform shirt was untucked, the back spotted with sweat, and his inexplicably brown socks sagged down by the polished black leather of his boots. Someone was screaming at him through his radio. He vanished back into the mist, his head ducked with defeat.

At long last, cars started up around Evan and tires peeled off into the night. The vehicle above him erupted as the engine turned over, laying a soothing blanket of warmth across his shoulders. It pulled forward and drove off, leaving him alone lying in the middle of the park.

He stood and brushed off his knees. The branches of the Gomero de la Recoleta ranged and twisted overhead, cloaked in mist like the cobweb-draped arms of a skeleton.

It was mostly silent, just the gentle whoosh of the wind and the sound of a couple bickering in Spanish somewhere in the soupy air. He recognized the calmer of the two voices.

He strolled over, their words coming clear. Veronica had switched to English. "— your jealousy isn't nearly as charming as you think it is."

Evan walked up to where they sat on a low bench near the base of the behemoth tree. The man at her side was exceedingly handsome, late fifties, a curl of thick black hair laid across his forehead with timeless matinee-idol aplomb. He rose abruptly. His posture, ramrod-straight, compensated for the fact that he was not as tall as he seemed to think he was.

"This is him?" he said, showing his teeth. "This is the *puta madre* who injured my men?" He stepped toward Evan. "Give me one reason not to have you thrown in prison and leave you to rot."

Veronica rose and rested a hand on the ledge of Matías's shoulder. "You'll have to forgive him, Evan," she said. "He's been working on his people skills for years, and

114

he's gotten them to the point where they're merely terrible."

Matías took out his phone, dialed, and pressed it to his cheek.

Veronica said, "Hang up the phone."

His dark eyes swiveled over to her. "Or what?"

"Or you'll never see me again."

His jaw clenched, bone rising at the hinges. Through the line a voice said, *"¿Hola? ¿Hola?"*

Matías took a breath, then said into the phone, *"Perdón. Estaba tratando de llamar a Francine."* He hung up and clenched his mouth with irritation.

Veronica said, "Evan, this is Chancellor Matías Quiroga. Matías, this is my . . . friend, Evan."

Matías glared at Evan.

"He's a former fútbol star," she told Evan. "You know how they get."

"No," Evan said. "Not really."

She turned to Matías. "Give us a minute."

"I am not leaving you alone with this man."

"I'm not asking," she said, giving him a nudge to get him moving.

Matías strode a few paces off, lit a cigarette, and glowered over at them. She flicked her hand at him, and he ambled a few steps

115

farther away.

Evan said, "Are you always like this?"

"No, dear," she said. "Sometimes I'm assertive."

"You two fight a lot?"

"*He* does. I don't show up to every argument."

"What are you doing here?"

"Argentina?" She sighed. "I'm here on a lark." She shot a glance at Matías, who was locked onto them and smoking aggressively. "I bore easily."

"Who do you need me to help?"

She lowered her voice. "His name is Andrew Duran. You'll have to find him."

"Who is he to you?"

"I made a promise to someone, his mother, to look after him if anything ever —"

Matías called over. "I need to know what the hell is going on."

She ignored him, and Evan followed her lead.

Evan asked, "Why should I help him?"

"You just need to. Go. You'll see." She reached to shake his hand. He felt something pressed between their palms — a scrap of paper. "This is a starting point. He's somewhere in Los Angeles."

That struck Evan as a hell of a coincidence.

He glanced down at the paper, saw an address scrawled in a feminine hand, and slid the scrap into his pocket.

"After this little fiasco, I'd imagine that airport security will be a problem," she said. "Get down to Saladillo Airport, Paramount Jets. I have a private charter standing by. It's a Bombardier Global 6000, but you'll make do."

"And you?"

"There's a bit to untangle here after all this, so I'll be coming a few days behind you. I have a gentleman friend with an estate in Bel Air."

"Another gentleman friend," Evan said, in a tone he did not recognize. "Is he as much of an asshole as Chancellor Matías?"

"Of course." She blinked once, indulgently. "No one wants to have polite sex, darling." She took in his reaction, amused. "What?"

"I'm trying to figure out what to say that won't make everything worse."

"And?"

"I can't think of any good options."

She leaned forward, perched on her toes, and kissed him on the cheek. He pulled away, the lipstick imprint of her lips cool on his skin, the scent of lilac lingering.

Matías was storming over, brow twisted, face red. She turned calmly to receive him as he came at her with pride-bruised grievances.

Evan took two steps back, vanishing into the haze.

13
A TEST

The handball court and the dark sedan lurch into view as Evan rounds the corner, sprinting, feeling much younger than his twelve years. The Mystery Man jerks around from his languid pose by the fence.

"Listen, listen —" Evan stops, panting, leaning over. "I know you want Van Sciver, but there's stuff about him that's . . . that's . . ." He shakes his head, agitated.

The Mystery Man walks toward him, annoyed. "What's this about? What's wrong with Charles?"

Van Sciver is currently doubled over on his bed, clutching his gut. Late last night Evan emptied two bottles of Papa Z's Ex-Lax onto the kitchen counter, crushed the pills, and mixed the residue into Van Sciver's protein powder. The cramping set in a half hour after Charles downed his morning shake, and he'd since alternated between toilet and bedroom, awash in a cold sweat.

119

"This some jealousy thing, kid? Believe me, you don't want to fuck with me. I told you. You're not good enough. You're not strong enough. You're not gonna surprise m—"

As the Mystery Man nears, Evan sinks to his haunches, pivots, and kicks the back of the guy's lead ankle with as much force as he can, sweeping the leg. Mystery Man goes horizontal and lands hard, cigarette ash scattering across his face as his head audibly strikes the asphalt.

Evan pulls himself up, all five feet and three inches, and drops the blue bandanna on the Mystery Man's chest. "You surprised now?"

In a flash the Mystery Man is on his feet, fist twisted in Evan's collar, knuckles grinding Evan's chin. His other hand draws back, blotting out the sun, and Evan realizes for the first time just how much he is willing to be hurt.

To the side the dark sedan's headlights flare. Just once.

But it's enough to freeze that fist in midair. The Ray-Bans are off kilter from the fall, dangling off one ear, and Evan sees now why the man wears them day and night — he has a lazy eye. The left pupil, slightly misaligned, peers past Evan's shoulder even as the right lasers a hole through his forehead.

The Mystery Man shoves Evan away, adjusts his shades, and walks over to the sedan. The driver's window eases down with an electric purr, but Evan can see nothing and hear nothing from inside. He stares at the tinted windshield as if it might magically turn transparent.

"But he's too small." The Mystery Man is doing his best to keep his voice hushed. He rubs the back of his head gingerly, notices Evan watching, and lowers his hand. "You want to waste two years waiting on him to grow? I can get you *dozens* who are better than him. Why's this one worth it?" A pause, and then he draws his head back sharply. "Maybe he did, but I still would've beat the shit out of him after." He listens intently for a moment, then shrugs. "It's your life."

The Mystery Man walks over, passing Evan without slowing. "Well," he says, without looking behind him. "You coming?"

Evan keeps at his heels across the handball courts.

"You wanna go home, say good-bye to your friends, your Papa Z?"

Evan pictures Van Sciver dragging himself along the wall to the bathroom, his hands balled into fists. "Nah," he says.

"You got stuff?"

"Nuthin' I need."

A few blocks away, they reach a beige

Crown Victoria, and the Mystery Man says, "Get in."

Evan obeys. The heavy door shuts behind him. He reminds himself to keep breathing.

The engine shudders to life, and they loop back through the neighborhood, passing Mr. Wong's dry cleaner that has the dish of Tootsie Pops the boys plunder with regularity. Mystery Man cuts around the corner, and Evan realizes with a stab of fear that they're going to pass right by Pride House and its big front window. And sure enough there they are, crowding against the pane just as Evan himself has done so many times.

Even though they are partially lost in the reflection, Evan identifies them by posture and silhouette. Ramón looming tall like a stick figure, bony arms poking out from his knockoff Timberland shirt. Tyrell stooped in that way of his, eyes lowered, hand swiping the wisps on his chin. Andre's head craning as he watches the Crown Vic coast by, looking lost, left behind, as far from those "California Dreamin' " roller-skating girls as ever.

Evan slumps down in his seat. The Mystery Man looks over with a sadistic smile, eases his foot off the gas a bit more to prolong the torture.

Evan risks one last glance before the row house slides out of view, just in time for him to make out Charles Van Sciver staggering to the glass, elbowing the others aside. He looks pale and sickly, his Redskins jersey askew, as if he'd pulled it on hastily. While Evan stares back in horror, Charles slams his palm against the window hard enough to make Evan wince inside the air-conditioned sedan.

At last the Crown Victoria drifts away. Charles's face, twisted in anger, remains like an imprint on the backs of Evan's eyelids.

His lips pursed with contentment, the Mystery Man focuses on the business of steering. They drive out of the city, heading north, passing drab concrete overpasses and interstate exits Evan has never seen. His excitement morphs into terror and then back again. The line between opportunity and ruin seems wafer thin.

They pull off the interstate. Evan can no longer hold his mouth. "Where are we going?"

The Mystery Man earns his moniker. He keeps his fist atop the wheel, a cigarette protruding from his knuckles, an endless ribbon of smoke sucked out the crack of the window.

They pull in to a gas station, but rather than head toward the pumps the Mystery Man idles behind the convenience mart near the air hoses. Evan eyes the meter, notes that the tank is still three-quarters full.

Mystery Man reaches for Evan, and Evan jerks back, but the hand continues past his thighs to the glove box. The lid thuds open. Inside, a gleaming handgun. The man removes it, the barrel jogging loosely toward Evan. He has gone board-stiff in the passenger seat, his hamstrings and calf muscles turned to piano wire. He tells himself to exhale, and a moment later he does.

The man smirks, enjoying this, then reverses the gun in his hand with an expert flip. Offering it to Evan. "Take it."

Evan does.

"Go inside," the Mystery Man says. "Aim it at the checkout clerk."

"Then what?"

"Oh," he says with knowing amusement. "That's all you'll need to do."

Evan feels the heft of the gun, this neat metal contraption that contains the power of the universe. This is a test — it *must* be — but for what, he does not know. Is it a test he even wants to pass? If he does, will that make him the golden boy or a calf ripe for slaughter?

For the first time, his nerve deserts him.

"I, um . . . I can't. I can't do this."

"Okay. Let's get you back home." The Mystery Man slots the gearshift into drive, and the tires creep into motion.

Evan pictures his mattress on the floor of

the crowded bedroom. Mac and cheese from the pot five or six nights a week. Ramón's brother, who left Pride House two years ago and now works at the mall, mopping floors and hauling trash. The size of Van Sciver's clenched fist.

They pull out onto the main road when Evan says, "Hang on."

The brakes chirp. Evan feels Mystery Man's eyes on him, and a moment later he gives a little nod.

The man drives him back. Idles again in the same spot. Evan takes two deep breaths, then two more.

"Well?" the man says.

Evan finds his voice. "Can you take the bullets outta the gun?"

Another smirk. The man drops the magazine, pops the round from the chamber, hands back the weapon. Reaching across Evan's waist, he flings the passenger door open.

Evan gets out. His blood thunders in his head. He holds the gun low at his side. The glass door approaches in a haze. A grating chime announces his entrance. The man behind the counter looks up. Middle Eastern maybe, or Indian, with kind eyes. He looks like someone's father.

Evan approaches the counter. "Sorry," he says, and lifts the gun.

The man rears back, knocking packs of Dentyne from the display. His hands go up in front of him, fingers wavering. "Please, please, just take. Just take."

Before Evan can react, the front door smashes open and two cops barrel at him, guns drawn. "Hands! Hands! On the floor!"

He sees them approach as if in a dream. His gorge presses up through his throat. And then his cheek is smacking the floor, his arms wrenched back so hard he thinks the shoulder sockets might pop. Metal cinches his thin wrists. He's hauled out, his head lolling weakly, and hurled into the rear of the squad car.

The beige Crown Vic is nowhere in sight.

14
WILDLY OUT OF CONTEXT

The house matching the address Veronica had palmed off to Evan was a shade of green that was better suited to peppermint frosting. The xeriscaped front yard featured little more than a few dead cacti and some square concrete blocks embedded in a sea of wood-chip mulch. The place was tiny, nestled between other Mid-Century houses, most of them Spanish style, heavy on stucco and adobe-tile roofs. A ladder, a few buckets of paint, and a bundle of detached rain gutters rusted by the side of the house, evidence of a remodel that had run out of steam. A collection of take-out menus had gathered on the doormat, a few weeks' residue.

After retrieving a backup vehicle from one of his safe houses, Evan had circled the El Sereno block a few times, checking for strategically parted curtains, lookouts in parked cars, or binoculars flashing from neighboring roofs. Once he was convinced that the approach to Duran's home was clear, Evan had left his silver Nissan Versa four blocks away in a parking garage beneath a strip mall and strolled back. He dressed generically as always — gray long-sleeved T-shirt, jeans, and an Angels hat pulled low enough to shadow his face.

A spin through the databases in the Vault had given him some insight into the man Veronica wanted him to find. Andrew Duran was of average build, not unlike Evan, and he'd checked "Some Other Race" on the last census form. From his record he seemed like another hard-luck guy who couldn't get his act together. Information on his childhood was sparse, but his sealed juvenile records showed the usual small-time busts in his late teens — possession of pot, vandalism, truancy. He'd seemingly cleaned up around the time most young men go to college or to prison, knocking around a number of jobs, the kind that put grease under the nails. Since then he'd collected an ex-wife, Brianna Cruz, and an eleven-year-old daughter named Sofia. A credit report showed a canceled Mastercard and a bank account that had hovered between seventeen and thirty-two dollars for a few months before it was closed. He'd struggled with debt and traffic fines, but the

DCSS database showed no issues with his paying child support. He was currently an attendant at a parking lot for impounded vehicles.

"Currently" meaning up until a month ago, when a murder was committed at his workplace and he went missing.

It was the kind of shocking news that — given how Evan had arrived at his doorstep — wasn't shocking at all.

The impound lot's security footage had been conveniently knocked out for seven minutes around the time of the attack, which had taken place at 3:09 A.M. In the wake of the killing, the city had begun to shutter the lot after six at night, a precautionary response to stave off potential lawsuits. The *Los Angeles Times* suggested that the murder might have been an inside job.

Duran was wanted for questioning in connection with the death of Jake Hargreave, but law enforcement had failed to locate him. Evan had perused the reports and the crime-scene photos. Hargreave's body had wound up sprawled on the asphalt, eyes open in an unnerving stare. As he'd fallen, his wrist had snapped under his weight, the hand swan-necked down as if Hargreave were displaying his fingernails. A bulky guy, air force, lots of gym muscle. A cross pendant had snagged on the collar of his shirt, caught in a nest of thin gold chain. One pant leg was hiked up, revealing the smooth-shaved calf of a triathlete. More blood had leaked from the gash in his neck than seemed possible, darkness spread beneath his body like a blanket.

A BOLO had been issued for Duran through multiple agencies, but nothing had trickled in. Evan had also checked his credit cards, banks, and cell-phone number, but Duran had done a fine job keeping invisible.

Or he was already dead.

The cops had presumably checked his house already, but Evan wanted to nose around himself.

He paused at the end of the walkway now, staring at the path of stones leading to the front door. So many questions.

Why had Jake Hargreave been killed?

Had Andrew Duran killed him?

Or had Duran witnessed the murder and fled Hargreave's killers?

And the big question resting beneath the others: Who was Andrew Duran to Veronica?

Starting up the front walk, Evan reminded himself that he was just looking into the matter informally. He'd not done anything except fly to Buenos Aires and have a conversation with a long-lost relative. He'd yet to cross any lines that would put him back on anyone's radar and void his presidential pardon.

Like, say, breaking and entering at the house of a murder suspect in a high-profile case.

Reconsidering the consequences, he veered off from the front door to the side of the house. He'd just check the backyard, peek in a few windows, nothing invasive.

Blackout shades protected the panes, giving up nothing. The small backyard was a work in progress, too, the crumbling patio replaced at one corner with new tiles. The remaining tiles waited in a lowboy dumpster puddled with rainwater. A jungle gym, half assembled by the rear fence, collected spiderwebs. As with the rain gutters, these projects had been halted abruptly sometime ago — certainly well before Duran had disappeared. What had caused him to abandon the home repairs? And the jungle gym, clearly purchased with eleven-year-old Sofia in mind?

A yellowed newspaper fluttered beneath an unlit citronella candle on the patio table. It was written in a foreign alphabet rich with circles and right-angle strokes. Korean.

Was Duran dating a Korean woman?

Did he have a Korean houseguest?

Keeping an eye on the drawn shades of the back windows, Evan stepped beneath the lattice roof of the porch and slid the newspaper free. The date at the top was rendered in both Hangul and English. Five weeks old. Beneath the paper was a junk flyer with a yellow post-office sticker forwarding the mail of Chang-Hoon Baek to this address.

Evan assembled a theory. In need of money, Duran had sublet his house to Mr. Baek, abandoning his home-improvement projects when he moved out. Judging from the take-out menus accruing on the front porch and the five-week-old newspaper, Mr. Baek had been out of town since before Duran went underground.

The cops would've already searched the house for Duran, figuring out what Evan was only now learning: that they were in the wrong place.

Evan paused abruptly, sensing something amiss. Was someone watching him from the darkness at the yard's edge?

He looked for a crack of light beneath the drawn shades. A breeze picked up, whispering through the yellow leaves gathered at the base of the porch. They silenced.

He heard it then, a telltale buzz branded into the memory center of his brain.

You never forgot that sound.

Not even here, wildly out of context, eight thousand miles and an ocean away.

It was as faint as a bee, now a touch louder.

Incoming.

He stood frozen, staring up through the lattice roof at the clear night sky.

Then his knees unlocked.

He took three big strides across the porch and launched himself at the lowboy dumpster.

A whooshing noise filled the air all around now, as if the sky itself had drawn a massive breath.

He cleared the 18-gauge-steel lip and crashed down on top of the stacked tiles an instant before the house exploded.

15
A MILLION PIECES OF EVAN

The lowboy dumpster rocked up nearly onto one side and then crashed back down, a cascade of tiles battering Evan's shoulders. He boxed his head with his arms, blinking against the dust. The sky had turned desert brown, the air filled with flecks and splinters.

He dragged himself over the edge of the dumpster and flopped flat on the ground, his head throbbing. The house was gone, a heap of tinder and flame in its place. Half a bathtub nosed up from the rubble like a breaching whale. A tangle of ducting, twisted improbably into a yarnlike ball, smoldered inside flapping sheaths of insulation. A crater dented the earth at the center where the house had taken the full force of the missile. Black smoke lingered over the site, a miasma of gloom.

Shrapnel was embedded in the outside wall of the dumpster, protruding like porcupine quills. The jungle gym by the rear fence was gone, as was the rear fence itself; the wreckage of both floated in the neighbor's pool. The air tasted poisonous. It smelled of burning rubber and plastic, a scent familiar to Evan. The only thing missing was the acrid reek of burning flesh. His head hummed, his eardrums throbbing distinctly enough that he could feel the pressure of each heartbeat.

A drone strike. On U.S. soil.

He pictured it circling invisibly two miles overhead waiting for the blossoming smoke to clear, a seamless extraterrestrial aircraft the size of a Volvo, held aloft by a modified snowmobile engine. A silver-gray assassination weapon with a smooth windowless bulb where a cockpit would be, at once eerily blind and all-seeing. Gauging the blast radius, he figured the missile to be a Hellfire launched from a Predator. Fifteen to twenty meters of damage meant they were intent on getting the job done. Even if that meant deploying a seventy-thousand-dollar missile.

They could have gone with a Reaper, faster and smaller, and its Small Diameter Smart Bomb, which could kill a man in the bedroom while sparing his wife in the neighboring kitchen. But here at Andrew

Duran's house, they clearly didn't want to take any chances.

The ultra-high-resolution infrared camera in the rotating sensor ball beneath the Predator's nose would be scanning the area now, heat-sensing body outlines, while other surveillance gear searched cell-phone signals, logged SIM cards, even read license plates on the surrounding streets. At the first sign of life, a software program aptly named BugSplat would calculate the best angle of attack and analyze collateral damage. Then a pilot in a trailer somewhere would be cleared hot to deploy the second Hellfire, a sensor operator would sparkle the target with an infrared flash, and a million pieces of Evan would join the incinerated debris filling the air.

Unless he moved fast.

The dust cloud continued to mushroom, and Evan knew he had to stagger free before it dissipated. His shirt was torn, the brim of his baseball cap scorched. He reached into his pocket and thumbed the RoamZone off, removing any digital signature from consideration. Rather than stumble out of the splash zone, he clawed his way into the heart of the wreckage, using the smoke as cover. His palms and knees burned as he fumbled around for what he was looking for. Over the sound of his own hacking, he could hear people shouting from the street, tires screeching, car alarms shrilling all up the block.

A crowd would be useful to lose himself in.

Grit lodged in his eyes, tears streaming down his face. At last his hands sank into something soft and scratchy.

The duct insulation.

One-inch fiberglass with foil facing.

He tore a massive sheet free. Wrapped it around himself to block his body's heat signature. The fiberglass dug at his raw skin and his scalp as he hobbled across the ruins, finally reaching level ground.

He moved across the backyard, through the blown-down fence, past the neighbor's pool, and up the side yard. Emerging on the far street, he shot up an alley, drawing a few stares. Ditching the fiberglass cape, he tossed his baseball cap into a trash can and popped out another block over, walking leisurely up the sidewalk, keeping tight to the storefronts, tucked beneath awnings.

He imagined the Predator ten or fifteen thousand feet up, watching bodies streaming around the accident site in real time, trying to locate which one was Evan.

And that's when it occurred to him.

They hadn't been aiming at Evan.

With his hat pulled low, his long-sleeved shirt, and his average build, he resembled Andrew Duran. They'd been watching the house from above, waiting on Duran's return. And the instant he'd surfaced, they hadn't been willing to delay to deploy an assassin for a controlled neutralization. They were willing to risk tens of thousands of dollars and a massive cover-up just to take Andrew Duran off the chessboard.

Which prompted the question, what the hell did that guy know?

They'd no doubt watched Evan circle the house earlier and disappear beneath the roof of the back porch.

It took a missile between fifteen and thirty seconds to reach its target, during which they assumed he'd entered the house.

He'd survived for only one reason, and that was because he'd been held up on the patio, reading Mr. Chang-Hoon Baek's newspaper.

Evan finally reached the covered parking garage, ducked into his low-end Nissan, and gripped the wheel. It was shaded and quiet down here. He realized he was breathing hard, his chest heaving. That his clothes were smudged with ash. That his eyes were still watering.

Eight knuckles lined on the top of the steering wheel, all of them squeezed to pale. His hands trembled slightly. He stared at them. Made them stop.

Any drone strike on U.S. soil had to have been ordered from within the deepest recesses of the government. It would be a full-black, fully deniable operation. He knew the drill: Tomorrow's news would say it was a water-heater explosion. As if a water heater could unleash a blast wave sufficient to crush internal organs, turn a house inside out, and aerate a concrete foundation with high-velocity steel shrapnel.

When General Atomics weaponized a drone in 2001, the state of warfare had been irreversibly altered. Pilots assumed a god-like power, hovering above the fray looking down, unleashing a thunderbolt from the heavens when they saw fit. For them it was a bloodless, odorless, soundless affair, more like hunting than fighting. Drones were what the DoD had hoped would make Orphans defunct, but they'd learned soon enough that human operators were still required on the ground. Those who would bear the risk and the cost. Those willing to get close enough to feel the warmth of the blood, to hear the suck of lungs through a slit throat, to smell the wreckage of voided bowels, the last hot fumes of life expiring.

The only good news was that they'd taken their shot — a norm-destroying illicit operation on U.S. soil — and they were unlikely to risk another cover-up. There were only so many atomic water heaters they could claim in the news.

Evan wiped the sweat off his forehead, left a streak of blood and ash. He'd have to clean up at the safe house before showing his face at Castle Heights. Then he'd regroup and figure out just what the hell was going on.

He thumbed on his RoamZone and called Veronica's prepaid phone.

She answered quickly. "Hello, Private Caller."

"Are you trying to have me killed?"

"What? Of course not."

Evan made out voices in the background — a dinner party? He thought he recognized the sharp timbre of former fútbol star Chancellor Matías Quiroga's voice fussing about something.

Veronica hushed whoever it was, came back to Evan. "Why would you ask that?"

"Because I went to your guy's house and it blew up."

"It doesn't help to exaggerate, dear. But I'm sorry you're finding it troubling." Then,

140

sharply, her mouth off the receiver, "I said I'll be there in a minute." Back to Evan. "I'm doing my best to get to Los Angeles tomorrow." She rattled off a Bel Air address. "I should be there by midday. Why don't you come by around one? A little mother-son time."

He could hear the smile in her voice, but he wasn't in the mood.

"What kind of trouble is this guy in?" Evan asked. "Duran?"

"I honestly don't know," she said. "He was terrified when we spoke and not making much sense. All I know is that there are people after him. And that he's scared for his life."

Evan said, "He should be," and hung up.

16
OUTSIZE MONIKERS AND WELL-HONED SKILLS

A long-term-storage shed with a roll-down orange door was admittedly an uninspired place to commit torture. But one had to work with what one had. And it was quiet enough here, with the oceanic roar of the 110 Freeway a stone's throw away, to work on a human body without worrying about being overheard.

The space was mostly empty.

A toolkit.

A sufficiently heavy chair.

And the man zip-tied to it.

To avoid getting blood on his slim-tailored suit jacket, Declan Gentner had removed it before entering and had left it with his sister outside as she preened in her little red Corvette. Queenie could stomach a good deal of violence, but she lacked stamina for the slowly escalating infliction of pain.

While the man in the chair whimpered, Declan removed his platinum cuff links and rolled up the sleeves of his nonwrinkle royal oxford shirt. Growing up broke-ass in east Philly, he and his sister had risen through the ranks of Irish organized crime as wet-work contractors before they outgrew the operations employing them — and the city itself. They both had nicknames, as was a prerequisite for working with any self-respecting East Coast outfit. Given Declan's sartorial proficiency and the resonance of his surname, he earned the title of "The Gentleman." And due to Queenie's talent for bloodletting and her penchant for the color red, they called her "The Queen of Hearts."

Just another pair of unwanted siblings from Kensington with outsize monikers and well-honed skills. Their mercilessness drove their asking price ever skyward until they were renowned on both coasts. Now they didn't get out their implements for a job that paid less than seven figures. This narrowed their client base to venture capitalists inclined toward creative accounting, socio-pathic scions with inadequate prenups, moguls tangled in inconvenient partner-ships. It had been a long climb from the gutter, but they'd arrived, shouldering up to the trough, elbow to elbow with the elite. Local kids done good.

Declan stroked the thin, meticulous lines of beard that edged his jaw. Zip-tied in the chair, Johnny "Mac" Macmanus shuddered. He wore his thinning hair scraped back tightly over his scalp, secured with a man-bun at the nape. It had the unfortunate effect of making it look as though he were wearing a hairnet. "I wish I had anything to tell you, man. *Anything.* And believe me I would. I don't give a shit about him. Do I look like someone with honor?"

"He worked with you for seventeen months. He let you borrow his car." Declan made a conscious effort, as always, to deepen his voice. He had all the musculature of a welterweight boxer, with the voice of Mike Tyson. He wet his lips, the tip of his tongue brushing the fine strip of mustache riding the bottom edge of his upper lip. "I don't let anyone borrow my car."

"Talk to his wife, man." Johnny was sobbing now, drooling freely onto his matted T-shirt. "She'd know."

"His wife despises him. They're rarely in touch. She knows nothing."

"And neither do I. I *swear.* I don't know any more than her. Why isn't she here instead of me?"

"I trust in the predictability of angry women," Declan said.

144

He crouched and laid the fine leather toolkit open. Johnny made a moan deep in his chest, like a cow lowing.

Declan ran his fingers across the tools. Surgical steel, smoother than every last thing found in nature.

And sharper.

"There are two hundred and six bones in the adult human body," he said. "More at birth, but of course they fuse over time." He removed a tenpenny box nail, ideal for installing clapboard siding, and held it up to the streetlight glow creeping around the edges of the rolling door. "The smallest bone is the stapes, the third of the three ossicles in the middle ear." Next he lifted a hammer from the toolkit. "It's tough to get to. But we'll manage."

Johnny Mac dipped his head, shadow curtaining his eyes. "Oh, God."

"The *largest* bone is the femur," Declan said. "But I only got to it once. And that was with the aid of an anesthesiologist."

He stood, hammer in one hand, nail in the other. The more sophisticated equipment he'd save for later. After all, there were 205 more bones that might need tending to. He made sure to square his posture, to pull his shoulders back. He wasn't as tall as he'd like to have been, so he compensated consciously with ramrod posture, earning every centimeter.

Johnny's face came apart a little then, wild around the eyes, the lips downpulled and wavering, the mouth of a tragedy theater mask.

There was always this moment when they realize you're going to submerge them in the world of pain and that there's not a thing they can do. When you have them trussed so well you could put a nail through any part of them, not hard, just *tap-tap-tap* until their nerves start speaking in tongues. When the skin of their face tightens to show the structure of the skull beneath, a death mask presaging what is to come.

Declan walked over to the rolling door, shouldered into it, and put his mouth near the edge. "Queenie," he said, "you might want to turn on your radio."

Her voice wafted through. "Okay, baby brother," and a moment later there was Prince, wondering if he had enough class.

When Declan came off the door, the steel slats undulated like water.

He stood over Johnny, but Johnny wouldn't lift his eyes to meet his. Johnny tried to breathe, but it just came out a series of hiccups.

"Wait," he said.

"Please," he said.

Declan closed his eyes, the insides of his lids glowing bloodred. "I'm sorry. There's really nothing I can do. It's not fair to you. But it's not fair to me either."

Johnny gagged a little.

The bloodred spread from Declan's eyelids through his entire body, firing him with a bone-deep heat. He no longer had to pay attention to his voice. It came as he knew it would, deep and resonant and rich. "There's a man who lives inside me. And he takes charge and does this until I get the answers I need."

"But what can I do?" Johnny's voice now hushed with horror. "What can I do? What can I do if I *really* don't know where Andrew Duran is?"

"You know what, pal?" Declan said, leaning in. "Together we're gonna find out."

17
THE SOCIAL ROOM

Despite a steaming shower at the Mar Vista safe house, Evan couldn't get the last bits of ash out from beneath his nails. Temples aching, eardrums pulsing, cheeks glowing with sunburn intensity, he trudged through the lobby of Castle Heights, heading for the elevator.

He made it inside without being assailed by anyone.

For once the doors closed without any chatty residents insinuating their way through the bumpers.

He tilted his head to the ceiling, let out a breath through clenched teeth.

A ding interrupted his momentary relief.

The doors parted on the tenth floor, revealing strung-up streamers in the social room across the hall, paper-cone hats, and a banner exclaiming HAPPY TRAILS, LORILEE! embellished with a cartoon cowgirl riding off into a sunset. The banner had been lovingly assembled, formed by a row of printed computer papers pieced together. The last page sported a black crayon signature at the bottom: *"Peter Hall, Age 9."*

"Ev!" Lorilee Smithson, Condo 3F, squealed with delight, extracting him from the safety of the elevator by cinching two hands around his arm. She was wearing a sparkly silver tiara. "You made it! I didn't have your Snapchat handle, so I wasn't sure where to send your invite!"

Her skin, taut from plastic surgery, took on a copper hue beneath the fluorescents. She'd had a rib resected on either side and looked as though she were perennially wedged into a Victorian corset. Evan tried to retreat into the elevator, but her French-manicured nails were unrelenting on his biceps. She dragged him into the mix.

Plastic wine cups abounded. A party blower in every mouth. "Oh, What a Night" crackle-hissing from dated speakers.

There was Johnny Middleton, 8E, ensconced in his ubiquitous Krav Maga sweat suit, teaching one of the divorcées incorrectly how to do a hand strike. And there was the Honorable Pat Johnson, 12F, wearing a lumbar-support brace because he'd thrown out his back sneezing last week. Resident elder Ida Rosenbaum, 6G, dolled up with bleeding maroon lipstick and her beloved marcasite amethyst necklace, tapped an orthotic sneaker, her trademark scowl diminished only microscopically by the celebration. Hugh Walters, 20C, had cornered a few new Castle Heights denizens by the fruit platter, regaling them with cautionary tales of HOA regulations gone ignored.

There was a fucking cake.

Lorilee sashayed off onto the makeshift dance floor, twirling like a Woodstock exile — both arms overhead, bracelets jangling, hips circling like she was working a hula hoop. Her age was undeterminable — late fifties? seventy? — but she comported herself like a twenty-something. The effect was mildly unsettling, like watching a lizard try to crawl back into its shed skin.

Evan looked around, discomfort rising through his chest, cold and claustrophobic.

"Evan Smoak!"

A blur through the crowd clarified into Peter, leaping up at Evan, clamping him in a hug. The nine-year-old was fifty pounds soaking wet, but his momentum, combined with Evan's assemblage of drone-inflicted bruises, made the embrace eye-wateringly painful.

Even so, Evan was surprised at the relief

he felt in being with Peter, one of only two people in the building he actually looked *forward* to seeing. Wincing against the discomfort, Evan set the boy down and searched the party for the other.

"Looking for my mom?" Peter asked.

Evan said, "No."

Peter grabbed an apple from a nearby table and mashed it into his upper teeth where it remained, impaled on his braces. His voice came out muffled. "Do I have something in my teeth?"

Evan said, "A bit of spinach."

Peter's laugh, like his voice, was raspy. Though most of his mouth wasn't visible behind the apple, his big charcoal eyes pinched up at the corners in a smile.

Evan plucked the apple from Peter's braces and handed it back to him. Without missing a beat, Peter returned it to the bowl. Evan grimaced.

"How's school?" he asked, having a hard time taking his eyes from the spit-glistening fruit.

Peter wore a man's button-up shirt that drooped to the tops of his knees. "Today was crazy," he said animatedly, the cuffed sleeves swaying like the ones on a magician's robe. "Sebastian? The tall kid with BO that smells like onion rings? He dropped the

F-bomb in music, and Ms. Lipshutz got super mad and tripped over the brass section . . ."

Conga-lining by, Lorilee plucked Peter's apple from the bowl and took a hearty bite, winking at Evan. He manufactured a smile, though he had little doubt it looked pained.

As she twirled beneath the HAPPY TRAILS banner, he had to admit a pang of envy at the seeming ease with which she was launching into a new life. What would it be like to feel so free to leave the past behind?

Peter was still going, talking loud over the music. ". . . it was Sebby's second strike after he got in trouble in Spanish, 'cuz he says 'grassy ass' — get it? Like 'thank you'? And so one more and he's out, which would suck, 'cuz he's the only one who knows how to pitch in kickball, so —"

Evan sensed someone approaching, the scent of lemongrass. A warm hand pressed into the small of his back, and he felt a jolt of something like adrenaline. He turned a bit too quickly, his face nearly knocking into Mia's.

As always, her curly chestnut hair was a bit wild. She was still dressed from work — not her court suit but a suit nonetheless. The top button of her blouse was undone, a delicate silver necklace resting across her sternum, a few freckles faintly visible against her olive skin.

Her smile came, as always, unannounced, as if it were catching her by surprise. "I have to say, you're the last person I'd expected to see at Lorilee Smithson's farewell party."

"I didn't know there was a party," Evan said. "I didn't even know she was moving."

"You just came for the boxed merlot?"

"I got dragged off the elevator."

"Poor defenseless baby."

"Mom?" Peter tugged at Mia's sleeve indelicately. "I have to get a poster board for that stupid family report."

Mia said, "Poster board. Stupid family report. Got it."

"And, Mom? Mom? You said we could get the Christmas tree this weekend."

"Christmas tree. Weekend. Copy that."

"And, Mom?"

"That's it. You'll get your poster board for the stupid family report and a Christmas tree, but that's where I'm drawing the line. Mom's closed."

Peter's lank blond hair swirled in the front, a cowlick that served almost as a side part. It gave him a bit of gravitas, though it was undercut by the smear of chocolate on his chin. "I was just gonna ask if I could have a Coke."

"Sprite. No caffeine."

He scrambled off toward the drink cooler, his shirttails swaying.

"What's with the shirt?" Evan asked.

"It was Roger's," Mia said. "Peter got into my closet and started wearing them last month."

Mia's husband had passed away when Peter was three. Adopted by Mia and Roger as a baby, Peter had always grappled with questions about his lineage.

"I'm not sure how to handle it. He doesn't want to talk about it. He just says he likes the shirts." Mia ran a hand through her curls, heaped them on the other side. "Maybe I should've thrown them out? The shirts?" She leaned close, put her mouth to Evan's ear to talk over the music. "There's no handbook for this stuff, you know?"

"No."

"What do you think? You said you never knew your birth parents, right?"

Evan flashed on Veronica crouching by that ancient statue of a lost baby in the cemetery, her head bowed as if in prayer. How he could see the mirror of his own features in hers. The way she'd rested her hands on his shoulders. Maternally.

He cleared his throat uncomfortably. "No."

In the background, even over the tumbao rhythm, he could hear Hugh Walters holding forth about his perplexing new symptoms of gastrointestinal distress.

It was difficult to fathom that hours ago Evan had flung himself into a dumpster to avoid disintegration by Hellfire missile.

"I know it's different, but maybe you could talk to him about whatever he's working through," Mia said. "Whether it's about where he came from or Roger's death or whatever."

Hugh's voice rose again above the music. "And tuna," he said. "It just moves right through me."

Lorilee had stopped dancing to refill her drink. She paused over by the table, arms crossed, one hand cupping the opposite elbow, staring at nothing. She looked suddenly lost. Despite the work she'd had done, Evan could see the worry lines beneath her eyes. He wondered what would drive her to alter her body continuously and drastically, to fight against time, against who she was.

She looked lonely, so lonely, as if the veil had dropped and he was seeing her true self. He felt a pang of empathy. And it struck him that since looking into Veronica's face, he'd felt more adrift. It wasn't a feeling of homecoming but a reminder of what he'd never had.

Lorilee was now studying the big going-away banner — that cartoon cowgirl riding off into a better tomorrow — with wistfulness. And fear. Johnny touched her arm, an invitation to dance, and she suddenly snapped back into form, an openmouthed smile and a whoop as she allowed herself to be spun.

How unmoored they all were, how helpless, how courageous. Lorilee struggling to present her best face to an unsure world. Peter struggling to know a father who'd died before he could solidify into memory. Mia struggling to help her son.

And Evan.

Mia had said something. "Well?"

"What?"

"Will you talk to him?"

Evan felt the slightest pressure behind his face. "Sure."

She reached out gently and touched his cheek. "What happened here? You look scraped up." This was the plausible-deniability dance they always did, former assassin and district attorney skirting the edge of the truth. He started to answer, but she cut him off. "I know, I know. You fell down the stairs, walked into a door —"

"— dodged an air-to-surface missile."

156

She laughed. "Okay, Mr. Danger."

Johnny spun Lorilee, and she let go of his hand, allowing herself to accidentally brush Mia aside and fall into Evan, her breasts hard and synthetic against his chest. Her perfume had been applied with biblical intensity.

Lorilee beamed into Evan's face. "Who's a single Pringle ready to mingle?"

She grabbed Evan's hand and spun back to dance-point at Johnny and jiggle her hips.

At Evan's side Mia covered her mouth in a poor attempt to hide her schadenfreude. Evan had an instant to say, "Kill me," before Lorilee yanked him into a cha-cha.

18
PICKING A FIGHT WITH VODKA

Upstairs, Evan stripped naked and burned his clothes and boots in the freestanding fireplace that sprouted from the expanse of the gunmetal-gray concrete floor, its flue a sleek metal trunk. Despite the fact that he'd already changed outfits once at the safe house, habit was habit. As the Second Commandment decreed, *How you do anything is how you do everything.*

He clipped his nails, taking them to the quick, and used a toothpick to scrape out the last remnants of ash. Then he took another shower, scouring with a silicone scrubber. There was virtually no chance that trace evidence remained on his skin, but he found the cleansing ritual calming; it soothed the OCD compulsions coiling around his brain, squeezing like a python.

He had plenty to be stressed about. He had met the woman who'd given birth to him and been asked to help a man who was either a murderer or a murder witness. He had been set upon by a crew of bodyguards and half the Argentine police force. He had survived a drone attack and a cha-cha with Lorilee Smithson.

He required vodka.

First he dressed, pulling his usual items from the dresser. He kept ten of each piece of clothing, all identical, folded with razor-sharp precision. From the top of each stack, he peeled one fresh item — boxer briefs, gray V-necked T-shirt, dark jeans. A new pair of Original S.W.A.T. boots from the tower of boxes in the closet. A Victorinox watch fob.

Then on to the kitchen.

He entered the freezer room, a cool waft finding his singed cheeks. The door sucked shut behind him, the rubber seals whispering an airtight *foomp.* The bottles stood in perfect parallel on the shelves like cartridges on an ammunition belt. Through the wall of exterior glass, a thousand pinpoint lights glistened in Century City, the world at bay for the moment.

He started to reach for the Guillotine Vodka but hesitated, his fingertips brushing the cool glass.

This was not a formal mission — and he was retired. He deserved to relax, take the night off, and resume in the morning. He'd offered to look into Andrew Duran for Veronica, but that didn't mean he had to devote himself to it with his usual fervor. It had already nearly cost him his life and had the potential to cost him his unofficial presidential pardon.

Whatever Duran knew, it was dangerous enough that they were willing to bring a Hellfire down on his head.

"So what?" Evan asked the chilled bottle.

He thought about the next step. When he got back on Duran's trail in the morning, Evan would make sure not to wear a hat so the eyes in the sky wouldn't mistake him again for the target and convert him into pink mist.

But the longer he waited, the more at risk Duran was.

Evan thought back to Veronica's voice over the phone. *All I know is that there are people after him. And that he's scared for his life.*

"This isn't my concern," he said.

"I don't owe her anything," he said.

The bottle did not respond. The liquid gazed demurely back at him, delightfully clouded, impatient. He didn't know what was more pathetic, that he was picking a fight with vodka or that he was losing.

He shoved out of the freezer, cursed, and headed for the front door.

He shoved out of the freezer, bruised, and headed for the front door.

19
END OF THE LINE

Sitting in the back of the police car, Evan watches the free world roll by outside his window. His cheek is swollen. Blood works its way down his slender neck, mingling with panic sweat. He feels sticky all over. His clothes cling. In his twelve years, he has never known this kind of terror, this kind of total dislocation.

As they drive, the cops up front banter, arguing about how much the Orioles suck. Another day, another bust.

But for Evan it's the end of the line.

And yet it makes no sense. Why go to all this trouble for a simple frame-up? The puzzle pieces don't fit no matter how many ways he turns them in his head.

They pull off the interstate at a deserted rest stop, and he assumes one of the cops has to take a leak. But then the rear door opens and he's yanked out onto the curb. The bigger cop sidles behind him, hands low.

"Wait," Evan says, panic rising. *"Wait."*

But the cuffs fall free with a clink. A knee bumps his kidneys, and he stumbles onto the little patch of browning lawn beside the restrooms.

The cop circles back to the driver's side, and the squad car takes off.

Evan stands there alone, a breeze cooling the sweat on his back. The air smells of cleaning solution, exhaust, and sewage. Blood hardens on his cheek. He watches the cars zoom by on the interstate below and has absolutely no fucking idea what to do next.

A familiar dark sedan turns off and climbs the slow arc of road to where he stands. The windows are tinted. All of them.

It stops before him.

The passenger window slides down, accompanied by an electronic purr.

Evan cannot see the driver, not across the passenger seat and the dark interior.

The voice that calls across is as smoky as a pilfered swig of bourbon from Papa Z's liquor cabinet.

"My name is Jack," it says. "Are you ready to begin?"

20
BAD COMPANY

Duran's old apartment complex had gone to hell in the months since he'd laid eyes on it. He lurked in the darkness beneath the sagging carport of the meth house next door, a black wave of guilt roiling through him. How could he let his Sofia live like this? How could his ex-wife not have told him how bad the neighborhood had gotten since he'd left?

He knew the answer to that already.

Because he was unreliable. Because he hadn't shown up. Because he couldn't do much to help aside from mail most of his measly paycheck to her every month.

Because he wasn't good for much and never had been.

It was colder than L.A. had any right to be, even at night, even in December.

He stared at the window of Bri's apartment. A halogen floor lamp illuminated the living room, giving him a decent vantage through the security screens. That old-timey travel poster of Paris still hung on the wall. Bri had always dreamed of going to France but hadn't gotten any farther east than Phoenix once for a human-resources conference. Among other laundry a pink sweatshirt rested over the couch back, which was the closest he'd gotten to seeing Sofia in one year, five months, and thirteen days.

She'd been so little when they'd moved in. Back then the apartment smelled of fresh paint, new carpet, and promise. When he'd get home from work, she'd toddle out and hold her arms up to him. She'd put her bare feet on top of his shoes and they would dance in the kitchen, and the stove would smell like fresh tortillas and spiced beans, would smell like home.

His throat was closing up, and he looked down and blinked till the ground stopped blurring. How far the fall from grace, from that kitchen filled with life to a rickety not-to-code room in El Sereno. One night, lubricated with a pint of the cheap stuff, he'd drawn a sketch of his daughter, re-creating her features one by one, each line a love letter, every curve a memory etched into his brain. He kept it tacked to the wall as a comfort and a punishment, a reminder that he'd left a mark on the planet but had been too flawed to build on that foundation.

His thoughts pulled to the smooth, smooth taste of rum and the feeling when it hit the blood, how it eased the cramps in the chest and loosened his focus so that for a few precious moments everything seemed warm and touched by grace. Even him.

He reached for the mantra, worn threadbare from repetition in his mind: *An alcoholic alone is in bad company.*

There was a crash from the backyard behind him. In trying to stand up, one of the meth heads had knocked over a barbecue. The man had a beard and no visible lips, an unsettling effect, as if his wiry facial hair had sprouted teeth. Red charcoal lumps dotted the concrete of the backyard and the six or so broken spirits stared down at them as if they were tea leaves prophesying the future.

The party unfroze, the people rumbling back into motion. The bearded man hit a pipe and then let a wasted girl shotgun the smoke right out of his mouth. She slumped back against a torn lawn chair, a sack of bones topped with straw hair. The other tweakers did hot rails of crushed meth, snorting it off what looked like an amputated tennis racket handle, eyes rolling white, hands jittering, tongues poking Morse-code patterns in their cheeks.

It brought Duran back to his childhood, where he'd seen a lot of things kids weren't meant to see and some stuff beyond that. It had been like a tour of duty, his childhood, a state of mind to be endured. His senses had been alive then, that was for sure. So much unrealized potential, so many dreams of who he could be and what he'd do when he got there.

And here he was hunted and terrified, hiding under the cover of a meth house, looking at the apartment where his lost wife and daughter lived, a zippered pouch in his back pocket holding ninety-nine dollars and change.

How was it possible to fuck up this badly?

The cat-piss and paint-thinner scent of meth was making his brain hurt. He stepped out from beneath the carport, leaning against a decrepit oak tree, its bark cracked like the skin of a wizened elder.

A car rolled past, deep bass bumping, the headlights illuminating a rusty knife discarded in the gutter amid scattered squares of aluminum foil. Each square had a dark patch in the middle, heroin residue staring up like a cyclops's eye.

Duran wanted to cry. He wanted to vanish through his shoes into the dirt and never come back. He wanted to see his daughter and say good-bye before they — whoever *they* were — caught up to him.

He hadn't dared to go to his house, holing up in the off-the-books sublet. And he knew he shouldn't be here either. But he couldn't help it. He didn't want to go out without looking Sofia in her deep brown eyes and telling her that having her as a daughter was the one true thing this life had given him.

A flicker of movement caught his attention, and he looked across into the apartment. Sofia spun into view holding a basket of laundry, approximating a ballerina's pirouette. Her dark hair whipped across her face. She hoisted the basket onto a hip the way Bri always did and vanished through the front door into the hall.

Duran had forgotten to breathe.

Eleven years old and still a kid. A few inches taller, sure, but her face had barely changed. Her features hadn't yet started to shift with the run-up to the teen years. Beautiful round cheeks still padded with baby fat. Those long eyelashes. That awkward child's grace as she danced, fluid and unbalanced all at once, a glorious spinning top that could capsize at any second.

Still his little girl.

For a moment he forgot himself, taking a step away from the tree toward the apartment building. And then he halted, the circumstances crushing in on him.

What was he thinking? If he had any contact with Bri and Sofia, that would put the fake deputy marshals on their tail. The same people who'd used dark magic to open up Jake Hargreave's carotid and bleed him dry.

All these long, lonely months, Duran could have swallowed his shame and shown up, could've given Sofia a Daddy Hug, the one where he picked her up and swung her around till her Crocs flew off. And now when every last instinct tugged at him to cross the dark alley and knock on that door, he couldn't.

Not without putting her at risk. Her mother, too.

He started to turn away when a flicker of movement caught his eye. A man melting from the shadows along the front of the building. He stood before the very window Duran had been watching, his hands in his pockets, staring into the living room through the security screen.

The man was perfectly still. Thirty yards away beneath the ancient oak, Duran stayed perfectly still, too.

Then the man headed for the apartment's entrance.

Duran stepped forward, plucked the rusty knife from the gutter, and started after him.

21
BUSTED CREATURES

Evan kept his hat off and wore short sleeves, the better to distinguish himself from Andrew Duran in the event that a guided missile was watching from ten thousand feet above.

How odd that after so many years spent flying below the radar, he now had to make himself visible for his own safety.

The hardware-store Schlage on the apartment building's front door yielded to a rake pick and a tension wrench, the pins popping into alignment with a readiness that suggested they'd been compromised enough times to know the drill. A rectangle of unpainted wood delineated where the latchguard plate had been snapped off with a crowbar.

The hall smelled of onions and garlic, someone's dinner hanging heavy in the unventilated air. Laughing and gossiping issued from a lit room with a wide doorless entry up the hall — a lounge? a communal kitchen? As Evan neared, he heard the thump of machines, the scent of laundry detergent cutting through the stale air.

The conversation became audible. "What's Jimmy up to?"

"Twenty-five to life."

Laughter. "You know how to pick 'em, girl!"

"Don't I, though?"

"Lemme guess. Armed robbery."

"Nothing so glam. Check kiting. Seventh offense. Se-*vunth*. Got him on RICO or some shit 'cuz of his dumb-ass cousin Renny."

"Renny? He the peach who said LuLu's diapered baby had 'junk in her trunk'?"

"The very one."

Evan reached the doorway and peered inside at four women and a girl sorting their laundry from various mismatched machines. Brianna stood at the end, thumping a shuddering dryer with the heel of her hand; he recognized her from the DMV photo he'd pulled up. At her side Sofia held a basket brimming with more clothes.

"Thing's been broke two weeks now," Brianna lamented.

A woman with copper skin and well-kept hair the color of snow *mm-mm-mm*-ed her agreement. "Busted lock on the front door, gang tags spray-painted above the garage."

Another woman in an ill-fitting spandex dress chimed in. "Yeah, well, the squeaky wheel don't get shit if it ain't in a zip code where rich folk hear it."

"Language, ladies," Brianna said, giving up on the dryer. "Can't you see this innocent child here?"

Sofia had secured one of her mother's bras over her head, the cups rising on either side like mouse ears. "Who, *moi?*"

As the other ladies laughed, Brianna tugged the bra free and flopped it back into the basket. "See what I deal with?" As Brianna spoke, Sofia mouthed her mom's words, engendering more laughter.

Brianna swatted her daughter on the arm, then planted a kiss on her forehead.

Evan stepped forward into a rush of warm air. Specks of lint snowflaked over the dryers, and a softener sheet remained impossibly airborne above a leaky vent, a feather riding a cartoon character's snores.

"Excuse me, Mrs. Duran?"

Brianna stiffened. *"Miss,"* she said. "Ramirez. My maiden name." She took the basket from Sofia and set it on a cocked hip. "What's he done now?"

"I wanted to talk to you about that," Evan said.

"Is he okay?" Sofia's dark eyes were wide, glazed with fear.

"I don't know. I'm trying to help him."

Brianna bulldozed at him, leading with the basket, forcing him to step aside. "You can talk while I fold in my apartment. And don't get no ideas. You try anything stupid, all these ladies up in here saw your face, ain't that right, ladies?"

Evan was treated to a chorus of suspicious glares and disapproving clucks.

He said, "I will be the picture of chivalry."

As he followed Brianna and Sofia up the hall, he heard one of the ladies say, "Chivalry, hell. My ass would settle for *employed.*"

Brianna's apartment was tidy and well kept, a contrast to what he'd seen of the building. Vacuum marks in the carpet, dishes neatly stacked on the kitchen shelves, photos of Sofia lined on a side table. A rickety desk held an outdated laptop and a pile of bills.

"Sofia," Brianna said. "Go to your room."

Sofia looked at Evan. "Just tell me if he's okay."

"I don't know," Evan said.

Sofia took her index finger in her opposite

fist, bent it till the knuckle cracked. "Did he kill that man?"

Brianna said, "Sof. Room. Now."

"I'm guessing it's more complicated than that," Evan told Sofia.

Sofia retreated down the brief hall, closed the door, then silently opened it a crack and peered out. She saw Evan looking, raised a finger to her lips, and winked.

He winked back at her, returned his focus to Brianna. She dumped the laundry on the couch, got on her knees, and started folding. "Talk," she said.

"I'm a friend of a friend of Andrew's."

"No you're not. Andrew doesn't have friends like you. Clean shirt, clean clothes, smell like soap. You need a better lie."

Evan didn't rise to the challenge. "I'm told he's in some real trouble."

She snapped a T-shirt harder than seemed necessary and folded it crisply. "You think?"

"I'm trying to find him."

"Yeah? Good luck. I been trying to pin down that man for a year and change. Like when he used to go on them benders. Gone. Just gone." She hunted through the mound before her. "How does that girl always lose *one sock*? Does she take it off at school?"

Evan had never lost a sock, though Mia had made him aware that this was a domestic epidemic. He glanced up the hall again. From behind her door, Sofia mimed dramatic remorse, pressing her palm to her forehead. He bit down a grin.

When he looked back, Brianna tossed the orphaned sock aside and held a T-shirt to her face. Evan thought she was smelling it. But then he saw her shoulders trembling and understood.

"Ms. Ramirez?"

When she lowered the shirt, her protective toughness had dropped from her face, and now there was just grief, pure and simple. "He's such an idiot," she whispered. "But he's Sofia's father, and I still love him despite himself, and if he got himself killed, I'll never forgive him."

Evan stood there quietly.

"I mean, no one's perfect, right?" she continued, talking at the shirt. "We're just these . . . I dunno, busted creatures. And then you have a child. A daughter. And you realize you're it — you're the mold, the model, the example. God help them. And you pray so hard that they're not doomed to fail like you. You're so desperate for them not to repeat your mistakes. Marry the wrong guy. Wind up . . . wind up here. Like you."

She threw down the shirt and rose, knees

cracking. "What's your name?"

"Evan."

"Evan. Do you really think you could help him?"

"I'm willing to try."

"What do you need from me?"

"You don't know where he lives?"

"He had a house. But he sublet it. Couldn't afford it no more, I guess. And he's been living somewhere else. Won't say where. For a guy without any pride, he sure has a lot of pride."

"Any regular hangouts?"

"I wouldn't know. Not anymore."

"Friends?"

She shook her head. "That's part of what goes wrong, right? You fold into yourself, your family. And then when it implodes, it's just you standing there."

"No one at all?"

"He did have a childhood friend. But you won't be able to talk to him."

"Why not?"

"He's in Kern Valley. State prison. Another fine influence."

"What's his name?"

"I don't know. Denny? Donnie? I wasn't exactly supportive of the friendship." She sighed, blew a lock of sleek hair out of her eye. "Andrew had a tough past. And I guess

177

I wanted him looking forward instead of backward. But what the hell do I know? Maybe we all need to do both."

"Do you have any way of remembering his friend's name? Would it be written down anywhere?"

She bit her lip, shook her head. "I'm sorry. I wish I could help."

"Okay," Evan said. "Thank you for your time. I'm sorry to disturb your Wednesday night."

"No problem. Wednesday ain't exactly bumpin' around here."

As he turned to go, he saw Sofia still spying through a crack in her bedroom door. She gave him a sad little wave, just her fingers fluttering.

"If I find anything out," he said, a bit more loudly than he needed to, "I'll let you know."

Brianna nodded.

He'd just reached the door when she said, "Hang on."

She waved him over to the desk. As he drew nearer, he saw that many of the bills were overdue. The rickety desk looked to be garage-sale quality, scratched and chipped and marred with stray pen marks. Brianna pointed to a scrawled series of letters and numbers on the rear ledge: *TG3328.*

"He wrote this on here," she said. "For

when he used to log in to send a message to his friend. It's the C-something number."

"CDCR," Evan said. "California Department of Corrections and Rehabilitation."

"Yeah, that," she said. "The inmate number."

Evan looked down at the wizened Dell laptop. "Is that his computer?"

"Hail no," she said, snatching it up and holding it to her chest. "Don't get no ideas. Just bought it new off eBay. Used. But new to me."

He showed his palms. "Just asking. I appreciate your help."

"Don't know how much help it was."

"Plenty," he said.

She showed him out.

He walked down the hall, tipping an imaginary hat to the ladies in the laundry room, who side-eyed him with distrust.

He'd just stepped out the front door and down the steps when he sensed movement behind him and felt a blade against his throat.

22
A LIFETIME AGO

The pressure of the knife on Evan's Adam's apple was light, unsure. A professional would have placed it to the side, resting over the stem of the carotid just before it split. Plus, a professional would be standing offset to protect his stomach and groin from a backward strike.

All in all a poor showing.

Evan cleared his throat. "You're gonna want to grab my head and pull it back to bare the neck," he said. "Or you'll get hung up in the sternocleidomastoid."

"The fuck?" the guy said, the knife tension easing. "You fucking crazy?"

Evan grabbed the wrist, rolled it outward, shot an elbow back into the sternum, and stepped to the side.

The guy stumbled back a few steps, doubled over, coughing. To his credit he kept the knife. When he straightened up, Evan blinked twice to stimulate his night vision and make sure he was seeing correctly.

It was Duran.

He waved the blade in front of him. The handle was chipped, the steel rusted.

Evan said, "Is that a *bread knife?*"

Duran regarded it. "Steak knife, I think."

"No," Evan said. "I'm pretty sure it's a bread knife. That curved end is gonna give you problems unless you plan to saw me to death."

Duran considered. "Maybe I'll just nick you and let you die of tetanus in five months."

Evan glanced up at the stars, listened for that buzz announcing impending doom, but there was nothing in the air except a few amorous crickets chirping away. He doubted that whoever was behind all this would risk another Hellfire on domestic soil, especially near a populated apartment building, but nearly having his ass incinerated had dented his confidence in his ability to prognosticate.

Evan said, "We should get off the street."

"Why?"

"So you can stab me in private."

"No," Duran said. "Not until you answer a few questions first. Like, why you stalking my wife and kid?"

"I'm looking for you."

"You with them other folks? The ones who

killed Jake Hargreave?"

"No."

Regarding Duran directly, Evan experienced the same unnerving déjà vu he'd felt when he'd caught his first clear glimpse of Veronica. Some flicker of recognition beneath the surface, a dreamlike recollection at once foreign and familiar. Duran's handsome face looked worn beyond its years, brown skin, stubble flecked with white. An accent mark of a keloid scar punctuated his right eyebrow, a darker shade of brown than the surrounding skin.

"Then what the fuck you want with me?" With each word Duran jabbed the rusty knife in the air.

"I was asked to help you."

"By who?"

"Veronica LeGrande."

Duran moved back, his step faltering, and lowered the knife to his side. Just then the front door hinged open and the white-haired woman from the laundry room ambled out, gargantuan purse swaying from the crook of her elbow. She labored down the stairs, grunting from the effort, and paused when she spotted Duran.

"Andrew Esau Duran," she said, wagging a finger. "Is that you? Where you been, boy?

Don't you know your daughter needs a father?"

Duran held his knife hand behind his back, looking exceptionally suspicious standing among the plants that framed the front of the building. "You're right, Mrs. Hamilton. I'm gonna set that right. I just . . . can't right now."

Mrs. Hamilton's face made clear what she thought of that. "One of these days, you gonna run outta tomorrows, son."

Duran nodded sheepishly. Under other circumstances his transformation from would-be badass to humbled little boy would have been amusing. But he looked so heartbroken it was hard for Evan to find humor in it. "Please don't mention to Bri you saw me here."

Mrs. Hamilton held a withering glare on him for a few moments, though his eyes stayed lowered. Then she bestowed her disdain on Evan. Finally she hiked her purse higher on her arm and ambled off.

Something she'd said to Duran stirred a memory in Evan.

"Look," Duran said, jarring him back to the here and now. "Ms. LeGrande's always looked out for me, but she has no idea what this is."

Evan said, "I'm guessing you don't either."

"I never shoulda called her. I need to stay underground. You're just gonna put me at risk. My family, too. You shouldn't have come here."

"You shouldn't have either."

That seemed to hit a nerve, Duran's lip curling. "Lemme make this clear: I didn't ask for your help. I don't want your help. Leave me the fuck alone."

Evan took Duran's measure. Found no chink in the armor. Again and again his experience had proved the old adage that you can't help someone who doesn't want to be helped.

From the stubborn set of Duran's face, Evan realized that his little detour from retirement had drawn to a close.

"Okay," he said, and started off up the walk.

He got two steps before a bolt of recognition pinned him where he stood.

He pictured Mrs. Hamilton's wagging finger. *Andrew Esau Duran.*

And he thought back a lifetime ago to a boy with a crazy-ass biblical middle name that no one knew how to pronounce. And to the time Danny had shoved that kid into the kitchen counter, opening up his forehead. The wound had required seven stitches and left a scar like an accent mark over the right eyebrow.

Evan turned around. Duran was still there among the fronds, waiting for him to leave.

Evan said, "Andre?"

Duran didn't move, but his face rippled with emotion, his scalp shifting. He looked confused, undone.

Andrew. Dr. Dre. Dre-Dre. Andre.

"It's Evan."

"Evan? *Evan.*" His pupils dilated, the dime dropping. "What the hell are you . . . ?" His voice trailed off into a husky rasp, as if his throat had dried up. "Why are you here?"

Evan wasn't sure which layer of the question to address first.

"I wound up in L.A. because of you," Evan said. It was, he realized, more of a statement than an answer.

"What?" Andre's forehead was shiny, sweat trickling toward his eyes. "Why?"

"The palm trees. The big-ass Cadillac." Evan could hear his voice falling into an age-old cadence he thought he'd long outgrown. "Did you ever find them? The blondes on Rollerblades?"

Andre dipped his head, his lips twitching as if he might smile, and all of a sudden Evan saw him clear as day, the boy with the spiral sketchbook and the infectious grin.

185

"Not like in my head," Andre said. "I went to Venice Beach, sure. And there they were. But they smelled like weed. And they had no interest in a fool like me."

"What happened to you?" Evan asked.

Andre recoiled, amusement freezing on his face, turning hard, and Evan could see the shame beneath. Andre had mistaken the question as a judgment on how he looked, who he'd become, rather than as the inquiry Evan had intended.

Andre's mouth twisted. "You don't know me. Not anymore. You don't know shit about me." He flung the knife down at his side, where it stuck in the soil. "Like I said, leave me the fuck alone."

He shoved through the plants and darted up the alley. Evan pursued him. A gate clanged open and shut loudly at the end, and as Evan neared, Andre twisted a padlock back into place and sank the U shackle home with a click.

Evan looked up, but the gate was topped with razor wire.

They stared at each other through the chain-link, close enough that Evan could smell the fear on him.

Andre was panting, more from emotion than exertion, it seemed, his face awash in fear and humiliation and confusion. He

186

looked utterly lost. A guy whose bank account couldn't break forty bucks. Banished from his own home. A half-assembled jungle gym in his backyard, built for a daughter who never visited. So much hope, so much grief. And despair running beneath it, dimming his eyes, the eyes of a man who'd fallen off the edge of the earth.

"Wait," Evan said. "Slow down. Just talk to me."

Andre stepped back, sweat gleaming at his hairline. Lozenge-shaped shadows from the fence broke his face into diamonds. "You can't help me," he said. "No one can."

He stepped back again, darkness enveloping him, and then there was nothing but the *tap-tap-tap* of his footsteps sprinting away.

23
A STATUE GARDEN OF ZOMBIES

By the time Evan neared the side street where he'd stashed his vehicle, his heart rate had settled no more than his thoughts. The F-150 wasn't just a truck, it was a war machine, every last security measure invisible to the untrained eye. Like the laminated armor windows. The custom push-bumper assembly up front. The run-flat self-sealing tires. The flat vaults in the bed stocked with a virtual arsenal.

The vehicle had been built to spec by his trusted friend Tommy Stojack, a nine-fingered armorer who worked out of Vegas. Tommy provided Evan ghost weaponry as well: guns with no serial numbers, taggant-free explosives, innovative tech a half breath out of DARPA.

The streetlights all up the block had been shot out, no doubt a tactical choice given the deals going down on various porches in the vicinity. A few guys called after Evan in

Spanish, and a lady whistled an invitation through sloppy orange lipstick, but he kept his head down, hands in his pockets. His eyes picked over the surroundings, scanning for threats, but part of his brain floated in years past. The gritty taste of generic mac and cheese. Andre on his top bunk, sketch pad propped on his knees, gnawed pencil scratching on paper. Van Sciver leering down at Evan, his knuckles scraped. The taste of blood in Evan's mouth, cracked asphalt skinning his palms, his knees, his chin.

He'd done his best to lock himself off from the past, and yet here it was again, rearing its head, threatening to buck him like a horse. Why Andre? And how the hell did Veronica know him?

He dialed her prepaid phone, but the number had been disconnected. If she were to be believed, she'd be in the air now heading to Los Angeles. He'd have to wait until their meet time tomorrow to get any further information from her.

As much as he was loath to admit it, the mission had sunk its fangs into him. He could see no acceptable response except to return the favor.

He knew what would have to come next. Figuring out who Inmate TG3328 was in

Kern Valley State Prison, which would be relatively easy. And then getting in to visit him, which would be relatively not.

To do so he'd require the help of the best hacker he knew. Who also happened to be an incredibly obstinate sixteen-year-old girl.

Curiosity crept up on him, a tingle beneath the scalp. What had Brianna called inmate TG3328? A *childhood friend*. The tingle grew warmer, unpleasant, turned to an itch.

The more he scratched, the deeper into his childhood this venture seemed to dig. He had no answers, not yet, just a clot of questions.

He halted, shouldering against a brick wall, and called up the serviceable CDCR website on his RoamZone. As he thumbed in the inmate number, he noticed a burn in his chest, a held breath growing impatient.

The screen reloaded and spit out a result. *Daniel Gallo.*

A complete shock and totally predictable all at once.

Danny who flew in and out of juvie like it was a revolving door. Danny who'd play-shoved Andre into the counter, giving him that beauty gash on the forehead. Danny who last Evan had heard was serving out a ten-year term in Chesapeake Detention

Facility for armed robbery.

He and Evan hadn't been particularly close. They'd moved at the periphery of the circle, Evan keeping his head low to dodge Van Sciver's wrath, Danny occupied with untangling his own various strands of trouble. One time Danny had shared with Evan a Coke he'd bought at the gas station using pennies salvaged from a wishing fountain in a strip-mall pupusa joint. With crystalline clarity Evan remembered the coolness of the bottle, the intoxicating fizz, how it had offered a few moments' respite from the baking Baltimore sun. It had been a small act of kindness, delivered with no pomp and circumstance, but small acts of kindness were all they had to give or receive in that summer heat. A few sips of Coke might as well have been a king's ransom.

The past could be so fickle, a moment boomeranging home twenty-seven years later with a palpability greater than the concrete beneath his boots.

The woman who'd given birth to him. Winging to L.A.

Andre Duran. In the wind.

Danny Gallo. Locked in a box.

How would these threads knit together?

Evan shoved off the wall and resumed his course, cutting between two banged-up low-

191

riders onto the side street.

As he neared his truck, he spotted the bearded meth head and his crew from the house neighboring Brianna and Sofia's apartment complex. They'd circled the F-150, peering in the windows hungrily. The bearded man bent over, plumber's crack on full display above filthy sagging jeans, and pried a loose cinder block from a low barrier blocking in a dirt yard.

He held it overhead, staggering back toward Evan's truck.

Evan stepped into sight. "I wouldn't do that."

The man sneered, yellow teeth seeming to spring from the beard itself. Most of them had caved inward, but his incisors remained in place, pronounced and tusklike. His crew tittered, rippling around him.

"You gonna stop us?" he asked.

Evan paused, hands still in his pockets. He tilted his forehead to the truck. An invitation to proceed.

The man smiled again, eyes glistening. Then he let the cinder block's weight tug him toward the passenger window. He let go at the last moment. The cinder block struck the polycarbonate thermoplastic resin glass with an impotent thud, bounced back, and knocked him square in the forehead. He tripped over the curb and lay sprawled on the sidewalk, unconscious.

Evan removed his key fob from his pocket and gave it the chirp-chirp.

The others stood frozen, a statue garden of zombies, unblinking eyes and crooked shoulders.

"Excuse me," Evan said.

He threaded delicately through them, stepped over the unconscious man, got into his truck, and drove away.

24
AN UNUSUAL RELATIONSHIP

Evan watched the peephole for a shadow, but Joey opened the door of her apartment without checking.

He said, "How many times have I told you to look who's at the door before you open it?"

"How many times have I told you I have pinhole cameras installed in all the heating vents so I can watch you shuffle up here all unannounced like you own the place?" She waved her Big Gulp at him. "Oh, wait, that's right. You *do* own the place."

After Joey had washed out from the Orphan Program, a series of unlikely circumstances had landed her in Evan's charge. Eventually he'd gotten her to California and set her up in a Westwood apartment building that had failed to meet his standards for security. So — through an array of shell corporations — he'd bought the place to make improvements and keep her safe, an arrangement he believed he could hide from her. But outwitting Joey was a virtual impossibility; she'd not only deduced the chain of ownership but hacked into the legal records, intent on reassigning ownership to herself.

He'd found out and threatened to ground her.

She'd relented.

It was an unusual relationship.

She was wearing eyeliner for the first time, just a hint that made her emerald eyes pop even more. Curious. Her hair was styled with a more severe undercut than usual, shaved tight on the right side, a black-brown wave waterfalling across her cheek in an uncharacteristically styled fashion. She'd traded in her wife-beater undershirt and baggy flannel for something resembling an actual blouse. And a scent wafted off her, different from her usual fragrance of Dr Pepper and Red Vines.

He said, "Why do you smell like orange blossom?"

"What?" Her blink rate picked up, a nonverbal tell. "It's nothing. Probably just soda."

"It's not soda. More . . . flowery."

"There's nothing flowery. You're hallucinating. C'mon, X. Hugs not drugs."

A Rhodesian ridgeback snout shoved between Joey's thigh and the doorframe, the dog whimpering to get at Evan. Evan had placed the dog in Joey's care thinking the companionship would be good for them both, and Joey feigned resentment at the responsibility. It was one of many dances she and Evan did around unspoken emotions and unacknowledged stakes.

"Can I come in?" Evan asked.

"I'm kinda busy," she said. "Plans."

"Since when do you have plans?"

"Since I'm an independent young woman who doesn't have to answer to a controlling uncle-person type."

"Josephine," he said.

She returned his glare. Then sighed, her shoulders rolling forward. *"Fii-nuh."* She drew the word into two syllables. "But it better be quick."

She stepped back, retreating to her workstation, a pod of monitors and computers that served as her hacking nerve center. The ridgeback went crazy, wiggling against Evan, shoving into his thighs, demanding to be petted. The pup had bulked up to at least a hundred pounds, his coat looked shiny and healthy, and the scars from his bait-dog days had healed nicely. An expensive-looking fabric collar, candy-cane-striped for the holidays, gleamed against his russet-tan fur. Contented with Evan's affection, he trotted away and plopped down on his plush bolster bed.

He hoisted his hound eyes at Joey, who was already typing away at her station, and gave a gentle whine for her attention.

"Quiet, Dog," she said. She'd refused to name the dog because she didn't want to grow attached to him.

Which she definitely wasn't. Attached to him. Not at all.

"Fancy new collar," Evan observed.

Joey kept her gaze unbroken on the monitors. "It was on sale."

"And the bed. Is that a pillowtop?"

"It's just what some website recommended for big dogs. 'Cuz their joints or something. I don't know."

She looked up finally to scowl at Evan.

At her shift in focus, Dog the dog's tail went *thump-thump-thump* against the bolster bed.

She went back to work. Snuck another look at the dog.

Thump-thump-thump.

Joey's face softened with affection.

Evan pretended not to notice the lovefest. One of the many arcane rules he'd learned when it came to dealing with a sixteen-year-old girl was to let her express herself in her own time.

"How are your courses going?" he asked.

One of the conditions of her living in here under his unofficial supervision was that she stay enrolled at UCLA. She'd chosen a computer-science major, promptly tested out of a raft of classes, and was struggling to slow her brain down enough to tolerate the remaining ones.

She guffawed. "Dull and last-gen theoretical. They're way outta date on machine learning, neural networks, and neuromorphic computing. The other day in lecture, the prof was going on — *incorrectly* — about PyTorch with some boring-ass PowerPoint, and I was, like, *dying* of tedium, so I thought I'd, ya know, crack the staff-only Wi-Fi. I did a quick deauth attack to force a reconnect and then sent the captured key hashes to the CrackStation critters, and next thing you know I'm inside the network and then into his laptop using a handy Metasploit payload, so I replaced one of his PowerPoint slides with a pic I found in his Photos of him and his wife in puppy-play sex outfits at the Folsom Street Fair. And it came up, and everyone was all like, 'Ah, kill that shit with fire,' and then he knocked over the laptop and it broke, and then lecture got canceled."

Evan cleared his throat. Staved off the ice-pick headache threatening to bore through his frontal lobe. "Let's just pretend I didn't ask."

"Or . . ." Fingers templed like a Bond villain's, she swiveled magisterially in her gamer chair to face him. "We could sit here and bask in your discomfort until the heat death of the universe."

"You need to stay in school."

"Even though I could, like, teach the professors?"

"We're not having this discussion again. Pick another major."

"But then I'd have to do *work*. When we both know that — especially now that you're in your dotage — my talents would be better spent taking over for you. I'd be a *way* better Orphan X. You're a middle-aged white dude. Get with the times. C'mon, X, tell me the world's not ready for a rebrand."

That ice pick made further headway, burrowing toward the brain stem. "The world's not ready for a rebrand," he said wearily. "*I'm* not even Orphan X anymore. We've discussed this. I retired."

"Then what are you doing here?"

"I just need help on a . . . thing I'm looking into."

She rolled her eyes, shot a glance at the wall clock. "Can we get on with whatever it is you need?"

"I need to hack into the CDCR website —"

"Even a two-digit-IQ noob like you should be able to manage that."

"— and get cleared as a visitor to Kern Valley State Prison. And get put on the log under one of my fake IDs to meet with the inmate. For tomorrow."

She frowned. "Hmm. Which ID you wanna use?"

He told her. As his unofficial in-house hacker, she kept files on his various identities and papers.

She whipped back around in her chair and pounded away on one of myriad keyboards. A cluster of monitors hovering around her lit up with code. She went at it for a while, fingers blurring, pausing only to slurp from her Big Gulp and once to strain herself into an awkward half hug so she could massage out a knot beneath her shoulder blade. Dog the dog shifted on his bolster bed, emitting a contented groan.

At last Joey's hands slowed. She tapped the mouse. Rolled the sensor ball. Tapped it again. She spun to him and chef-kissed her fingers, complete with a *"Muah!"*

"Done?"

"You're on the books for seven a.m. under the name 'Frank Kassel.' Bring the appropriate photo ID and filled-out waivers. I sent you a link. I assume you can figure the rest out all by yourself like a big boy. Now, is that it?"

Her urgency caught him off guard; he was used to her prying for details, not rushing him out.

He thought about the impound lot where the murder of Jake Hargreave took place. How the surveillance cameras had magically gone down during the key seven minutes. If Joey could coax some other electronic eyes out of the ether, there might be a way to piece together a picture of what happened.

"Can you find geotagged cameras in a specific area?"

She snickered. "Is Putin an alpha?"

"One straight answer would be so lovely."

She did robot voice and robot arms. "Yes. I can. I'm so sorry, Mr. X." Her posture reverted to her characteristic slump, as if she had no bones and the chair was her exoskeleton. "I'll just hack up some code to hit the Shodan device discovery API and filter results for our target area. It already comes back geotagged for every device it finds. Then we fire up five hundo Amazon EC2 instances and automate the crap out of sploiting them with pro_exploit from Metasploit again. We bust into that shit, we're looking at the world through their eyeholes."

"I have an idea for your new major."

"What's that?"

"English as a second language."

"Wow. Dad joke. Maybe you could start wearing plaid shorts and T-shirts with golf puns on them. And, like, wearing shower sandals with socks. And drinking Arnold Palmers. And —"

"Joey."

"Fii-nuh."

As he stepped into her circular work area, he sensed an immediate rise in temperature, the burned-wire smell of electronics working overtime. He commandeered a keyboard to search out the impound lot's address, but the monitors were stacked three high all around and he wasn't sure which one to look at. Joey reached up, cupped his chin, and pivoted his focus to the appropriate screen.

He pulled up the lot on Google Maps. "A murder took place there three weeks ago, but the security system was knocked out. I need to know if there are any other cameras with a partial view of that parking lot that we can get into and grab archived footage from."

"I need specifics, X. Date, times. And what's the story with this? A prison visit, a murder scene. That's a lotta shit for a retired dude instead of . . . ya know, bingo."

He stared at her, his mouth shifting. He had no one else he could talk to about something like this. Someone who had the same points of reference to understand how tricky this was for him to navigate. He mustered the words. "The woman who gave birth to me contacted me."

Joey's eyebrows shot up, disappeared beneath a fringe of hair. "You don't have a mother. I mean, you know what I mean. No wonder you decided to risk your whole presidential immunity setup. Must be super emotional, right?"

He said, "No."

"But I mean, it's gotta be weird, right? Like it must've rocked your world?"

He said, "No."

"C'mon. Everything you thought you knew about yourself is different. I bet you're *freaking out.* I mean, *internally* obviously, since you're all No Affect Guy outside and incapable of expressing human emotion."

He said, "No."

"X," she said. "It's your *mother*. What's she like?"

He grimaced. Leaned back against one of the curved desks. Crossed his arms. "Can we skip all that so I can read you in on the mission?"

"Ah. It *is* a mission. I *knew* it."

"I misspoke."

She started her next retort, but he raised his palm emphatically. "Joey. Do whatever you need to do to get to those cameras. Shut your piehole. And let me fill you in."

As quickly as he could, he gave her a just-the-facts intel dump. When he finished, she stared at him, eyes wide, her surprised face looking impossibly youthful.

Before she could respond, someone rapped on the door, and she stiffened as if she'd been hit with a cattle prod.

25
THE WIDE WORLD OF FUCK

Evan couldn't read Joey's face. She kept her gaze at the monitors, not looking over at the door.

The rapping came again, more insistently.

"You expecting someone?" Evan said.

"Nah. Just ignore it. They'll go away."

"Joey. Is someone harassing you?"

She shot him a look, her green eyes blazing, emphasized all the more by that eyeliner. "Harassing *me*?" she said. "Have you *met* me?"

"I'm gonna answer it."

"Don't answer it."

Already he'd exited the workstation. He put his body to the left of the jamb and cracked the door.

A young guy stood outside. Sagging jeans, wide-collar shirt, thumbs looped in a distressed leather belt. A tuft of rigorously mussed hair with a hard side part razored in. He was ridiculously good-looking, no doubt a future actor or a Starbucks barista.

"Oh," Evan said.

Joey's makeup. The blouse. The orange-blossom perfume.

"Oh," Evan said again.

"Hey, man. I'm Bridger. Joey here?"

Evan heard a thunk behind him. Joey's forehead hitting the desk.

"Where do you know Joey from?" Evan asked. *"Bridger."*

"Like, lecture class."

"Lecture class," Evan said. "How old are you?"

"Uh, eighteen."

"Eighteen," Evan repeated. "You know it's illegal for you to —"

"Evan." Joey was suddenly at his shoulder, tugging his arm. Behind his back she gathered his hand in a pronating wrist lock to steer him away from the door. He reached back with his other hand and deployed a countergrip, prying her hand off his.

They both kept their faces pointed at Bridger, maintaining smiles as he rubbed at an honest-to-God soul patch on his chin.

Dog the dog was up, growling. Seeming to sense that Evan had the situation in hand, he padded back to the Red Vines tub that served as his bowl, lapped up some

206

water, and huffed down onto the pillowtop again.

Evan kept his stare level on Bridger. "I didn't catch a last name."

"Bickley. But I go by Bicks sometimes, ya know." He shoved his hands into his pockets, rose up on his tiptoes, rocked back on his heels. "Anyhoo. Joey and I were supposed to, like, hang out."

"Hang out?" Evan said. "It's two in the morning."

"So it's a bad time?"

"Yes," Evan said as Joey said, "No."

"Okay. Cool, cool." Bridger bobbed his head, managed eye contact with Evan. "And you are . . . ?"

"My uncle," Joey said in a rush. "This is my uncle. He's protective — *really annoyingly protective* — and I guess he needs to talk to me now about some stuff, so could we, like, reschedule?"

"No worries," Bridger said. "Grab you tomorrow? Like eight o'clock?"

"Surethat'dbegreatthanksbye."

Joey ratcheted the door closed in Bridger's nonplussed face and delivered Evan an extra-pointed glare; on the receiving end, it felt like a shiv to the chest. "What the actual hell, X?"

At her tone Dog the dog lifted his head,

collar tags jangling. Joey went on tilt, coming at Evan, driving him away from the door.

Evan said, "Language."

"I cannot *believe* you. You're such a dipshit."

"Joey," he said. "That's offensive."

"Yeah, to dipshits for having to be compared to you."

"He's eighteen years old."

"I'm in college. Who am I supposed to date? Middle-schoolers?"

"Because that's the only other option."

"You can't just come in here like you own the place — insert punch line here — and be all *controlling*."

"It's not about being controlling. It's about making a few inquiries about a guy named Bicks with a soul patch who says 'anyhoo' and wants to hang out with you at two in the morning."

"We were gonna go to a party!" she said, again digging furiously at that muscle knot near her shoulder blade. "Oh, my God. I should just give up on ever being normal and enter a nunnery."

"Before that can you help me with the geotagged cameras?"

She made a noise like a horse whinny but more rageful and then stomped off to her workstation, where she began pounding on the keyboards.

Evan retreated to the bolster bed and sat on the floor next to Dog the dog, who offered him a sympathetic gaze. For a while Evan scratched at his scruff, the dog grumbling with pleasure, a sonorous groan-snore.

Finally Joey said, "Get over here."

He obeyed. Dog the dog obeyed as well, getting halfway across the room before realizing that the command had not been directed at him. With relief he slunk off.

Evan took up a position behind Joey. "What am I looking at?"

"A variety of digital footage from cameras around the block cued up and frozen the night your boy was killed. We're starting here." She pointed at a monitor behind Evan's head, her fingernail barely missing his cheek, a near gouging that seemed not unintentional. "An EyeSky Web-connected cam at a First Union Bank of SoCal ATM."

She tapped the mouse and the frozen black-and-white scene thawed to life, a silent winter film. Leaves scuttling across a sidewalk. A city bus hogging both lanes, there and then gone. A Hasidic Jew shuffling by wearing his wisdom on his face, a twelve-inch charcoal beard, brittle and ragged.

And then a Corvette drifting into the

camera's purview, creeping along at a pedestrian's pace. Tinted windows. Blank license plates.

It eased from the frame, and Joey clicked again. The neighboring monitor picked up the Corvette from a different angle, capturing it pulling up to the curb across the street from the tall chain-link fence of the impound lot. It idled opposite the open gate. No sign of movement except fog wisping from the exhaust pipe.

Nothing happened. And then more nothing.

Joey nudged the footage of both screens forward, the time-stamp numbers flipping like slot-machine reels, closing in on 3:00 A.M.

Back on the previous screen, a Prius darted into view on fast-forward and then swept into the new field of vision. Joey slowed down the world as the car turned in to the parking lot.

In the dark Corvette, no one moved. It sat there heavily, breathing exhaust, lights gleaming across the impenetrable windshield.

Joey's fingers rattled across her Das Keyboard, and then she flicked her chin at yet another screen up on the third row of monitors. A slice of a view onto the impound lot from a neighboring rooftop camera allowed them to track the Prius. It pulled up the main lane carved through the wrecked vehicles, creeping toward the kiosk. The kiosk door was ajar, the big window mirroring a fireworks burst of skyscraper lights.

The Prius halted midway up the lane. A man climbed out.

Jake Hargreave.

No idea he was being watched.

He walked over to a totaled Bronco and tried the caved-in driver's door, but it wouldn't budge. He circled to the passenger seat, tugged it open, and ducked inside.

Evan sensed movement and pivoted back to the second monitor, which held the parked Corvette in view. He snapped his fingers. "Look."

A man and a woman finished climbing out of the car. They kept to the shadows on the opposite side of the street, holding tight to the buildings. The man wore a fine-tailored suit that seemed at odds with the sense of menace he projected. The woman, too, was done up, fluffy hair, jeans, a fitted top. They could have been heading to a night at the theater.

The man's elbow was bent, a hand held out to the side as if bearing an invisible butler tray. Nothing on his palm.

Together they strode a few paces up the sidewalk, presumably to gain a better vantage on Hargreave. They paused, partially illuminated by a streetlight. The man was locked on, a predator's stare pointed off frame, staring through the darkness at Hargreave.

But that's not what lifted the hair on the back of Evan's neck. It was how the man was holding his palm up, as if it contained something incredibly dangerous and delicate.

The woman gave a nod, walked calmly back to the idling Corvette, and sat behind the wheel. Ready to take off.

The man remained in the outer throw of the streetlight, hand still raised. And then he lowered it to his side.

Monitor Three: Hargreave backed out of the truck abruptly. He stared in the opposite direction of the couple — toward the depths of the impound lot.

"What's he looking at?" Evan asked. "Do we have an angle there?"

Joey shook her head, transfixed.

Hargreave stood with his back to the street, staring at someone or something. Head tilted to one side with curiosity.

There was an awful calm, the breath-held moment before calamity.

Hargreave turned partially.

And then he seized, muscles jerking.

Blood shot up from his neck.

With a hand he tried to stem it, to no avail.

He crumpled.

And wound up in the crescent pose Evan recognized from the crime-scene photos.

The man in the suit observed calmly. Then held his palm upturned in the position he'd had it before.

Monitor Three: The kiosk door flew shut. It was right at the edge of the camera's purview, so they couldn't see who or what had struck it. The same invisible force that had opened up Hargreave's neck?

But no, the man on Screen Two lowered his arm again, frustrated. Glared into the darkness. Something had not gone according to plan.

In the Corvette the woman's mouth was moving. Her face strained, cords in her neck. Anger? No — concern.

The man jogged back to the Corvette and jumped in.

It zipped out as if on fast-forward.

Quiet street. Quiet compound lot. A black, icelike sheet spreading beneath Hargreave.

Joey cocked back violently in her chair, laced her hands at the nape of her neck. "What in the wide world of fuck."

Evan couldn't muster the focus to give her a reprimand. Plus, she'd expressed his thoughts exactly.

"What do you think's up with Merlin?" she said. "Some super-secret CIA program to harness energy and, like, kill people with invisible rays?"

Tingling spread beneath Evan's face, a sunburn prickling from the Hellfire's afterglow.

"No," he said.

"What, then?"

It seemed too far-fetched and yet made perfect sense at the same time. He shook his head. "I'm not sure yet. We need to dig into this more."

"Where do we start?" she asked.

"Can you run facial ID on the two from the Corvette?"

"At this distance with grainy footage?" She shrugged. "They kept to the shadows pretty well. I don't know if we'll have enough sensor points."

"Is that a no?"

She furrowed her brow at the challenge. "Have you heard of model-based feature extraction for GRS?"

"No, but if you hum a few bars, I can fake it."

"You know the only thing missing from

this social train wreck of an evening? Even more Lame Dad Humor. I mean, *really*, X?"

"GRS," he said, steering her back on track.

"Gait-recognition software." She was typing. "China's been kicking ass in this arena — shocking what you can accomplish with, like, zero regard for privacy — and I might have left myself a backdoor . . . in case I ever . . ."

She trailed off, typing in quick bursts, pulling imagery of the man and woman from one monitor to another, a virtual wireframe encasing them as they walked. Evan admired her trancelike calm, all that brainpower churning beneath the surface.

The screens to Evan's right flashed up rap sheets and booking photos.

Declan Gentner.

Queenie Gentner.

A brother-and-sister team out of Philly, laureled with requisite hard-bitten monikers. They'd been investigated for unlawful detention, homicide, continuing criminal enterprise. A scattering of plea deals for lesser charges like tax evasion and assault. No last-knowns, no current utility bills, no phone numbers on record.

"They seem pleasant," Joey said. "This thing keeps getting weirder and weirder.

What the hell did your mom hook you into?"

Mom.

The unfamiliarity of the word hung in the air like something tangible. He didn't have a mom. He had a woman who had given birth to him. And who'd led him into a set of circumstances seemingly designed to end the life she'd created.

He rubbed his eyes hard, spots of light blotching the darkness. So many fronts to tackle.

He had to locate Andre Duran as soon as possible.

He had a prison meeting with Danny Gallo in a few hours.

He had to sit down with Veronica and pry more details out of her.

He had to figure out why Hargreave had been killed.

He had to determine who the Gentner siblings were working for.

He had to uncover who had authorized the use of a Hellfire missile on U.S. soil.

"I'm going to head to Kern Valley Prison," Evan said. "Can you look into Hargreave for me? I checked him out a bit, know he's air force. I want know more about his newer postings and deployments, but they're behind a second DoD firewall."

216

He rubbed his eyes some more.

"X?" Joey sounded concerned. "You look tired."

"I'm fine."

"I mean, just . . . watch out for yourself. This kind of stuff — I mean, your mother, childhood shit — it hits deeper than a normal mission. It breaks the Fourth."

The Fourth Commandment: *Never make it personal.*

He said, "Just get me the stuff on Hargreave."

She nodded and for once didn't offer a retort.

He headed out. Paused outside, keeping the door cracked. Joey didn't notice. She looked over at Dog the dog, who lifted his head, tags jangling on his fancy new collar.

Joey said, "Who's such a good boy? Who's such a *good, good, good boy?*"

A big warm baby voice, devoid of its usual sardonic underlay. That long ridgeback tail thwapped the luxurious bed, a steady beat of affection.

Joey ran over and sprawled on top of him, the dog large enough to take her weight. She buried her face in his neck. "Who loves you? Who loves you the most in the world?"

Syrupy and embarrassing. And yet Evan found himself grinning.

He eased the door gently shut, strolled to his truck, and started the long drive to prison.

26
PICK YOUR POISON

Terror came black and dense, an oil slick. Declan Gentner woke up into it. It filled his rib cage, compressing his heart, paralyzing his limbs. Couldn't call out, couldn't lift an arm to knock on the hotel wall to beckon his sister in the connecting room.

No oxygen in his lungs.

Muscles strained to the breaking point.

A graininess in the dead-of-night air, pixelated with hyperclarity.

Eyes bulging to pop.

Sheets already kicked down, briefs clinging to him, air hot-cold on his bare chest.

He felt the vein squiggling across the front of his neck surge with his heartbeat — *still alive, still alive* — and the heat of his face purpling.

He strained and strained but couldn't produce a twitch of a single muscle.

Like being buried alive inside his own body.

And then it began.

Someone scraping on the locked door.

It bulged inward like rubber, fingernails splintering through, lifting the paint.

The door opened, hinges moaning.

She was there as always, framed in the doorway. Those long nails silhouetted at her sides, manicured to bitter-housewife perfection.

Still couldn't move.

But blood was shoving through his veins — *still alive, still alive.*

Not real. Not. Real.

Now she was over the bed, looking down at him. She didn't move, just teleported here when he blinked.

A pure-black cutout. A-line dress and hair done up in a bob, even her curves somehow anachronistic. She reached out, fingers splayed. Didn't even have to touch him. She just mimed the clawing.

Gouges rose on his arms, his neck.

No air. Lungs nothing more than deflated bags. Muscles knotted, the arches of his feet crocheted into stitches.

Her head cocked, that neat bob bobbing, the Virginia Slims–sanded voice, deep and sexy and rageful: *Not going to raise you to be like* him.

Cigarette burns sizzled to life on the

insides of his thighs.

Running around to prove he's still a man, and all I get left over is that little-boy temper.

She leaned closer yet, those womanly cheekbones, eyes glowing white as bone.

No matter how spotless a house I keep.

Fingernail scrapes flared to life on his chest —

No money, two kids underfoot, and still looking like I do.

— drifting down the hollow of his sucked-tight belly, lower, lower, lower —

Teach you what he won't learn.

At last breath came in a screech.

"Queenie!"

Declan choked out the word and then curled up, fetal and shuddering.

He heard his big sister's feet hitting the carpet one room over, the connecting door flying open, the heel of her hand striking the light switch.

And then he was back in the world, unclouded, the apparition gone. Panic sweat cooled across his ribs.

Queenie was on the bed, cradling him, his head limp in her lap. She wore a red silk chemise, and his cheek was against her bare thigh, her breasts pressed to the top of his head, but it wasn't fucked up and weird, it was just comforting, and she was rocking him, rocking him, her lips pursed as she shushed him like shushing a child.

They were Irish twins, Declan born eleven months after her, and sometimes it seemed they could communicate telepathically.

Like now: *I'm here. I'm here. I'm here.*

The warmth of her flesh, like his own. The sway of her arms.

Breathing. Oxygen catching up to his head, his bloodstream. Transforming him from child to adult.

He kick-shoved himself so he was leaning against the upholstered headboard. She moved to sit at his side, both of them staring straight ahead. Her fingertips gently traced up and down the underside of his arm, calming him.

The Four Seasons on Doheny was one of his favorites, with its plush furnishings and Beverly Hills–obsequious service. He stared at the fringed throw pillows, the textured cream walls, the plush bath sheets visible on the warming rack through the bathroom door and let the luxury soothe him. Let it seep into his bones and warm him back to life.

He could taste his breath, sleep-stale and hot. His inhalations still came in jerks. He willed them to slow, to steady out, and finally they did.

They sat in silence, breathing.

After a time Queenie said, "Mom?"

He nodded.

"You caught all of that," she said softly. "And I caught none."

"Thank God for that." Sweat beaded on his chest. He smeared it across his slick skin. "She wanted to make me different than him. And she did. Can't take the blessing without the curse, right?"

Queenie nodded. She smelled like sugar, a candied overlay to her nightly lip gloss. "Mom did adore me."

Declan said, "Dad, too, when we saw him."

"But Mom, she really tucked me under her wing. Flesh of her flesh. Shaped me right down to the thoughts in my head. She's still in there." Queenie rolled her lips. "Sometimes the blessing *is* the curse."

She was right. There was no way to get through a household like theirs without damage. Pick your poison. Pick your medicine. And bury it beneath a polished-clean veneer.

Queenie's hand slid down to clasp his, and they squeezed their palms together like they'd been doing for twenty-eight years, their knuckles aligned to form a single big fist, two halves of one whole as they'd always been and would always be. They'd gotten each other through their childhood, day after terrible day.

The burner phone rattled loudly against the nightstand, making him start.

Never a good sign at 3:42 A.M.

He and Queenie exchanged a look.

Late-night call. We haven't performed adequately. The doctor is unhappy.

He picked up the phone, rested it on his bare stomach, clicked to speaker. "Yes?"

"Because of your inability to handle the situation," the doctor said, "I had to take more drastic measures. A high-visibility strike."

Declan cleared his throat. "Did you get him?"

Andrew Duran had to be killed by Declan or Queenie's hand, or they wouldn't get the back half of the payment.

"We couldn't determine in the immediate aftermath," the doctor said. "Too much detritus for visibility and too hot for thermal imaging. But the news reported no human remains."

Declan exhaled. His jaw ached.

"I can't risk another strike like that," the doctor said. "Too much exposure. We missed our chance."

Declan felt Queenie's hand warm in his.

Why didn't you call us in instead? We could've handled it.

"Why didn't you call us in instead?" Declan said. "We could've handled it."

"Why weren't you staking out the house?"

"We're laying pipe to get to the other name you tasked us with," Declan said. "There are two of us. We can't cover every base."

"Why not? I do. You demanded a premium to get the job done. Can you deliver the cleanup we negotiated, or do I need to find another contractor?"

Queenie rustled at his side. *We'll need more operators.*

"We'll need more operators," Declan said. "We'll have to keep eyes on the wife's place, the kid's school, the site of his old house —"

The impound lot.

"— the impound lot and any other prior places of employment. We've already questioned a few of his former associates, and nothing's yielding. We need to sit on every location we can think of till he pops up. And that's gonna take manpower."

"You'll have whatever you need to end this," the doctor said, and severed the line.

27
Lost Boys

Security procedures at Kern Valley State Prison were understandably rigid. Government ID at the towering front gate. No chewing gum, no cell phones, no medications, no wallet, no cash, coins, or credit cards. To avoid being mistaken for a prisoner, no blue, gray, or orange clothes, no denim of any shade or monochromatic outfits. To avoid being mistaken for a correctional officer, no green or camouflage. To avoid exciting any of the inmates, no shorts, tank tops, or V-necked shirts. To avoid getting an eyeball gouged out, no jewelry with sharp edges, nonprescription glasses, or clothes with metal snaps. To avoid getting strangled, no belts or sweatpants with drawstrings.

Make no promises to inmates. Never run on prison grounds. Don't deliver any messages.

Only car keys, a valid picture ID, and a

foldable umbrella that collapsed to no more than eighteen inches were allowed inside. The lack of rain cut the item count by a third.

At 6:57 A.M. Evan entered the front building, gave a driver's license in the name of Frank Kassel, and signed in. Joey had scheduled the appointment outside normal visiting hours, part of the reason for the vigorous guidelines.

Hours ahead of the family visitation period, relatives were lined up. Evan took a seat between an ancient Hispanic matriarch with sagging, grief-battered eyes and a hefty single mother with two toddlers at her ankles and a wailing baby in her arms. Within seconds his fake name was called, and he advanced with a correctional officer through a series of security doors and metal detectors, emerging into a sally-port pen composed of concertina-topped fences stretching thirty feet high.

The solid-metal door locked behind him with an electronic thump.

About thirty seconds passed.

And then the tall gate before him rumbled open.

A desert-flat plain of asphalt and dirt housed a broad, sprawling throw of buildings coated in dust.

The CO led Evan a good distance up a paved road with no vehicles, the dry wind chapping his face. He entered another building containing a scattering of bright orange picnic tables bolted to the floor, a raised stage, and little else. The lights were off, no doubt to save energy, the walls bare, lifeless. Six single-stall toilet rooms lined the east side, doors ajar, sink outside. No hiding places here.

A few guards manned a station at the rear of the auditorium, an elevated platform that gave them ample oversight. They spoke in low voices, ignoring Evan and his escort.

"Wait here," the CO told him, and vanished.

Evan sat at the nearest table. It stank of bleach.

Ten minutes passed and then another ten.

The double doors clanged open, and there was the CO with a man stooped to accommodate the belly-chain cuffs, one shoulder riding higher than the other, head lowered. They were backlit by the thin blue glow of morning, features masked in shadow. The CO halted there and prodded Danny forward, and he came walking that dead man's prison walk. As the dark outline approached, Evan studied it for anything familiar — gait, posture, bearing — but came up blank.

The man reached the picnic table and wobbled a bit as he threw one leg over the bench and then the other, his hands pinned low at his sides.

The CO called out, "You got twenty minutes," and withdrew.

The doors hinged shut slowly, taking the glare with them, and Evan got his first clear look at Danny Gallo. Nothing about him was recognizable except for the pockmarks and the blue eyes, now watery and dulled. Evan scanned him for any other signs of the boy he'd once known, but there was nothing to distinguish him from any of the other five thousand inmates stored within these walls. He wore signs of poverty on his face — crooked chipped teeth, papery skin, sunken eyes that spoke to malnutrition or opiate use or both. It wasn't just damage but overuse, ninety years of hard living forced through a forty-year-old body.

"I don't know no Frank Kassel," he said.

"Me neither," Evan said. "I used a fake name to sneak in to see you."

"Well, I must be more important than I thought." Amused, Danny rasped a hand across scraggly patches of facial hair. For an instant his eyes caught a glint of inner life, and Evan could see through all the wreckage to Danny beneath. But just as quickly he was gone. "Who are you, then?"

"Evan," he said. "From Pride House."

Danny leaned forward, pronating his hands so he could prop an elbow on the table's ledge. "Evan?" he said. "You'd better be kidding me, now."

"No, sir, I am not."

"Holy shit."

Danny rose in excitement, chains rattling, as if to greet Evan properly, but then remembered himself and sat back down. His movement sent a faint breeze across the table, carrying the sour tinge of body odor. Over on the platform, the COs had gone guard-dog stiff, suddenly on point. They assessed Danny for a moment, then relaxed and went back to chatting softly.

"What happened to you after that guy took you?" Danny said. "Where'd you go, man? Where'd you go?"

Evan said, "It's a long story."

"Ain't they all."

"How 'bout you?" It was creeping back into Evan's voice, that street inflection. What a bizarre and unsettling subconscious shift. He reined in his diction. "Last I heard you were serving time back east."

"Yeah, that was some bullshit. I was just the lookout."

"How'd you land here?"

"More bullshit. I couriered some stuff from KC to Visalia. Yeah, I helped rock it up, but it was less than five hundred grams. I got paid three hundred fifty bucks. You believe that shit? Three hundred fifty bucks. The supplier flipped on me, reduced sentence for him giving up low-level guys like me. Never fucking trust the sambos. Me, I had priors, judge's hands tied 'cuz of mandatory sentencing, you know the drill. Fifteen years. It's the little fish gets fucked, right?" He shook his head. His hair was stringy, greasy, swaying across those pock-marked cheeks. "Three hundred fifty bucks. Fifteen years."

"Fifteen years is rough," Evan said. "But you'll still have enough life left after to have a third act."

Danny exhaled, a waft of halitosis and stale cigarettes. Evan blinked against it, held a poker face.

"I got in a tussle in the yard last June," Danny said. "Guy got his head caved in on a dumbbell. Wudn't my fault. They tacked on ten more years."

Evan let it settle, the weight of another lost decade. "Maybe good behavior," he said.

Danny looked up through the curtain of bangs, his eyes flashing blue. "Nah," he said.

"I ain't gonna behave good. Not for all them days." He noted something in Evan's face, drew himself up as best he could, shoulders pinned back as far as the chains allowed. "Don't you fucking pity me. I'm fine in here. Better, even. Last I was out, it was all fucked up. People walking around with the Internet in their pockets now. Little phones smarter than I am. Don't make no sense."

Evan nodded, lowered his eyes. Heat in his fingertips, his neck. It took a moment for him to identify the sensation.

Grief.

For what? For the wasted life sitting before him? Or for the fact that it could just as easily have been him on the other side of the table? If Jack hadn't shown up. If Evan hadn't gotten himself chosen. If he'd been found lacking.

He pictured the polished shine of his seven-thousand-square-foot penthouse. The freezer room containing tens of thousands of dollars of vodka. Stocked bank accounts in nonreporting territories. Safe houses and vehicles. The floating bed.

"I put in forty hours a week," Danny continued, a hint of boastfulness creeping in. "Prison furniture. I spray the polyurethane and shit. Sometimes I sew mailbags, too. Puts seventeen cents a hour toward my commissary account." He caught himself, seeming to realize that seventeen cents wasn't worth bragging about. A quiet cough shuddered his shoulders, a loose, wet rattle like a car engine that refused to turn over. He finished and lifted his eyebrows, his ears shifting back, the left lobe lost to a smear of burn tissue. "You heard about Ramón?"

Evan nodded. "Overdose."

"And Tyrell? Finally got his dumb ass in the army, shot to shit over in Buttfuckistan somewhere, poor fool. Served him right." Danny's face loosened with emotion. "May he rest in peace."

So many lost boys.

Evan said, "Yeah."

"We used to ride him hard about his sister being a whore." Danny cocked his head a bit too severely, a med-induced twitch. "You think she was a pro or we just liked to give him shit?"

"Probably the latter," Evan said.

The old camaraderie felt good, a comfort he had never known to seek. The fact that his life shared a common stream of history with someone, anyone.

"Man, she was fine, wasn't she?" Danny said. "That caboose."

"She was. More woman than any of us could handle. Easier to call her a whore

233

than admit she scared the shit out of us."

Danny's head jerked a few more times. He scratched at his hair. "Maybe you're right. Maybe she was just hot and that showed us for the weak-ass little boys we were."

Evan felt a smile coming up beneath the surface. "Remember when Papa Z went to the hospital that time with gastritis?"

"That fat motherfucker *always* had gastritis."

"He was gone for — what? — two weeks?"

"And he didn't want to tell nobody 'cuz the state'd cut off the checks. So there we were, a buncha savages in the house —"

"Inmates running the asylum."

"Shit, brother, that whole month we had sleep for dinner." With a flick of his head, Danny cleared his hair from his eyes. "And 'member we used to steal plums off Old Man Pinkerton's tree?"

Evan smiled, gave his best Ewelius Pinkerton voice. " 'You motherless bastards get offa my lot 'fore I give you the whupping your long-gone daddies never did.' "

Danny rocked a bit and laughed. "Those plums, shit they was good." The grin faded. "Till they weren't," he said. "It's like that in here. It was like that for Tyrell and Ramón and the rest of us, too. There's a season fruit is ripe, right? But if you miss it, it goes all rotten. We didn't get picked. So we went rotten." He cleared his throat. "You got picked, though, didn't you?"

A coughing fit seized him. He tried to raise a fist to his mouth, but a metallic clank stopped it at his sternum.

Evan leaned back, away, picturing a mist of germs settling across the table between them. His OCD revved up, that internal scanning software that assessed infection, contamination, decay. He tried to keep the disgust from his face, but Danny locked onto it.

"You ain't no better'n me."

"No," Evan said. "I'm not."

Danny drew back his head haughtily. "Okay. So long as we have that shit straight."

"We have it straight."

"So why are you here?"

"Andre. He's in trouble."

"What's it to you?"

The explanation came haltingly, the words jumbling up at Evan's mouth. "I . . . used to help people —"

"Help people how?"

"— but I'm retired."

"Then why are you —"

"Because Andre . . ." Evan couldn't grab hold of the thought to finish it.

"That's what they took you to go do?" Danny asked. "Help people?"

An Estonian arms dealer sprawled on the floor, chest sucking blood, a mist of blood speckling his lips. An NGO worker garroted in a public bathroom in Cairo, slumped beneath a shattered urinal. A drug lord sitting lifelike in a São Paulo steam room, terry towel twisted around his neck, marbled white skin glistening with condensation.

Evan said, "Yes."

"And what's up with Andre?"

"Some highly connected people are trying to kill him. I want to find him first."

"You try Bri? The ex?"

"I did. She doesn't know. She said he visits you."

"Yeah. You add it all up, I been inside twenty-three years." Danny's stare was unrelenting, accusatory. "He's the only visitor I ever had."

"When's the last time he came?"

"Fifty-three days ago."

The thought of Danny's tracking each day since was too distressing to linger on, so Evan pushed past it. "Did he say where he was living?"

"No. Well, wait. Yeah, El Sereno somewhere. Not that that helps narrow shit down much."

236

"Did he mention anything about it? Anything at all?"

"Rented some shitty room he complained about. You know Dr. Dre, always bitchin'." Danny smiled affectionately. "Upstairs from a Chinese restaurant, said he always reeked of kung pao chicken or some shit. I told him I'd sell my left nut for Chink food."

"He ever write to you?"

"He sent me some sketches — you 'member how that boy could draw? But that was years back."

"Has he been in touch any other ways?"

"Wires money to my commissary account now and again. Even when he's broke. Twenty bucks here. Twenty bucks there." Danny wet his chapped lips. He had a sore at the edge of his mouth, cracked and runny. "Takes me a hundred eighteen hours of work to make that much. Twenty bucks."

"When's the last time he sent you something?"

"Right before his last visit."

"How'd he send it?"

"MoneyGram. It's all the assholes allow here. Costs four-fifty at Walmart for up to fifty bucks. Fuckin' waste. Twenty-six and a half hours' work just for the fee — I done the math." Danny tried to clear his throat, but it turned into another coughfest. It seemed to go on forever. When he finally settled down, he said, "You still never told me what exactly you do. Or why you snuck in here under some fake name."

The double doors behind him clanged loudly once more and swung open, letting in a spill of morning light.

"Time's up," the CO called out.

Evan stood as Danny managed to extract himself from the picnic bench without the benefit of his hands. They faced each other.

Evan could smell him even at three feet away. It was hard to look him in his ruinous face. This living, breathing part of his past. Like a piece of himself he didn't want to acknowledge.

Danny leaned forward on his soft orange canvas deck step-ins and for an awful moment Evan thought he was going to hug him. But instead he looked at Evan through strands of sweat-darkened hair and said, "You're the lucky one. That's all that separates you and Ramón. Or you and Andre. Or you 'n' me. *Luck.*"

Evan said, "Okay."

"So look in the mirror, boy. And smile that you're on the right side of the glass."

"Gallo!" the CO yelled. "Move it."

But Danny stayed put. The skin of his forehead, taut with emotion, went lax, giving way to furrows. "They lock that cell door at eight forty-five P.M., that's when you feel it. The hours and minutes and years waiting on you ahead. It's like the sun. Can't look straight at it. Probably the same for you. Where you came from. What you left behind. Look too hard and you'll go blind."

Evan said, "Thanks for the info on Andre."

Danny's hostile expression loosened, the buried-deep hurt showing through. For a moment he just looked like what he was, an accumulation of vulnerabilities armored over with resentment. His eyes darted away. "You take care of yourself, Evan."

He trudged toward the door, disappearing into a shaft of late-morning glare.

28
PENANCE

Driving away from the prison on the flat line of Interstate 5, Evan maxed the air conditioner to keep his body temp steady. He wasn't sweating, but discomfort hummed beneath his skin, a kind of friction heat.

He could still feel Danny's presence, a soul-deep filth that had rubbed off on him. A vision of the road not taken. Locked behind bars. Dead with a needle in his arm. Blasted to pieces on the hot sand of a desert halfway around the world.

You ain't no better'n me.

You're the lucky one.

So look in the mirror, boy. And smile that you're on the right side of the glass.

In two hours and change, he was supposed to meet Veronica, another reflection of a past he preferred not to see. If he drove at the speed limit, he'd reach the designated Bel Air address with time to spare. And finally he'd get some answers about how the hell she knew Andre. And figure out what other pieces of his best-forgotten childhood she held.

Tension built in his chest until his inhalations burned. At the next exit, he screeched off, parked at the Flying J truck stop, and hustled inside. A hefty man lumbered out of the bathroom. On his way in, Evan elbowed the swinging door so as not to touch the handle.

He slathered his hands with powder soap and washed them under hot water and then washed them again until his palms chafed lobster red. He cuffed his sleeves and scrubbed up his forearms next and then ducked his head to the tap and shoveled hot water across his face, scouring away Danny's scent, his words, the bleach and BO of the prison air.

He knew it was in his head, a user error that flared up when he was under emotional duress — a need to control, to purify, to set his world in order. He wouldn't feel properly disinfected until he had a proper shower, but this would be enough to get him home.

He hit the lever for a paper towel but then sensed the germs on his fingertips from touching the plastic so he rinsed his hands again and then turned off the faucet using the wadded paper towel. He didn't want to touch the plastic lever again, so he mashed the soggy wad to release another scroll of paper towel, which he ripped free and used to open the bathroom door. He exited and stood for a moment, breath still coming hard.

Then he walked outside.

Fresh midday air, the sun like a klieg light to the east, boring through a fuzzy blue sky.

He dug his RoamZone out from the center console, fired it up, and dialed.

Joey picked up through her computer; he could hear the last chimes of the ringtone on a delay. "I tried you twice, but it went straight to voice mail," she said.

"I was in prison."

"Excuses, excuses. I have the background on Jake Hargreave you wanted."

"Go."

"Air force, like you said. Senior airman, active warfighter, all that. Then — get this — he got moved to Creech Air Force Base to work on . . . guess what?"

Evan said, "Unmanned aircraft testing."

A rare moment of speechlessness from Joey. "How'd you know that?"

"Lucky guess."

"Yeah, he was with the 556th Test and Evaluation Squadron. Till he and his sensor operator ran into some trouble."

"What kind of trouble?"

She snapped her gum with gunshot vehemence. "Dunno. Honorable discharge for Hargreave a few months back. His partner got ODPMC, whatever that means."

"Other Designated Physical and Mental Conditions Discharge."

"Headcase, then?"

"Where is he? The sensor operator?"

"In Fresno. California Veterans Reintegration Center. It's like a compound to help vets get their heads right or something like that. But get this, it's got crazy security — cameras and guards and whatnot. What's up with that?"

"The DoD prefers to keep drone-warfare intel in a dark box," he said. "A lot of these operations aren't even under air force command. They hook it under JSOC or the CIA."

Joey said, "So I guess when you have people who know lots of classified shit but might be losing their minds, you gotta lock them up."

"Or kill them."

"Ha." A pause. "You weren't joking."

"No."

"So?" she said. "That's it. Another job exceptionally handled by *moi.*" More loud gum chewing. "Pretend you got a personality transplant and say, 'Thank you, Joey. You're amazeballs.' "

"I would never say 'amazeballs.' "

"You just did."

Evan grimaced, pinched his eyes. "I need you to find something else for me."

"No thanks," she said. "I'm busy not studying."

"Andre Duran is living in El Sereno renting a room above a Chinese restaurant."

"Sounds glam."

"He sent a MoneyGram payment to Daniel Gallo's commissary account at the prison about two months ago. The database should have wire details on all financial transactions, including where the money originated from."

"You want me to hack into the CDCR databases again, find the MoneyGram store that Duran sent the cash from, and cross-correlate with two-story Chinese restaurants in El Sereno?"

"I want you to do precisely that."

"What was it like seeing Danny Gallo?" Her voice was hushed, respectful. She was such a pain-in-the-ass teenager that it was sometimes easy to forget she'd been a foster kid like him, floating through a system, devoid of past or future. "Was it weird?"

He lowered his head, bit his lip. Pictured Danny's pockmarked face, the tic that jerked his head to one side, that burn that had robbed his left earlobe. The image took his voice away.

Joey came through the RoamZone, tinny over the receiver. "X?"

"Thanks, Joey," Evan said, and hung up.

He walked over to where he'd left his rig at the pump station and filled the tank.

He pictured Andre as a kid, sitting up on his bunk, sketching away. *You wait and see, fools. Mystery Man's gonna choose me 'cuz he got some taste. Then I'll drive a big-ass Cadillac and move to Cali. They got palm trees and shit and blonde girls with juicy booties who Rollerblade in bikinis all day long.*

He thought about Danny trolling the wishing well for pennies, the wet change dumped on the counter in front of the displeased clerk. Sitting on the curb, sharing a Coke, just another two East Baltimore kids no one wanted.

He pictured Veronica crouched by the marble carving of a newborn in the cemetery. She'd driven through the night, she'd said. Across the border from Lancaster, Pennsylvania. To dump him off with a couple unable to care for him.

He pinched his eyes, blinked hard around

his thumb and forefinger. That sensation of pressure he'd felt in the prison arose once more.

Not just grief, he realized, but guilt, too. For making it out? For surviving? For being intact?

The Pride House Group Home had been life or death. Jockey for food. Claw up the dominance hierarchy. Fight for any shred of hope and guard it with everything you had.

And yet Danny had shared his hard-earned Coke with him.

The gas pump clacked off, snapping Evan back to the present. He holstered the nozzle, his eye catching on a neon sign in the travel-plaza window across the lot. Squashed between signs for Bud Light and Skoal Bandits, it glowed yellow through the grimy pane.

MoneyGram.

Evan twisted on the gas cap, climbed into his truck, and fired up the engine. He sat a moment, knuckles ledging the steering wheel, just breathing.

Then he slotted the gear stick back into park.

The glass door chimed "Jingle Bells" when he walked through into a rush of air-conditioning. He found his way to the counter and wired a thousand dollars to

Inmate TG3328.

Rumbling along the interstate toward the towering hills of the Grapevine and Bel Air beyond, it struck him that the payment was an atonement of sorts.

A penance he owed for not turning out like Danny.

29
BROKEN HEART

The half-acre setback in the Bel Air hills featured holly ferns and palm trees and a trickling river-moat hosting swans. A stone wall hemmed in the vast front yard, the iron gate giving way beneath Evan's hand with a creak.

He crossed a fairy-tale footbridge over the moat, approaching the imposing granite façade. The air carried the sickly-sweet scent of gardenias. A bright red door with a speakeasy grille confronted him. He lifted a brass knocker shaped like a sprinting greyhound, gave it a few whacks, and waited in the perfumed breeze.

Nothing.

He shifted, feeling the reassuring pressure of his ARES 1911 snugged to his flesh. He wore an appendix holster, the fastest concealed-carry method. The Kydex was tightly molded for retention, which could cause a striker-fire pistol like a Glock to kaboom when seating the gun but worked beautifully for a 1911 with external grip and thumb safeties. The pistol itself, engineered from a solid aluminum forging, was designed to spec and impossible to trace.

Once again he checked the street, the sky, the surrounding rooftops.

He knocked again, a touch louder.

The yapping of a pair of little dogs, the scrabble of paws on hard surfaces, and Veronica's voice from within. "Okay, okay. I'm coming!"

Another twenty seconds passed, and then the towering architectural door yawned inward, a slit in a castle wall. Veronica wore a light gray shift dress — not revealing but not modest either — a champagne flute in one hand. The dogs, who looked to be some sort of Chihuahua-Pomeranian mix, vibrated around her ankles, emitting earsplitting barks.

She took a moment to admire him. "Evan." She downed the rest of her mimosa, set the glass aside, and spread her arms for an embrace.

He offered a hand.

A flicker of hurt crossed her face, quickly gone beneath a smile. Her hand was cool and dry. "Would you like a drink?"

A tang of champagne on her breath.

"No thank you," he said.

"So polite. You were brought up right." She seemed to realize her poor choice of words, her eyebrows pinching in with dismay, but she quickly dismissed any discomfort — his or hers — with a wave of her manicured hand as she headed into the interior.

The dogs scurried alongside her, glancing nervously back at Evan, pink triangle tongues hanging out from all the excitement.

At second glance Evan realized the foyer was a dark-tiled pool, wide concrete blocks serving as stepping-stones zigzagging across still water. The dogs bounced from one to the next with practiced agility. Shaved hindquarters, scrawny legs, a poofy mane rimming beady features and sharp snouts.

"Barry's obsessed with animals," Veronica called over her shoulder, "but I have to say, these dogs look like they were put together by committee."

They threaded through a kitchen and then down several wide steps to a sunken living room, complete with a fully stocked bar and a flat-screen television the size of a billboard. A stainless-steel bucket held a tilted magnum of Perrier-Jouët, the belle epoque bottle wrapped with painted flowers. Beside it a glass pitcher of fresh-squeezed orange juice.

Veronica filled another flute and then flopped down on an endless curved couch that formed a parenthesis across the savanna-tan carpet. He took a seat opposite her at the edge of a silver-gray chaise longue.

She gestured with her glass. "You'll have to forgive the nouveau riche mishmash of . . . can we call it 'styles'? Barry's a movie producer. He's on location now. It's just me and his staff and these awful little dogs."

At the mention the dogs sat and gazed up at her needily, panting.

A majordomo floated into sight in the vast doorway, wearing a black button-up with an Asian collar. His shiny bald head reflected the muted light of the kitchen. "Girls, come now," he said, in some kind of a Slavic accent. He patted the thigh of his dark linen pants, and the dogs padded out after him, the trio vanishing.

For a moment Evan wondered if the man had been an illusion.

Veronica tucked her legs beneath her, folding them to one side, and ran a fingertip absentmindedly around the rim of the champagne flute. "I assume by now you've done some digging on me."

Evan had indeed spent a few hours in the

Vault prying into Veronica LeGrande. What she'd told him had checked out, and he'd unearthed a bit more. An only child, she'd grown up in Lancaster, Pennsylvania. Veronica's father, the grandiosely named Bernard LeGrande, had been a structural-steel fabrication magnate. Her homemaker mother, Maryelizabeth, had spent years in and out of psychiatric hospitals for crippling phobia disorders before early-onset dementia had taken her out in her late forties.

Veronica had lived a privileged life, spending her high-school years at Linden Hall — the oldest all-girls boarding school in the country, established a full three decades before the nation's birth. Three years of college at Vassar before dropping out and then patchwork records showing a gypsy lifestyle. Her father's profligate spending had drained much of the family money before his death. Veronica had run through the rest rather quickly, it seemed, leaving her to rely on the kindness of strangers. Lots of passport activity, no mortgages, decent credit rating.

No children on record.

"Not really," Evan said.

"I have a long history with not much to show for it." She knocked back the rest of her drink and stretched her arms overhead.

Firm neckline, smooth skin, youthful hazel eyes.

"Are you really sixty-two?" he asked.

She smirked. "Parts of me." She brushed a lock of chestnut hair from her eyes. "Were you really trained to kill people?"

"I was."

"I didn't call you to do that."

"You called me to help Andre."

"Andre? I thought it was Andrew." She rose to refill her glass. "I want you to help him. Not do whatever horrible things you've done in your past."

He hadn't considered wanting her approval, and yet her words twisted something inside him, something with jagged edges. "People are trying to kill him."

"I'm not sure I believe *that.* He just needs a hand to get himself out of trouble. Got tangled up in the wrong situation. Maybe he owes some money. Needs some legal counsel."

"You don't understand anything about me," Evan said. "What I do, what I don't do."

She kept her back turned, her hands resting at the bar, but he could see her shoulder blades tense. She paused a moment. Poured champagne without the OJ this time and downed it. When she turned around, she'd

253

collected herself.

She replenished her glass once more, glided across the thick carpet, and set herself down on the cushions again a bit more heavily.

"How do you know Andre?" Evan asked.

Her eyes stayed low, on the rim of the flute. Hint of lilac in the air, the faintest trace of her perfume.

"Veronica. This is where you give me some answers."

He could see a flutter to the side of her throat, her heartbeat making itself known. She looked into her glass as if the bubbles might tell her something.

"I went to an elite high school," she said. "But we did have a few underprivileged students. There was a Puerto Rican girl I was friendly with. My father gave a lot, scholarship funds, that kind of thing, so there was some overlap. I wouldn't say we were friends, but we were friend*ly*. And we stayed in touch vaguely after graduation, a letter now and again, a card at the holidays. She wound up studying at Union a hundred miles or so up the Hudson from me." She pursed her lips. "I was in my junior year at college when she showed up at my dorm room. I supposed she had nowhere else to go. No one she trusted. She'd been . . ."

"What?"

Veronica shook her head, an etchwork of lines surrounding her tense mouth showing her age at last. "She had bruises around her wrists where they'd been held down." Her own hands rose and mimed gripping someone. "And she was still wearing the shirt, torn at the collar where it had been . . ." Her lips trembled, though barely. "Broken fingernails from trying to fight back. A clump of hair missing where it had been yanked out. It was brutal. Savage."

Evan swallowed. Kept perfectly still.

"And she was worried that . . . that she could be expecting. And she stayed with me, and she took those damn tests every day, like playing a lottery you don't want to win. But sure enough she won. And even though this was a child born of violence, it was still a child. People don't always understand that these days. It's not some political statement, but it's different when it happens to you, I suppose. And she decided she wanted to bring this child to term."

Evan remembered Andre's skipping out every chance he could to search for his birth parents. And how he'd returned empty-handed time and again. A kid seeking a truth that would wreck him if he ever found it.

Evan said, "Jesus."

"Well, she didn't have much money. And there was school debt, too. And when the baby came . . ." Veronica cleared her throat, straightened up. "When Andrew came, she didn't have the resources to support him. And I told her that sometimes, sometimes with children, your desire to care for them can ruin them."

The words came before Evan could stop them. "How would you know that?"

The depth of feeling beneath the words caught him off guard.

She shook her head. "You're right. Bear in mind I was a twenty-two-year-old kid myself. But she didn't follow my advice, not initially. She tried to raise this baby who'd done nothing wrong, who deserved so much more. But she found she didn't have the strength to look in that child's face every day. I remember her telling me that she could see in his features the face of the man who'd attacked her. Imagine living with that."

"So she put him up for adoption."

"Not at first. She fought herself for a year. And gave this child care. But she also detested him. And it was tearing her apart. I've never seen a person so conflicted. So yes. But by then he was a toddler, and the problem with that is —"

"The older a kid is, the less anyone wants him." Again Evan's words came sharper than he'd intended.

She blinked at him a few times, her eyes glassy from the alcohol. "Yes."

"Why didn't you tell me this?" he said. "At the Recoleta Cemetery?"

"It was more than I could get out," she said. "With the police closing in and all. And I was worried you wouldn't help. That you wouldn't want to go back to that time."

"So you thought you'd manipulate me instead."

"I suppose if you frame it that way . . ."

"Does Andre know this story? About the rape?"

She shook her head excessively, like a little girl. "It would destroy him."

"Where's his mother now?"

"Two years after she parted with him, she took a ferry from Essex one night and slipped overboard with stones in her pockets. Very Kate Chopin."

Despite the crack, Evan could see the pain in her eyes. A small burst of blood vessels colored her cheek just in front of her left ear, a spiderlike pattern where her concealer had faded. He could sense her years more now than he had in the Buenos Aires night when she'd seemed to glow in the haze of their shared anticipation.

Veronica said, "Her last correspondence to me was to look after him if he ever needed anything. A dying wish. Very dramatic. But impossible to ignore."

He tugged at his mouth, felt the fleshy pinch of his lower lip. "How did Andre know to get in touch with you?"

"I was the one who dropped him off at the first foster home. After all the legal steps, the paperwork. She couldn't bear to. And after she was . . . gone, when he needed to be placed in a facility for older boys, I made sure he was moved to Pride House. That's how I knew about it. . . ."

"To pull strings and move me there later." He caught himself before he could add, *After you dumped me off with an incapable couple.*

She nodded. "When he came searching for his mother years later, I was the only name he could find. I suppose I'm the only connection to family he ever found."

"What did you tell him?"

"That his mother had passed away of cancer. He's contacted me sporadically over the years. When he wanted advice. When he needed bail money. When he was in trouble."

"All these years you knew I was there. And

you knew about him. But you kept us both in the dark."

"I bore that burden."

"Did you? Or did we?"

She sighed. "I don't know. It's one of the awful secrets to getting older. You don't ever get the answers. Every time I consider myself an adult, I think back five years to when I also thought of myself as an adult. And I'm aghast at how staggeringly blind I was. Maybe what I hold to be true right now will seem just as ignorant when I reflect back on it years from now." She arched an eyebrow. "If I'm around." She examined the flute once more. "Maybe that's all growing up is. Knowing in real time that you don't know anything."

"So you think we'd have been worse off if we were told the truth?"

"Don't you?"

Evan looked down at the union of his hands. Fingers linked, pressure at the knuckles, like he was holding on to nothing too tightly. He considered her question for a very long time.

She watched him think. "It's a lost art." Her voice carried a blend of admiration and approval.

"What's that?"

"Entertaining an idea before rejecting it."

"I don't know the answer," he said. "Whether I'd have been better off. My background was tough in most ways. I was diminished by it. And strengthened by it. I don't think you get to have one without the other."

She nodded several times too many. "What would you have preferred? Growing up riding horses and sailing? The finest schools? Like the boys I grew up with, my friends' children and now grandchildren? I can see right into them. They're as solid as a plank of birch and just as deep. Ninety percent deadwood. Catch a spark and they go up in flame. No. You had challenge. Purpose. Honed by hardship."

"I did."

"And yet." Her eyes, abruptly, were moist. "I wish I could have given you so much more." She blinked rapidly, reached for her glass on the acrylic side table, but saw that it was empty.

He said, "Why . . ."

. . . didn't you want me?

He caught himself.

"Why did you decide to give up the baby?"

She blinked a few more times, confused, and he realized he'd left out the possessive. "What baby?"

One syllable, but it was hard to choke out. "Me."

She'd regained her composure, her words smooth and breezy. "My circumstances weren't suited to it."

"It?"

"Being a mother. Having a child."

"I see."

"I suppose you want to know about your father."

Jack sitting across the dining table from twelve-year-old Evan in the low light of the farmhouse, twirling his pasta around his fork: The hard part isn't turning you into a killer. The hard part is keeping you human. *That square, rugged face. Blue flannel and classical music.*

"My father is the man who rescued me from the foster home," Evan said. "My father is the man who raised me."

"It's just as well," she said. "I don't know much about your birth father anyway."

"One-night stand?" Evan said.

"No." Her eyes twinkled. "A whole lost weekend."

"Sounds classy. Let me guess, outlaw biker."

"Rodeo cowboy. Bronc rider."

"You're not as funny as you think you are."

"Well," she said, "sometimes I am." She

tilted her glass at him. "Would you be a dear and freshen this up for me?"

He could tell that if she stood, she'd be unsteady on her feet from the alcohol. And she didn't want him to see.

He rose and plucked the glass from her hand. The Perrier-Jouët bottle was frigid to the touch, and it lifted from the bucket trailing ice water. It was mostly empty. He poured.

Behind the bar a few pill bottles rested beside Veronica's clutch purse. Vitamin K. Calcium. And a prescription written under her name for rifaximin, an antibiotic used to soothe stomach problems from traveling. Veronica presented such a resilient and polished façade that he hadn't considered the human fragility beneath.

The plush carpet muted his steps as he returned the glass to her. She took it with a nod of thanks, a flush sitting high on her cheeks and her throat. She patted the cushion at her side. He took a seat but left a good amount of space between their hips.

She said, "Okay." She sipped. Sipped again.

The ARES dug into his ribs. He shifted the holster anchoring on the belt to make sure it wasn't pointing at his femoral artery or more sensitive anatomy yet.

He watched Veronica looking at him and had trouble reading her expression. Intrigue? Wariness? *My son, the assassin.*

He mustered his nerve. The words felt like pulling barbed wire through a closed fist. "You said I had a middle name. It wasn't on any of the paperwork. What was it?"

She said, "Bartholomew."

"Really?"

"No." Her lips pursed, a not-quite smile.

"Forget it."

"I'm sorry," she said. "It wasn't . . . it wasn't on the paperwork because I didn't want to name you. I thought if I named you, I couldn't bear to part with you. I called you baby boy. For the week I had you, I called you baby boy."

The words came into him as such, unattached to the greater meaning they dragged beneath the surface. He could register them consciously, but the emotional impact felt numbed, dull, like sound traveling underwater.

She'd had him a week. She'd been terrified of bonding with him or parting with him. She'd called him *baby boy.*

She continued, "But when I left you with the Krausses, the paperwork, I needed to put down something, a name. And I realized I'd already named you even though I didn't know it. Evan."

"What . . . what was I like?"

"You barely cried. The doctor thought something was wrong with you. But I knew there wasn't. I could see how sensitive you were, how much you were taking in, that you were overcome by it. And to survive you had to shut off parts of yourself, what you felt, what you reacted to. God, what do I know? Maybe it was all projection. My own broken heart mapped onto a newborn."

His RoamZone chimed in his pocket, and he fished it out. A text from Joey listing five Chinese restaurants in El Sereno that fit the search parameters.

He stood. "I need to go find Andre."

Her face was lowered, flushed with alcohol. She lifted a hand clumsily for him to take. He stared at it, slender fingers, soft pale skin, manicured nails. Her eyes, imploring.

He nodded at her and walked out.

30
FROM NOTHING TO SOMETHING

Evan hit the target at the fourth location. The Szechuan Rose, enticingly sandwiched between a Chevron station and a pawnshop, had glazed red roof tiles and a glossy plastic dragon standing sentry at the entrance. The place bustled, the dinner shift in full swing. After several requests got lost in translation, the hostess sent Evan up the chain of command, pointing him to the kitchen. The inexplicably Japanese owner, busy orchestrating a massive take-out order, waved him up a back flight of stairs.

Evan knocked on the flimsy door at the top. A chain rustled, and a moment later Andre's face appeared at the gap. His features contracted.

"How the hell'd you find me?"

"Long story."

Andre's eyes darted to look over Evan's shoulder. "Your dumb ass was prob'ly followed here."

"I wasn't followed."

"How would you know?"

"I'd know."

Andre glared at him. "I told you to leave me alone."

"Look. I'm here. No point in putting this off. Let's just sit down and talk."

"It's a bad time."

Evan said, "No shit."

He held an unremitting gaze until Andre rolled his head back, cursed, and opened the door. When Evan stepped inside, the cooking aromas from the kitchen only intensified. He looked at the heating vents, and Andre nodded and said, "All day long I'm breathin' egg foo yong up in here."

Unmade bed. Dirty clothes heaped on the floor. A folding closet raked open to reveal a few crooked shelves. Evan could have spread his arms and touched opposite walls. In the far corner, a hot plate, basin sink, card table, and single chair composed a woeful kitchenette. A bathroom the size of a coat closet.

The only note of grace was a beautifully rendered sketch thumbtacked to the wall. Sofia gazing out with lifelike eyes, an open-mouthed smile. She seemed happy to see whoever she was looking at. Even all these years later, Evan recognized Andre's hand behind it.

He imagined that the drawing was precisely how an estranged father would want to remember his daughter.

Set before Sofia's sketch on a chair, like an offering at an altar, was a bottle of drugstore rum.

Unopened.

Evan said, "What's this about?"

"It's about none of your business."

Evan lifted the full bottle. Beneath, hidden from view, rested an Alcoholics Anonymous medallion. 1 MONTH. GOD GRANT ME THE SERENITY TO ACCEPT THE THINGS I CANNOT CHANGE, THE COURAGE TO CHANGE THE THINGS I CAN, AND THE WISDOM TO KNOW THE DIFFERENCE.

Andre kept his eyes lowered to the floor.

Evan said, "Want me to pour this out?"

"No." Andre wiped his nose. And then, "Yeah."

Evan unscrewed the cap and glugged the cheap rum into the basin sink.

He dropped the bottle into a mound of fast-food wrappers at the base of the bed and looked for somewhere to sit. The room stank of alcohol, unwashed clothes, and Chinese spices. The walls seemed to lean inward. It was hard to breathe.

Andre picked at his nails, cleaning dirt

from beneath them and flicking it onto the floor.

Evan felt it again, that black fog of disgust that had choked up his chest when he'd sat across from Danny at the prison. He felt that same urge to pull away, to scrape their shared history off himself, the primordial sludge from which he'd emerged.

Andre said, "I didn't always live like this."

"Okay."

Andre bustled around, tidying up, which really only meant moving items from one crowded surface to another. "This is just temporary."

"Okay."

Beneath the bed a sheaf of sketches lay half visible. Andre crouched and gathered them up lovingly. "I'm better than this."

"I know."

He rose sharply. "No you don't. I can see it in your eyes. I'm used to folks lookin' at me that way."

"Why's that?"

The question put Andre back on his heels. "I dunno. Where we came from. No money. My race or whatever."

"Or whatever?"

"Who knows what I am? Some kinda mutt. I'm earth-colored and beautiful. That's what I am."

"Okay."

"And we wear it." He slapped his chest with an open palm. "White boys like you don't get it. You can outgrow your shitty upbringing. Can't outgrow your skin. We wear it when we get pulled over and some asshole cop wants to break our balls. You don't know shit. How hard it is to get from nothing to something. How sixty-five dollars can be the end of you."

"Sixty-five dollars?" Evan said. "What are you talking about?"

"Nothing. Christ, nothing." Andre swiped his hand across the back of his neck, aggravated. "How much you got in your pockets?"

Evan said, "I don't know."

"Count."

Evan pulled out his folded bills, freed the money clip, and counted. "Three hundred eighty dollars."

"See." Andre gestured at a yellow zippered pouch by his pillow. "Seventy-three dollars, twenty-two cents. That's all I have in the world."

"I don't understand what conversation we're having."

"Course you don't. That's what I'm saying. Someone like you can't understand someone like me."

"There's nothing more dangerous than thinking you're a victim."

Andre snorted. "Ain't that some shit. How 'bout the people who want to kill my ass? They more dangerous'n me?"

"They think they're victims, too," Evan said. "That's where it gets you."

"Listen to your judgmental ass."

"Without judgment," Evan said, "we've got nowhere to go."

"I don't need you." Andre jabbed a finger at him, a threat of violence underscoring the gesture. "The hell you do anyhow? You some kinda what? Social worker?"

"I don't do anything," Evan said. "I'm retired."

"Right. You're here 'cuz of Ms. LeGrande. Working a charity case. Like you know a damn thing about what I'm into."

"I know Jake Hargreave was murdered that night at the impound lot. I know something materialized out of thin air to open his throat. I know that two well-dressed siblings, Declan and Queenie Gentner, were behind it. I know very powerful people are looking for you. I know you're not safe anywhere you go."

Andre's eyes bulged, bloodshot squiggles showing in the sclera. Unguarded, stunned — a flicker of the face Evan recalled from childhood. Andre rested a quavering hand on the mattress and lowered himself to sit. Head bowed, cords of his neck pronounced, breathing. His voice much softer. "What else you know?"

Evan told him the rest, from his trip to Buenos Aires to the Hellfire blowing up the house.

Recalling all those field trips Andre had taken as a young man in search of his parents, Evan did not divulge his own relationship to Veronica. And he honored Veronica's request, leaving out the part about Andre's disturbing provenance.

When he finished, Andre said nothing.

Evan asked, "What *don't* I know?"

Andre filled him in on some remaining details — the visit by the Gentners, the fake U.S. Marshals phone number, how he'd watched from the darkness as Jake Hargreave bled out.

Evan said, "Have you been back to the impound lot?"

"Nope."

"Still have the keys?"

Andre flicked his chin at a plastic hook on the wall where his key chain dangled.

Evan checked the watch fob dangling from his belt loop. "The lot closes in an hour and a half. Once it's empty, I'll go look around."

Andre popped up and snatched the keys from their hook. "I'm coming with you."

"No."

"You think I'm just gonna wait around here? Hail no." He scrambled to tug on his shoes. "This is my life. You want to help me? Then help me. But you ain't taking over."

"Andre. No way."

"You said it yourself. I'm not safe anywhere I go. Might as well be with your white-knighting ass." He finished lacing up, his knuckles brushing the empty bottle of rum. He picked it up. Sniffed it, eyes closed. Hearing the siren song. He seemed to realize what he was doing and dropped the bottle again. "I need to go to a meeting. Or I gotta call my sponsor."

"You're not calling anyone," Evan said. "Zero contact. You'll put us both at risk. Understand?"

Andre smiled. "So that means I'm going with you?"

31
CHASING GOOD

Evan parked in the precise spot across from the impound lot where Declan and Queenie Gentner had positioned their Corvette as they'd lain in wait for Jake Hargreave, a good distance back from the surveillance-camera scope of the First Union Bank's ATM. Though it wasn't yet six o'clock, the sky was nearing full dark, December early twilight crowding ever earlier. This stretch of downtown, mostly factories and plants, was already largely deserted.

Through the facing chain-link, the wrecked vehicles slumbered in imperfect rows, strobing into view between streamers of low-lying fog. Evan kept the headlights and dome light off, the engine killed, his door cracked to prevent the windshield from fogging with his and Andre's breath.

"Why don't you just roll down a window?" Andre asked.

Because the laminate armor glass didn't

retract, and even if it did, there'd be nowhere for it to go given the Kevlar-plate reinforcements filling the door panels.

"Broken," Evan said.

Andre shivered. "Fancy-ass truck like this, I'd figure you could afford to get that shit fixed."

"I'll look into it."

The kiosk was lit from within, illuminating a man in a Carhartt jacket chewing a pen and watching a tiny portable television that looked decades old. Evan checked his watch fob again. Ten minutes to closing.

He retrieved a tube of superglue from the center console and spread a thin layer across his finger pads.

"Why're you doing that?" Andre asked.

"Cover my prints."

"Shouldn't I do that, too?"

Evan looked at him. "You worked here. Your prints *should* be all over the place."

Andre said, "Good point."

A white Mazda drifted past and a few moments later a Tesla Model S with tinted windows. Evan noted the plates, watched them turn at the intersection ahead and vanish. He adjusted the side mirror to better capture the street behind them.

Andre was at it again, prying dirt from beneath his fingernails.

Evan grimaced. "Can you stop doing that?"

Andre peered over at him. "Why?"

"Because it's gross. And you're in my truck."

Andre blew an annoyed puff of breath through his lips. "You're so fastidious. All anal retentive and shit. Even your *hair's* fastidious."

"Big word."

"Says the guy with fastidious hair." Andre shifted in his seat, enjoying himself now. "Is a little bit of dirt bothering you?" He waggled his dirty finger in the air. "How 'bout this? Oh, no! *Oops.*" He wiped it on Evan's thigh.

Evan resisted the urge to administer a kenpo ridge hand strike to the bottom of Andre's chin, shattering his jaw. Instead he shoved Andre's arm away. "And you could use a shower. You smell like hot-and-sour soup."

Andre laughed. "Don't I know it." His eyes warmed. "Shit, Evan. There you are. For one second you're almost like your old self. That little-ass kid always getting knocked around. But I'll give you this. You always got back up." He shook his head. "I used to be like that, too. I used to get up every time they knocked me down. Till I couldn't no more."

" 'Cuz of the booze?" Again there was the loose articulation, the street slang, coming out of Evan's own mouth, catching him off guard.

Andre shrugged. "When you're young, you self-medicate and shit without knowing it. Just to feel better. Good times. Loosens you up. Why not? Then you get older, you do it with *purpose*. Try combinations. Rum and Xanax. Get pharmacological and shit. You start out chasing good but end up just trying to dull the bad. Till one day . . ."

"What?"

"You wake up with blood on you, don't know from what or from who." Andre rubbed at the scar over his eyebrow. "Had to get in the shower to find out it wasn't mine. Didn't know what I'd done till I'd done it. Looked in the mirror, saw a fuckup staring back. Husband in name. Father in name. But really? God's truth? Just a fuckup."

Evan didn't know what to say. Over at the kiosk, the worker had moved on to picking his nose with vigor. The fog crept and bloomed, turning the lot swampy.

"We were all fuckups, weren't we?" Andre said. "Kids no one wanted."

Evan thought about Andre's mother looking down at him as a newborn, seeing the features of her rapist looking back. "Yeah."

"When you're outside life, it's hard to get in. Know what I mean?"

Evan pictured Mia's condo, candles and throw blankets, laundry and a stocked fridge, TV blaring cartoons, Peter fussing or cracking up, Mia sipping red wine and listening to Miles Davis.

So much warmth. And color. Like looking through the aquarium glass at a wondrous new world.

Evan said, "Not really."

"Like, ever watch some sports match you don't understand? On one a' them second-rate ESPNs — international or something? Like, I dunno, rugby. Or Australian football. It takes you out, right? All those people cheering, crying, chanting, like their lives depend on it, like they've been empty their entire lives and now they're full, brimming with life, with *triumph.* And you're outside, right? You don't know this game. You don't give a shit. But you envy them being so god-damned alive, for knowing what they care about and what they want and for trying to get at it. For being *in it,* man. And you're just sitting there watching." Andre's voice grew hoarse. "When you're like us, that's how everything feels sometimes."

Evan caught the words before they came out. *I'm not like you.*

Andre said, "You're never jealous of folks like that? People who can just be . . . you know, happy."

"You think happiness is the point?"

"Of what?"

"Of life."

"Ain't it?"

Evan shrugged. "I don't know if you can build anything on it."

"What do you build on, then?"

"Responsibility," Evan said. "Duty."

The air seeped through the cracked door, tightening Evan's skin. He thought about the calm nights since he'd retired, sipping vodka at his kitchen counter in his climate-controlled penthouse. Then he thought about strolling through a mist-draped South American cemetery, tracking and being tracked, a police-force battalion waiting in the wings; the heat blast of a Hellfire missile putting him on the brink of disintegration, every cell screamingly alive; and the sensation filling him sitting here now on the razor's edge of a mission, each step a high-wire act, lives hanging in the balance, danger coiling itself around him, fork-tongued whispering in his ear.

One trajectory offered what he wanted.

The other what he needed.

He didn't want to hold them up side by side in his mind, because then he'd have to admit which one spoke to his truest self.

Over in the passenger seat, Andre was still musing. Evan checked the mirrors, the intersection ahead, the weight of the dilemma tugging at him.

"Maybe happiness is overrated," Evan said. "Freedom, too. Maybe the only way to get anywhere worth being is to pick up the heaviest thing you can carry. And carry it."

"Easy for you to say."

"Is it?"

"The heaviest thing to carry is family. A marriage. A kid. You ever try?" Andre glared at Evan, reading his silence. "What I thought. You don't know how hard it is."

An edge of resentment rose inside Evan. It felt unfamiliar, toxic. "I know it was too hard for you."

"Hell, man. You think it'll be different, you'll be different, but you're not. Our honeymoon we went camping, up the hill, just me and Bri and her PMS. We fought from the beginning. Had fun, too. Then it was all one and not the other. Women all wind up the same."

"You mean the piece of them you know how to interact with is the same."

But Andre didn't even hear him. "And you got no idea what it means to make a baby. People say it's a miracle. Sure. But you see them, man. They have knuckles. You put your pinkie finger out and they grip it. And it's just you, man. It's just you. And what if you're not up for it?"

Evan thought about Veronica, buzzed and breezy on the wide Bel Air couch. *My circumstances weren't suited to it.* His voice came hard. "You get up for it."

"I didn't know how to be a father, man. I kept thinking, 'What if she winds up like me?' " Andre wiped his mouth. "Shit, maybe the best thing I did was remove myself from the equation."

Evan pictured Sofia spying on his conversation with Brianna, the worried furrows in her brow, how desperately she wanted to know that her dad was okay.

He said, "I doubt she sees it that way."

"I want to see her. I do. But I been afraid that I'm not . . . good enough."

"If you don't do it, where will you be in five years?" Evan said. "Where will she be?"

Andre's eyes moistened. He shook his head. "All this talk 'bout responsibility, and you here running around in the shadows, won't even say who you are."

"I didn't say I was any good at responsibility."

Andre chuckled, the tension dissolving between them. He palmed the back of Evan's neck affectionately. Evan had to force himself not to wipe off his skin.

A Ford Explorer turned onto the street, headlights flaring the side mirror, but it lumbered by without incident.

Andre exhaled, his breath fogging. "It's freezing here. Can't we turn on the motor, get some heat?"

"No."

"Why not?"

"We don't want to signal that we're in the truck."

"Signal to who?"

"The people trying to kill you."

"Right." Andre shivered. " 'Member that broken window in Papa Z's laundry room?"

Evan smirked. "How could I forget?"

"We had to get our wet clothes into the dryer *fast,* or that shit would freeze."

"That one time Ramón snapped his sock in half —"

"His big-ass feet. Size thirteens."

Evan said, "At least he got his own gym shoes."

"Right. We had them two pairs we had to share depending on who had gym that day.

Size-eights and size-tens. We'd rotate that shit."

"Man, those things stank."

"What are you complaining about? When we were overcrowded, I had to share a bed with Tyrell, and he'd wet the sheets, and I'd smell like piss all the next school day."

Evan was laughing now. "I remember that."

"Shower off with that Boraxo powder hand soap Papa Z lifted from the gas-station bathroom, be like scraping my skin off with sandpaper."

"And what was with that generic mac and cheese?" Evan said. "Yellow box with black lettering. Tasted like cardboard and cheddar."

"And we couldn't even eat that when Papa Z would go out 'cuz our dumb asses couldn't figure out how to turn on the stove." Andre laughed. "Wait. Van Sciver knew how to turn on the stove."

"Then he'd eat all the food, though," Evan said.

"Charles Van Sciver. Shit. 'Member that fool?"

Evan's smile faded. "I do."

"He left a bit after you. Same guy came for him. Mystery Man. Van Sciver was all puffed up. Left one day, and we never saw him again, just like you. Wonder what ever happened to him? You ever see him again?"

"We had to work some shit out," Evan said. "Later."

"And?"

He hesitated. "It didn't go well for him."

"What does that mean?"

Evan could feel the heat of Andre's stare on the side of his face. He studied the lot across the street, hoping for the line of questioning to die.

"At least tell me what you guys did," Andre said. "After they took you. Where'd y'all go?"

The kiosk went dark.

Evan held up a hand to silence Andre.

The worker emerged, locked the door behind him, and trudged to the front gate. He slid it shut, looped a chain through the bars several times, and secured it with a heavy-duty padlock. Then he climbed into an ancient BMW 2002 covered with more rust than paint, and the vehicle coughed its way up the street and around the corner.

Evan and Andre sat in the relative quiet for a moment. Then Evan slid a laptop from the backseat and pried the lid open. The impound lot's Web video server had a serious vulnerability. Its string input parameters hadn't been type-checked or checked for length, so Joey had crafted an overly long POST request for Evan to deploy when he needed it. It would cause a buffer overflow, escalate privileges using another vulnerability on the system, execute Joey's shellcode as root, and let Evan intercept and replace the video stream.

With a few clicks, he did that, and the footage showed the empty impound lot on a perennial loop. He could lead a marching band up the main aisle of wrecked cars and the stream would show nothing but a deserted tract of vehicles.

Andre watched, his mouth ajar.

Evan exited the truck. Andre trailed him to the gate, fumbling with his keys. They got through the padlock and entered. Evan paused, sensing a note of danger vibrating the night air.

He went back and left the gate open in case they needed to beat a quick retreat.

32
LIFELIKE

Andre stood at the spot where Hargreave had bled out, staring at the dark blotch on the asphalt. His cheeks looked heavy, shiny with sweat. "He died right here," he said, his voice strangled, like he had to push out the words. "And it was my fault."

But Evan had no interest in Andre's guilt. He scanned the street once more and then moved cautiously to the kiosk. A shiny new lock assembly secured the door. As Andre came up behind him, Evan lifted the tiny rake pick and tension wrench from his back pocket.

"Don't have that key," Andre said. "I broke off the old key in the lock, so they replaced —"

Evan twisted, and the lock released with a click.

Andre said, "Dayum."

They entered the tight space, the motion-activated light clicking on overhead. Triangle

285

desk in one corner. Tall file cabinet. Security monitors showing hacked surveillance footage — an abandoned lot, a locked front gate, and a dark, empty kiosk. The room hadn't been cleaned anytime recently, which was good given what Evan was looking for. The scent of musky cologne lingered.

Andre waved a hand in front of his nose. "That'd be Juan. Motherfucker smell like he bathed in Old Spice."

Evan crouched by the crappy rolling chair and searched the linoleum, running his fingers along the seams where floor met wall. He assumed the cops would have missed it, because they wouldn't have known to look for it. And he figured the Gentners wouldn't risk returning to a crime scene to get rid of a dispensable item. Even so, it could've been thrown out or stepped on.

"What are we looking for?" Andre said.

"Eyes up," Evan said. "Watch the street."

He rose so his gaze came level to the desk. Crumbs, mouse pad, keyboard, outdated Dell Inspiron desktop, chipped coffee mug, legal pad shaved down to a few sheets and covered with doodles. He checked behind the computer and then turned, frustrated.

The file cabinet.

Rising on tiptoes, he gazed across the

dust-layered metal top.

There it was, resting toward the back, expended.

He reached carefully, picked it up by a fragile metallic wing, and placed it on his palm.

When he pivoted in the tight space, Andre was waiting, his stare locked on the item resting in Evan's hand. "Did you just find a motherfucking *metal dragonfly*?"

"It's a KAM."

"Come again?"

"A kamikaze assassination microdrone." Evan gazed down at the delicate robot on his palm. Amazingly lifelike, easily mistaken for an actual dragonfly. It weighed no more than an AAA battery. The slender body, the size of a snap pea, wore a tiny processor like a backpack. Beautiful translucent wings veined with carbon-fiber, camera and microphone mounted on the head, copper electrodes visible beneath the metallic blue polyamide coating.

Protruding from the face was a wicked-looking stiletto blade, about an inch and a half in length, its silver tip colored with bright arterial blood.

Hargreave's.

Andre reached a finger to poke at the dragonfly but couldn't seem to muster the courage to actually touch it. "They stabbed him with *this*?"

Evan pictured the surveillance footage Joey had produced, Declan holding out his hand as a launch pad, the near-invisible KAM taking flight from his palm. And his attempt to recall it after it had taken out Hargreave.

"Yes," Evan said, tilting the wings to the light. On the underside a tiny etched logo featured an *M* with wings sprouting from the letter's outer downstrokes. "These things can fly, hover, and perch. Some of them can even store a solar charge and stay afloat indefinitely. We got lucky that you locked it inside the kiosk. And that you weren't in there when it came in to puncture your throat."

"Who the hell *are* these people?"

Evan slid the microdrone into one of his cargo pockets and pressed past Andre, relieved at the rush of fresh air greeting his face. "That's what we have to figure out."

Andre skip-stepped to hold pace at Evan's side. "So drone people killed Hargreave. And drone people blew up my house. And Hargreave was a drone pilot."

"Which is why I have to talk to his sensor operator ASAP, find out why they were discharged a few months ago." Evan approached the wrecked Bronco bookending the nearest row of vehicles. It was a sorry lineup: a VW Bug missing two tires, a Ferrari with a front trunk twisted open from a collision, the carbon-fiber lining giving off a stoical gleam.

"I'm going with you," Andre said. "To talk to the sensor operator."

A MINI Cooper puttered by on the road ahead, and Evan halted, reaching back to put a hand on Andre's chest. He waited for the car to pass and then resumed walking.

"No," Evan said. "And watch the street."

He passed in front of the Bronco's smashed grille, his Original S.W.A.T. boots grinding over glass pebbles. He tugged at the passenger door, which gave with some resistance.

Andre hovered at his back. "What are you doing now?"

"This is where Hargreave was looking before you interrupted him."

"Right," Andre said.

Evan knuckle-tapped the pine-tree air fresheners dangling from the rearview, sending them into a twirl, and then searched the top of the dashboard. Nothing.

His gaze caught on a sticker adhered to the inside of the windshield. He swung out of the truck and looked at it through the glass. An elaborate security hologram of the air force base's insignia — a robotic set of wings rising from a five-pointed star.

He leaned close. The hologram was elaborate and — given the drone innovators' capability with and fondness for lasers — no doubt embedded with covert laser readable imagery. The features hidden inside the hologram could be verified only at a security checkpoint with a control device endowed with proper input illumination.

They'd let Hargreave keep it on his windshield to lure him back.

It had worked.

Rendered in white against white at the bottom corner, as subtle as a watermark: INS NORTH.

It took a moment for Evan to recognize the capital letters as the Federal Aviation Administration three-letter identifier for Creech Air Force Base.

But this was slightly different.

Not Creech. Creech *North.* Evan had never heard of it.

He whipped the Strider out of his pocket, the refined-grain particle blade clicking open, and Andre took a step back. "Whoa, Nelly," he said.

"Watch the street." Evan leaned back into the cabin and gently sawed the knife beneath the sticker's edge. The corner popped up, and then he was able to pinch it and peel it free intact.

It disappeared into another cargo pocket.

Andre slapped one hand with the other. "So *that's* what Hargreave came back for."

Leaning back, Evan saw that the Little Tree air fresheners had stopped spinning, revealing a visitor parking pass hung in their midst.

He slipped the permit hanger free. CALIFORNIA VETERANS REINTEGRATION CENTER. One-day pass. The heavily guarded compound in Fresno where Hargreave's sensor operator was being rehabilitated.

Something behind Evan clicked, shifting the shadows.

His head snapped over, his hand moving toward his holster, but it was just the motion-sensor lights turning themselves off in the kiosk. He untensed his back muscles, then straightened up.

Over Andre's shoulder a set of headlights flared at the intersection. As the car continued in the direction of the open front gate, Evan made out the model.

A Tesla Model S.

Tinted windows.

Like the one that had passed them earlier.

Midnight silver instead of pearl white. Different license plate. Los Angeles was lousy with Teslas.

And yet the First Commandment spoke up in the back of Evan's mind: *Assume nothing.*

His body stayed on alert, Andre keying to it. "What?"

"I told you to watch the street," Evan said.

At the far end of the facing road, another Tesla turned into view. And then another. The third plate Evan recognized.

The vehicles sped up, converging on the open front gate.

33
SEARCH AND DESTROY

Evan's pistol was in his hand instantly, his Woolrich tactical shirt still gaping at the belly where he'd reached straight through it for his holster. The faux buttons were held together by magnetic closure, the halves now refinding their mates, the shirtfront clapping back together.

At his side Andre made a strangled noise that barely emerged from his lips.

Evan pulled him down behind the Bronco and ran a quick calculation. Eight rounds in the magazine, one in the spout. His cargo pants had low-profile inner pockets on either side hiding an extra mag, which put twenty-five rounds within reach.

He'd recently upgraded to Gorilla Silverbacks. The Silverbacks had excellent terminal ballistics with huge cavities in the ogive and premachined fracture lines that allowed them to expand rapidly to two and a half times the original caliber. When the hygroscopic effect was elicited, they basically turned into grappling hooks, punching a hole big enough to vastly increase the chances of hitting something vital. A downside of the expansion was that they didn't always defeat soft body armor, which called for precision shooting — throat, head, pelvic girdle. But he preferred them in situations with noncombatants present, since he didn't want his rounds going through walls into the next room or through the intended target into a no-shoot.

Right now he would have taken something with more penetrating power. An assault team this well coordinated would come with body armor.

He stared at his Ford F-150 through the gate and across the street. The job of his pistol was to get him to that truck, because the locked vaults in the bed held World War III. But within seconds the Teslas would be between him and it.

Outnumbered. Less-than-optimal ammo. Cut off from a munitions upgrade.

This would go down very fast, one way or another.

He ran a quick tap-and-tug on the ARES to quadruple-check that the magazine was full. Taking a high, firm grip on the pistol to disengage the grip safety, he snapped off the manual safety with his thumb and swung up to peek over the hood of the Bronco, tracking the vehicles over the barrel. He liked a narrow front-sight blade and a lot of light around the blade in the rear-sight notch. The Teslas breached the front gate, flashing into the lot — one, two, three.

Evan ducked back down. Andre was looking at him as if he'd never seen him before.

"Are these guys here to kill me?"

Evan said, "Probably."

"What are you gonna do?"

"Ascertain whether they are. And if so, kill them first."

Andre's mouth gaped a bit.

Behind them headlight beams strobed through myriad shattered windshields, the vehicles nearing.

Evan head-tilted at the Ferrari backed into the space next to them, the maw of the front trunk low and beckoning and reinforced with bullet-resistant carbon-fiber. "I need you to get in."

"What? There's no fucking way I'm gonna —"

Still crouching, Evan grabbed Andre in a wrist lock, forced the joint to urge him off the ground, and flipped him into the trunk.

"Stay here. Don't move."

Andre blinked up at him as Evan slammed

the lid. It wedged shut with a grinding of metal.

Staying low, Evan pivoted back to the Bronco and peered through the side windows.

The Teslas neared the dark kiosk, spreading out.

Driver and passenger doors opened in concert. Two men spilled out of each car.

Gym-burly, dark polo shirts, black Polartec masks covering the lower halves of their faces — everything about these men screamed private military contractors.

Down to their slung MP5s and the Browning Hi-Power clones on their hips.

The six men fanned out, forming a semicircle around the kiosk.

Raised their submachine guns.

And aerated the kiosk.

The sound was thunderous. Glass shattering, wood splintering, the flimsy paneling yielding under the barrage until the kiosk sagged to one side.

No concern about being heard or seen — they were here to neutralize Andre at any cost and kill anyone else who got in the way.

One of the men — the team leader? — moved to the door and kicked it open. Surveyed the interior. Shook his head. Backed out.

His voice carried to Evan. "We need the scene completely cleaned. Witnesses and — if need be — first responders." He nodded at his partner. "Diaz, hold center position at the kiosk. Go." He gave a quick circle of his upturned finger, a command to search and destroy, and then climbed into his Tesla and got on the phone. Reporting back.

The other five operators pivoted to the rows of cars, spreading out, each taking a different corridor through the wreckage. Evan flattened to the ground, praying that Andre would stay silent.

The Bronco was high enough that he could roll beneath it to note the men's positions. The heftiest operator and the two heading to the darker outskirts of the lot flipped down monocular night-vision headgear for hands-free. The two staying nearest the kiosk held tactical LED high-lumen flashlights; the tallest shoved his Polartec mask down around his neck, holding the flashlight between his teeth so he could wield his MP5 with both hands. The team leader waited in the Tesla, his form visible behind the windshield, phone pressed to his cheek.

Outnumbered six to one, Evan would have to delay giving away his position as long as possible. And determine who to pick off first.

Jack's voice came to him as a memory-whisper: *The Ninth Commandment: Always play offense.*

Evan gauged the men as they started to disperse, watching their chests and the mist pattern through the Polartec masks to assess their breathing. The hefty guy sweeping the aisle on the north side of the lot and the tall man with the flashlight in his mouth were both jerking in breaths, not quite panicked but not far from it either. The team leader's partner, Diaz, was circling the kiosk. He looked dead calm, like he'd done this too many times with a positive result, cocky enough to let his guard slip. The other two with monocular night-vision displayed good combat breathing, shuddering intakes, slow exhalations. Appropriately alert but not too nervous.

They'd be the most dangerous.

Evan rolled out from under the Bronco, darting low through the next row of cars, threading past a jagged bumper, and planting himself along the trajectory of the tall operator with the readied MP5 and the flashlight clenched between his teeth. Evan sank low behind a Pathfinder with half its hood sheared off.

He listened to the footfall. Shards of glass crusted the asphalt like jewels, providing a nice crunch that broadcast the man's position.

Fifteen yards away.

Now ten.

The tight cone of the flashlight appeared at Evan's side, a cold white beam sweeping left to right. Shadows stretched and warped as the man neared. His nervous inhalations, barely audible, sounded quick and shallow.

Five yards.

Two.

Evan waited for the cone to rotate to the far side of the aisle, which required the man's face to rotate with it. The beam illuminated the tire inches from Evan's heel and then swept slowly away.

Evan held until it reached the vehicles across the aisle and then rose, setting his legs and hips to generate power for the punch.

He was standing just beyond the point of the man's peripheral vision. The silhouette of the flashlight protruded from the guy's mouth like an anodized-aluminum cigar.

Evan said, "Psst."

As the man pivoted, Evan hammered the end of the flashlight with a palm-heel strike, his hand flexed back, fingers pointing up.

The shaft rocketed back into the man's mouth and through the soft tissue at the rear of the throat, and there was a crackle as the spinal cord gave way. Evan caught his sagging weight.

He slid the flashlight free of the man's ruined mouth, clicked it off, and slipped it into his thigh cargo pocket. He thought about taking the MP5 but preferred his own pistol for agility.

The man's glassy eyes stared up at Evan, tears running down his temples. The stink of his panic breath rose with each fading exhalation. He blinked and then blinked again.

Evan whispered, "It's okay, now. It's okay."

The man stopped blinking.

Evan let him pour to the ground and then was up, scooting between cars, circling the kiosk from a distance and assessing the locations of the remaining five men. The team leader had turned the Tesla around to aim it at the open front gate, ready for a getaway.

Diaz kept a tight rotation around the kiosk, MP5 held casually, aimed outward. Still too confident.

No sounds of approaching bystanders. No distant sirens. Just a car alarm screaming somewhere in the distance. Given the men's kill orders, Evan hoped the lot was sufficiently isolated not to draw bystanders. Still, he didn't want to take his time and find out.

Creeping through the maze of cars, making his way around the kiosk, he stuck his head up at intervals to track the men's movements around the lot. The night air chilled his throat, his lungs. He finally reached the back side of the kiosk, taking a position so it blocked him from view of the team leader's idling Tesla.

The other three men moved steadily through the property's periphery, one behind Evan, the others to either side of him. Beneath the sharp ridge of the masks' nose lines, their breath puffed through the thermal fabric.

Evan timed Diaz's pace as Diaz vanished around the corner of the kiosk. Counted to three. Then emerged from the cover of the damaged vehicles, bearing down on Diaz as he came back into sight.

Approaching swiftly, Evan shot him three times in rapid succession — thigh, hip, and right shoulder. Diaz managed to depress the trigger, but given his destroyed shooting arm it was nothing more than a spray-and-pray to the side, the rounds sparking off the nearby cars before the MP5 kicked from his hand of its own volition. The bullet that had shattered his hip had also knocked the still-holstered Hi-Power clean off his belt, the Silverback round doing what it did best.

With his left hand, Diaz ripped a KA-BAR straight-edge from a thigh sheath and swiped at Evan's face, but Evan trapped the wrist against the wall, caught the falling knife, and slammed it through Diaz's palm, pinning his hand to the wood.

They were eye to eye, Diaz shoved up against the kiosk, his good leg taking his weight. He made a stuttering sound, a series of "t"s that couldn't find a vowel.

"Wait here," Evan said.

Gunfire strafed the top of the kiosk, and Evan sprinted back to cover amid the damaged cars, returning fire to hold them off. He caught a glimpse of the operators closing in, their monocular night-vision headgear turning them to cyclopes.

The three men were hustling toward him from different vectors. A round chipped the asphalt behind him, and then his leg blew to the side, the ricochet catching his heel.

34
TASTE OF COPPER IN THE AIR

The force of the bullet spun Evan around, dumping him onto a throw of pebbled glass between two reasonably intact Town Cars. He grabbed for his leg to assess the damage. The round hadn't in fact struck his foot but had bitten a chunk of rubber from the heel of his boot, leaving the steel shank in the sole exposed.

Quick exhale of relief.

The slide of his 1911 was locked to the rear, the nine rounds spent. As he hit the slide release and reached for a new magazine, bursts of gunfire from both directions riddled the Town Cars on either side of him, degrading them to the condition of the surrounding vehicles. Evan flattened to the ground, caging his head, glass raining down.

When the barrage ceased, he shouted, "Wait!" — graveling his voice to disguise it. "We're shooting at each other."

He took advantage of the momentary

pause to scramble on all fours up the lane. He was still gripping the empty ARES, bits of glass sticking to his knuckles and the palm of his other hand.

Behind him the Town Cars lit up again, rocking on their chassis. He hit a streak of oil, his arm flying out, his chest slapping the ground. The tactical flashlight rolled free from his cargo pocket but thankfully did not illuminate and give away his position.

Rolling to his side, he reached again for the spare mag in his left inner cargo pocket, but then he made out the sound of labored breathing just beyond the neighboring row of vehicles. The sounds grew nearer, and he froze.

Silence.

With an MP5 in the immediate vicinity, Evan didn't dare move, let alone wrestle out the magazine and click it home.

A voice shouted over. "You okay, Keller?"

"Good!" The answer came from the far side of the Mustang that Evan was sprawled behind. Six feet away, maybe less.

The sound of heavy breathing resumed, the same anxious cadence Evan had observed from afar. The light crackle of a boot setting down. Then Keller edged into sight, his image fragmented through the Mustang's cracked side windows. He led with the MP5, hunched over the stock. The black mask wrapped the bottom of his face, his forehead seeming to float, the night-vision lens — which looked to be a cheap Russian knockoff — lowered over one eye. Severely shadowed, he looked like an apparition of steam and iron.

Another step brought him to the hood of the Mustang. The next would carry him into the aisle where Evan lay unfurled in plain view. The backup magazines shoved into his skin, beckoning. But by the time he ripped one free, seated it in the gun, and raised the barrel, he'd be on the receiving end of six hundred rounds per minute.

The tactical flashlight rested three feet from his head.

The Unofficial Eleventh Commandment: *Don't fall in love with Plan A.*

Evan strained for the flashlight. Plucked it silently from the ground.

As Keller stepped around the car, Evan's fist pulsed around the flashlight, the beam shooting directly up into the man's face.

Keller yelped and reeled back, swatting at the night-vision lens that compounded the glare into a spike of light through his eyes. Evan swept himself up off the ground, a spin kick connecting with the MP5 and knocking it free. As Keller drew his handgun, Evan laced his fist around his empty ARES and brass-knuckled it into his face. Keller's nose cracked beneath the mask, but he didn't drop his own pistol. Rather than back off, Evan skipped inside the hefty man's arm span, his head parallel to the Hi-Power as it fired. Inches away, the gunshot was deafening, but he was safely inside its range. Evan ducked and swung behind Keller, slipping one arm around his neck in a rear naked choke and clamping his gun with his other hand.

Keller's head was bent forward painfully, his torso curled, leaving him bellowing into his own chest. Holding pressure on the head, Evan goosenecked Keller's wrist, locked the elbow, and torqued his arm so the pistol was aimed sideways. Evan laced his forefinger through the trigger guard on top of Keller's.

The remaining operators were sprinting toward them from two offset trajectories, each about thirty yards away. Evan cranked Keller's hefty arm upward, captured the lead man in the off-kilter sights, and fired three times. One of the rounds caught him in the face, clotheslining him, his body landing flat on the asphalt with a deadweight thud.

Evan swung Keller's arm thirty degrees to

the right. Before he could aim at the second operator, the man opened fire, one of the rounds striking Keller in the shoulder. Spray of warmth across Evan's cheek, taste of copper in the air, the impact sending a thunderclap through Keller's flesh and bone. The domino effect nearly knocked Evan onto his ass, but he managed to hold on, keeping Keller's arm captured and maintaining the choke.

Steering Keller from behind, Evan kicked his Achilles tendon. Keller jerked his foot forward with a zombie step and grunted, lips fluttering wetly beneath the mask. Then Evan kneed the back of Keller's other leg, manipulating the big man like a doll, force-walking him around the front of the Mustang for cover. Keller tried to rear up, but Evan slammed his forehead down onto the hood, denting the metal and cracking the Tiffany-blue paint job. He kept his grip on Keller's arm, fighting their shared gun hand up and over to aim.

The operator was still coming, rounds sparking off the body of the Mustang, one of the tires going with a pop, air hissing angrily through the puncture. Keller was screaming into the hood. Evan wrenched the Hi-Power over another inch and fired,

fired, fired, finally clipping the operator's cheek.

The guy halted at last, the MP5 tumbling from his hands. Evan took a moment to sight carefully and shot him through the forehead.

There was a single instant of quiet, powder smoke stratified in the air.

Then, somewhere behind the kiosk, the Tesla hummed to life, headlights sweeping the perimeter fence as the team leader whipped the car around to charge into the fray.

Keller was sobbing, his words muted given Evan's ringing ears. "— my friends, made me shoot my friends —"

His neck was slick with blood, making it harder for Evan to maintain the rear naked choke. Keller tried to twist his gun hand free, but Evan kept his hold, pulling the Browning inward and forcing it up, up, the muzzle nearing Keller's face. Evan's biceps strained, his forearm burning. The Hi-Power trembled in their shared grasp. Keller was stronger, his arm so much meatier than Evan's; if this went on much longer, Evan would lose the battle.

Halfway across the lot, the Tesla fishtailed into sight around the kiosk, headlights blazing, and rocketed toward them.

With his last ounce of strength, Evan ripped the pistol inward one final inch, the muzzle coming parallel to Keller's temple. His forefinger overrode Keller's, forcing him to pull the trigger.

A dry click.

Evan had lost track of the rounds.

Inexcusable.

Keller's hoarse gagging sounded like a laugh. He stomped Evan's foot, twisting away. Evan released the pistol and jammed his thumb into the mandibular angle under Keller's ear behind the lower jawbone, the tender intersection of three major nerves.

The Tesla was closing, city lights cascading across its windshield.

Keller lurched away from the pressure point, screeching.

The Tesla accelerated. Close enough now that Evan could make out the team leader inside, readying his sidearm, aiming straight over the steering wheel so he could fire through the windshield.

The hiss of the electric motor crescendoed.

Keller bucked violently, setting his weight, Evan's hold weakening.

The Tesla's headlights bore down.

Digging his thumb even harder into the pressure point, Evan swung Keller in the opposite direction from what the big man would have expected.

Out into the open lane and directly into the path of the looming Tesla.

Keller shook loose from Evan's hold. The high beams caught them both in the face, bleaching them white, freezing them as if against the wrath of an atomic bomb.

For an instant it was certain they'd both die.

Keller raised his functional arm in front of his face, bracing for the collision. But Evan knew something he did not.

That the Tesla Model S featured the finest automatic braking system on the market.

The brakes stutter-clamped to slow the vehicle, smoke shooting from the tire wells. The squeal was earsplitting, the reek of burned rubber shooting forward on a pressure wave of air, hitting them in the face.

The Tesla swiveled left and then right, finally centering as it came to a steaming halt no more than a foot in front of Evan and Keller.

Keller was stooped, his arm swaying from the wrecked shoulder, foam flecking his lips. He coughed out a single note of relief.

The team leader had been tossed forward into the wheel, his handgun thrown onto the dash. He pried himself back, met Evan's eyes, reached for his pistol.

Evan took hold of Keller's ruined limb, twisted it into an arm bar, dropped his full weight into the joint lock, and swung the man down and around, tripping him as they fell.

Their shared momentum accelerated Keller's face as it slammed into the Tesla's grille.

The air bag deployed, the gun inside the car giving a muffled pop.

Keller slid off the hood and slumped to the ground, his arm striking the asphalt with a moist slap.

A hissing sound issued from the air bag as it deflated, speckled with grit and white powder, a firework burst of crimson across the sturdy nylon. Evan stayed on his knees, panting as the air bag diminished further, revealing the team leader slumped back in the driver's seat, mouth ajar as if he were sleeping. The air bag's explosion had propelled the gun upward, causing him to shoot himself in the face.

The autobrakes had delivered him to Evan.

And the air bag had done the rest.

Evan's ribs ached. His right side was doused in Keller's blood. The close-range gunshot had reduced his hearing to a ringing whine, and cotton filled his head. Enough adrenaline had dumped into his bloodstream to make him light-headed.

He allowed himself the luxury of three full breaths. Then he pulled himself upright, his lower back aching.

No bystanders. No sirens. Not yet.

First step, he told himself. *Secure your weapon.*

He trudged over behind the Mustang, the blown-out heel of his boot lopsiding his gait. The metallic rasp of the exposed shank against the asphalt accompanied every other step. He picked up the ARES where he'd dropped it and slotted a fresh magazine in. Heading back to the kiosk, he staggered a bit but then regained his balance.

Next in the gear checklist was the Roam-Zone. Not surprisingly, it had cracked in the brawl, turning the screen into a mosaic. As he moved through the labyrinth of cars, he placed both his thumbs over the fault lines and applied pressure, the self-repairing polyether-thiourea knitting itself back together before he reached the clearing.

Diaz was right where Evan had left him, pinned to the wall by his hand, his weapons on the ground just out of reach. Fighting the pain in his impaled palm and quaking on his intact right leg, he strained to reach

312

the MP5.

There was no way.

Evan approached, the steel shank click-click-clicking on the ground. As he neared, Diaz gave up, sagging back against the wall. He'd tugged the Polartec mask down around his neck, pained breaths huffing in the cold air. A bib of drool sheened his chin. The damage to his hip was severe, arterial blood snaking down his leg. It wouldn't be long.

Diaz looked down, tried to stem the bleeding with his good hand.

"You're a private military contractor," Evan told him.

". . . did good, too . . ." Diaz's chest juddered as it rose. ". . . everyone thinks . . . bad . . . but we're the ones . . . call in when they need . . . demine a field in Mosul . . . Kurmal . . ."

"That doesn't interest me," Evan said. "Who do you work for?"

Diaz licked his lips, his eyes halfway gone. "Every cleared mine a saved life or . . . Every one. . . . I'm not bad . . . not bad . . ."

"Who do you work for?" Evan asked again.

"We come back here. . . . What are we s'posed to do . . . ?"

His head lolled, his hand slipping from the ragged wound on his hip, the life running out of him, pooling in his boot.

Evan stepped forward, gripped Diaz's chin, lifted his face. "Who do you work for?"

The dark lashes parted sluggishly. ". . . don't know . . . call him . . . the doctor . . . All I know." He was crying now. "I'm not all bad . . . helped people, too . . . help me now . . . help me. . . ."

"You were willing to kill witnesses," Evan told him. "Cops."

Diaz's large brown eyes held a depth of sorrow that seemed bottomless. ". . . not all bad."

"Okay," Evan said. "I understand."

Diaz slumped forward, his good leg giving out, his body sagging from the impaled hand. An ignoble pose, even grotesque.

Evan stared down at the top of Diaz's head. Then he ripped the KA-BAR free of his hand, Diaz's body spilling to the ground. His lips were tensed in a crooked scowl, eyes glossed with a lifeless film. Evan reached down and closed his lids.

Then hustled across the lot, trying not to limp.

He reached the Ferrari and pried up the lid of the trunk. Andre roared something unintelligible, swinging and kicking wildly.

Evan stepped back, none of the blows landing. "You're safe. We need to move."

cake to the onlookers. Even from here Declan could make out the white lettering across the dark chocolate frosting: HAPPY TWO YEAR BIRTHDAY. KEEP COMING BACK!!

The burner phone in the cup holder animated. Queenie had Bluetoothed it to her Corvette, her custom ringtone issuing through the speakers: "99 Red Balloons" in German.

Careful not to smear her nail polish, she pressed a button on the steering wheel to answer.

Declan said, "Yes, sir."

"Six dead."

Declan said, "Excuse me?"

"Six dead," the doctor repeated. "I'm considering it an R 'n' D expenditure. This many lost assets make clear that someone's helping Duran."

"Who?"

"I'm looking into it. This elevates the priority level, the urgency. I need you to produce results."

"We're almost ready to move on the second target."

"No," the doctor said. "Duran first. He actually saw it."

Queenie flipped the visor back up, dropped the car into gear, and crept out from the curb. *We're doing everything we can.*

"We're doing everything we can," Declan said. "Right now we're staking out —"

"Maybe you have a different understanding of what 'results' means," the doctor said, calm as ever. "Do you need me to acquaint you with my definition of the word?"

Declan clenched his teeth, his neck cording, and let the silent scream vibrate his whole head.

Queenie reached over, stroked his thigh. *No. No, sir.*

Declan exhaled until he felt the purple leave his face. "No. No, sir."

"I have teams watching the ex's place and the child's school. They've been alerted to the escalation. If he rears his head, they'll take it clean off. In the meantime you'd better figure out another approach. Friends, co-workers, distant family."

"We've looked at everyone and everything," Declan said.

Queenie banked hard onto the freeway ramp and opened up the 650 horses. *Don't argue with him. He wants blood. We need to give it to him.*

Declan looked at her. *We already took that one guy apart top to bottom.*

Then we'll take another apart. And send

pictures.

That won't get us anywhere.

You're being too literal. It's not about getting somewhere right now. It's about satisfying the doctor.

The doctor had said nothing. Not a pleasant silence.

Declan said, "We have another person we can talk to."

"Good," the doctor said. "Because you won't like it if I run out of patience."

He hung up.

A few minutes later, Queenie exited the freeway and crawled through a dark neighborhood. Prefab houses set imprecisely down on plots of dead weed. Flaking paint. Rusted mailboxes. Disgust curdled in Declan's chest. As hideous as their childhood had been, Mom had always made sure the house was a place of pride. Spit-shined counters. Beds made with boot-camp precision. Kitchen floor you could eat off.

These people lived like animals.

Queenie coasted up on a double-wide positioned crookedly at the far edge of a dirt lot. Vinyl siding splayed up at intervals, exposing rotting wood-chip board sheathing beneath. A decrepit BMW at the curb.

As Declan climbed out, Queenie popped the trunk. He slid off his Brioni jacket, gave it a dead-man's fold to avoid wrinkles, and laid it precisely across the leather backseats. The trunk held his fine-leather kit. He'd sterilized the tools and the nails since their last use. It was a matter of professionalism.

A surgeon had to keep his implements pristine.

Queenie had her personal phone out, the iPhone case studded with crusted faux rubies. Its camera had an array of filters and HDR that really brought a tableau to life.

She handed it off. "I'll wait out here. Whistle if you need me."

"You know we won't get any answers." His voice came high and wheezy, irritating even to his own ears.

"I know, baby brother. But sometime you just gotta feed the beast."

Declan took the phone and crossed the dirt lot, cautious not to scuff his Ferragamos. He removed his cuff links and rolled his sleeves above the forearms.

The front door was open to vent the heat of the stovetop — something reheated and preservative-intensive. A TV murmured calmingly inside, a game show with lots of applause: *I'll take Science for two hundred, Alex.* The screen yawned open with the groan of a rusty coil.

The man sat on a ripped La-Z-Boy facing

away, watching *Jeopardy!,* the volume too loud.

Toolkit in hand, Declan glided through the narrow galley kitchen into the living room. The threadbare carpet silenced his loafers as he approached. He paused right behind the man's chair, watching the TV over the back of his head.

The scent of Old Spice was strong here, overpowering the kitchen smells. The man stayed fixated on the screen, oblivious. Declan rubbed the catch of the leather kit with his thumb, closing his eyes into that bloodred glow, letting the other part of himself take charge.

The game-show host wore a two-button herringbone Ted Baker. He rested an elbow on his podium. "There are two hundred and six of *these* in the adult human body."

"Wait, I know this one," Declan said, and Juan just about fell out of his chair. Declan flicked the catch, the weight of the implements causing the leather kit to unfurl with a snap.

Now his words came forth low-pitched and sonorous. "What are 'bones'?"

36
FOUR-LETTER WORD

Coasting through light traffic into West-wood, Evan dialed Joey's number again. He'd delivered Andre to his woeful room above the Chinese restaurant. After rinsing off Keller's blood and changing into a new set of clothes from his truck vaults, Evan had extracted a promise from Andre that he wouldn't leave except to eat. Andre had been shaken enough to concede with minimal complaining, especially after Evan pointed out that takeout was literally a flight of stairs away. He'd left him with a few hundred dollars to cover anything he'd need until Evan could return, and Andre had placed the bills in the zippered pouch that he handled with great care.

Halting at a stoplight, Evan glanced over to the passenger seat where he'd rested the dragonfly drone, the encrypted clearance sticker for Creech North Air Force Base, and the parking hanger for the veterans' facility.

The spoils of victory.

Joey's line rang and rang. Just when he was certain the call would dump into voice mail once more, she picked up. *"What?"*

"Why aren't you answering?"

"Uh, 'cuz I'm not, like, a child slave sitting around all day stitching Nikes and just waiting for you to —"

Evan said, "I need you to get my name on the visitor's log at the California Veterans Reintegration Center for tomorrow."

"I'm gonna write some dialogue for you," Joey said. "This is what it sounds like when *actual humans* call each other. 'Hi, Joey. How are you? How were classes today?' "

"How *were* classes today?"

"I dunno. I cut."

"Josephine."

"Okay, okay. Let's go back to nonhuman talking. The California Veterans Reintegration Center — and by the way, that name? like, Eastern European communist creepy much? — has no-fooling-around security, like I told you."

"You got me into *prison.*"

"Prison is easy by comparison. No one wants to sneak *into* prison. Well, except you. Like you said, this is a military compound protecting vulnerable human assets who know confidential shit. They're not trying to keep people in. They're trying to keep people out."

"I have the best forged passports in the world —"

"Oh, well, then. Maybe bring a note from your first-grade teacher, too? Pin it to your sweater?"

"What are you talking about?"

"You're gonna need more than a fake ID. You're a military-age male, X. You're exactly the demo they'd be on high alert for. Even if you *are* getting long in the tooth."

He rubbed his forehead. "I'm not getting long in the tooth."

"Says the prune-juice-drinking retiree. Look. I gotta go. I'll call you later."

"I'm almost at your place."

"What? No. *No.*"

"Yes. I found a microdrone with a logo on it —"

"A friggin' *microdrone* now?"

"— and I already ran an image search on Google, but nothing's coming up. I need to identify it ASAP. Guess what else doesn't come up anywhere online? Creech *North* Air Force Base. Which is what the parking sticker from Hargreave's rig says."

"Wait — you went to the lot?"

"With Andre. They were watching that rig, that sticker, and ready to kill anyone who came near it. Six private military contractors followed us in."

"How many came out?"

Evan let that pass. "We need to figure out what exactly Creech North is and who the person is behind all this — a guy who they call 'the doctor.' I need you to —"

He thought he heard a doorbell in the background, and then Joey said, "Don't comeovercallyoulaterwhenIhavemoretime bye," and hung up.

It took a moment for the quarter to drop.

Bridger "Bicks" Bickley.

With his soul patch and his distressed leather black belt and his boy-band jawline. *Grab you tomorrow? Like eight o'clock?* To "hang out." With Joey.

Evan glared at the dashboard clock. It was 8:13 P.M. Bicks couldn't even be on time.

He noted that his hands had gone bloodless atop the steering wheel.

He ran the red light, eliciting a few honks, and accelerated through Westwood Village, cutting off a guy with robust hair in a Jag convertible who gave him what-the-fuck hands. He leaned into the pedal, the Ford F-150 zooming around the corner just as Joey and eighteen-year-old Bridger emerged from her building.

Joey wore a sleeveless shirt, cypress green to bring out her eyes. It took a moment for Evan's brain to process the fact that she was wearing high heels. Bridger ran a hand across her shoulders and took a hit from a vape pen.

Joey's shoulders.

A fucking vape pen.

Evan tucked into the curb behind an SUV and kept the engine running.

Up ahead Joey pointed a key fob at a Ford Focus with a ZIPCAR.COM sticker emblazoned across the back. The brake lights bleeped twice, and then she opened the passenger door for Bridger.

Her. Holding the door. For him.

She climbed into the car-share vehicle and drove off.

Evan transitioned into a rolling surveillance position, leaving two vehicles and a half block between them. He tightened up at the choke points and fed her more leash once she banked onto Wilshire Boulevard.

A few blocks up, Joey threw a right-hand signal but drove straight through the light.

She'd spotted him.

Damn Orphan training.

With nothing to lose, he swept into position behind her, giving her a few car lengths.

At the next light, she stopped even though it was green. Evan stopped behind her. He could see her angry eyes skewering him in the rearview. Vehicles clogged up behind him, horns blaring.

He waited. The light turned yellow.

"Don't do it, Josephine," he said.

Now red.

Cross traffic flooded the intersection from either direction. At the last moment, Joey punched the gas and shot through the gap, motoring away and leaving Evan stranded at the light.

He seethed.

As the Ford Focus drifted off, the brake lights flared. It took a moment for him to realize that she was tapping them in a pattern.

Tap-tap-tap-tap.

Then *tap-hold.*

Morse code.

For "ha."

Joey zipped through the next intersection and was gone.

Rather than wait for the light, Evan cut right, inserting himself into the traffic flow, then jogged left, ran a parallel street hard for five blocks, and popped back over onto Wilshire.

There she was ahead, her signal broadcasting a right turn.

Overconfident.

After she went, he crept to the turning lane, counted off thirty seconds, and then eased up the same street. She'd just parked ahead in front of a newsstand. He watched her get out and hesitate at the meter.

She patted her pockets. No change. She looked at Bridger, who was predictably useless. She walked to the newspaper stand, liberated a brown paper bag while the worker was distracted helping a customer, and put it over the parking meter upside down.

A quick and easy out-of-service scam.

Evan felt his temperature tick up another degree.

Bridger led her into the Italian restaurant next door.

Evan moved to the opposite curb and parked, watching across two lanes of traffic as they were shown to a window table.

A poor countersurveillance move. Joey still had much to learn.

Which was precisely why she shouldn't be out on a date with an eighteen-year-old named "Bicks."

Bridger hit his vape pen once more and handed it across the table. Joey stared a moment. Then took it. She gave a few puffs.

Even at this distance, Evan could see the effort it took for her to pretend to enjoy it.

Last straw.

He climbed out, unlocked one of his truck vaults, and removed a long-range laser listening device, headphones, and Steiner tactical binoculars. Back in the driver's seat, he rested the apparatus in the V between the slightly open door and the frame of the truck, training the microphone on the restaurant window.

Inside, Bridger took back the vape pen, then removed something from his pocket and set it on the table in front of Joey.

The invisible infrared beam detected vibrations in glass, translating them into sound, amplifying them, and filtering out ambient noise. "— oh, nice," Joey was saying in a hyperfeminine tone Evan barely recognized. "A candle. Thank you *so much.*"

Evan lifted the binocs, put the stadia crosshairs on the gift: Misty Cashmere, fancy glass vessel, forty hours' burn time.

Cloying.

As Joey and Bridger made cute-talk, Evan held the mic steady with one hand and scrolled through his RoamZone with the other, running a background check.

" 'Scuse me one sec," Bridger said. "Gotta drain the main vein."

331

As he headed to the bathroom, Joey picked up the candle and sniffed it, closing her eyes.

Evan dialed. Watched her expression harden as she glanced down at her phone. She screwed a Bluetooth earbud into her ear angrily and tapped the screen to answer.

He watched her lips move, the sound reaching him on a slight delay. "What do you want? I lost you for a reason."

"Misty Cashmere," Evan said, "sounds like a stripper name."

Her head jerked over. She scanned the street. It took a moment for her glare to zero in on him, but when it did, he felt it like a retaliatory laser.

"You take one more hit off that vape pen," Evan said, "and Bridger's gonna wake up tonight knowing what a choke hold feels like."

"That's so perfect. I make my *own choices* as a woman —"

"You're not a woman —"

"— and you blame the *man*. Like, I have no agency."

"You have more agency than I can keep track of," Evan said. "But you don't even know this guy."

"That's the point of dating," she said. "To, like, get to know someone."

"The guy's a communications major —

ironic given his lack of verbal acuity — and he barely maintains a two-point-oh. Been on academic probation twice. And he had a jaywalking ticket —"

"Uh, you just *butchered six dudes in an impound lot.*"

"Context is everything."

"Yeah?" Joey said. "Well, maybe he was jaywalking to help a nun not get run over by a bus."

"An unlikely array of circumstances. Plus, that would've been on the ticket write-up."

Her face was red. "Pulled that up already, did you?"

"Yes. And he has an outstanding speeding ticket. Not exactly responsible."

"Not exactly Ted Bundy."

"That's your standard now, Orange Blossom Girl?"

Bridger stepped back to the table, drying his hands on his pants in a manner unbefitting a legal adult.

Joey said, "This is me hanging up on you."

"He'd better pay for dinner," Evan said. "He's got a five-thousand-dollar limit on his Mastercard, and he hasn't even used half of it this month."

He watched her reach for her phone.

"Wait," he said. "Don't you want to know his late-payment history?"

Click.

Joey smiled at Bridger as he slid into his chair. When he adjusted his napkin in his lap, the grin vanished and she shot a death stare over at Evan.

Bridger looked back up, caught the tail end of her expression before she produced a new radiant smile. "You okay?" he asked.

"Oh, yeah," Joey said, swirling her straw in her water glass. "It's nothing."

A truck passed between them, disrupting the reception. Evan adjusted his headphones and picked her back up again.

"— just issues with my uncle."

Bridger said, "That angry guy?"

"Yes," Joey said. "I agree that he comes off real angry. He doesn't think so, but he lacks self-awareness."

"Yeah? That sucks. My dad's like that. He doesn't get what a dickhead he is all the time, like, 'I'm not paying for you to get C's,' you know?"

But Joey was barely paying attention to her date, instead casually letting her gaze sweep the street. It stuck for a moment on Evan, her defiant smile magnified through the Steiners. "And lack of self-awareness isn't even his worst trait."

"What *is,* then?" Bridger, ever the conversationalist.

"He's really demanding. I work for him, kind of. But he needs everything on *his* time frame."

"I hate that shit."

"And he's not appreciative," Joey continued. "Barely at all. And right now he needs me to arrange an appointment for him tomorrow, but I made clear there's *no way I'll help him* if he doesn't give me the night off tonight. So." She smiled once more, flashing that hair-thin gap in her front teeth, a dimple indenting her right cheek. It was ridiculous how elegant she looked across the table from that mouth-breathing reprobate. "We'll just see if he's smart enough to not disturb me for the rest of dinner . . ."

Bridger looked confused. Or that was just his resting facial expression.

". . . and to remember that I will handle any work that needs to be handled the way I always do, which is with earth-shattering competence —"

"Uh —"

"— before he comes over tomorrow morning. At, like, seven A.M., 'cuz I know it's pressing. Anything my uncle and I have to deal with we can deal with then."

"O-*kay*," Bridger said.

"And he should know me well enough by now to trust that I can take care of *myself*,"

Joey continued. "And that I will get home safely tonight, isn't that right, Bicks?"

Bridger said, "Sure?"

Evan lowered the binoculars into his lap. She was his charge, and he had to look out for her and keep her safe. Didn't he? What was the right amount of protective and what was too much? A low burn started in his chest like an overstretched muscle. Anger? Concern? He didn't have a good sense for things like this, not the way Mia did.

He tugged off his headphones and threw them and the surveillance device into the passenger seat. Pulling the truck out into traffic, he flipped a U-turn. When he passed the front of the restaurant, Bridger had his face buried in the menu, but Joey's eyes flicked up and watched him sail past.

She mouthed, *Thank you.*

As he headed back to Castle Heights, that burn in his chest spread out, descending the rungs of his ribs, creeping up his neck. An image came to him unbidden, Veronica on that endless sweep of a couch, her gaze lowered to the rim of her champagne glass: *I thought if I named you, I couldn't bear to part with you.* And then it slammed home, the name for the warmth expanding from his torso, the realization making him wince.

No wonder they called it a four-letter word.

37
To Be Continued

Mia answered the door wearing a Columbia Law School T-shirt that drooped to midthigh. She smelled fresh from the shower, green-apple shampoo or conditioner, her mop of wavy chestnut hair brushed back and for once subdued.

"Yes," she said. "I checked the peephole."

Evan said, "And you answered anyway."

"You look a little banged up."

Given the ringing in his ears from the close-proximity gunshot, her words came in slightly muted. "Rough day at the office."

She opened the door and offered a hug. Her body felt distinct beneath the T-shirt, every contour of her pressed against him. For a moment he lost himself in the familiarity of her. His mind cast back to the warmth of her bare stomach against his, her mouth at his ear, the arch of her spine. He felt an urge to slide his hand off the midline of her back to the dip of her waist and wrap her into him.

Instead he patted her shoulder blade once and stepped back. Behind her he could hear the TV, something cartoony and symphonic.

"To what do I owe the pleasure?" Mia said.

"You asked me to talk to Peter. About the stuff he's been grappling with. Your husband — he died when Peter was three, right?"

"Good memory."

Evan had gone upstairs only to burn his clothes from the impound lot and grab a shower. Standing under the pounding heat of the jets, he'd realized that if he felt lost in regard to Veronica, Peter must have felt the same way about his father. But was trying to process it with a nine-year-old brain.

And that no matter how busy Evan was dodging missiles and mercenaries, he owed it to the boy to try to clear a few obstacles from his path.

Not that he had any idea how to do that.

Mia beckoned him in. "He earned a bit of screen time this week," she said somewhat defensively. "And tomorrow's an admin day, so no school."

Evan said, "I won't tell anyone."

Peter's head popped up above the back of the sofa. "Evan Smoak!"

As Peter zipped into full view, Evan saw

339

he was wearing pajama bottoms and another man's dress shirt, the tail and front hems swaying down past his knees. The fabric was wrinkled, the collar out of whack, and Evan wondered if he'd been sleeping in his father's shirts, too.

Peter tried to engage Evan in an elaborate handshake that he couldn't keep up with. "No," Peter said, seizing his hand and forcing it into various contortions. His fingers were grubby, sticky with some sugar residue, but Evan restrained himself from drawing away or commenting.

He blundered his way through the ritual, looking over at Mia, who grinned at his discomfort. "I'm gonna finish the dishes," she said. "Why don't you two watch TV."

Peter made a fist, yanked it back beside his waist. *"Yesss."* He grabbed Evan's arm and pulled him around the couch, flopping onto the cushion.

Jerked down next to the boy, Evan grimaced against a rib bruise he'd sustained in his death match with Keller.

On the television a donkey-boy cried out, "Mama, Mama!" braying and kicking everything in sight, and then Pinocchio sprouted equine ears and tugged at them in horror.

It was one of the few children's movies Evan was familiar with. He remembered watching it on Papa Z's crappy console TV with its wooden frame, the reception fuzzed by static. How the lost boys of Pride House had fanned out around the screen on the worn carpet of the living room, transfixed like toddlers at story time. What had the movie of a motherless boy meant to them all? To Andre?

What had it meant to Evan?

On the floor beside the couch rested a poster board with color-printer photos pasted haphazardly on it, apparently drying. A crayoned oak tree with the pictures dangling like fruit from the limbs — Mia; Peter's father, Roger; Mia's brother and parents; and so on.

The stupid family report.

Evan snuck a peek at Peter, but he was focused intently on the movie. They watched a few minutes, Evan glancing over at Peter from time to time, gauging an opening. His own childhood, devoid of heart-to-heart talks, had left him ill-prepared for this.

"He's a puppet," Peter said. "But he wants to be a real boy."

Evan nodded. "Why do you think that is?"

"Duh," Peter said. "Everyone wants to be real. But I guess . . ."

"What?"

"I guess you could get hurt more. 'Cuz

341

wood, you know? But once you're real, it's scarier."

Evan thought about the Ten Commandments, how they wrangled the world into a rigid order. His penthouse upstairs, airtight and defended against intrusion. Clean hard surfaces, every item in place, accounted for. So comforting and so lifeless. Not a single mess or splinter, every rough edge sanded down, smooth as the limbs of a marionette.

Very much opposite to the chaos engendered in him at the thought of Veronica. This person he was bound to, human and flawed, blood of her blood, flesh of her flesh. He recalled her hands on his shoulders, the tinge of chardonnay on her breath. She'd gazed at him with maternal adoration. And recoiled from him in disgust when he told her what he'd been trained to be.

Maybe that's what intimacy was, a discomfort like the burning he'd felt in his chest when Joey had told him she could take care of herself. A sense of dread at what could go wrong, a stifling of fear, a baring of the vulnerable self to the judgment of someone else. The jagged edge of one soul meeting another, tearing and rending, a connection and a diminishment both. All that imperfection, all that friction — it wore

down the tread, expending rather than pre-
serving.

What if that was the point?

To expend ourselves in the care of people
who mattered?

Without that, what was there to preserve?

He felt a rush of grief that he'd taken this
long — the better part of four decades —
not even to learn this but to consider it.
Once again he pictured Veronica crouched
over that marble newborn in the cemetery.
He was so much like that inanimate likeness rendered in stone, carved into a facsim-
ile of a human being. What had Veronica
told him in Bel Air? *To survive you had to
shut off parts of yourself, what you felt, what
you reacted to.* He'd certainly expended
himself in the service of others, for Andre
and those he helped, but now all those missions lay revealed to him for what they were
— proxies for actual intimacy, surrogates
for real connections that could pierce
through his defenses and touch him at the
tender core.

Joey mouthing, *Thank you,* as he drove
away from her.

Veronica's hazel eyes glazed with emotion
and champagne.

Peter swimming in the rumpled pinstripe

shirt of his dead father: *Once you're real, it's scarier.*

Evan felt that heat moving through him once again and blinked a few times to regain his focus. He noticed he was clenching his jaw and relaxed it, bringing himself back to this couch, this living room.

Pinocchio was following Jiminy Cricket now, pursuing his conscience up a craggy hillside and leaping into the black, black sea.

Peter was watching Evan. "What are you thinking about?"

Evan cleared his throat, which he was surprised to find needed clearing. "How much wiser you are than me."

"When you were my age?"

"Maybe now, too," Evan said.

Peter beamed.

Evan tried to find what to say next, but this wasn't his language. His head felt murky, words just out of grasp. He picked a starting point. "Your shirt's big."

Peter looked down, picked at it. "It was my dad's."

"Do you remember him well?"

"Not really." That raspy nine-year-old voice still upbeat, contemplative. "I remember the scruffles on his cheeks when he kissed me. And some kind of whaddayacallit he wore. Like, to smell good?"

"Aftershave?"

"Whatever. Some guy at the mall had it once when he walked by, and I remembered." His charcoal eyes looked impossibly large, and Evan sensed an opening into something bigger. Peter tugged at a button. "But . . ."

Evan's mouth was dry. He stayed hushed, his muscles tight with anticipation. He waited. Waited some more.

"But how do you know someone you never knew?" Peter said.

The question left Evan breathless. An image flashed into his mind, the moment when Veronica's wide cheeks and dark, shimmering eyes had first come clear beneath the brim of that black summer hat, how he'd known that it was her without knowing her at all. Something twisted free inside him, an unknotting into a new space.

He'd been drawn down here for Peter. But for himself, too. His head was pounding, his senses fired.

"I don't know," Evan said. "But your dad knew you. And maybe . . . maybe that went into your cells. I think you know him in there. Deep."

"Why do you think that?"

"Because I know what kind of kid you are.

345

Open and confident and . . ." Evan searched for the word in the murk. "Secure." The conversation was moving fast and required terrific focus, like skiing a black diamond where any second he could catch an edge and it would all go horribly wrong. "And a lot of that is from your mom. But I'm pretty sure it's from him, too."

"How do you know?"

Evan thought about it. "Because I know your mom. And I know what kind of mom she is."

Peter blinked up at him. Nodded.

"Which means we know what kind of man she'd marry," Evan said. "Don't we?"

Peter nodded again.

"And that's why you're wearing his shirts, I think. To be close to him."

"But . . ."

"What?"

Peter said, "Even if that's true . . ."

Pinocchio and Jiminy had made their way home across dark cobblestone streets, pounding on the front door with frustration. But no one was home.

"Even if that's true . . ." Peter took a deep breath and scratched his nose, hiding his eyes. "I don't have anyone to be proud of me."

There were a hundred pat answers, none

346

of them suitable. Evan sat with the words Peter had entrusted to him. Then he reached over. His hand looked so big resting on Peter's knee.

"I know what you're gonna say." Peter kept his face tilted down, away. "But Mom doesn't count. She *has* to be proud of me. She's my *mom.*"

Evan marveled that Peter could take something like that for granted.

Again he pictured Veronica on that big white couch.

Why didn't you want me?

My circumstances weren't suited to it.

Peter placed his hand on Evan's, a double stack atop his knee. He returned his focus to the movie, and Evan followed suit.

They watched for a time, the boy's hand warm against his.

Finally Mia called over from the kitchen: "Okay. *Bedtime for Bonzo.* Brush, floss, pee."

"Mom! Evan Smoak's here! Twenty more minutes."

"Are you kidding? You are way past bedtime already."

"*Ten* more minutes?"

"Hmm. Let me consider. How about . . ." Mia came around to the front of the couch, a finger rested alongside her cheek, pondering theatrically. ". . . *no* more minutes. You know why?"

Peter singsonged, "You don't negotiate with terrorists."

"That's right."

"Can I have a glass of eggnog?"

"No. Too much sugar. And besides, it's expired."

Peter slouched off toward his bedroom. "Like my *dreams.*"

Mia pursed her lips, rolled her eyes. Evan followed her back to the kitchen and helped her put away the last few dishes. A Post-it stuck next to the telephone had another quotation from that Jordan Peterson book she was always reading: *Do not hide unwanted things in the fog.*

She often scattered notes around the condo as parental touchstones for Peter. It was always a challenge for Evan to wrap his head around the notion of a childhood guided by carefully curated life lessons. Especially in contrast to his own, shaped by the rule of the foster-home pack and a set of Commandments designed to sharpen him into a lethal implement.

She gestured to a top shelf in the cupboard, out of her reach, and then handed him a salad bowl. He took it, their fingers brushing, and set it high in its place.

"Did that go okay?" she asked, head tilting toward the couch.

"I think so."

"Just getting him to talk about it is a help," she said. "It's hard for him to bring it up to me. I think he thinks it's . . . disloyal somehow. Like I'll take it that he's saying I'm not enough for him as a parent. And I'll let you in on a secret." She leaned close, and again Evan caught the scent of green apple from her damp hair. "*No one's* enough as a parent."

"I'd argue you're pretty close."

She swung around, leaning back against the sink, her arm pressing into his as he dried a water glass. "You're pretty helpful for a tough guy. Do you do windows, too?"

"You couldn't afford me."

"Is that so."

Amused, she rolled her lips to moisten them. Her bottom lip, even fuller than the top, protruded just slightly. He remembered having it between his teeth, her legs outside his, heels sliding on his calves, slick with sweat.

"You know, we never really talked about it," she said.

"What's that?"

"You saved my life. And you saved his life."

He had. And she was right. They'd never addressed it. They couldn't without compromising her as a district attorney and introducing something between them that could never be taken back.

"And I can't thank you properly," she said. "And I can't be with you." She came off the sink to face him. They were standing very close. Her gaze dropped to his mouth. "But I *want* to be with you."

Keeping his eyes on hers, he set down the glass on the counter. "What would you do if you could be with me?"

A sparkle behind her eyes, a playful crease in her cheek as her lips pulled to one side. "For starters?" She lifted a finger, brushed the side of his throat. "I'd put my mouth right *there.*"

Only at this proximity could he make out the sprinkling of light freckles across the bridge of her nose. "And then?"

She moved her finger up, placed it against his lips.

Close enough now that he could see the rust-colored flecks in her irises, could feel her breath against his chin. The pressure of her finger was warm, insistent.

She lowered her hand. Shifted onto her tiptoes. Their foreheads touched.

"Mo-om!" A two-syllable bellow from across the condo. *"I'm out of toothpaste!"*

They drew apart, smiling as if they'd been

caught at something. "Hang on, Black Hole of Need!" she shouted.

"And not the minty one that makes my tongue all bumpy! The bubble-gum-flavored one!"

"Be right there!" she called out. Then, apologetically to Evan, "I need to get him down."

He said, "Of course."

"Thank you again. For talking with him."

She walked Evan to the door and leaned on it as he started out, letting her weight sway on the hinges. He stopped, looked back across the threshold. They both wanted to say something else, but he was all out of those kinds of words for the evening.

She cleared her throat. "To be continued?"

He looked at her.

She looked back as she closed the door.

38
ROAD TRIP

At 6:59 A.M. Joey bounded down the steps of her apartment, visible through the glass front doors. Overnight bag slung across one shoulder, she scurried out to the curb and hopped into Evan's truck.

"What are you doing?" he said. "I was just about to come up."

"I know. Being Mr. Punctual-to-the-Second makes you predictable. Which is another improvement I'll put in place when I take over as — dun-dun-*dunnn* — Orphana X."

"I don't think there's a feminine form."

"There is now."

"And when you assume my role, you'll save the day with tactical lateness?"

"I shall do precisely that."

"Why are you in my passenger seat?"

" 'Cuz you told me to handle everything. And I have. You said you needed to see Hargreave's sensor operator, one Senior Air-

352

man Rafael Gomez, which means you have to get into Das Veterans Reintegration Ministry for Better Zociety und Citizenry."

"Impressive German or Russian accent, I think."

"Eet vas both." She dropped the Eastern European guise. "As I said, security's intense, so there's no way you're getting in alone. Too suspicious. I mean, look at you. Military-age man, beady eyes, overcompensatory truck — you just scream shady."

"I do not have beady —"

"Whereas with your daughter, Almudena" — she hit the accent hard and in this case correctly — "who is also conveniently Rafael's seventeen-year-old niece, you are a far less suspicious presence to visit the facility on — wait for it — Family Friday!" She threw jazz hands, mouth ajar, eyebrows hoisted.

"My daughter," Evan said. "Have you *seen* us?"

"Yes. You married Consuelo née Gomez, Rafael's older sister, in 1998. Congratulations. Wishing you a lifetime of love and happiness. Oh, by the way, your name is Harold Blasely."

"Harold Blasely? Sounds like a traveling brush salesman."

"A fine option for your imminent re-

retirement."

He gritted his teeth. He was due to meet his armorer en route to the Fresno veterans' compound, but his inimitable and tenacious forger was over in Northridge. Bruising had come up overnight around his right eye, and his lower back ached from the confrontation in the impound lot. The last thing he was in the mood for was Joey and her three-hundred-mile-per-hour mouth.

"Joey," he said, mustering as much forbearance as he could, "we don't have ID to pull this off. You said so yourself."

"I figured we don't have time to see your badass Paper Dragon Lady — see what I did there? — to get the real deal, so I made us virtual ones, which is, like, *way* easier. I uploaded scans of doctored passports and licenses and stuff when I put us on the visitor's log. They're all in the system."

"We'll still have to show ID at the gate."

"It's a new preclearance process. They'll just smile and wave."

"And what's Rafael gonna say if he's expecting his niece and brother-in-law?"

"Oh, you're right." She shook her head with mock consternation. "That's way too daunting a situation for you to socially engineer in your fragile sunset years. Want me to get you back to the home for pinochle?"

"If it gets me out of *this* conversation, yes."

"Come on, X. It's a Harry and Almu Blasely road trip!"

"You can't come," Evan said. "It's too dangerous."

"One: Then you won't get in. Two: It's not dangerous. It's a military facility. The worst that'll happen is you'll get arrested and renditioned somewhere, and I'll just cry and make sad-girl eyes, and they'll feel sorry for me for being drawn under the spell of your bad influence —"

"*My* bad influence —"

"*Three.*" She was bending back her fingers, the nails painted a vivacious pink, no doubt due to Bicks's arrival on the scene. "If we don't do this, then your boy Andre's gonna get killed, and so you're *literally* choosing being uptight over saving his life."

The muscles of his neck had tightened up. He let his head sag, feeling a sudden kinship with Mia. "I don't negotiate with terrorists."

"Clearly," she said. "You just got *out* negotiated by a terrorist." She snapped her fingers and pointed through the windshield. "Drive or we'll be late."

He looked over at her. She smiled that winning smile, flipped her hair to the left to show off that shaved strip over her right ear, her thumbprint dimple indenting one cheek. She was irresistible. And entirely infuriating.

He drove.

"Can we listen to music?"

"No."

"Can we stop for road snacks?"

"No."

"Ug. You're so . . . *uuuug.*" Joey slouched in the passenger seat, dirty boot resting against the glove box. She chewed the side of her thumbnail.

With her molars.

Evan glanced over. "You need help with that? I could get you gardening shears."

She removed her thumb from her mouth and glowered at him. Then she contorted herself in the seat, trying to dig her thumb into her shoulder blade.

"You should get that looked at," Evan said. "Too much keyboard time."

"Yeah, well my uncle-dad-boss-person is super demanding so I'm not sure I can get time off for, like, a massage."

"It's okay. Boss-person provides medical."

Her face sagged with an inadvertent pout, and she crossed her arms and slumped down, suddenly looking five years younger.

He wondered how old she'd be when he'd no longer be able to see the kid in her. What would that feel like? It was relentless, time stretching out ahead, full of loss and opportunity. Every step left behind a world of options but set you on new ground. He pictured Mia leaning on her door, letting her body sway with the hinges, one foot raised behind her as if for a cinema kiss. *To be continued.*

The truck wound across the Tejon Pass, a five-mile ascent up the Tehachapi Mountains and across the San Emigdios. Finally they eased down into the vast bowl of the Central Valley. Fresno and Rafael Gomez waited a hundred and fifty miles to the north, but Evan had set a truck-stop meet with Tommy Stojack at the base of the Grapevine. Winter rain had greened the hillside in patches, but browns and yellows predominated, chaparral and weedy grasslands. A scorched rise darkened a hillock to the left where a fire had taken the earth down to the dermis. The air leaking through the vents smelled of diesel and sagebrush.

"How was your date with . . ." Evan couldn't bring himself to say "Bicks" in nonmocking fashion.

"Fun," Joey said. "Till it got annoying."

His heart lifted. "Annoying?"

"Well, he and I are, like, solid, you know? But we went to a club after dinner with some of his girl-*space*-friends and they were so annoying. Like a different species."

"How so?"

"Like the kind of girls who talk in baby voices and ugly cry at Hallmark movies."

"What's a Hallmark movie?"

"Right. I forgot you're frozen in time like Captain America."

"Who's Captain America?"

"You're kidding, right?"

"Right."

"Thank bejesus. So anyway, this one girl named — of course — *Sloane* totally karaoke-filibustered with Diana Ross. And she was 'Ain't No Mountain High Enough'-ing Bicks, all leaning over him, and I was all like, 'I'm *right here,* bitch.' "

Evan tried to shape the words Joey was saying into some sort of meaning that he could comprehend but came up short.

Fortunately, she was on a roll, undeterred by his silence. "So I'm realizing that *Sloane* doesn't *just* want to be Bicks's girl-*space*-friend, so I finally grabbed the mic and had them cue up 'Total Eclipse of the Heart,' and I was like, 'I got this,' but —"

"You didn't get this."

She sighed. "I didn't get this."

"You have many talents," Evan said. "Singing is not one of them."

"In my haste to show up *Sloane,* I might have forgotten that. And she was all like, 'What?' — acting like she didn't know what she was doing, which she *totally* did. And her friends all rallied around her, playing the victim. And then she got all in my face and I told her to back off and she didn't so I moved her away. And I barely even used an elbow lock —"

"You used an *elbow lock* on a girl named Sloane?"

"Not really. More like a gesture. Certainly not enough to 'trigger' her or whatever she said. So then it was the crybully Olympics all over again with rich white-girl snowflakery on full display."

Wind buffeted the truck, the steering wheel insistent against his palms. "So," Evan said. "An eventful night."

"I can only hope that Bicks will find my lack of talent and rough edges charming in a hapless rom-com-heroine kind of way."

"Was that your read on him after?"

She considered. "He seemed simultaneously attracted to and terrified of me."

"That's a good description of how most guys feel around an impressive young woman."

" 'Impressive young woman.' Gawd. You're so geriatric."

But he could read her face, the way her eyes pinched up by the temples — she was taken with the compliment.

They reached the truck stop, and he exited the freeway and drifted to the parking lot. In the middle of a lineup of eighteen-wheelers, a semi-trailer waited with its rear roll-up door hoisted. Tommy Stojack sat in the back with his jungle boots dangling, Camel Wide screwed into his mouth beneath that biker's mustache.

As they coasted up to him, he flicked the butt away and rose creakingly. Aggrieved knees and ankles from too many rough parachute landings, bad hearing from too many demolition charges, a half finger missing on his left hand from some undisclosed mishap — Tommy had made it through his service reduced but undaunted. Evan and Tommy had never shared particulars about their respective pasts, but since their first meeting they'd understood that they were birds of a feather. Tommy provided weapon prototyping, fabrication, proof of concept, and R&D to a number of government-sanctioned spec-ops groups and did the same for Evan despite his highly unsanctioned status.

Before getting out of his truck, Evan leaned into the backseat and grabbed a red medical sharps-waste-disposal container, which gave off a weighty clunk. As he and Joey approached, Tommy stood on the high tailgate, another cigarette already plugged into his face. His bottom lip bulged out with chewing tobacco, and a cup of coffee rested on the metal at his feet; he was never one to skimp on stimulants.

Backlit, Tommy crossed his arms and gazed down at them, his stare lighting on Evan's swollen eye. "You look like a bag of smashed asshole."

At Evan's back Joey giggled.

Evan said, wearily, "Language."

39
HOLD THIS

Tommy hoisted Evan and Joey up into the back of the semi-trailer. Four feet inside, a steel partition rose like a vault door. As with everything else in Tommy's orbit, the trailer was customized.

"You're lucky to catch me on my way to Santa Maria." Tommy winked. "Seeing a man about a horse."

Evan knew the costs of allowing Tommy to get off topic, but Joey, relatively new to him, said, "What's that mean?"

"Got a crusty old designated marksman buddy, been around since Jesus was a corporal." Tommy waved an arm, giving off a waft of tobacco, heavily leaded coffee, and Ivory soap. "Got his early training with MAC/SOG in Vietnam. He engineered the new polymer-cased ammo that DoD is all hot and bothered about and invited me to test-fire it."

Joey's eyes widened with delight. Evan just

shook his head.

"So that's, like, your life?" she said. "You get to just cruise around and test cool new stuff for the government?"

"Hell, D.C. needs all the help they can get," Tommy said. "Half of those oxygen thieves are peacenik bliss-ninnies, and the other half's busy moonlighting as Putin's cockholster."

Evan was going to protest, but he'd run out of energy, and besides, Joey was rapt. Her excited eyes flashed over to him. "This guy's a total upgrade from you, X."

Tommy gave her an approving tap on the shoulder. "Yeah, well, unless you're the lead sled dog, the view never changes."

He shot Evan a smirk, then fussed with a huge ring of keys, found one to his liking, and unlocked the metal door. Before opening it he sucked his Camel Wide down a good half inch, the cherry crackling, then dropped it out onto the pile of butts below the tailgate. "Can't be doing respiratory therapy in the boom room." His grin showed off the gap between his two front teeth. "Step into my office."

The walls inside the trailer were lined with weaponry and ammo crates, plastic explosives and rocket launchers, everything strapped down.

As Tommy closed the door behind them, Joey looked around with wonder. "Is that detasheet? You can't have that much explosive just, like, out on the road."

"Whoa, girlie." Again with that gap-toothed grin, a gleam coming up beneath his watery blue eyes. "Better pack a lunch, I want to keep up with this one, huh, Evan?"

Evan held out the red sharps waste bucket, the used ARES frames rattling inside. "Tommy, we're on a clock. I need you to slag these and get me new —"

But Tommy's attention had fastened onto Joey, his worn-leather face softening. "An old Zen master once told me that high explosives are sorta like relationships. You either get too much too soon or not enough when you really need it. Either way you're screwed — and not how you want to be."

Evan said, "Old Zen masters are into explosives, are they?"

"Hey, you don't gotta wear saffron robes to practice the Lotus Blossom."

"I think that's a Kama Sutra position."

Tommy waved him off. "Same difference."

Joey had moved deeper into the trailer, running her fingers across a wooden box of Chinese antitank blast mines. "How do you get all this?"

Tommy turned his focus to a set of built-in

metal drawers on the starboard side. "I been pressing trigger since Lyndon Johnson was showing off his donkey cock in the Oval —"

"Uh, *gross.*"

"— which means I've earned the trust of a lotta the secret-handshake folks. I got more BATFE permits than I can shake a middle finger at. And the land-mine trade" — Tommy nodded at the Chinese crates — "has been pickin' up lately. U.S. installations have been peppering the surrounding land with those puppies to dissuade curious lefty protestor types." He leaned over with a groan, slid open the bottom drawer, pried a matte black ARES 1911 from a foam bed, and held it out to Evan. "I was up at stupid o'clock, so I only had time to machine you up one. I'll get you more later."

Evan weighed the pistol's heft. Fierce eighteen-lines-per-inch front-frame checkering, specialized Simonich gunner grips, high-ride beavertail grip safety. Designed to Evan's specs, it fit in his palm like an extension of his hand.

"I need new ammo, too," Evan said. "Something soft-armor defeating."

"Soft-armor defeating? You got some serious mugwumps after you, huh? I thought you retired."

"So did we all," Joey said.

"I *am* retired," Evan said.

"Well, as a retirement gift, how 'bout some barrier-blind Black Hills HoneyBadgers." Tommy toed open another drawer and produced several cartons of ammo. "Picked these puppies up at SHOT Show last year. Designed to penetrate intermediate light barriers and not break up. We're talking windshields, doors, Sheetrock, body armor — they fly true straight through to point of aim. A hotter load'll get you through both sides of a IIA vest. But when they hit anything gelatinous?" A whistle escaped that front-tooth gap. "They go hollow-point." He slammed the cartons down into Evan's arms. "You'll be stacking bodies like they're cordwood."

"Appreciate it," Evan said.

"Hey, it's good to have an uncle in the furniture business."

Evan loaded his magazines, slipped them into his cargo pockets, and snugged the ARES into his Kydex holster.

"I want a pistol, too," Joey said. "I prefer a subcompact like a SIG P238, same reliability as a large frame —"

Evan said, "No."

"You never let me do *anything.*"

"You're standing in a semi-trailer filled with enough munitions to take out a Panzer division, and we're riding off next to break into a military installation."

"Right." Joey popped her mouth. "Fair point."

Evan squared to head out. "Tommy, you know anything about Creech North?"

Tommy paused, palm resting on the handle of the vault door, his face suddenly serious. "Where'd you hear about Creech North?"

"Thing I'm looking into."

Tommy's bird-nest eyebrows rose. "You'd best watch your taillights. We're talking Area 6 now."

"Area 6?" Joey said. "That like Area 51 — Nevada and alien remains?"

Tommy nodded somberly. "Best way to cover a conspiracy is with a conspiracy. And 6 has long been a high-security testing site for unmanned aerial vehicles. Deep-black R 'n' D with lots of private-sector overlap. That place doesn't exist."

"That's okay," Evan said. "Neither do I."

"So where *is* Area 6?" Joey asked.

"Remote detachment northeast of the Yucca Flat test site," Tommy said. "Right in that big expanse of bumfuckery between the 93 and the 95. Undeveloped, unincorporated, short private-jet flight to the geekdom of Silicon Valley and all that tech. You playin' around with drones?"

"No," Evan said. "But they've been playing around with me."

"Hold up." Tommy ambled past Evan, flattening him to a rise of crates with Hebrew lettering, and started digging through a trunk in the back. "Hold this." He handed Joey a rocket-propelled grenade, which she admired gingerly. "And this." Now she bobbled a white-phosphorus grenade. "Ah. Here we are."

He walked back to Evan and pinched a thin rubber device no bigger than a money clip to the hem of his shirt. "You're dealing with drones, you need infrared sensor protection."

Joey came over. "No way. Is that a miniaturized coarse head Laser Warning Receiver?"

Tommy's wiry eyebrows rose, his forehead wrinkling. "You ain't the average girl."

"No shit."

He frowned respectfully. "It is. Since pretty much all military targeting systems use a short-wavelength IR laser —"

Joey: "— that are around 1550 nanometers —"

"— this tiny receiver here" — Tommy thumbed up the clipped device to show a pinhead lens — "uses Indium Gallium Arsenide sensors —"

"InGaAs, right!" Joey said.

"— to detect if you've been lit up by a covert illuminator, and then . . ." Tommy squeezed the device between thumb and finger stub, and it gave off a three-note bugle salute.

"Taps?" Evan said. "Really?"

Tommy shrugged. "Hey, they let me customize it. Besides, when it's warning that you've got incoming, you think your ass is gonna get finicky about musical selection?"

"Like you have any taste in tunes anyways, X," Joey said.

They were shoulder to shoulder, staring at him, their heads on parallel derisive tilts. They even blinked in tandem.

"Your sudden rapport is alarming," Evan said.

Together they said, "What do you mean?"

Then they cracked up.

"Hey," Tommy said. "It's just refreshing to be around someone without a room-temp IQ for a change."

Joey said, *"Seriously."*

Evan turned to open the metal door, realized it was locked.

"What'd I tell you?" Tommy said. "Case in point."

He held up a four-and-a-half-finger hand, and Joey high-fived it.

40
PROPER IDENTIFICATION

Evan left the truck a few miles from the California Veterans Reintegration Center at a Zipcar location where Joey had reserved a homely white Nissan Sentra under a fake name. He locked the holstered ARES and his ammunition in the truck vaults in anticipation of high security at the military compound.

Sure enough, as they passed through the exterior parking lot, two layers of chain-link rose into view, thirty-foot barriers encircling the center. Armed military police officers oversaw all points of entry, showing off blue berets and impressive firepower. A soft wind spiraled gusts of dirt up off the ground.

As Evan approached the main guard station, he pulled on a cheap pair of gas-station sunglasses and clicked on the radio, scrolling through until he found an easy-listening station. Air Supply leaked through the crappy speakers. Joey shot him a pained look.

Evan said, "It's hard to find someone who listens to crap like this suspicious."

"Copy that." Joey mussed up her hair, removed her shoes, and propped her bare feet on the dashboard. Cranking her seat back, she popped a piece of gum into her mouth, converting herself into a disaffected teen with alarming authenticity.

Evan coasted into the sally port. The gate rattled shut behind them, trapping them inside. He eyed the half dozen armed air force MPs within view. "You'd better hope they don't ask for ID," he said.

Joey smiled at the approaching MP, talking through her teeth. "I uploaded everything to their preclearance system."

"I'd prefer backup behind that," he said, grinning back. "The Second Commandment: How you do anything is —"

"— how you do everything." Joey rolled her eyes. "Gawd. I can't wait to take over for you so I *never have to hear another Commandment again.*"

The MP knuckle-tapped the window, and Evan rolled it down, smoothing his face into an expression suited to a middle-aged dad from Carlsbad, California.

"Howdy," Evan said. "I'm Harold Blasely,

and this is my daughter, Almudena." He did his best with the accent but out of the corner of his eye he could detect Joey's smirk. "We're here to visit my brother-in-law."

"His name?"

"Rafael Gomez."

The MP exhaled a breath that smelled of sunflower seeds and withdrew into the station, where he stared into a computer monitor, the greenish glow uplighting his features.

After a moment he lumbered back out. "See some ID?"

"Oh, darn it," Evan said, offering Joey a grin rife with disguised told-you-so irritation. "We left our personal stuff back at the hotel. We were told that we'd be okay since we uploaded everything into the preclearance system."

The MP rested a beefy forearm on the roof of the Sentra and leaned down. "It's never a good idea to drive without ID," he said. "In fact, it's illegal."

"You got me there, sir," Evan said. "We woke up so early this morning to catch the flight up that my head isn't screwed on right."

"I can't let you onto the base without confirming proper identification."

"But I was told" — Evan risked another veiled glare at Joey — "that our passports uploaded to the system would be sufficient. Can't you just check us against those?"

"Go back to your hotel. And get your ID."

"Our hotel's all the way in San Jose," Evan said, "where we flew in. And our flight out's this afternoon. If we go back to pick up ID, we won't have time to make it back down."

The MP looked away, swallowed. "Not my problem, sir."

"Such a bummer," Joey said, leaning forward, suddenly speaking with a full-blown Latina accent. "We haven't been able to see Uncle Raffy since Mom's diagnosis. And I made him this."

She twisted around to her overnight bag in the backseat, producing a folded poster board covered with LaserJet-printed color pictures. Evan did a double take at the images of himself and Joey with Rafael and a Hispanic woman Evan figured for Rafael's older sister, Consuelo, Harold's wife. There they were — in a Jacuzzi together, enjoying a meal on a backyard patio, standing on what looked to be a Caribbean beach with various other family members scattered around. The tableaus of Evan and Joey inserted into a regular American family were surreal and seamless, like a vision of some prior life. It took a moment for Evan to register fully that they had been Photoshopped.

Across the bottom glitter-glue lettering read WE MISS YOU, UNCLE RAFFY!

When a sniffle sounded from the passenger seat, Evan and the MP looked over with equal startlement to see Joey's bottom lip wavering, tears spilling from her eyes.

"I promised Mom we'd check on him before her last chemo," she said. "I can at least do that. I know I've sucked as a daughter —"

"We never said that," Evan assured her, warming to the role of Harold Blasley, prospective traveling brush salesman. "Your mother never thought —"

"— but if I could just do this *one thing* for her. And now with the rectal cancer spreading to her lymph nodes . . ." Joey sucked in a wobbly breath and broke down sobbing.

It was so convincing that Evan barely had to act at all to comfort her, patting her knee. The MP looked past him at Joey. "Hey," he said. "Hey."

Joey looked up, eyes brimming.

"I'm sorry about your *mamá*," he said. "Lost mine to breast cancer when I was in high school."

She nodded stoically.

He withdrew a small tablet from a belt holster and scrolled through. Evan watched him pull up their scanned passports. He caught Evan looking and tilted the screen away.

"Pop your trunk."

As Evan obliged, the MP made a circle with his upraised finger, and two more officers came out and searched beneath the car with under-vehicle inspection mirrors.

The MP checked the trunk, slammed it, and came back around. "Magnolia South Residential Building, room fifteen," he said. "Edge of the compound that way. Next time bring ID."

The gate ahead of them rattled open. Evan thanked him and drove through, keeping his gaze ahead. As the guard station receded, he said, "Rectal cancer?"

Joey's tears evanesced, and she smacked the radio to turn it off. "Of course. Who would ever make *that* up?"

He slotted the car into a space outside the residential building. "You."

"And — *wa-la* — look where it got us," she said. "What would you do without me?"

"I would arrange for proper ID instead of badly singing karaoke with Bicks."

He was out of the car before she could retort.

Another MP guarded the entrance to the building, wanding them down even after they'd stepped through a metal detector. They padded their way along a carpeted hall. A few doors opened into spaces with a dorm-room vibe, veterans slouched in beanbags, reading books or playing first-person shooter video games.

The door to Room 15 was closed.

Evan knocked.

A voice issued from within. "Harry! You made it!"

The thump-thump of footsteps, and then the door swung inward to reveal Rafael Gomez. Lean, muscular build, clean-shaven, backward baseball cap. His boyishly handsome face registered them, the smile flattening into shock, and his features contracted.

"So you motherfuckers finally got to me." He showed his palms, backing away. "Go on, then, and kill me quick."

41
A Dark-as-Fuck Rabbit Hole

Evan and Joey stepped inside, Evan pulling the door closed behind them. Rafael backed to the far wall, head lifted with dignity, still glaring.

The small space was neatly kept, photos thumbtacked to the walls in perfect parallel, shirts precision-folded on shelves, stack of *Air Force Times* newspapers on a nightstand, edges aligned. The room's conformity — so opposite the wreckage of Andre's place — felt soothing to Evan, the environment of a like soul.

"We're not the ones who killed Jake Hargreave," Evan said. "We're trying to figure out who did. We need your help."

Rafael held his position flattened to the wall. Then his ramrod posture softened, a breath easing out of him. He sat on the bed, joined his hands between his knees, and lowered his head. His arms started shaking uncontrollably.

Joey said, "You okay?"

Rafael said, "Don't talk."

He sat like that for a time, limbs vibrating, until the tremors receded. He cleared his throat, tugged at his mouth, and finally looked up. "You're not here to kill me?"

Evan said, "No. We want to —"

Rafael held up his hand, a hard stop. "It's not safe. They could be listening." He reached beneath the bed, dug out a soft black pouch the size of a binder, unzipped it, and held it open. "Phones."

Evan and Joey dropped their phones into the flexible metallic fabric of the Faraday bag, and Rafael closed it and tossed it on the bed.

"You have no idea the reach of these people," he said. "What they're capable of."

"Why don't you tell us?" Evan said.

"Who the fuck are you?"

"I promised someone I would look into Jake's death. That's all I can tell you."

"You know they'll kill you."

"I'm willing to take that risk," Evan said. "If it gets me to the people who murdered Jake."

Rafael sat back down on the mattress, yanked off his baseball cap, and worked the brim in his hands. The San Diego Padres emblem, gold against brown, looked worn and faded. "No one listens to me anymore, man. Got me locked up in here. A cot and three squares. Once a week I get a pass, go to the shooting range, get some trigger time just to remember I'm still alive. Then they put the horse back in the stable. These four walls." His shaved scalp was sweating, beads standing out against the taut skin. "They ruined me, man."

Joey said, "How?"

"Hacked my social media, put up fake posts." Rafael raised his stare, a sudden anger edging his words. "Islamophobic shit. Red Pill MGTOW male-power psycho stuff. QAnon. Then a rant on my Facebook page that sounded like some kinda delusional schizophrenic snap. Doesn't take nothing to ruin a guy's reputation. A shitty-ass hacker with twenty minutes on his hands can take a motherfucker down. Think how ready you all are to believe."

"Believe what?" Evan asked.

"That us military guys are fucked up, one Tinder rejection away from losing our shit. Internet's a dark-as-fuck rabbit hole, and they made it look like my stupid ass dove down there. All of a sudden, I'm discharged, diagnosed, all my pay and benefits tied up unless I take accountability for some shit I never said and prove I'm fit to reenter society. They wanted to take me off the board, you copy? Make it so no one would believe anything I have to say." Rafael ran his hand over his head. "It's not like I don't have . . . it's not like I don't get it that my head isn't always right, you know? But I don't deserve this. I *don't* deserve this. No one'll listen, and anytime I talk, I dig a deeper hole, and I have no one to talk to, and they got Jake, man, they got Jake."

He lowered his head, pinched his eyes. His shoulders shook.

Joey started to say something, but Evan cut her off with a look, wanting to give Rafael more space. He'd been locked up inside his own thoughts for months and needed them out.

When Rafael lifted his head again, his eyes were dry. "You know how hard our job is? Flying hunter-killer drones? How fucking *confusing*?"

"Tell us," Evan said.

"You kill so much it gets *monotonous*. Think about that. You're playing a video game that never ends, man. You live at home, sleep in clean sheets. Drive through Starbucks on the way into base. And there they are. Ground control stations lined up like fancy-ass shipping containers. You walk into your GCS and you're not in California no more. You're in Fallujah. You're in Kunar. Or Al-Baghuz Fawqani or Mosul or . . . or fucking Yemen. Cushioned seats, man, A/C, and your latte right there by your mouse pad. And you don't have fear, right? Your own life's not on the line. So you don't get that . . . dunno, that skin in the game, that you might lose an arm or get your guts spilled all over your lap. I mean, some Taliban motherfucker ain't gonna come here and snuff you in the Starbucks drive-through, right? So what are you doing? To you it's target practice, putting warheads on foreheads. But on *their* end? Feels like fucking war."

"Will you tell us about Jake?" Joey asked.

Rafael's head snapped over. "I *am* telling you about Jake."

"Okay," Evan said. "Okay."

"You need to *listen,* a'right?"

"I will," Joey said. "I'm sorry."

Rafael palmed his skull and rubbed some more. "What I'm telling you is, you're in a box halfway around the world for twelve hours, and then your girlfriend's mad you didn't pick up milk on the way home. You understand what I'm telling you?"

"We do," Evan said.

"And who bears that responsibility? Jake Hargreave does. I do. It's all on us. And the fact that it's not . . . dunno, *dangerous* makes it even worse, you understand? Makes it *harder.* Like I said, you don't have fear. You have *dread.* Dread at what you're doing, what it's doing to you. The choices. The *decisions.* You copy?"

The heater clicked on with a low hum, and Rafael's eyes shot over at the noise. A warm, dusty air breathed through the room, thick and claustrophobic. The window fogged from the bottom up, a patchwork of clouds. He licked his lips, settled his tensed shoulders.

"Know my favorite euphemism for this shit? 'Loitering munitions.' 'Cuz that's what we do. We loiter. Days, sometimes. Even weeks. You're not looking into their eyes, but you know them. You're following them. Their habits, chores. See them kiss their wife good-bye. Buy bread at the market." Rafael breathed wetly a few times. "There's a delay after you launch. Most people don't know that." He closed his eyes, held out one arm like an airplane wing. "The UAV yaws from the thrust of the missile, pixelates the screen for a sec. And then it feels like an eternity, hoping no one wanders into the screen. You know, civilians, nonhostiles." He paused. "A kid on a tricycle."

Rafael's shoulders shook some more, but

his eyes stayed dry. It occurred to Evan that whatever meds they had him on interfered with his ability to generate tears. He looked numb and wrecked at the same time.

"Then you have splash, right? Moment of impact. Dust cloud. And when it settles, you can't always tell if you got just the one or two you was aiming at, right? Could be three, could be four. 'Cuz body parts, you copy? A fucking detached torso." A strained sound rose from deep in Rafael's chest, part cry, part gasp. "Little kid's sneaker. Or they're flapping around bleeding out, the heat signature fading and fading till they're the same color as the ground they died on. No one talks about that shit neither. And then you got *more* decisions, you understand? The squirters, too, at the periphery, piss themselves with fear. And maybe you gotta clean *them* up, too. Second missile. Third. Who makes that choice? Who steers those in? We do." He smacked his chest hard with a fist. "*We* do."

He pounded his chest again and again and again and finally stopped, catching his breath. The heater shut off with a dying wheeze. The air felt sharp and arid at the back of Evan's throat.

"And everyone else, they give us *all* the shit. 'Chair Force.' 'Stick Monkeys.' 'The

Chairborne Rangers.' " Rafael gave a dry laugh that lifted the hairs at the back of Evan's neck. "Doesn't feel like combat, but it is. You carry it, carry the same burden. You make the choices, you hear me? We at least bear that. What happens when you don't anymore? What happens then?"

"I'm not sure I understand," Evan said carefully.

"Course you don't," Rafael said. "Course you don't. 'Cuz you're not paying attention. No one's *paying attention.*"

"To what?"

"What'd the Russians just put up at the Abu Dhabi defense exhibition?" Rafael stood, agitated, finger-jabbing at Evan. "A Kalashnikov drone. Size of a coffee table, six pounds of explosives on its back. Mother-fucking Kalashnikov, man. You can't take a piss in the desert without hitting one'a their rifles. And now they want to do that for drones. 'Democratizing smart bombs,' they say. It's their response to our RQ-11 Raven, hand-launched motherfucker the army uses. They answered that shit with an upgrade. Mutually assured ruination. So what's our *answer* to their answer?"

"I don't know," Joey said.

"We go smaller. And *smarter.*" Rafael slung his Padres cap on backward once more. "The third revolution."

"Third revolution?" she said.

Rafael ticked off the points on his fingers. "Gunpowder. Nukes. And now this."

"What's 'this,' Rafael?" Evan asked, careful to keep the impatience from his voice.

"Autonomous weapons." Rafael blinked at them. "Suicide drones that *think for themselves.* Kamikaze UAVs with their own moral code. 'Ethical adaptors,' they call them. Ones and zeros arranged to create a sense of compassion." An ugly laugh like a sneer. "To *robo-think* through using lethal force. To learn from past missions. From mistakes. Like, say, someone logged the wrong guy's SIM card in our database. Sorry, Muhammad Number Twelve. The algorithm'll get that shit right next time. You feel me?"

Joey said, "Jesus."

"Jesus can't help no more. They even got teams of roboticists figuring out how to engineer *guilt.* But — go figure — it's a bitch making robots feel guilty. So now say that some shit goes down wrong, someone bombs a . . . a fucking baby-naming ceremony in Paktia —" Rafael cut off with another series of silent, tearless sobs. "Whose fault is it? Is it Jake's? Is it mine? Nope. 'Cuz we're no longer in the mix.

We've evolved past needing humans to make war, right? So who bears the cost? The weight of it? Does the coder? The pogue who placed the order for the drone? The fucking contractor sales rep?"

"And that's what Jake got onto?" Evan asked.

"They pulled him up to Creech North." Despite the Faraday bags sealing their phones, despite the fact that they were alone, when Rafael said the base name, he still spoke in hushed tones from fear or reverence or both. "They needed pilots for testing. Don't need sensor operators 'cuz that's what the drones do, right? Make us redundant. Hell, man, it's just life-and-death decisions, right? The hell you need me for?"

"What do they look like?" Evan asked, though he already knew. "The drones?"

"Insects. We're talking swarms. One collective brain distributed across a thousand of them. They're securely data-linked. Anything one knows, they *all* know. You got — wha'd they call it? — diffusion of responsibility even for motherfucking microdrones. Take one out, the other ninety-nine finish the job. And the shit these things can do. Coordinate their movements, chose optimal formations, navigate to targets. And we ain't even talked about cluster bombs yet. Shoot a thousand of these fuckers out of an F-16 flare canister, they disperse to dodge radar, head to a congested urban environment, then join up to maximize their payload. Navigate to multiple precision strikes . . . Hell, you could wipe out an entire presidential cabinet at the same time in their beds."

Rafael breathed for a time, and Evan and Joey breathed with him.

"They can do all that shit without a *single human* in the decision loop," he finally said softly. All the anger had drained from his voice. "They just need the start order. 'Circle that black pickup truck.' 'Land on the roof of that hospital.' 'Eliminate these two dudes inside that house.' "

Evan pictured Declan Gentner holding his palm aloft. The spurt of blood from Jake Hargreave's neck.

Evan looked over at Joey. "Kill everyone at the impound lot."

Rafael stared at him, wide-eyed. "That's what they used to get Jake?"

"A KAM," Evan said. "Yeah."

Rafael nodded. "Dragonfly?"

"That's right."

Evan started toward Rafael, who flinched, hands hovering tense above his thighs, ready to lift into a high guard. A reflex of the traumatized. After a moment he relaxed his arms again and looked away, tongue running inside his bottom lip, his eyes averted, embarrassed. Evan nodded reassuringly and moved past him to the fogged-up windowpane.

He drew the letter *M* on the glass, his fingertip cutting through the fog. Then he added wings to the sides. "This logo was stamped on the dragonfly," he said. "Recognize it?"

"Mimeticom." Rafael's nod looked like a twitch. "That's them all right."

Using his sleeve, Evan wiped the logo from the pane. "Who's *them*?"

"The company providing the tech for this shit at Creech North. Serious top-secret, need-to-know shit buried in Area 6." He blinked rapidly four times, his nose scrunching. "It's the Area 6 of Area 6. When Jake was up there, they found out there were glitches in the ethical-adaptor software."

"Glitches," Joey said.

"They programmed five unarmed dragonflies to surveil an office with 'maximum efficiency.' A reality-based tactical scenario. Had a E-1 in there at his desk, you know, playing his role. Just a kid, three steps out of basic. So they set him up in the room and pulled back to the observation bay." A spasm caught Rafael's eye, twitching it once. He wet his lips again, staring off into the middle distance. "When the drill went live, the first drone flew itself through his eye into his brain."

Joey let a breath out through her teeth.

"The other four took perches in the corners of the room," Rafael said. " 'Maximum efficiency.' Easier to provide comprehensive surveillance if no one's moving, right? Problem solved. And hey, no worries. Like I said, the algorithm'll get it right next time."

Evan forced a swallow down his dry throat. "And Jake was going to blow the whistle on this?"

"Man, Jake came back from Creech North *shaken*. Was looking into options within Command, but you think the inspector general's gonna give a shit? They're not inclined to open up the kimono 'bout anything related to the drone program. They discharged him, threatened him legally, all that. Sent a signal loud and clear. You talk, we own your ass and you die in Leavenworth. But Mimeticom's not content to leave it there. They're staring at a five-hundred-million-dollar contract with the DoD, and I'm thinking those motherfuckers weren't willing to risk it on one guy keeping his mouth shut. I'll tell you something that's *not* programmable. Jake Hargreave's soul. You try rendering *that* outta ones and zeros."

Evan felt Rafael's outrage keenly. With the advent of drones, the Orphan Program had been downsized drastically. Why bother with the expense and uncertainty of deploying an expendable living, breathing weapon when you could merely push a button to disintegrate a target in another hemisphere? But Evan's training, like Rafael's, was about more than ease. It was about a willingness to shoulder the human consequences. To use pain and fear and grief and guilt as guardrails. To *feel* that which you were willing to inflict. Or at least risk that you might. And to carry the cost the rest of your waking days.

"What was Jake's plan?" Evan asked.

"He was figuring shit out. Maybe a journalist. Or an ombudsman over at Defense. Thought about protest ads in the *Air Force Times.* Had to talk it through, 'cuz if you don't talk about stuff like this, it eats you from the inside." Rafael raised his arms, a gesture encompassing the base, the four walls of his room, himself.

Evan pictured that plastic parking permit hung over the rearview mirror of Jake's

Bronco, lost among the air fresheners. "He came to see you here," he said.

Rafael gave a nod. "Once. His head wasn't right. Talking 'bout he's gonna break into Creech North and get evidence. No one breaks in there, man. And if they did, they'd never break back out."

Evan thought about that shot-up Bronco. They'd tried to kill Jake on the 110 Freeway. He'd fled his vehicle and returned to the impound lot later to peel the security-hologrammed Creech North parking sticker off his windshield. The sticker now burning a hole through Evan's cargo pocket. Hargreave had been planning to use it to gain access to Creech North again.

"Did he ever mention someone called 'the doctor'?" Evan asked.

Rafael wrinkled his nose, shook his head. "I warned him you can't go up against this kind of power and keep breathing." He hesitated.

Joey sidled a half step closer. "What?"

"Since his visit I feel like I've been *watched*. I don't know how to explain it. Just . . . eyes on me." He scratched at his arm. "But of course who am I gonna tell *that* to?" His posture slumped, and his shoulders rolled forward, defeated. "Looking back, I wish he hadn't told me any of it."

"Do they know that you know anything?" Evan asked.

"Well, them getting my ass landed in here means they wanted to make sure no one would listen to my delusional schizophrenic ass. But Jake didn't let up, and they killed him. So they're moving, cleaning up. Who knows what kinda risk those motherfuckers consider me *now*?"

Evan crossed to the tiny desk, where a pad of paper rested squared to its right side. He jotted down a phone number, handed it to Rafael. "If you need me."

Rafael looked down at the paper: *"1-855-2-NOWHERE."*

"Wait," he said. *"No.* I heard about you. You're really out there? You're really you?"

"Not anymore," Evan said. "Just seeing through this one last thing."

Rafael said, "For Jake?"

The question, obvious as it was, caught Evan off guard. Why *was* he doing this? Since that first phone call from Veronica, he hadn't really stopped to consider.

I heard you help people.

Was that it? Was that why he was here? To do a favor for the woman who hadn't wanted him? Why? To be close to her? There was something more, something in all this he needed to know.

He recalled her words once more: *You barely cried. The doctor thought something was wrong with you. But I knew there wasn't. I could see how sensitive you were, how much you were taking in, that you were overcome by it. And to survive you had to shut off parts of yourself, what you felt, what you reacted to.*

He felt suddenly hyperaware of the bones of his feet and how imperfectly they balanced him. His breath moving through the channel of his throat. His heartbeat up from its resting rate, body temperature also on the rise.

Emotion.

And then it struck him.

Veronica was the only one who'd ever seen him purely, who'd held him in his first vulnerable minutes and looked into the wide-open slate of his face before trauma and loss had been written over it. Before he'd closed up and armored himself, scar tissue growing around a vulnerable core until nothing could pierce it.

He recalled the chill air of the Recoleta Cemetery, Veronica laying her hands on his shoulders, hazel eyes appraising him from beneath the brim of that hat like she was seeing more of him than he knew existed.

His mother's gaze held the totality of him. It was the only place he'd ever seen it reflected. She was the mirror by which he might be able to know himself.

It sounded so pathetic and small, a childish hope as futile as Andre's parental quest. That this final mission, set in motion by his long-lost mother, might prove to be the path to himself.

His *mother.*

He'd used the word now, if only in his mind, the realization sending him further afield.

"X?" Joey said. "You okay?"

Evan came back to the present, mildly surprised to find himself here in Room 15 of the Magnolia South Residential Building. He swayed once more on his feet. Joey's eyebrows were furled; she was watching him with concern. He shook off his thoughts, seated himself in the present.

"I need an address for Mimeticom," he said.

"The lab don't got no address," Rafael said. "But I can steer you to the founder. Brendan Molleken."

"A tech guy," Evan said. "He have a Ph.D.?"

"Handful of them, I'd guess."

Evan's eyes snapped to Joey's as quickly

as hers found his. "The doctor?" she said.

Rafael said, "He lives in Atherton."

Evan firmed his legs, locked in his composure, looked over at Joey.

She shrugged. "I packed for an overnight."

42
THE STRANGER

Declan firmed the camera once more to his face. The zoom lens, a Canon EF 70-200, was a workhorse. Depth control, image stabilization, even a Super Spectra Coating to reduce lens flare. Best of all it was great at distance with its telephoto lens, ideal for wildlife portraiture.

Or spying on a high-security Veterans Reintegration Center from a half mile away. They were in a rented sedan, Queenie behind the wheel. The red Corvette was too conspicuous even for the outer parking lot. She'd gone with a Corolla from Avis, a muted maroon to match today's nail polish.

He adjusted the lens, zeroing in once more on the window of Room 15 of Magnolia South. A smear of transparency cleared the fogged pane where the stranger had mopped off the logo he'd drawn.

A familiar logo.

"You sure?" Queenie asked. She tugged at

her Big Red gum, let it snap back against her front teeth. She smelled of cinnamon and hair spray. You can take the girl out of Philly.

"I'm sure," Declan said.

"Well, I'd say that's a red flag. Should we call the doc?"

Declan lowered the camera, kept his gaze locked on the chain-link fence and the building's back side beyond. "We should."

Two rings to a pickup. That infuriatingly calm voice. "Yes?"

"We're in position to move on the second target," Declan said. "Someone intriguing swam into our net."

"Duran?" Even the doctor couldn't hide his eagerness.

He'd backed off a bit after Declan had texted him pictures of the co-worker's fragmented body. Barely a trace of blood, since most of the damage was skeletal. Declan had posed the man flat on his own carpet next to his La-Z-Boy, a chalk outline gone cubist. The doctor wasn't bloodthirsty, not per se, but he was willing to be in the name of ambition. He had concerns, and they had to be sated.

If Declan and Queenie didn't deliver Duran soon, they would pay a price. Declan clicked the phone to speaker, set it in the cup holder.

"Not Duran," Declan said carefully. "A stranger. Who is familiar with Mimeticom."

"How do you know that?"

"I saw it with my own eyes."

"Who is this stranger?"

"I don't know. Couldn't get a clear view."

"Is he alone?"

"From our vantage he appears to be."

"Did you see his face?"

Declan watched the vehicles exiting the base. A Humvee filled with airmen. Fat guy on a motorcycle. Family in a Suburban. "Not clearly. Watched him through a fogged-up window."

"And your assumption is that he is the one helping Duran?"

"That is indeed my assumption."

Queenie laced her fingers, reversed them, and stretched like a cat, her arms stiff over the steering wheel.

"Well," the doctor said, "it's a good thing I delayed you in getting to the second target. Now we have more data."

"Yes we do," Declan said. "We are so very appreciative of you."

Queenie side-eyed him. *Careful, little brother.*

"Can you follow the stranger?" the doctor asked.

More vehicles flashed through the gate, drifting up the blacktop and past the parking lot. Officer in a spit-shined Lexus. Two dykes in a pickup. A food-services truck driven by a wetback.

"We can't get a surveillance position to identify him when he exits the building, so it's unlikely."

"I'll provide you with more dragonflies. So you're better equipped for your next run-in. And there'd better be a next run-in."

"Understood."

"When are you handling the second target?"

The gate arm lifted once more, letting out an old-school van filled to the brim with kids. Guy and his teenage daughter in a white Sentra. Elderly dude in a boat of a Caddy.

"Tomorrow," Declan said. "First thing."

43
CUDDLE HUDDLE

Joey's online excavations had revealed Dr. Brendan Molleken to be an enigmatic man. Grew up in Akron, Ohio, dueling Ph.D.s from Caltech and a raft of honorary doctorates on top of those. He'd founded and sold a string of artificial-intelligence companies, each for mogul-size hunks of cash. *Wired* magazine had termed him "the reclusive visionary."

Joey had dug up relatively little aside from that. No interviews, no TED Talks, no rousing commencement addresses. As opposed to many of his fellow tech luminaries, Molleken seemed to make a point of remaining low-profile.

Evan and Joey had scouted his three-story Atherton mansion at dusk, taking note of the catering trucks and party planners rolling up to the residence. A Friday-night soiree would provide complications. But also opportunities.

They'd bolted back to the Stanford Park Hotel and made arrangements for Evan's solo return. Another quick online spin had acquainted Evan with what to expect at the event: the founder and venture-capital crowd on full sybaritic display.

He coasted back up the street in an Uber now, the estates looking even more stately at night, uplit and grandiose.

A San Francisco chill had crept down the peninsula, giving him a good excuse to wear gloves. His looked sleek and stylish, fine leather disguising the steel shot stitched into the knuckles for maximum impact in the event the evening got sporty. At Molleken's place the party was already in full swing, luxury cars rotating through the quartz-stone circular driveway. A gaggle of snow machines turned the manicured front garden into a winter wonderland, a red carpet carving through the faux powder, fringed with models dressed as sexy Santa's helpers. A platoon of publicists manning a *Citizen Kane*–worthy banquet table out front checked IDs assiduously.

Evan thanked his driver and got out at the street, passing through the massive wrought-iron front gates unmolested. He'd left his truck a few blocks away, wanting to arrive under other cover. His attire was Bay Area founder-casual, a Giants hat low over his eyes, a pair of well-loved 501s, and a hoodie he'd picked up at the Gap. He'd shoved a thin line of chewing gum beneath his upper lip to thwart any facial-recognition software that might be in play and put in contacts that turned his eyes an arresting blue.

The contact lenses, which Evan had acquired from a connection at a global corporation's augmented-reality lab, served an additional function as a digital camera. The sensors embedded in the flexible electronics could differentiate between conscious and unconscious blinking patterns. Every time he blinked purposefully, a live stream would be fed to Joey's laptop.

When in Silicon Valley, do as the Silicon Valleyites.

The ratio of women to men was extreme, as much as five to one, and there seemed to be a radical aesthetic differential as well. Evan drifted toward the red carpet with a stream of others who'd arrived via ride-hailing services. The portly guy ahead of him threaded through the high-end cars that the valet had left displayed in the driveway, four stunning younger women in a tight orbit around him. A swirl of hair bird's-nested the man's bald crown, which he patted with a handkerchief as he leered at the other women on the check-in line.

"Now, those girls," he announced. "*Those girls* know how to dress up."

His dates tittered vacantly.

A few bouncers were interspersed with the Santa's naughty helpers, who cooed from beneath bright red caps and adjusted their fishnets. A photo area was set up outside, a guy pouring Remy Martin Louis XIII cognac into the mouths of a trio of women on their knees, the tableau strobing at intervals under the mounted flash heads. The yard reeked of weed and expensive perfume, the party spilling out across the driveway. Electronic dance music pulsed from the interior, the bass thrumming deep enough to vibrate the petals of the massive poinsettia displays rimming the porch. A couple was having sex behind a hedge.

Evan shuffled forward toward the check-in table, passing a champagne metallic Maserati Quattroporte, a vintage Aston Martin, a bright orange McLaren 570S Spider.

Two bros in line behind him were arguing. "A Nissan GT-R will eat a Ferrari for breakfast and a Porsche for lunch."

"Yeah," the other said. "But then you have to drive a *Nissan*."

The publicists handed iPads across the desk for guests to sign, their calming mur-

murs reaching Evan across the crowd. "— basic nondisclosure, just initial here —"

"— of course you're on the list and your female friends are welcome, but we're not admitting any male plus-ones who aren't preapproved —"

There were about ten people in front of Evan, but nearly as many publicists at the long table, the line moving quickly.

Someone stumbled past them, dropped a Baggie filled with capsules. A few broke open, puffing white powder out across the toe of Evan's boot, mixing with the fake snow.

"Shit." The guy looked up at Evan, red-eyed, then gathered the intact capsules. "Chief, your foot just did five snorts of Molly. Your shoe's gonna be seriously rolling in a half hour." He cracked up, sagging weakly into his friend, who shouldered his weight and hauled him back inside.

The EDM kicked up another gear, and the guy with the cognac fell over, taking one of the light stands with him.

As everyone turned to the commotion, Evan thumbed up the key to his truck, dug it into the side panel of the McLaren, and scraped a two-foot line through the bright orange paint.

He stepped wide of the line, waving his

hands and shouting over the music. "Hey. *Hey!* You see this shit? That fucking bitch just keyed my car." He pointed toward the side yard, where partiers gathered in clusters beyond the throw of lights, snorting and laughing.

The bouncers stepped forward, on alert.

"That's a fucking McLaren 570s Spider," Evan said, releasing his inner asshole. "You'd better find her. Red sequined dress, big nose, no shoes."

A pair of bouncers headed off, another touching Evan's elbow. "I'm sorry, sir. We'll track her down."

"You'd better." Evan pulled his arm away. "I'll be back inside," he said. "At the bar."

He shouldered through the line and stormed past the publicists. The bouncers on the front porch parted deferentially.

The foyer was packed, champagne flowing, dancers jumping to the music. Evan pushed through into an immense sitting room. People were paired off, making out on couches. Slicing through the bar, he wistfully noted the Stoli Andean Elit on offer. He scanned the room for any sign of Mimeticom's mysterious founder, but Brendan Molleken was nowhere in sight.

Evan headed down one of a half dozen halls. A long line for the bathroom, women rubbing their bare shoulder blades against the wall. A clot of men with honest-to-God pocket protectors blocked the far end, jittering in their Converse sneakers, noses in their phones.

Evan squirmed through the hall, passing a home theater remade as a tiki lounge. One guy sat in a potted plant, licking his Breitling watch.

Someone bumped Evan hard, spilling him into a conversation pit. The cushions caught his fall, plopping him between two women with blown-open pupils and massive press-on eyelashes. They took no note of him whatsoever.

"You're pregnant?" one continued, talking right across Evan's face. "With Sergei's kid?"

"I had a miscarriage," the other woman said. Evan pushed himself up, noting a glint of emotion in her eyes before they went flat again. She wiped a single tear off her cheek. Her face hadn't so much as quivered. She laughed, a drunken bray. "Did you steal my lighter, you bitch?"

"Hey," Evan said, interrupting. "Have you seen Brendan?"

The women turned blank gazes to him. "Who?"

He hauled himself out and into the press

of bodies by the bar. He asked a few people if they'd seen Molleken and got shrugs. A sweaty guy with a hairpiece said, "No. Hell, man. You know Molleken. Guy's a fucking hermit."

An older man wheeled around. "Don't run him down, asshole. You're here, aren't you? Drinking his booze, enjoying his house? Don't take advantage of Brendan's good nature."

Evan left them to their dispute, finding a drunk woman at the fringe leaning over a vase, preparing to vomit. "Do you know where Molleken is?"

She pointed to the ceiling, which Evan took to mean upstairs.

The elevator was off-limits from the look of the no-neck bodyguard blocking it. It took a solid five minutes for Evan to make it through the crowd to the sweeping staircase, and he fought his way up.

The second floor was quiet by comparison, the sounds of sex emanating through a few closed doors. A woman with glossy lipstick looked at Evan from a phone alcove, her mouth parted with pleasure. It took a beat for him to see the man on his knees in the shadows before her, her dress bunched up around her hips, his face buried between her legs. She looked at Evan, panting.

He moved on.

At the end of the thickly carpeted hall, a door, presumably to the master suite, rested ajar. Evan headed to it silently, pressed his glove to the wood panel, and slipped inside.

Dim space, candlelight livening the walls with an aquarium glow. In the center a massive four-poster bed, the canopy drapes pulled wide. On the mattress there were two naked men and five women — no, six. A dozen guests waited half undressed on the dark-upholstered chaise longues rimming the room's periphery like bleachers. The air smelled of sex, but the couples on the bed appeared to be resting for now, flesh sparkly with sweat.

The women were all substantially younger and more attractive than the men. The vibe had all the subtlety of a Playboy Mansion party. Or a cattle auction.

Three of the men at the periphery had naked women sprawled across their laps. They rested highball or martini glasses on the curved flanks before them, conversing as if the women weren't there. A few additional girls, no older than teenagers, huddled together on the adjacent chaise longues, grinning nervously. One had long dark hair in a throwback center part. She wore a red off-the-shoulder blouse and aggressively ripped designer jeans, her hands clasped tightly on her bare knee.

The man closest to Evan had an overdone gym body. He ran a hand up his thick beard, holding forth to his comrades. "— got to know your lines. The baseline runs from the jaw corners around the Adam's apple. Gotta keep that shit clean so you don't have a neck beard, right?"

The others listened intently. One slugged back the rest of his drink. "We hitting the cocktail festival again this July, Rishi?"

The densely bearded guy dismissively waved his martini glass, filled with an iridescent green liquid. "Fuck that. You know New Orleans has the most cases of STDs per capita of any city in the world? That's like putting your dick in a roulette wheel. You know one of the *best* cities? Salt Lake. We're gonna go there and bang Mormon chicks."

Evan watched the women giggle. The teenagers joined in on a delay. Except the one in the red blouse.

An electronic chime sounded, and Rishi pulled out his Google Pixel phone and thumbed at it, his log-thick arm flexing. He groaned. The woman in his lap flicked her head to clear her hair over her shoulder and looked up at him. "What?"

"New bullshit out of Sacramento. Look at this shit, Zack." He showed off the screen to the friend sitting next to him. "Americans love drones. Over *there.* Kill a bunch of mujis, everyone's on board. But God forbid a UAV gives you a speeding ticket *here.* Then it's all moral outrage and restrictions and the fucking Constitution."

Evan stepped forward into the guttering candlelight, drawing their attention.

Rishi looked up at him. "No more dudes in our cuddle huddle, man. We're not turning this shit into a sausage party."

Evan said, "I'm looking for Molleken."

"What the fuck for?"

"That's not your business."

"He's my boss. You'd bet your ass it's my business. Do you know who I am?"

"If you have to tell people you're important," Evan said, "then you're not important."

The girl in the red blouse said, "I heard someone say Brendan's prob'ly upstairs in his office."

"You," Rishi said. "What's your name?"

The girl said, "Cammy."

"I tell you to talk, Cammy?"

She lowered her eyes.

Evan took a step back. Hesitated. Looked at the young woman. "You okay?"

411

Cammy said, "Yup, fine."

Rishi laughed. "Got us a nice guy here, boys. A white knight." He smacked the woman's ass resting in his lap, and she shifted off him. He looked dense, muscle-bound, a gold s-chain nestled in carefully manscaped chest hair. "These girls are founder hounders." He spread a hand, a waiter displaying the dessert tray. "They know what they're looking for."

"Maybe they don't."

"Oh. You're a mind-reader, right? You know what's best for the ladies?" Rishi sucked his front teeth, flicked his head at the door. "Go on back to the kiddie table now."

Evan didn't move.

Rishi tensed, flicking his martini glass at Evan, the green liquid striping his shirt, his chin, his mouth. A few drops landed on his lips, apple liquor overlaying a grape-based vodka, either Chopin or Finlandia.

He didn't want to fight Rishi. But the guy *was* drinking an appletini.

As Evan wiped his face, his OCD ramped up and he breathed steadily to tamp it down. He steadied his gaze at Cammy. "Do you want me to leave?"

Her eyes, heavily made up, darted away. "Yeah. I said I'm fine."

"Cammy," Rishi said. "Come."

She rose and walked over to him.

He reached up and fondled her breast through her top, then grabbed it and pulled her in for a kiss. The whole time he kept his eyes on Evan.

Rishi released her. She was breathing hard and not, it seemed, from pleasure.

"Now kiss Astrid," Rishi commanded.

Reluctantly Cammy leaned down and kissed the woman who'd previously been in his lap. Rishi pushed the backs of their heads together, laughing. Evan imagined Joey, just a few years younger. His hands had tightened, the buckshot rolling across his knuckles.

Cammy straightened up, wiped her mouth, tried on a laugh.

"Run along, now," Rishi said.

Evan looked at Cammy once more.

"I'm okay," she said. "Leave me alone. Just go."

Rishi's sidekick piped up, "You heard her."

Evan left.

Across the floor, up another stairwell. The third-story hall was adorned with display cases showing off a collection of preserved insects pinned to black velvet. Butterflies, beetles, dragonflies.

Evan was so focused on the collection that

413

it took him a moment to notice the two bodyguards at the end of the hall, framing a doorway like pillars, as motionless as the impaled specimens.

"This floor is off-limits," one of them said, his mouth barely moving.

"I'm looking for Brendan Molleken," Evan said.

"What makes you think he's not busy with his guests?"

"If he's up here," Evan said, "I'm guessing he's as bored with the guests as I am."

A flat laugh issued through the doorway behind the bodyguards. "Finally," a voice called out. "Someone interesting enough to talk to. Let him in."

The bodyguards didn't move.

Evan walked between them, entering a vast high-ceilinged study, and came face-to-face with Brendan Molleken.

44
RORSCHACH BLOT

Molleken sat behind an expansive walnut desk, polished sufficiently to reflect his upper body and the panes of the towering window behind him. He wore round spectacles that complemented round, boyish features, a face sufficiently likable to make Evan want to smack it with envy. A rumpled oxford shirt bore his initials over the breast. The lighting was cigar-parlor dim, a few scattered sconces warmed to a dull glow.

Molleken's elbow rested on the desk, one loosely clenched fist held before his face for no apparent reason. His other hand was placed over what looked like a flat, square computer mouse of sorts, a finger lazily tracing patterns on the sensor screen.

Though the desk was spotless, the rest of the study was cluttered with filing boxes, stacks of computational notebooks, robotics parts, and discarded electronics. The walls held diagrams of various insects, their anatomic parts labeled down to the last seta. Various degrees framed in gold hung to the left of the window, which looked out across the parklike grounds of his backyard.

"Sit," Molleken said, and Evan entered and lowered himself into a plush leather armchair facing the desk. Only then did he notice Molleken's unusual eyes, the pupils seemingly forming figure eights.

Polycoria: multiple pupils.

Fitting for an inventor of all-seeing drones.

"You're ordinary-looking," Molleken said with a flatness that made him seem either stoned or on the spectrum.

"That's what I'm told," Evan said.

"Your eyes. That isn't a real color."

"No," Evan said. "I wear contacts."

"I don't know you."

"No."

A feminine voice issued from behind Evan, startling him. "Why don't you ask who he is and what he wants?"

He turned and saw an Asian woman — Korean? — sitting on a worn chesterfield to the hinge side of the door he'd just entered. Her legs tucked beneath her, she flipped disinterestedly through a magazine.

"That's Soo-jin Kim," Molleken said. "She's here to help me interpret social situations."

Soo-jin didn't look up. Her sleek black hair draped past the bend of her elbow. She swept it over a swanlike neck and continued flipping pages.

"Who are you and what do you want?" Molleken asked.

"I'm a tech journalist for *Medium*," Evan said. "My name's Marc Specter."

Joey had ginned up a profile and thwacked it onto the website, putting Evan's image and fake name on the byline of a scattering of existing articles.

Something emerged from the loose curl of Molleken's fist. It crept around his pinkie and then scuttled across his knuckles.

A giant flower beetle.

"And what do you want?" Molleken asked, admiring his pet.

"I'm writing a story on your technology."

The beetle hopped off Molleken's hand onto the desktop. His finger moved pointedly on the sensor pad, and the beetle skittered around the desk, adhering to the very edge. As it passed before Evan, he caught a reflective flash from its thorax, a metallic circle no bigger than a dime.

A remote-controlled insect.

When he looked up, Molleken was watching him. "It's real," he said. "A living machine. You might think of it as a cyborg.

417

I equipped it with a microprocessor and implanted six tiny electrodes."

The beetle reached the corner of the desk, made a cadet-tight pivot, and scampered back toward its master. Molleken's finger lifted from the sensor pad, then tapped it once, the beetle freezing at attention, its antennae bristling.

He pressed his fingertip again to the pad, and the beetle's wings slid out, beat themselves into a blur. Another movement of Molleken's hand and it took off so abruptly Evan had to duck to avoid catching it with his face. It hummed around the room, Evan marveling at it. Over on the regal sofa, Soojin looked unimpressed.

Molleken said, "With tiny jolts of electricity to its brain and wing muscles, I can control —"

He frowned and stared at the pad, making adjustments. The flower beetle sped up, looping around the room, out of control. It buzzed past Evan's ear, zipped past the desk, and struck the window with a thud. It dropped lifelessly from sight, leaving a Rorschach blot of its innards on the pane.

"Oh," Molleken said. "Well. Still working out the kinks. The biological ones aren't very smart either." He knuckled his glasses back up the bridge of his nose. "So," he said, the beetle forgotten. "A story. On my technology."

"The military applications in particular."

In her same casual tone, Soo-jin said, "You want me to get Legal in here?"

"No, no," Molleken said. Back to Evan, that same focused nonfocus, as if those extra pupils were attuning themselves to invisible signals Evan was giving off rather than to Evan himself. "Do you understand what I do, Mr. Specter?"

Evan stared at the splotch on the windowpane above Molleken's head. "You're a software engineer and a founder."

"He's a biomimeticist," Soo-jin called out from the shadows behind Evan. "He takes biological inspiration from nature and incorporates it into technological design."

"Like, say, a dragonfly drone," Evan said.

"Like precisely that." Molleken brightened. "Us humans, we love to revel in our technological superiority. Deep data-mining and artificial intelligence. But nature's been playing this game a lot longer than we have."

"What game is that?"

Design. Molleken smiled, his face lighting with a childlike wonder.

Evan thought about Molleken's defender downstairs in the bar: *Don't take advantage of Brendan's good nature.* There was some-

419

thing immensely appealing about him, an unshielded youthfulness that elicited an almost protective instinct. Wide-eyed, uncensored, pathologically direct.

"Dragonfly wings beat in a basic Lissajous pattern with exceedingly high efficiency. They have separate muscles for their front and back wings. That design element eliminates the need for discrete tilt and attitude controls. They can hover."

"Don't you think you should mingle a bit downstairs?" Soo-jin said. "It is your party."

Molleken waved her off, his eyes never leaving Evan's. "Abalone," he continued. "Their shells are made out of calcium carbonate. Know what else is made of that?"

Behind Evan, Soo-jin flicked another page of her magazine. "Chalk," she said, in a been-there voice.

"But by subtly adjusting proteins, they build it into staggered walls of nanoscale brick to create an armoring harder than Kevlar." Molleken grinned. "A blowfly can make a near-instantaneous right-angle turn in less than fifty milliseconds. A maneuver like that would rip a Stealth fighter to pieces. A gecko can walk straight up a wall. We can model high-tech camera optics off the eyes of praying mantises. When I was figuring out how to efficiently move mari-

420

time drones through water, I looked to eels. Want to know how they swim?"

"I think I get it," Evan said. "You use animal design to build better weapons."

Molleken rubbed his face, exasperated, his eyeglasses bobbing up above his fingertips. "No. That stuff's boring. It's just for funding. That's not where it's at for me."

"No? Where's it at?"

"Imagine a hummingbird drone, nineteen grams, wingspan less than seven inches, highly efficient electronic motor. Now imagine it lives on a single 1.2v Li-Ion coin-cell battery that can keep it airborne forever through regenerative wireless charging. You could direct it through radio telemetry, fly it into the Fukushima reactor to assess the radiological threat level. Hell, it could recharge itself off the radiation in the air." He leaned forward, his eyes shining. "Now imagine we equip it with thermal cameras and FPV capabilities —"

"First-person view," Soo-jin said lazily from the perimeter.

"— and fly it into inaccessible earthquake disaster zones to locate trapped survivors. Or to track endangered wildlife populations. Or to catch poachers in Africa or South Asia. It could read wind patterns inside wildfires, guide water hoses to the source of a conflagration. Imagine crawling a centipede through the wreckage of 9/11 —"

Soo-jin sat forward. "Brendan, perhaps just a quick hi to your other guests —"

"They're here drinking my alcohol, eating my food, making use of my house. That's sufficient social reciprocity to help our people leverage relationships moving forward." Without so much as a change in his cadence, Molleken kept on his previous track with Evan. "— or a solar-powered octocopter that could provide wireless Internet in remote poverty-stricken regions in Haiti or Lesotho. What if a fleet of them delivered food? Vaccinations? Brought blood samples to medical labs to help thwart disease outbreaks? Tested for harmful gases and chemicals in the air? Imagine being liberated from size, from range, from power sources."

"It that achievable?"

Molleken brushed back his lank bangs, which had fallen to touch the top of his eyeglasses. Then he reached in a drawer and pulled out a bigger touch pad.

"Brendan," Soo-jin said. "Don't."

"Why not?"

"Because it's creepy."

"Mr. Specter won't find it creepy," Molleken said. "He's a curious man. Unlike

422

the drunkards downstairs."

He placed four of his fingers on the pad. Evan heard a faint hum from the corner over by Soo-jin. He turned, and she rolled her eyes and pulled her feet up onto the chesterfield. A metal trunk in the shadows juddered slightly, its latch rattling.

Then the lid popped open a sliver. Something seemed to pour out of the interior, but Evan couldn't make out what it was.

It spread across the floor, a wave dispersing into individual drops that scuttled toward him. He felt his stomach turn in revulsion, a precursor to fear. The edge of the flood swept beneath Soo-jin's stockinged feet.

A faint ticking of tiny legs against floorboards, multiplied by a thousand. The surge swept to Evan's chair, enclosing it. He resisted the urge to leap up. He looked down.

Robotic ants.

Thousands of them.

He looked back at Molleken, who was still grinning, his fingers manipulating the pad, spread as if gripping a bowling ball.

Evan's chair shuddered. And then lifted unevenly. His arms flared as he kept his balance.

The army of ants conveyed him in his

chair around the huge desk. He stared at Molleken, who seemed to approach lurchingly. Evan's chair was deposited next to Molleken's. He looked down as the ants peeled themselves off the wooden legs, lowering him to the floor.

That awful skittering noise resumed as the robotic ants retreated back into the shadows. Soo-jin watched him from across the room, the pale skin of her face the only part of her visible in the shadows, her expression unreadable.

Evan heard the latch rattle once more, the lid of the metal trunk click upward. A pouring sound, like ball bearings dumping into a bin. The waterfall sound went on for much longer than seemed plausible. Then the lid clanked down once more and silence reasserted itself in the study.

Evan realized he'd been holding his breath.

He and Molleken sat facing each other, their knees almost touching, not more than a few feet between their faces. Molleken seemed unbothered by the lack of personal space. Those duplicate pupils gazed into Evan, and again Evan had the unsettling feeling that Molleken was seeing more of him than he wanted to reveal. He resisted the urge to adjust the chewing gum beneath his upper lip.

"No wonder the military wants in on this," Evan said. "The applications are spectacular."

"The military is small-minded," Molleken said. "But they do spend an awful lot of money."

"I'd like to make clear," Soo-jin called out, "that this discussion is strictly off the record. Do you understand, Mr. Specter?"

"I understand."

Evan kept his focus on Molleken as Molleken did on him when addressing Soo-jin. She was an external embodiment of her boss's concerns more than an actual person in the room with them. She seemed like a figment of Molleken's imagination. The fact that she was East Asian and submissive, lurking in the shadows, gave Evan the same discomfort he'd felt downstairs at the young women on passive display before the male partygoers.

"The potential is spectacular," Evan said. "But the military applications present some moral challenges."

"Of course they do." Molleken's gaze was steady, penetrating. "But you can't stop progress."

"That's what Oppenheimer thought."

"And he was right."

"A swarm of your microdrones could overwhelm enemy air defenses."

Molleken smiled. Up close his skin looked impossibly smooth, devoid of wrinkles. "They could do more than that. Sensor systems like AWACS, they're oriented toward larger airborne assets. If they were sensitive enough to detect one of my microdrones, they'd also alert at every mosquito or dandelion puffball caught on a breeze. My dragonflies benefit from inherent cloaking by dint of their size. And they have a negligible heat signature, which renders thermal imaging useless. So they are essentially invisible. They are everywhere and nowhere. They are divisible and additive. They are collaborative and think for themselves."

Molleken leaned forward, his nose no more than a few inches from Evan's, seemingly unaware that he was crowding him. "Imagine waging war without home-team casualties," Molleken said. "No more Americans coming back in caskets. And imagine outsourcing the negative emotion associated with killing so our soldiers don't have to feel it."

Evan recalled Rafael rubbing his shaved scalp with agitation. *You make the choices, you hear me? We at least bear that. What happens when you don't anymore? What happens then?*

Evan leaned back, gathered his thoughts. "In the past decade or so, the number of skiers who wear helmets has tripled," he said. "Do you know the effect that's had on the number of head injuries?"

Molleken's features broadened with pleasure, a smile without the smile, this style of banter seemingly to his liking. "I do not."

"They've stayed exactly the same. Do you know why that is?"

"The added protection gives skiers incentive to take more risks."

Again Evan pictured Rafael, trapped inside his own conscience and the four walls of his room. *I'll tell you something that's* not *programmable. Jake Hargreave's soul. You try rendering* that *outta ones and zeros.*

"There's a moral hazard to avoiding cost," Evan said. "Making war less painful for one side makes it a lot easier to sell. Which means we'll see more of it."

"There's no halting progress," Molleken said. "There's no halting this technology. It's being developed around the world. The safest thing we can do is make sure everyone has it."

"Mutually assured destruction."

"How many thermonuclear bombs have

427

been used in war?"

"None," Evan said. "Yet."

Soo-jin's voice floated across to them. "Go to your party, Brendan. Circulate."

"Fuck you, Soo-jin." There it was, a peek at the child-tyrant behind the curtain. Molleken rose abruptly, staring down at Evan. "Enough talk. Want to go play?"

45
THE WAITING DARKNESS

Evan exited the study with Molleken. Soo-jin didn't even look up from her magazine as they passed by. They moved through the bodyguards and headed up a private hall. The electronic dance music rumbled through the bones of the house, vibrating the royal-blue Anatolian silk runner beneath Evan's feet. They reached the elevator and stepped inside. The house was only three stories, but Molleken thumbed a fourth button at the bottom.

The elevator car's mirrored interior threw endless fun-house reflections of Molleken and Evan as they rode down, down, down. When the elevator peeled itself open, they were in an underground garage that smelled of gasoline and cleaning products. A dozen or so cars slumbered beneath covers, enough to require a staff for maintenance. But there was no one here now.

Molleken led the way to a thick steel door,

where he placed his palm on a sensor that hummed, reading his vein patterns. The door clicked open.

Beyond was a passage bored through the earth like a subway tunnel. Evan barely had time to register his surprise before Molleken ushered him across the threshold. A single open-topped shuttle car rested on a monorail. The space was claustrophobic, tight enough that Evan had to stoop to get aboard after Molleken.

Molleken threw the lever, and they whipped off, shot up the horizontal shaft. A few lights flew by overhead at wide intervals, intensifying the coal-mine effect. Evan pressed a palm atop his Giants hat to avoid losing it. He had kept his bearings, noting their northwest heading, which was launching them into a commercial zone of Redwood City. Molleken looked over at Evan, hair riffling, and said, "I traded for one of Elon's tunneling machines."

"What did you give him?"

Molleken smiled and did not answer.

Almost as soon as the ride started, it began to slow, halting at an abbreviated platform facing a similar door. The jaunt had been maybe three-quarters of a mile.

Another palm-reading sensor, and then they entered a pitch-black space.

"Welcome to my battle lab," Molleken said.

He stepped forward, and motion-activated lights clicked on, illuminating the cavernlike space in segments. The lights kept going, the lab stretching out and out as it unfolded into view, an awe-inspiring reveal.

There seemed to be no rear or side walls, just perimeters where the lights ceased illuminating.

Evan followed Molleken through various industrial workbenches, server racks, and enclosed spaces. The cold design and fascinating gear gave it a utilitarian cool-nerd aesthetic; Evan half expected to find a Tesla coil lurking behind a pony wall. The overheads began to shut off in their wake until they were entrapped in a solitary rectangle of light that moved with them, the rest of the battle lab hidden all around.

They moved past a variety of missile prototypes, and then a disassembled Predator drone came into sight. Evan felt a prickle at the back of his neck where the Hellfire missile had scorched his skin.

"Is that a Predator drone?" he asked. "Here in your private lab?"

"I'm engineering a superior carbon-and-quartz-fiber composite for the fuselage," Molleken said. "To reduce vibration and further decrease the sound signature."

"You must have crazy security clearances," Evan ventured.

But Molleken just kept walking, the lights clicking off behind them, shrouding the Predator in darkness.

They arrived at a bowling-alley stretch of polished tile leading to a bizarrely staged tableau: a variety of mannequins posed among furniture as if at a cocktail party. A masculine one in the middle had a bright red target painted on its smooth plastic skull. Molleken halted at the far end of the gallery before a lab bench. Atop the immaculate surface rested a plastic torso and head wearing a skin-tight skull-cap of sorts, the apparatus on display like a wig.

As Molleken peeled it up gingerly, Evan saw that it was studded with electrodes — hundreds of them. Molleken placed it on his head, making several minute adjustments as if smoothing a swim cap into place.

He looked ridiculous, his round face beaming beneath the apparatus. Sliding open a drawer in the bench, he removed a tiny robotic bee and set it down on the lab bench. A shiny little square of a backpack rose from its thorax. Next he took out a laptop and placed it open beside the torso. Code began to scroll across the screen.

Evan blinked pointedly, initiating the live-feed feature of his contact lenses. A graphic appeared, projected by the left contact and visible only to him. It indicated that there was no signal here; the recording would be saved and dispatched once he returned aboveground.

"I started developing neurofeedback to interface with robotic prosthetic limbs," Molleken said. "Turns out we can be trained to vary our neuro-wavelengths and use the brain-control interface to manipulate objects external to us."

He closed his eyes, settled his shoulders, took a breath. The bee hummed to life and rose, flying in circles around his head. Evan focused on the laptop, capturing as much of the code as he could without seeming obvious.

Molleken opened his eyes, his forehead furrowing with focus. The bee buzzed and buzzed overhead. "Would you like to guess the accuracy of bombs during World War II?"

Evan said, "Not good."

"An understatement. They had a fifty-percent chance of landing within two kilometers of the target."

A band of perspiration appeared at Molleken's forehead just below the rim of the cap. The bee zipped off into the darkness behind them, banked, and flew back around toward the posed party scene. It sliced between the peripheral mannequins, cut right, and struck the target painted on the plastic skull with a bang.

A sharp sizzling sound matched by a puff of black powder.

Molleken peeled off the cap and beckoned Evan forward. They reached the target mannequin. It had a quarter-size entry hole directly over the bull's-eye and a cone blown straight through the solid plastic skull.

"My precision munitions are accurate to within two inches," Molleken said. "A tiny bang sufficient to breach the skull and incinerate the contents. Think about the reduction in collateral damage. Life, property, infrastructure."

Evan circled the mannequin, peered back through the exit hole.

Impressive.

The force of the explosion hadn't even been sufficient to knock the mannequin off its feet.

When he came back around, Molleken was holding another robotic bee between his thumb and forefinger. "Now watch this." He aimed it at Evan, compressing its wings once, and it made a click like a camera taking a picture.

He threw the bee into the air, and it took flight, buzzing away.

"I've locked in your facial features as the target," he said. "Now it doesn't need brain waves. It doesn't need a database or an Internet connection. It does the thinking on its own."

A bead of sweat tracked down the back of Evan's neck. He heard the bee in the darkness somewhere, circling.

"Think how tiny it is," Molleken said. "And how helpless you are."

The buzzing changed pitch, Evan doing his best to track the noise in the darkness beyond their throw of light, but the echoes of the vast lab made it impossible.

"Call that thing off." Evan's voice was firm as he'd intended but a bit strangled, too.

"It's too late," Molleken said. "There's nothing we can do now."

A flash of movement to Evan's left. The bee zipping into view.

Evan lunged behind two of the mannequins, the bee whipping past overhead. It circled tightly and headed back. Evan dove and rolled over his shoulder blades, came up in time for the bee to smack him in the forehead and fall harmlessly to the floor.

No explosive charge.

His heart was hammering, his shirt doused in sweat. The metal bee hadn't broken the skin, but his forehead smarted from the impact.

Already Molleken was walking away.

"Hey." Evan hurried to catch up to him. "Hey. *Doctor.*"

Molleken paused. Turned around. "Doctor? *The* Doctor? From what I hear, that's someone whose attention you don't want."

His eyes glittered flatly. He looked unshaken. They could have been talking about the weather.

Evan tasted the bitter residue of adrenaline at the back of his throat. The air felt suddenly humid. He didn't dare push the topic further and make the connection overt. He was too vulnerable here, at Molleken's mercy.

"What the hell was that?" he said. "That stunt with the bee?"

The lights clanked off behind Evan, dousing the posed cocktail party in darkness. Evan spun around, and when he turned back, Molleken was walking away again. Evan pursued him across the battle lab, segments of the space illuminating around them, blackness all around. It felt claustrophobic, a virtual sally port encasing them as they strolled. Molleken ignored him. They both walked swiftly, shy of a jog.

Molleken took a different route back, passing workstations littered with parts and blueprints and hardware. Evan held his stare as long as he could on the passing technology, memorializing as much as he could with his contact lenses.

Molleken sped up until he was a half dozen strides ahead of Evan. He opened up more space yet. It took a moment for Evan to realize that Molleken was trying to leave him behind. He sensed an uptick in his body temperature, felt the heft of the gloves on his hands swinging at his sides. Weighted-knuckle gloves seemed absurdly low-tech for the threats he was facing here.

"Molleken. *Molleken.*"

About ten yards ahead, Molleken halted, his back still turned. "You're not who you say you are."

Evan paused as well. "Why do you say that?" It felt bizarre talking to the back of Molleken's head.

"That clip on your shirt. It's a miniaturized Laser Warning Receiver."

"You recognized it."

"I considered acquiring the company." Still facing away, Molleken reached over, cuffed his sleeve up once, twice. And then the other. "Who are you really?"

"I told you who I am."

Molleken was lit from above, a perfect silhouette, not an inch of him shadowed. A cardboard cutout of a man. Not being able to see his face felt creepy, discomfort crawling up Evan's spine, bringing to mind the legion of tiny footsteps that had presaged the arrival of the robotic ants in the study.

Molleken reached into his pocket and removed what appeared to be transparent gloves. He pulled one on, snapping the cuff. Then the other. A surgeon readying to enter the operating theater. Still he kept his back turned.

He lifted one finger and pressed it to the inside of the opposite forearm, which Evan now saw had a shiny clear patch overlaid onto it. Molleken seemed to scroll along the patch as one would on an iPhone. It took Evan a moment to register what it was.

Tommy had told him about electronic skin under development at Langley. Biocompatible silicone rubber embedded with touch-sensitive sensors.

Molleken tapped the wearable screen on his forearm, and then a recording boomed from hidden speakers: *You see this shit?*

It took Evan a moment to recognize his own voice.

"That fucking bitch just keyed my car."

"So I used a ruse to get in," Evan said. "So what?"

"That's a fucking McLaren 570s Spider."

Molleken's finger swiped to the side, and the recording cut off abruptly. "Pretty impressive ruse," he said. "For a tech journalist. Plus, the *Medium* articles under your name, Archive.org shows different bylines just a few hours before you showed up." He lifted his gloved hands and held them out, a magician laying on a spell. "Someone's been giving me trouble lately," he said. "Working against my interests."

Even from this distance, even from behind, Evan could see him wiggle his fingers.

A noise pitter-pattered in the darkness ahead. Thousands of tiny parts coaxed to life by the movements of Molleken's digits. It sounded like countless insect legs drumming the earth in eager anticipation.

Evan felt a tightness in his chest, a constriction in his throat. This whole time he'd been out of signal range, which meant that none of the images he'd recorded had been sent to Joey yet. No one knew where he was.

He was underground in an unknown location at the mercy of a mad scientist.

"You've seen what a bee can do. . . ." Molleken intensified the movement of his fingers, and all at once Evan heard the terrible humming of a multitude of wings. "But you haven't met my prize pets yet."

Now at last Molleken turned. He clenched his hands into fists, the clear gloves turning his flesh shiny, and a thousand tiny yellow-green lights illuminated in the darkness beyond him. The pinpricks were arranged in tight groupings of two, which — Evan realized with an irrational spike of fear — mimicked the compound eyes of an actual dragonfly. And they rose in neat rows from floor to ceiling, a wall of unseen micro-drones.

The tiny eyes rose and fell a few centimeters, mirroring the undulation of Molleken's fingers. The humming waxed and waned with their movement, the unseen metallic legs scratching horribly each time they found their perch.

A noise broke above the thrum of white noise — a bugle giving a three-note salute. It sounded once more, and Evan noticed the vibration of the Laser Warning Receiver on his shirt. The sound was coming from him.

He was lit up.

Molleken said, "Should we try this again?"

Evan stared at the robotic eyes staring back at him from the darkness, ready to launch. All those laser target designators locked on him. He wouldn't get two steps before they'd fill the air around him. For now they stayed in place, hovering in the darkness.

He held up his hands. "Okay," he said. "Okay."

Molleken lowered his hands. *Taps* stopped emanating from Evan's clip. The dragonflies settled back down. An instant later the lights of their eyes clicked off, and now it was just Evan and Molleken staring at each other in a cube of light.

"I'm an airman." Evan tried to exhale some of the tension that had knotted his shoulders into rock. "A friend of Jake Hargreave's."

"Who's Jake Hargreave?" Molleken asked.

Evan stared into his four pupils. No tell. "A drone pilot who was killed a few weeks ago."

"And he is relevant to me how?"

"He tested some of your technology. At Creech North. And then was killed."

Molleken mused on this for a moment. "I recall something about this. Unspecified training accident in Area 6. That's what I was told. I know nothing more about this Hargreaves incident —"

"Hargreave."

"— though I was informed that people die in training all the time."

"Not like this."

"Maybe not. But that's the official record. What are you going to do?" Molleken's lips twitched with amusement. "Take down the military-industrial complex?"

"I'd be happy just taking down the people who killed Hargreave."

Molleken stared at him for a long time, his face devoid of human emotion.

"Okay." He peeled off his gloves, stuffed them into his pockets. "Good luck." He started off at a different trajectory, piercing the waiting darkness to their side. "I have a party to get back to."

46

AND THEY LAUGHED

The elevator rose to the ground floor and opened. Molleken pressed his hand to the bumper. "You get out here."

Evan stepped out.

He turned around, but the doors were already closing, wiping Molleken from view.

Behind him he could hear the party in full swing, awed voices at the periphery.

"Was that him in the elevator?"

"I just saw him. Dude, that was *him.*"

A blinking green light in Evan's visual field indicated that the video he'd recorded in the battle lab had been sent to Joey. He exhaled. Time to split.

As he cut through the crowd, various gazes adhered to him: the man who had ridden a private elevator with Molleken. Beneath the hoodie his shirt constricted his ribs, stuck to him with dried sweat. He was eager to get outside into the fresh air, to get back to Joey at the hotel and see if she could make any sense from the live stream he'd initiated in the battle lab.

He shoved into the foyer, the scent of poinsettias riding the thin breeze from the porch, and then he spotted her.

Cammy, the girl in the ripped jeans.

Standing alone on the second-to-lowest step of the stairs, gripping an elbow with her opposite hand, a dazed look in her eyes. One cheek splotched red, maybe from being slapped. Her blouse ripped at the side seam, showing a bulge of tanned flesh. She was chewing her lip, looking at nothing.

After losing at hide-and-seek with a robotic bee, confronting a swarm of glowing eyes in the darkness, and standing down a genius who'd batted him through a subterranean lab like a cat toying with a mouse, this was not a complication Evan welcomed right now. The Seventh Commandment: *One mission at a time.*

He turned his back to the girl and started out. He neared the threshold, the December air cool and welcoming across his face, freedom just a few steps away.

Then he paused.

He thought about the bearded man — Rishi — tugging Cammy's breast. Ordering her to kiss the other girl. *They know what they're looking for.*

He gritted his teeth.

This wasn't really another mission.

More like a sub-mission.

He turned back around. A pair of drunken revelers stumbled down the stairs, knocking Cammy in the shoulder, shuddering her frame. She barely seemed to register them.

Evan walked back to her. She clung to the newel post. Her blouse hung low in the front as if it had been yanked and stretched out, her ribs visible above her breasts. She shifted, and the neckline tugged over, exposing a nipple.

Evan paused five feet from her, a safe distance back. "Excuse me?"

It took a moment for her eyes to settle on him.

"May I walk closer to you?"

Her hands gripped the newel post, thin arms trembling. She jerked her head up, down.

He walked near her. "Your shirt is out of place."

She looked down. She moved to reach for her collar but seemed to collapse forward; she needed the post to hold herself upright.

Evan said, "May I adjust your shirt back into place?"

She nodded.

He reached out slowly and tugged the

445

fabric up to cover her. He pulled his hoodie off and held it out. She nodded.

He drew it across her shoulders. She smelled clean and sweet, deodorant and perfume. He imagined her getting ready earlier — preparing for a fun night ahead, checking her lipstick in the mirror, maybe a bit of music on — and had to tamp down the simmering in his chest.

She said, "Will you get me out of here?"

Evan shouldered her weight and helped her off the stairs. He pushed through the people in the foyer with purpose, and they seemed to sense his mood and move aside.

On the porch one of the bouncers said, "Hope you had a good evening."

Evan caught his eye. "I have a feeling," he said, "that I'll be coming back."

As Evan moved Cammy toward the gates, someone crooned after them from the photo area. "Yeaaah, boy. Go get some!"

They walked in silence, Evan bearing her weight. Cammy kept her eyes down to check her footing and make sure she didn't stumble on her wedge heels. The air smelled of eucalyptus, the sidewalks littered with shed peels of bark. Slowly the noise of the party faded behind them, and then it was just the sound of her shoes ticktocking the concrete and her hoarse breathing.

They reached Evan's truck. He paused by the passenger door. "Are you comfortable getting in?"

She nodded.

He unlocked the door and helped her up and then circled around. As he pulled himself into the driver's seat, he noticed she was sobbing. Face tilted into her hands, shoulders trembling, deep, wrenching sobs. He let her cry.

Five minutes passed and then another five. He wondered if she wanted some physical reassurance, a rub of her back, but wasn't sure if that would be invasive. He wondered if men raised with mothers actually knew better what to do in circumstances like this. Veronica came into his mind, her cool, mysterious demeanor holding no answers.

At last Cammy lifted her head. "How do I stop crying?"

"You don't," Evan said. "You don't right now."

"What do I do?"

"How old are you?"

"I turned eighteen on Tuesday. They checked my ID before they let me on the list. Took a picture, even. For, like, evidence." A smile found her face, though it held no happiness. A resting grin, the kind that young women wore to cover whatever darkness was moving beneath the surface.

"Are you in school?"

"I'm a freshman. At Foothill."

A first-year at community college. Evan gripped the steering wheel, the steel shot rolling in the leather pouches at his knuckles. "Can you talk to your parents?"

She gave an ugly laugh. It hung there, an echo imprint on the air.

"I went to a biker bar in Los Gatos with some friends last week." She shoved fists across her red cheeks. "All these fat, bearded rednecks, and we were treated with respect, but these MIT assholes . . ." Her voice trailed off.

"I can take you to the ER," he said. "File a rape kit."

"No." She shook her head roughly, like a little girl. "No. They used condoms. Rishi threw them at his friends. Said, 'We don't wanna get cock rot.' And they laughed."

She hoisted the hood over her head and withdrew her hands into the sleeves, bunched the fabric to close it off, a sea anemone retreating into itself. Evan thought about all the creatures Molleken studied but how he only appropriated their strengths instead of learning from their vulnerabilities.

He pictured Joey's date offering her that vape pen on the patio and suddenly felt tired. How much courage it took to care for someone. He thought of Mia figuring it out alone. What had she said? *I'll let you in on a secret.* No one*'s enough as a parent.* And yet she was doing everything for Peter that she could — the way Cammy's parents likely had for her. Evan's training had taught him to cover every operational contingency, but the feat of laying bare one's heart seemed rife with greater dangers yet. There was nothing more wild and unpredictable than a human being.

"I knew what I was doing," Cammy said. "I did. At the front part at least." She sipped in a few breaths. "They slapped me. Rishi grabbed my mouth hard from behind, cut up the insides of my cheeks. These guys watch so much porn they think they know what turns girls on. Or maybe they don't care." She looked over at him, her eyes huge and unguarded. Her voice little more than a whisper: "I never said no."

"The crying should have been enough."

"Yeah," she said. "But it wasn't."

There wasn't anything to say to that.

"There's nothing to do," she said, her words hushed and cracked.

"Well," Evan said. "Maybe not nothing."

She looked at him.

"Are you okay to wait here a few min-

449

utes?" he asked.

"What if they come after me? Smash a window?"

"You'll be safe here. No one will get into this truck."

She hesitated. Gave a quick, nervous nod.

He handed her the key. "Don't drive off." No smile.

He climbed out and started back for the party.

47
WHITE KNIGHT

Cutting through the crowded foyer, Evan brushed against a partygoer and lifted a stainless-steel ballpoint pen from the guy's shirt pocket. It slid free of the pocket protector smoothly. Climbing the stairs, he thumbed the tip off and dropped the spring and the ink refill from the barrel so all that remained was a smooth metal tube.

As he headed up the second-floor hallway, he heard Rishi's voice carrying through the partially open door. "— and when you're on the prowl, pay attention to their eyes, Scotty. Women on the pill blink an average of nineteen times more a minute than women who aren't. That's how you know they're active, right?"

He stepped inside the room. The orgy bed was now empty, but Rishi and his compatriots — Zack and Scotty — remained in their chaise longues, half disrobed. To the side a trio of women were pulling on their clothes.

Evan said to them, "You might want to leave."

The women took one look at his expression and scurried away, clutching high heels and shirts to their chests.

Evan looked at Rishi and his two friends. "You hurt the young woman."

Rishi glanced over at him, stroking his beard, his biceps rippling. "Who are you talking about? The one with the ripped jeans?"

He didn't bother according her a name.

Evan felt his jaws tighten, an ache in the bone. "And the ripped shirt," he said.

"I think you're gonna want to move along before you get *yourself* hurt."

Rishi's two sidekicks looked more tentative, but they covered with lupine grins.

"Look, White Knight," Rishi said, "we don't procure the product."

"You mean the girls?"

"Women," Rishi said. "Don't be disrespectful." He leaned back, spreading his beefy arms along the top of the couch. "This Valley is about one thing. Resources. The right VC. The right engineers. You know the most valuable resource? Time. But young women who are DTF? They're inexhaustible resources. They're the one reward we get. So we outsource the selection process. That girl

— Cammy? — she gave her ID to the bouncers *yesterday,* man. She knew why she was here. You don't agree to come to a party like this looking like that and think it's for your personality."

"That's true," Evan said.

"I did nothing illegal."

Evan said, "No."

"She had a choice."

"Yes."

"She could have left at any time."

"Maybe."

"She's legal."

"By seventy-two hours."

"Hey, man." Rishi gave a big shrug. "If you're a hammer, everything looks like a nail."

Zack and Scotty laughed.

"No," Evan said.

"How would you know?" Rishi said.

"Because," Evan said, "I'm a hammer."

Rishi stared at him. Then he stood up, his shirt unbuttoned down the front. He was a thick guy, all muscle and bloat. His friends stood up, too.

"Okay," Rishi said. "So we're gonna do this?"

Evan's gaze stayed level. "Do you know what a tension pneumothorax is?"

Rishi rocked back on his heels. "A what?"

"A torn lung leaks air inside your chest cavity, increasing pressure. That prevents the lungs from filling. Then it prevents blood from getting to the heart."

Rishi looked at his friends. Back at Evan. Laughed. "You're a weird fucking dude. But that's okay. I like weird dudes."

He stepped forward and swung at Evan's head. Evan ducked and sidestepped.

Rishi regained his balance, turned, and tried another cross. Evan leaned back, the wind from the punch fanning his face.

Flustered, Rishi threw a haymaker. Evan weaved right and crouched, tightening his hand, the weighted knuckles of the glove stretched tight across his flesh.

He drove a compact punch into Rishi's right side just beneath the armpit.

There was a pleasing pop, and then Rishi drew in a screeching breath.

Evan pulled himself upright and looked at Rishi.

For a moment they were eye to eye.

And then Rishi toppled to a knee. He clutched his ribs, his mouth guppying.

"Your lung is collapsing right now," Evan told him. "I punctured it with your sixth rib. That drowning sensation? It's from negative pressure building in your chest cavity. It'll get worse."

Rishi fell back onto his rear end, his legs squirming on the carpet. His friends looked on in horror.

"You will suffocate from this," Evan said. "Unless."

He fished the stainless-steel pen tube from his pocket and held it up. Zack and Scotty watched him, their pale faces bathed in sweat. Evan flipped the tube at them. Zack bobbled it but managed to hang on.

"An emergency chest decompression." Evan stepped forward. "Excuse me."

Zack and Scotty parted, and Evan knelt over Rishi, whose mouth was stretched in an oval, his face purpling. Evan peeled Rishi's shirt aside and used his thumb to find the second rib space in the midclavicular line. He looked up.

"Come here."

Scotty fell to his knees.

"Put your finger right here. No. Here."

Scotty complied, his hand trembling.

"You need to punch the tube through into the chest cavity to relieve pressure," Evan said.

Tears dotted Rishi's cheeks. He waved his head back and forth, clawing the carpet, his lips struggling for words. He mouthed, *Do it. Do it.*

"One of you probably should," Evan said.

455

"Decide among yourselves. Because I'm not going to."

As Rishi thrashed from side to side, Zack and Scotty started shouting at each other, fumbling the pen tube between them. Rishi's Pixel phone had dribbled out of his pocket. Evan scooped it up and pressed Rishi's thumb to the screen to open it.

No one seemed to notice.

Evan stood up. Looked down at Rishi. His eyes bulged, the sclera pronounced.

"You could have left at any time," Evan said. "You had a choice. Until you didn't."

He walked out, Zack and Scotty still locked in a panicked argument behind him. He'd just reached the stairs when a bellow of pain rolled up the hall, Rishi's breath coming back online. Moving down the stairs, Evan entered the security setting of Rishi's phone and updated the thumbprint setting to match his own.

Crossing the front yard, he fished the gum out from beneath his upper lip with his tongue and blew a bubble.

Evan drove Cammy back to an apartment building worn down by too many generations of tenants with no stake in ownership. Stucco with missing chunks, weedy front lawn littered with cigarette butts and dog droppings, a bicycle wheel locked to a parking meter, the frame long liberated.

She hesitated in the driver's seat. "Can you walk me in?"

He climbed out and followed her up a set of splintering stairs to her apartment. She clicked on the lights, peering into the dark bedroom nervously.

Evan said, "Want me to check the space for you?"

"Yes, please. I'm gonna go change."

She cast off his hoodie and disappeared into the bathroom. The blinds were drawn, the sheets mussed, plastic water bottles collecting on the nightstand — the environment of someone who slept a lot. He searched the closet and looked beneath the bed to set her mind at ease. The place called to mind Andre's sad little room above the Chinese restaurant.

A thin stack of bills and work scholarship time sheets rested on an IKEA desk in the corner, laying out Cammy's hours and telling a familiar story of mounting student debt. A grade-school class picture of herself was tucked into the frame of a mirror above the bureau, a reminder of who she used to be.

One thing he'd learned time and again was that you never could tell what kind of

457

private hell people were fighting through.

He heard the hinges squeak behind him and turned around.

Cammy was standing in the bathroom doorway wearing only a bra and panties. She had a bruise on her lily-white skin across the strokes of her ribs.

He lowered his gaze.

Her toenails, painted baby-girl pink, were chipped. He thought about her paying for the pedicure out of the hours she spent working the front desk at the Foothill College Fitness Center. That school picture — third grade, maybe fourth.

So much humanity reduced to flesh and function.

"Do I owe you anything?" The question was strained; she'd had to force it out.

He felt the words like arrows to his sternum. He kept his eyes lowered. "What if everything you thought about yourself was wrong?"

"God, am I that fucked up?"

He crouched, picked up his hoodie where she'd sloughed it onto the floor, and offered it to her. She took it, her head drawn back. Then pulled it on, zipped it up. The waistband touched the tops of her knees.

"You were cursed with being pretty, which means the world told you what you were supposed to be before you could figure it out for yourself," he said. "But what if who you could be is something vastly more important and powerful? Some men are afraid of that. Especially in an attractive young woman. Do you want to let them write your story?"

"Important." Her nostrils flared. "Powerful."

"Sure." He held her gaze. "What if?"

Tears ran down her cheeks though she made no sound.

He crossed to the cheap desk, picked up the phone, and called the operator. He asked to be put through to a rape-crisis hotline.

After a few rings, an older woman's voice answered. "Counseling."

Evan said, "A young woman here has been through a traumatic experience."

The woman said, "Who's this?"

Evan turned and held out the phone to Cammy. She stood staring at him, her arms folded, tears still running silently down her face.

She uncrossed her arms.

She took the phone.

He walked past her to the door. As he shut it behind him, he heard her say tentatively, "Hello?"

A pause. He eased the door shut. Her voice carried faintly through the panels.

"My name is Cameron," she said. "Someone hurt me."

48
BETTER THAN REAL LIFE

Evan called Joey on his drive back to the Stanford Park Hotel.

She picked up with a full mouth and made some sort of vowel sound in greeting.

"What are you eating?"

"Room service," Joey said, "might be my favorite thing in the world."

"You got the footage from my contact lenses?"

"The good doctor's supervillain lair. Uh, yeah. His tech is *lit.*"

The streetlights of Palo Alto rolled by overhead, an upside-down river of LED blue. "It's less lit when it might be trying to kill you."

"You're such a drama queen," she said.

He felt a faint throb on his forehead where the defused robotic bee had struck him. After the evening he'd had, he could muster no retort.

Fortunately, Joey was not one to let a

silence linger. "I read some of the code off that laptop on his lab bench. A lot to dig through. I'll need a day or two and a Costco pallet of Red Bull."

"I have a Pixel phone for you, too," Evan said. "One of Molleken's guys. He looks to be logged in to a couple databases so you can poke around behind the firewall. I changed the security thumbprint to match mine so you can get in."

She snorted. "I can get in without that. Those things only record partials. I have a digital master fingerprint I built using the most common whorls, loops, and arches." She took another bite of something and mashed it around in her mouth. "Works seventy-two percent of the time."

"How come every time I talk to you, I feel less intelligent?"

"I just hold up a mirror, X."

"When he snapped my photo with the robotic bee, did my facial features go into the system?"

"No," she said. "That's the whole point. That shit is between you and the micro-drone. It doesn't need anything else. No records in the system, no accountability. And thank God. Your Scooby-Doo disguise — bubble gum in the lips and a hat — would've only gotten you so far."

"Molleken seems to have top-secret security clearances. Looks like he's even cleared to access sensitive compartment information."

"Judging from the Predator drone parts littering his lab, I'd say, 'Duh.' He should be the poster boy for the military-technological complex, but there's virtually no mention of his overlap anywhere. That Area 6 shit makes you fall off the map fast."

"Next stop is Creech North. I need your help prepping."

" 'Kay. I need to get home anyway. My neighbor's watching Dog. She's this lonely divorced Realtor with the worst ombre hair-dye job ever who, like, binges on home-improvement shows and subsists entirely on Truffle Kerfuffle —"

"Truffle . . . ?"

"It's an ice cream — hel*lo*? — and I told her I'd be back tomorrow for Dog."

"Look at you, all grown up."

"I'm sayin'. Adulting's hard business, X. But I gotta learn for when —"

"I know, I know. For when you take over for me."

"Glad you're finally on board with the plan."

"I'm not —"

"Hey, where'd you go after you left the

battle lab? You shut off the feed, like, an *hour* ago."

He thought of Cammy leaning on the newel post to hold herself up. *I never said no.* Standing in the doorway of her bathroom wearing nothing but a bra and panties, diminished and scared.

"Just had to handle something real quick."

" 'Kay. See ya here."

She clicked off.

When Evan entered his hotel suite, the connecting door to Joey's room was open, the TV blaring. He walked through to find her indelicately passed out, sprawled on the mattress, one arm flung over her head into the pillows, mouth ajar, drooling. Her laptop, the remote, and various plates littered the bedspread around her, the wreckage of a Caesar salad and a cheeseburger. A sole stubby french-fry survivor rested aslant on the plate next to a well-plowed mound of ketchup.

She often started when woken up, a panic reaction from her childhood, so he crossed the room as quietly as he could manage. He thumbed down the TV volume a few notches and then pulled a throw blanket gently over her.

One eye was crusted with sleep, and her

whistling exhalations carried the scent of onions, but he felt no ping of his OCD initiating disgust or aversion. There was no part of her that he didn't find endearing.

He wondered what that meant.

The realization cut him at the knees, and he lowered himself to sit on the bed to her side. He thought about Veronica looking at him, that flare of pride before she'd found out who he really was: *He told me that you were chosen out of the boys' home. To do good.* He thought about that sketch Andre kept thumbtacked to his wall, his daughter lovingly rendered, each line of her face resurrected from memory. He thought about Cammy's parents and everything they might have wished for. And then her on the stairs, blouse ripped, breast exposed.

"Damn it," he said softly.

Joey shifted, for once waking calmly. She stretched, wiped her mouth. "Language."

"Sorry."

She rolled over onto her side, yawned inelegantly.

His thoughts pulled to Andre. At one time he'd had something so precious. In Sofia, a daughter with life in her eyes. Evan pictured her in the laundry room of her building, wearing her mom's bra on her head and mugging for the other ladies. And Brianna, tough and smart enough to raise an eleven-year-old girl on her own. A kitchen table to share meals at and someone to tuck in at night.

Resentment stirred in him — no, something deeper. Envy? That Andre had all this and had thrown it away. And yet Evan was stuck with him. If he turned his back on Andre, he'd be turning his back on Veronica, and then he'd never find whatever he was looking for.

And yet he had something far more valuable right here in front of him. He watched Joey's back rise and fall with her breaths. Crumbs on her pillowcase.

"Can I . . . ?" Evan hesitated.

She said, "What?"

"Can I pet your hair?"

She looked up at him. "Uh, sure?"

He did.

She closed her eyes. Then opened them. "This is weird, isn't it?"

"Kind of," Evan said. "Should I stop?"

"No." She snuggled down into a pillow. "I might like it."

Her head was warm, her locks glossy and smooth. Her skull felt fragile and soft.

She kept her eyes closed. "We never . . . I don't know, just like get lunch. Go to a movie."

"You want to go to a movie?"

"That's not the point," she said. "The point is, what are we? You're not my dad. You're not my uncle. You're not my big brother." She opened her eyes, and as always he was taken by the depth of their green. "So, like, who are we? What are we good for?"

He kept stroking her hair. He knew what he was good for. He just wanted to be good for something else.

She arched her spine, lazed back into a fetal curl. "This isn't real life."

Evan pictured Cammy's dark room, the bills piling up, her chipped pink nails, the way she'd looked at him from the threshold of the bathroom.

He said, "Maybe this is better than real life."

But Joey was already asleep.

49
A NOBODY

The Fresno Valley Shooting Society was sunk in a vale between two desiccated hillsides in Visalia, far enough from society and Route 216 that no one could be bothered by the snap, crackle, and pop of gunfire from the outdoor ranges. Queenie parked the Avis Corolla at the edge of the parking lot, pointing downhill.

The location was remote and discreet, features becoming to a firing range.

For once Declan was dressed down, a pair of Ralph Lauren jeans and an untucked navy-blue T-shirt, the better to fit in.

They'd parked here a few minutes after sunrise, staking out the best surveillance position. Sure enough, their target had strolled in at 8:00 A.M. sharp, military punctual for his weekly outing.

They'd watched him disappear into the pro shop to check in and were waiting for him to emerge.

"The doctor's pretty unhinged," Queenie said. "I guess someone showed up yesterday asking questions about Hargreave."

"You know the doctor," Declan said. "He prefers playing offense to defense."

Queenie laughed a throaty, womanly laugh. "Don't we all."

"We have to figure out who the hell is helping Duran."

"Duran." Queenie shook her head. "It is weird that guy could get any kind of backup. I mean who the hell *is* he anyway?"

Declan shrugged. "He's a nobody."

"A nobody with a zero in his bank account and a job at an impound lot." Her sigh smelled of Big Red chewing gum, cinnamon and sugar. "God, what a life most people have."

Up ahead their target emerged from the pro shop, clutching his gun case and a few fresh boxes of ammo. Nodding at the range master, he headed up the walkway toward the open-air ranges, the Padres symbol showing on his backward baseball cap.

Queenie reached across and adjusted Declan's hair, smoothing a wayward lock down around his ear. *Time to go now, little brother.*

Declan got out, the firecracker fury of gunfire suddenly louder. A revolver *pop-pop-*

popped and then was drowned out by someone unloading a semiauto. He strolled toward the shower of noise.

Rather than head for the main walkway, he cut behind the toilet shack. The men's-room door was open, a waft from inside carrying a swirl of black flies and the fish-and-iodine stink of well-used urinal cakes. A sign warning of lead poisoning hung crookedly from the warped planks.

Declan emerged past a kink in the walkway, out of view of the range master, who he could hear giving instructions, his voice raised to be heard through ear protection.

All the shooters stood parallel on the firing line, sealed off on either side by sound-absorbing transmission barriers that blocked their view of one another. Declan drifted behind them, unseen and unheard. Each of them faced away, focused on the plastic Corflute targets affixed to bales of hay. A sloped sandbag backstop rimmed the retaining wall. The pistol ranges here were shorter, targets positioned from ten to twenty-five meters. Oblivious to Declan's movement behind them, the shooters fired away, cases spinning to the dirt below.

Simple tepees of shingles roofed the firing points, providing shelter from the San Joaquin Valley heat. Gunfire thundered all

470

around, punctuated with the flat thwack of rounds punching plastic and hay. Bright orange wind flags flopped lazily from thin flexible poles. The air smelled of gun oil and burning nitrocellulose. Declan turned his face to the sun. It was a beautiful day.

He found the target in the seventh firing lane, his back to the walkway.

Rafael Gomez stood in a modified Isosceles Stance, torso square to the range, knees slightly flexed to absorb recoil. Declan watched him shoot, watched the recoil shudder his shoulder blades and blur the Padres logo on the turned-around cap. He couldn't get a clear look at the pistol, but it sounded like a .22.

A gun case lay open on the bench behind him, the ammo dumped into a gray rubber tray. A few other handguns rested on the convoluted foam inside the case, including a SIG Sauer nine-mil, the air force service weapon of choice.

No more than five feet away, Rafael switched out his magazine and kept on firing. He'd chosen old-school Birchwood Casey targets and was dumping round after round through the nine ring, a few edging the red.

The shooters on either side thundered away, the percussion and echoes deafening even over the sound-absorbing transmission. Unlike Rafael's firing cadence, theirs were sporadic and uneven, recreational sportsmen doing their Saturday best.

Declan stepped beneath the floating roof. Using a gun-cleaning cloth, he plucked the SIG from the case. A pair of magazines rested on the bench, conveniently loaded. Manipulating the cloth like a glove, Declan slid the mag into the well.

He watched Rafael shooting, so proud, so consistent, timing the pops.

He waited for Rafael to fire again and clicked the magazine home, the noise disguised by the bang. The cloth formed a barrier between Declan's palm and the grip, his finger and the trigger.

Around them countless guns roared and roared.

Stepping forward, Declan raised the barrel so the muzzle floated two inches off the Padres logo at the back of Rafael's skull.

He fired.

Folding the cloth into his pocket, he crouched over Rafael and dug through his pockets.

Wallet, keys, a folded day pass granting him leave from the reintegration center. His back pockets were empty save for a small piece of folded paper.

It contained a phone number and nothing else.

1-855-2-NOWHERE.

Declan's veins turned to ice.

He walked away swiftly past the other firing lanes. Cutting back around the bathroom shack, he ducked inside, dropped the gun-cleaning cloth into the toilet, and heeled the metal prong of the flusher.

Across the parking lot, back into the maroon Corolla, his chest heaving.

Queenie looked over at him. *What's wrong?*

He said, "We've got a problem."

50

DUMMYPROOF

Evan walked Joey up to her apartment because he wanted to see Dog the dog. He waited in her place while she retrieved the ridgeback from up the hall. The boy lost his mind at the sight of Evan, wagging his tail so hard his whole body hot-dogged back and forth. He shoved his rear end into Evan so he could scratch him just above the tail, and Joey slumped into her oversize leopard-print beanbag and watched them with reluctant amusement.

"Gawd. Get a room."

She pulled her phone out and thumbed around, then flung it down next to her. The whole drive back to Los Angeles, she'd been checking it constantly with an undercurrent of irritation.

"It's a giant butt pain having that dog around, you know," she said. "Every time I want to go somewhere, I have to go deal with the neighbor lady, and she always invites me in and wants me to *drink tea.*"

"The horror."

"I should fix you up with her, since you're all schoolboy skittish about Mia. This lady's just your type. You two could be, like, the lamest-haircut couple ever."

Evan sat on the floor, the better to pet Dog. "What's wrong with my haircut?"

Joey rolled her eyes and flung her hands wide, apparently stunned at his inability to grasp the obvious. "It's just a total generic guy cut."

"I'm a generic guy. And it's good for you to have to interact with other humans. Weren't you just complaining that you long for 'real life'?"

Dog tilted his head up to slurp the underside of Evan's chin.

Joey scowled. "I meant real life without . . ."

"Responsibility?"

"I didn't say that!" She considered. "But yeah."

"Responsibility's where you find meaning."

"Oh, yeah, Fortune Cookie Head? If responsibility's so great, why are *you* retiring?"

"I'm not retiring today. I'm heading to Creech North."

"Yeah, right." Joey dug in her pocket, pulled out a vape pen.

Even from across the room, Evan caught a whiff of weed. "What the hell, Joey?"

"Chillax, X. This isn't what you think it is."

"It better not be."

"If we really want to know what's going on, we need you to get into the network at Creech North. We both know that Hargreave's parking sticker is only gonna buy you a little time. You said you need a cover —"

"I'm working on that."

"— and you'll need to sneak a hacking device inside the base. What's the least suspicious electronic device imaginable?" Joey twisted the vape pen, opening up a hidden inner core that showed off a circuit board.

"How do I use it?"

"You, like, toke."

"Josephine."

"JK! Don't worry. It's dummyproof. Even for you."

She snatched up her phone once more, glared at it, threw it back into the beanbag.

Evan said, "What's with your phone?"

"What?" She reached over her shoulder again and started digging at that spot on her back. "Nothing."

"You keep —"

"Look, it's fine, okay? Gawd." She stretched back, grabbed a Speed Cube from the windowsill, and started playing with it. It turned to a blur of colors in her capable hands, a magic orb. "Bicks is ghosting me. I was just checking if he texted me back, but he didn't. It doesn't matter. I don't care."

"Do you want to talk about it?"

"Hard pass."

Dog nosed his empty Red Vines water bowl and whimpered. Evan stood and carried it into the bathroom. On the counter an array of lipsticks rose like rockets, and there were two kinds of concealer despite the fact that Joey had flawless skin. The sight brought him up short. How hard she was trying to fit in.

He filled the water bowl and brought it back to Dog and sat down again as the ridgie slurped and drooled on the floor. Joey kept spinning the cube, eyes down. Easier to focus on the plastic toy than on a human.

Evan waited.

She solved the cube, spun it on her finger like a basketball, then attacked it again, fingers flying. Now it was checkered. Now striped. Her proficiency was staggering.

He waited some more.

"I mean, what do *I* care if he posted a picture of him with *Sloane* last night? It's his problem if he wants to date some stupid rich girl who exfoliates with whale semen and only eats panda meat."

"Whale semen? Is that a thing?"

"Duh. They're mammals."

"I meant the facial-care application."

"No, X. And she doesn't really eat panda meat either. I'm just saying. He can go back to his life and his mom landlord and fuck right off."

She winced, pulling her head to one side, contorting herself again to get at that knotted muscle by her shoulder blade. Her face looked suddenly full, a heaviness in the cheeks, beneath the eyes.

He remembered her once telling him about when she was fourteen, barely hanging on in the Orphan Program. After having an ear blown out from a demolition charge, she'd been left to find her own way to her pickup point. Stumbling along, she'd come across a father rocking his baby on a park bench, murmuring, *You are safe. You are loved.* After she'd conveyed this memory to Evan, she'd stared at him, her eyes glimmering, and said, *Can you imagine?*

He couldn't. But since knowing Joey, he'd

been starting to imagine how to impart something like that.

Right now it had to be without words. Without eye contact. For the millionth time, he wondered what Jack would have done. When Evan was young and guarded and lost, Jack had always known exactly how to find a way in, what not to say. This was the domain of other people — of Mia, of parents, even fathers like Andre who at one time had held the weight of Sofia's life in his arms.

Until he'd chosen not to.

Evan cleared his throat. "If you need —"

"I *don't* need anything, okay?" Flash of anger, her expression hard, impenetrable.

"Okay."

"I don't need you. I *don't*."

"Okay."

Dog slumped down on the floor with a harrumph and panted contentedly. He smelled like musk and sunshine. Over on the beanbag, Joey strained even harder to reach the sore spot in her back.

Evan said, "Can I help you get that?"

"No."

"You need to learn to accept help."

"Why? You never do."

Evan said, "So you can teach me."

She still didn't bother to look up. Meeting

479

his gaze would be too much for her, but he could tell that she was selling it to herself differently, that he wasn't worth looking at. Not a blemish on her face and two kinds of concealer on the bathroom counter. However hard it was for him to decipher the rules of ordinary life, it was harder for her. Sixteen years old with a labyrinth ahead and endless potential if she could just find the right route through.

She kept trying to get at that muscle. He sat, watching her frustration mount.

Finally she said, "*Fine.* Just 'cuz I can't reach."

He crossed to her and took her place on the beanbag, motioned for her to sit down on the floor in front of him. Facing away, no eye contact. That was good.

He set his hands on her shoulders. Her right one was a good two inches higher than the left, curled slightly forward, the muscle fiber locked up. He found the pressure point with his thumb. Applied pressure, the angry knot yielding nothing.

He gripped the ball of her shoulder, hunched and tight. The problem was there. He held it gently, set his knee in the space between her shoulder blades, and applied gentle pressure, peeling the shoulder back.

"Breathe," he said. "And release."

Her inhalations came in jerks, the exhalations shuddering. Her shoulder trembled, moved back a quarter inch. Fought forward again, muscles and tendons rippling beneath his fingers, in spasm.

"Steady," he said. "Let go. Just let go."

"I *am,*" she said, her voice wavering.

Joey let her head grow heavy, made a sound between a groan and a growl. Dog the dog's collar jangled as he lifted his head.

Her breath evened out. He kept the pressure on, gentle and insistent. Her skin grew suddenly hot. And then her shoulder peeled back and away, opening up, a sudden smooth movement that set it in line with the other.

She tipped her head forward more, let it go lax.

She shook a little. He wasn't sure what was happening until tears spotted her jeans.

"Damn it," she said softly. "Damn it damn it damn it."

Evan drove back to Castle Heights to gear up for the trip to Creech North. Any plan to get him in and out of the top-security compound in one piece would require maximum flexibility and a wildly inventive cover.

So far he had a vape pen and a parking sticker.

It was going to be a challenge.

He parked in the underground lot and made his way through the lobby, sufficiently preoccupied that he barely noticed the person sitting in the sofa area.

Lorilee Smithson.

For once she didn't leap up at the sight of company; she didn't even look over at him as he moved quietly to the elevator. She was staring out the windows onto Wilshire Boulevard, half her face painted with the late-morning sun. Her jaw was set in contemplation, a grave bearing he had not thought her capable of.

He could have continued on to the elevator unseen. But something about her expression made him pause.

He looked back at the elevator. Behind the security counter, Joaquin was watching him, eyebrows raised at this break in Evan's routine. Joaquin didn't speak or move, like a nature photographer gone motionless to avoid spooking the wildlife.

Cutout construction-paper snowflakes danced across the walnut facing of the security desk, Evan close enough to see the sloppy crayon penmanship signing the lowest one: PETER HALL, AGE 9.

That kid was constantly decorating the lobby, Easter Bunny piñatas and Thanksgiving tissue turkeys and customized drawings for every resident's birthday. Evan flashed on Peter sitting on the couch in his dead father's dress shirt — *I don't have anyone to be proud of me* — and the image about wrecked him. How could a kid that fundamentally good ever have to wonder if he was good enough for someone to be proud of?

With quiet awe Evan considered the upbringing Mia had given Peter that let him interact with the world so purely, so freely, so unabashedly. That was what kids were supposed to do: say how they felt and have fun and create joy before life wore them down and dulled their clarity. Joey had never had that chance, and neither had Evan.

Was his decision to leave the Nowhere Man behind some misguided attempt to fight his way backward to some kind of freedom? To the childhood he never had?

He thought about that moment at Lorilee's going-away party when she'd paused amid the dancing to stare balefully at her HAPPY TRAILS! banner, contemplating a future that was unsure and maybe even impossible.

Was that it, then? The thinnest thread connecting him to her? He'd always viewed her as a member of a different species. If they were alike in some distant, tiny way, what did that mean? Did he owe something different to her? To himself?

He was still standing there motionless in the lobby, Joaquin's eyes on him.

And then he reversed course.

He walked back to Lorilee and sat opposite her. He was unskilled at small talk, uncertain how to initiate it. But he was here, breathing the same air, tinged with her perfume.

She slowly registered him, more dazed than languid. "Oh. Hi, Ev."

"Are you okay?"

"Yeah, just . . . you know." She removed a tissue from a bright pink purse and dabbed at her eyes. "Just a lot going on."

"With the move?"

She looked back out the window again and considered the sidewalk, her Botox-smooth and filler-plump features helpless to hide the anguish beneath. "I'm not going anywhere, Evan."

For the first time, her voice had no youthful singsong element, no forced musicality. She was just a grown woman talking in her natural voice, and there was something bare

484

and human in it.

"I don't think I was ever gonna go through with it," she said. "Can't change who I am. Wherever I go, I'll still be me." She blotted her lower lids with the tissue, a practiced gesture that preserved her eyeliner. "Part of me didn't know. But part of me knew all along."

He was dumbfounded. "So why . . . ?"

"The party?" She gave a sad little laugh. "I guess . . . I guess I wanted the attention."

The sentence hung in the air between them, an ugly little confession that was also somehow graceful in its honesty. It was so revealing, so intimate, and he felt a quick counterweight pulling him to get up out of his chair, to head for Creech North, back into the mission where the rules were clear and distinct, governed by Ten Commandments handed down from on high.

And yet he fought back all those urges and remained. She was telling him something about herself, yes, but she was also telling him something about himself, something he couldn't understand but needed to know.

"Oh, God," she said. "I'm so ashamed. What am I gonna tell everyone?"

Evan dug deep in the quagmire of his feelings, sorting through the confusion for a single clear thought. But as always in these situations, he came up short.

He rose respectfully. She kept her gaze out the window. He walked away.

When he looked back from the elevator, she was sitting there silently staring at nothing, alone with the wreckage of her plans.

51
A BLOB OF UNDEFINED NOTHINGNESS

Area 6 was literally off the grid. Even Google Earth refrained from mapping the experimental military zone. Satellite imagery all around showed the pockmarked expanse of the Nevada National Security Site, the earth punished with untold devastation, but the forbidden sector itself appeared as a blob of undefined nothingness. Ironic that the Internet's only blind spot was a facility devoted to engineering all-seeing drones.

Creech North itself lay on the shore of Groom Lake, a two hour forge north from Creech proper. Evan chugged toward it in a well-used Honda Civic that he'd bought for cash three hours ago in Barstow. He'd adhered Hargreave's parking sticker to the windshield, the covert laser readable hologram throwing back the midday glare. He was all but certain that surveillance drones had noted his approach over the past few miles, along with any other movement in the area.

At last a series of compounds came into view, clustered like grapes along the vine of a paved road, each with its own perimeter and security. Creech North had a solid seven-foot-high concrete wall, the better to keep out inquiring eyes. Evan had no idea what lay beyond. Signs posted everywhere warned drivers not to leave the road under any circumstances.

He pulled alongside the security entrance, confronting a solid steel gate sandwiched by barriers on either side and a guard station composed of concrete slabs. Same drill as the Veterans Reintegration Center in Fresno, but on steroids. The Military Police toted M4 carbines, their eyes invisible behind reflective blade sunglasses. One casually brought his rifle to his shoulder. No warning shots here.

Evan coasted up to the checkpoint, and an MP stepped forward with a handheld laser to verify the hologram. It took a specific input illumination to allow the encoded information to appear.

Jake Hargreave had lost his life going back to the impound lot to recover the parking sticker, a strong indication it was still active. But now, in the jaws of facility security, the

First Commandment needled at Evan: *Assume nothing.*

The MP scanned the hologram unsuccessfully, shook the control device, and tried again.

Evan's hands tightened on the steering wheel, the trapped heat of the desert sun amplified through the windows, reflecting off the dash, soaking into the seat. His fingers were tipped with next-gen transparent silicone composite adhesives that sported a false set of prints. At fifty microns each adhesive was thinner than a piece of hair and nearly invisible. He'd pulled the impostor fingerprints off the FBI's IAFIS database, choosing an offender around his age with long shaggy hair, a ragged beard, the same-color eyes, and the most relevant rap sheet. Once again he'd molded chewing gum inside his cheeks and lips to alter his appearance, just enough to skew the facial-feature data points.

As the MP tried the scan once more, Evan steadied his breaths.

And then the steel gate was rumbling aside.

He exhaled through his teeth.

To his right a rabbit bounded along the perimeter fence, paused to nibble. The MP looked up at it, said, "Uh-oh."

The rabbit took another step. A click came audible even at this distance, and a landmine explosion hurled it into the air, its legs stretched wide, brown-gray with a slash of violent red. It hit the dirt with a puff.

The security signs posted on the road leading in made a lot more sense.

The MP shrugged. "Poor little guy." He waved Evan through. "I assume I don't have to remind you to stay on the prescribed paths."

"Not after that."

"Straight to parking. Third or fourth floor. Check in again at the guard station when you exit to verify your access level."

Evan entered the inner sanctum. A ribbon of road stretched ahead, the secure facilities placed at a far remove even from the remote perimeter, withdrawn that much farther from civilization. For a time he rumbled forward, kicking up a dust cloud, anticipating what would come next.

Fortunately, a big sign arrowed the way to the parking structure. He dutifully followed. The hologram had allowed him entry, sure, but that didn't mean that the powers-that-be weren't using the parking sticker as bait. They'd done so already with success at the impound lot.

Evan had to imagine that the hologram

scan had announced his presence — that someone was using Jake Hargreave's credentials — and that he was being watched from here on out. They'd give him some rope and hope he'd reveal what he was after.

Sure enough, within seconds a Humvee fell in behind him, maintaining a respectful distance. He kept his foot steady on the gas, heading for the parking structure like a good little soldier.

The interior roads seemed to be laid out like the spokes of a wheel, leading to the bunched buildings that served as base headquarters.

The central zone was bustling, fields and runways sprawling all around, teams jogging past in formation, unidentified objects of various sizes speckling the sky. It was all Evan could do not to crane his neck and stare out the window.

The four-story parking structure was covered, a stroke of much-needed luck. The guard station waited ten feet from the structure to receive anyone who walked out of parking from the stairwell or elevator. The Humvee following him was joined by a second, idling casually at the curb.

Evan pulled in and wound up to the third floor and chose a spot facing the open air, a good oversight position for the buildings to the east.

He had a loadout bag in the backseat filled with a change of clothes. Moving swiftly, he pulled on a white undershirt on which he had Magic Marker–ed several peace signs and written DRONES DESTROY OUR HUMANITY. Retrieving a Ziploc from the console, he cracked it open, releasing the skunky-sweet scent of weed. He took a hit, presidentially avoiding the inhale, and blew smoke all over himself. The windows were rolled up, the haze compounding.

A few more strategic puffs and the Civic was effectively hot-boxed, the smell suffusing his hair and his clothes. He twisted the vape pen open as Joey had instructed him and clicked an interior switch, the inner core illuminating with indicator lights. He rotated it closed once more and slipped it into his front pocket.

As Joey had promised, the vape pen wasn't what it looked like. It sent out wireless malware that targeted embedded devices — like printers and monitors — connected to the highly secured, air-gapped computers he really wanted to get into. It compromised those devices and acted as a hub linking them so they could speak to one another around an entire office over the Bluetooth connection nobody knew they had. The malware broadcast through the vape pen used Van Eck phreaking through a wide-band antenna, an ultraprecise oscilloscope, and an amplifier to measure the electromagnetic emissions of the embedded devices' video signals. Then it correlated those minute readings to the data being worked on to siphon out the passwords and security keys. Those were sent back to the vape pen, which in turn transmitted them to Joey. He just had to get the pen within twenty meters of the nearest embedded device.

Next he freed the long-range laser listening device from his bag, the same one he'd used to spy on Joey at the restaurant. He got out of the Honda, the intake of fresh air making him cough, and sat on the hood facing the compound three stories below. Leaning forward, he saw that the Humvees held position by the guard station, exhaust spiraling from their tailpipes.

At this point he was on borrowed time and had to move quickly. As he aimed the microphone on the buildings below, he let his Steiner binocs pick across the windows.

A jumble of voices came off the different panes.

"— supply chain clusterfuck getting in the way of our agile combat-support capabilities —"

"— issue for the VA. You're gonna have to contact your wife's doctor to —"

"— rather eat MREs than this shit. Smell this? You think that smells like beef stew?"

He zeroed in on the center building. Shaped like a hockey puck or — more aptly — a UFO. Dark windows along the curved exterior and not a lot of them. He could pick up only a few faint vibrations from the glass:

"— better encryption —"

"— in-flight repair —"

"— improved guidance algorithm for automated collision avoidance —"

That was the place.

He zipped up an air-force-blue Windbreaker over his shirt, dumped the surveillance device beneath the tarp of a pickup parked beside him, and checked his false fingerprints. He crossed to the north-facing edge of the structure, stepped over the rail, swung himself out and down to the concrete ledge of the next level. A tricky bit of parkour that hurt his ankles and knees, but it wasn't backbreaking.

Repeat to the second floor. And then the first.

He wound up winded on the packed sand behind the structure. Out of sight of the guard station and the waiting Humvees, positioned to face the stairs and bank of elevators. Peering around the corner, he waited until the foot traffic thickened along the path ahead. Then he swift-walked out to join it, circumventing the guard station, not daring to look behind him.

Walking rapidly now, the afternoon heat raising sweat across the small of his back. He neared the disk of the center building. Unlabeled like the others, the front doors a wall of tinted glass, black as obsidian.

He slowed his walk, timing his approach with a cluster of engineer types nearing the building, sipping coffee from plastic cups. In succession they held their electronic access cards to the panel, the doors unclicking electronically as they filed in.

Evan queued up behind them, tapping his hand to the sensor as if presenting a card, and caught the handle before the door resealed.

He entered.

A loud hum hit him immediately, the sound of a concealed server farm working overtime. The front lobby space was bathed in warmth from various vents suctioning air from a vast sunken area that constituted the building's inner core. A row of curved interior windows looked down and in, but

Evan wasn't close enough to see what lay below.

He passed through a security metal detector, tossing his keys and the vape pen into a plastic dish. The MP running security pulled him aside and wanded him from head to toe, checking every last zipper and metal eyelet on his boots. Joey had warned him to forgo the digital contact lenses for precisely this reason; they would have alerted beneath the metal detector.

The MP handed him back the dish with a smirk — smoking devices were clearly not in vogue at Creech North — and waved him through.

As Evan moved toward the rounded bank of windows, a giant lab three stories below drew gradually into view. The scope of the space was breathtaking — part factory floor, part Hieronymus Bosch painting. Uniformed airmen and white-coated scientists scurried insectlike between computer stations and lab benches. Robotic entrails and dissected drone parts lay scattered across virtually every surface. Banks of monitors blinking with code, UAVs hovering above test-launching pads, airmen in Operational Camouflage Pattern uniforms huddled around diagrams, in heated discussions with bespectacled engineers.

Signs indicated that the elevator bank waited to the left, but as Evan arced around the curve, he saw with dismay that two armed MPs were inspecting credentials before letting anyone on. Even worse, the lift wasn't summoned by button; it required an electronic access card for entry.

There was no way for Evan to even board the elevator, let alone get the vape pen within twenty meters of the data stations below.

That's when he sensed a flare of movement overhead and heard the three-note bugle of his Laser Warning Receiver playing *Taps*.

He'd been lit up.

52

DOGPILE

Overhead a diminutive quadcopter drone zipped around, holding its laser on Evan. He could only hope that it was unarmed, strictly for interior surveillance.

No time to delay.

He'd be in custody within seconds.

Already the MPs from the security checkpoint had alerted to him.

Evan ripped off his Windbreaker, releasing a miasma of marijuana fumes, and cast it aside. He shouted, "Drones can't hear the cries of children on the ground!"

The MPs started for him, and he freed the vape pen from his pocket and sprinted away. The air felt heavy, the heat drafted up from the lab floor venting along the elevated corridor.

Down below, the commotion went unnoticed, but people in the corridor froze all around him. A number of passing airmen keyed to him, going on point.

Evan feinted left, sprinting around an MP, and hurdled another coming in for a tackle. Suddenly a dozen people were in play, a wall of blue berets and camouflage, the noose closing fast.

He curled his hand around the vape pen, vectoring hard for the outer wall, aiming at one of the heating vents. Someone struck him from the side, and he rolled away like a running back evading a tackle. His momentum spun him 180 degrees, his forearm slamming into the concrete. His other hand, clenching the vape pen, swung around to absorb the impact, and he opened his fist just before it hit the vent. His palm slapped the metal rectangle, the slats digging into his skin. The vape pen rolled between his flesh and the metal, horizontally positioned but not popping through.

Someone rammed into his back, dragging him toward the floor.

He fought back, holding himself against the wall, his hand sliding down along the vent. The vape pen clanked unseen across each slat, and finally Evan felt the pressure in his palm release, the pen squeaking through. He heard it tick against the inside of the ducting as it plummeted downward, and then he was on the floor, buried beneath the dogpile.

■ ■ ■ ■

Evan had to dip his head to press the ice pack to his swollen cheek. His knee felt bruised, and the index finger of his left hand had been torn at the nail in the one-sided rumble. Raw skin ringed his wrists where he'd been steered hard by the handcuffs. His fingerprint adhesives were still smudged with ink from when they'd printed him, and dried blood from a nosebleed had crusted on his upper lip.

He'd been brought into a concrete box of a room in the neighboring building and deposited into a chair bolted to the floor, his cuffs locked to a metal ring on the table before him. His reflection gazed back woefully from the one-way mirror.

His activist high jinks had earned him two hours locked in this position. His arm muscles were cramping, his hamstrings tight from sitting on the hard chair for this long. He watched a fly crawl across the ceiling. He wondered if it was real.

At last he heard footsteps.

The door was flung open with seeming great annoyance, and then a major general entered and steadied an iron gaze on Evan. He had pale blue eyes that looked hard, chips of gemstone. Yellow-red mustache, blond-white hair in a dated center part, two-star insignia riding the shoulder of his pressed uniform. His rank showed that these people treated any intrusion as a national security threat.

At first assessment he seemed to be stalwart, one of those men whom the military had disassembled in basic and rebuilt from the boots up. He filled those boots now with a forward-tilting confidence that seemed righteous — or at least approximated righteousness with conviction.

Evan wondered if anyone at Creech North had an inkling of Molleken's extracurricular activities, that the good doctor was putting his considerable resources toward cleaning up those who might interfere with the massive government contract that the DoD was on the brink of awarding him.

"Every last thing on this base falls under my purview. My attention is valuable, Mr. . . ." A glance down at a printed report in his hand. "Paul Norris."

"I know what you're doing here," Evan said. "I know you're building drones that violate international law. I have a hundred and eighteen Freedom of Information Act requests in with the CIA, and as soon as I get those results" — he faked a tic that

501

jerked his head to one side, a mannerism he'd picked up from Danny when he'd visited him in prison — "I'm gonna whistle-blow on your whole operation."

The words seemed to wash over the major general without moving him in the least, tide over a boulder. He kept on his own track. "How'd you acquire a Creech North parking credential?"

"Our 4chan group keeps track of drone pilots. We know when someone goes down, gets arrested . . ." Evan paused coyly. "When their truck winds up in an impound lot. We won't stop until the killings do."

"I see you have previous arrests at other bases." The major general's eyes slotted to the paper and then assessed Evan once quickly, top to bottom, like a computer scanner. He folded his arms across his chest, his uniform starched and wrinkleless, as if it had been painted on. "So it shouldn't surprise you that sneaking onto a military installation is a federal offense. As is imper-sonating a member of the U.S. military."

"That's why I'm here. Arrest me."

"You've certainly given us good cause."

"I'm ready to go to trial." Evan gave with another series of twitches. "Let's let the American people hear about what you're doing here."

"It must be nice," the major general said, "to do so much complaining and offer no solutions. I need to get into that business, because God knows what I do here to protect idiots like you out there is a helluva lot harder." He snapped the sheet curtly to his side and turned to leave. "We're done, Mr. Norris."

53
BUMP IN THE NIGHT

For Declan, twilight was the hardest time of day. Morning and afternoon he moved with a predator's fearless stride, the world around him lit with clarity. Obstacles and opportunities. Prey moving obliviously before his all-knowing gaze, a living buffet. And at night he felt invisible, capable of doing things that one could do only when no one was watching.

But the transition froze him in a child's place, the gold leaching from the sky, the air murky like fog, promising uncertainty. During the gloaming he was neither the active hunter nor the one who lurked.

Queenie read this in him like she read everything, though they'd never discussed it. They sat in her Mustang now on stakeout, waiting for an opening to get their surveillance gear in place. They were also waiting for the doctor to return their call. They'd left two messages and finally texted him the new information about the Nowhere Man. He'd process it in his cold reptilian fashion, hostility tempered by logic, and then he'd toss the grenade back into their laps.

Declan stared at the moths gathering beneath the streetlight, feeling that constriction in his chest that presaged his night terrors. They wouldn't come on now, not while he was awake, but they'd flicker at the edges of his awareness, a reminder of the waiting nightmares.

Queenie reached over and took his hand. *Breathe deep, little brother.*

He said, "I am."

She adjusted the mirror for a better view of the building they were watching. "I know."

He placed a hand reassuringly on his stomach, felt the cotton twill soft against his skin. No fingernail scrapes there. The insides of his thighs smoldered, memory twitches of cigarette burns.

Queenie tightened her grip. *Not real. Not real.*

He would be okay. Just a few minutes as the earth turned, and then night would fall like a soothing blanket and he'd be invisible again, safe until sleep.

An obese woman in a pink pantsuit exited her minivan and walked past them on the sidewalk. He thought about the bones inside her holding up all that weight. The blood coursing through her veins, keeping the whole enterprise functioning. There was enough iron in a human body to make a three-inch nail. That's all anyone was. Parts and particles. Raw matter that could be re-arranged. You could dress it up with gym muscle or bespoke clothes or plastic surgery, but at the end of the tunnel people were just pain receptors and nerves, ligament and marrow.

The charade was exhausting.

He adjusted his cuff link, watched the orb of illumination hanging from the streetlamp grow more pronounced until it stood out against the darkness, a fishbowl holding a swirl of fluttering moths.

It was safe now for a while.

He exhaled, released his sister's hand.

"It's not our fault, you know," he said. "What we are."

She looked over at him. Snapped her gum. "That's the only thing scarier than if it *is* our fault."

"My first memories are her telling me I was toxic. Dangerous. Didn't care about anyone but myself. Maybe it wasn't true. But that's what I heard when my brain was just . . . when my brain was just clay. And now?" He held out his arms, biceps bulging beneath the tailored suit jacket. "Now it *is* true."

"You care about me," Queenie said.

"That doesn't count."

"Why's that?"

"You are me."

She pursed her lips, considered.

Declan said, "What if we don't get away with anything?"

"Mom did."

"No," he said. "Mom lived in hell. And now maybe we do, too."

The phone rang through the speakers. Once. Twice.

He and Queenie looked at each other.

Then he answered.

"Who the fuck is Andre Duran?" the doctor said.

"Nobody," Declan said. "He's a nobody."

"That's what you've been telling me. But now we have this — what? — private assassin on our hands?"

"The Nowhere Man."

"And what exactly is *he*?"

"A thing that goes bump in the night," Declan said.

Static crackled over the line, the pause drawn out long enough that he wasn't sure if the doctor had disconnected. "Is that trepidation I sense in your voice?"

Queenie glanced over through mascara-heavy lashes. *No.*

For the first time in memory, Declan didn't heed her advice. "Maybe part of me's scared," he said. "But another part of me's looking forward to it — staring into the face of something worth staring at. Something that might tell me what I am."

The doctor's breath rumbled across the line, a shush of white noise. "If this guy's what they say he is, you'll have your chance soon enough."

It took a few moments for them to realize that the call had ended.

Declan picked a string from his sleeve, flicked it out the window. Queenie splayed her fingers at the top of the steering wheel, admired her incarnadine nails. She looked over at him and grinned, lascivious red lips against too-white teeth. Something in her face was yearning, hungry, eager. He knew exactly what she felt, because he felt it, too.

He stared at that smile, a mirror of his own.

It said, *We're not the only hunters in the game anymore.*

54
THIS SHITTY LIFE

Limping into the empty Chinese restaurant, Evan was met with a hearty round of *"Irasshaimase"*'s from the largely Japanese waitstaff until he indicated he was merely going upstairs. Though the swelling on his cheek had diminished, his nose was still deciding whether or not it was broken, having bled sporadically for most of the drive back to Los Angeles. He'd taped his torn cuticle and popped a handful of Advil to back off the ache along his spine; he'd been the recipient of a few kidney punches in the dogpile.

The major general had ordered him quietly removed from the base to create minimal public splash. Evan had been frog-marched outside the main gate and reunited with his crappy Civic, which had been taken apart in a search and mostly put back together again, though one hubcap remained missing and the seat cushions were all slashed. He'd driven back to Barstow to pick up his truck, stashed the beat-to-shit Honda on a side street, and headed straight here.

He paused halfway up the creaky stairs to stretch out his elbow where a nasty contusion seeped down to clutch his forearm. His RoamZone chimed, and he glanced at the text from Joey: GOOD NEWZ. WHATEVER U DID @ CREECH NORTH WORKED. I'M IN THE DATABASES NOW.

Before he could register his relief, another chime sounded: BAD NEWZ.

Beneath, a forwarded article: "Senior Airman Fatally Shot at Gun Club." A sinking sensation overtook him, dread pulling at his insides. He didn't have to glance at the tiny photo on the text alert to know who it was.

He pictured Rafael in his tidy room, agitated and trapped, caught between his conscience and the drive to survive. *You can't go up against this kind of power and keep breathing.* They'd gaslighted him, gotten him discharged, destroyed his career, his honor. But they hadn't been content with that.

Evan wanted to feel sadness, but the only thing that came was anger.

A crash echoed down at him through Andre's flimsy door, and then the sound of someone bellowing.

Steeling himself, he sprinted up two stairs at a time and flew inside.

Lamp toppled, tilted shade throwing uneven light. Holes knocked through the drywall, the aftermath of a fight. A body hurled into the cramped space between the foot of the bed and the wall, legs and one arm sticking up into view, waving animatedly.

But no one else in the room.

It took a moment for Evan to construct the picture.

Upended bottle draining onto the floor. Another empty on the windowsill. Sugary scent of rum. Andre fuming into the side of the mattress. He seemed to be stuck.

Not a brawl, then.

A booze-induced tantrum.

Heeling the door shut behind him, Evan entered. He hoisted Andre up, and Andre swung at him drunkenly. "Offa me!"

Evan seized his shirt and shook him. "Knock it off."

Andre didn't stop so Evan shoved him onto the bed. He lay there a moment, then reached for the mostly empty bottle on the floor.

"I'm out there trying to save your ass, and this is what you're doing." Evan kicked the bottle away, out of reach. "You need to sober up, drink water."

The few glasses on the card table were dirty, crusted with residue. Evan tore through the crooked cabinet. A cracked mug on its side and a plastic cup with a pub logo. Not a single thing matched in this fucking place; it was as though Andre had designed it to maximally aggravate Evan's OCD. Evan grabbed the cup, filled it, and held it out to Andre.

Andre knocked it away, spraying droplets across Evan's face. He tried to push himself up, losing traction in the sheets, and wound up slumped against the wall. "I told you I wanted to call my sponsor."

"I see. It's *my* fault."

"— left me here for *two days* with a buncha Benjamins and nowhere to go."

"People are *dying.*" Evan was angry, angrier than made sense. "All you had to do is stay here and not screw up."

"That's rich coming from you." Andre threw himself up onto his feet, swaying unevenly. "You got chosen. *You* did."

"What does that mean?"

"They were gonna take another kid. Van Sciver and one other kid. That shoulda been me. *Me.*" Inexplicably, Andre was crying. "But you jumped the line. You got yourself picked. And then they took Van Sciver. And that was it. That was *it.* The rest of us got left behind. So how come you got to get fixed, huh?" He swung at Evan weakly, a halfhearted fist that struck him in the chest, more imploring than violent. "How come?"

The words came heated and urgent through Evan's clenched teeth. "I earned it."

"No. No. You *stole* it." Another loose swing connected with Evan's torso. "I coulda been so much more. I coulda been you. I didn't get a shot. You shoulda been here instead of me in this shitty room. In this shitty life."

Andre was sobbing openly now, his contorted face eliciting not empathy from Evan but a deep, heated embarrassment he didn't understand. The smell of booze and unwashed sheets, the vise grip of the four tight walls, the baleful drawing of Sofia — it all seemed to thicken the air, pressing in on him, compressing his chest, his judgment.

And then the words were pouring out of him. "You had a wife. You had a kid. A normal life. You had *everything* anyone could've wanted. And you threw it all away for what? This?" Evan plucked the empty rum bottle off the floor and shook it in Andre's face. "How useless do you have to

513

be? How much of a coward?"

Andre's face hardened. He swung at Evan again, but this time with intent. Evan sidestepped the cross and punched him in the solar plexus, all fleshy gut, careful not to snap a floating rib. Andre barked out a chunk of air, fell to his knees, and vomited on the threadbare carpet. He heaved again, the hot stink of alcohol and bile rising. His lips were open, sucking for air. And then it came, screeching intakes mixed with sobs, his face shiny with tears and mucus and puke.

He dragged himself into the bathroom in shame, kicking the door shut behind him, but it hit the frame and wobbled wide to show him clinging to the toilet, fighting for breath.

Evan lowered his face, his cheeks burning. It was the first time he'd lashed out in anger since his childhood. Jack had taken that part of him and hammered it into an implement he could keep sheathed, a weapon he drew only with great focus and caution and reverence.

He'd betrayed all three.

This mission — from Veronica to Danny to Andre — reached back to that youngest part of Evan. It had found the red-hot center of his vulnerability, the scarred-over wound that made him afraid to hope or belong or have dreams of his own.

He needed to go into the bathroom and set it right.

And yet his feet stayed rooted. His legs didn't obey.

He glared at Andre. Andre glared back, his chest heaving. "And what the fuck are *you*?" he said. "Always on the lookout for someone to save. You need it, feed off it. Other people's weaknesses. It's the only thing that defines you, 'cuz you don't have anything else. Deep down you know you're nothing on your own. Just like me."

Evan felt his heartbeat fluttering the skin at his temple. His breath stretching his intercostals. The low simmer of rage waiting for an excuse to bubble over.

He thought about what he'd been through, from the Buenos Aires Provincial Police to the Hellfire missile, from Kern Prison to the ambush at the impound lot, from Molleken's battle lab to the battering he'd taken at Creech North.

Andre wasn't worth it. Whatever duty-bound sentiment had pulled Evan out of retirement wasn't worth it. Even Veronica and the mysterious wisdom she might or might not hold wasn't worth it. The anger welling inside him felt fresh and pure, fu-

eled with all the vitality of youth, un-
tempered by age or wisdom.

"You don't care about me," Andre said.
"This is just some favor for Ms. LeGrande."

Evan just breathed. Fresh air in. Stale air
out. Holding himself at bay.

Andre scowled at him. "I never asked for
your help."

"No, you didn't."

"Like I said, leave me the fuck alone."

Evan took a step forward. Filled the
doorway of the bathroom. Andre recoiled in
fear, and Evan was ashamed at the twinge
of satisfaction that gave him.

He stared down at Andre, cringing against
the toilet, filthy and pathetic and lost.

"Gladly," he said, and moved from the
squalor down the stairs and out into the
clean night air.

55
LOST CAUSE

As Evan blazed across the city to Bel Air, his RoamZone rang. He smacked to answer, and Joey's voice came through the Bluetooth. "We have to talk."

"Not a good time."

"I've been combing through the code from Molleken's battle lab and the stuff from that Pixel phone you stole, but it wasn't the full picture. I'm getting my head into the Creech North databases now, and looks like Molleken's running most of their engineering initiatives. He's got whatever clearances he needs pertaining to" — and here Joey paused to put on her Important Voice — "remotely piloted, unmanned, and autonomous weapons systems."

"Joey —"

"Dude's got cray-cray access to do what he wants under the guise of training or R 'n' D and the database access to cover it up. Like take a Predator out for a spin or assess the high-value-target list or overwrite commands. Which means it's looking *way* worse for Andre than we thought."

"I don't care."

A confused pause. "What?"

"I'm aborting the mission."

"Why?"

"Because the guy is self-destructive. I can't help him."

"You're just gonna let them kill him?"

"It's not my business anymore," Evan said. "He never asked for my help. He never wanted my help. He's made that clear."

"What about your mother?"

"She's not my mother. You should understand that."

"Fine, okay." Joey's tone was, for once, accommodating, conciliatory. She was backpedaling and sounded unsettled, maybe even rattled. "But, like, you promised her you'd —"

"One week after she gave birth, she dumped me into the system. She left me there all those years until Jack saved me. Since she's reared her head, I've almost gotten killed at every turn. And for what? For *her*? I don't owe that woman a goddamned thing. And I'm going to tell her that."

"But Andre —"

"Joey. It's *over.*"

A stunned beat.

"This isn't you," she insisted, her voice little-girl brave.

"Maybe you don't know me," Evan said.

For the first time he recalled, she couldn't find words. As he screeched up in front of the Bel Air mansion, he severed the connection.

Storming up the walk through the iron gate, palm trees throwing jagged shade. In the river the swans were tucked into themselves, neat origami packages of white floating beneath bowing fronds. He banged the ridiculous greyhound door knocker, the yappy dogs exploding to life inside.

A minute later the architectural door opened, a split in the towering façade of the house. Veronica stood in the gap, heeling the dogs back, a gin and tonic bubbling in hand.

"Evan, I'm just visiting with a friend." She took in his face, the bruises, the scowl, her gaze sharpening. "Are you —"

He brushed past her into the house, the dogs scrabbling across the concrete stepping blocks, barking their high-pitched barks and barely avoiding tumbling into the dark-tiled pool.

Moving through the kitchen he said, *"Off,"* and they dispersed with great agitation and shot away into various halls.

Veronica hurried to catch up, and they entered the sunken living room together. A handsome woman around Veronica's age was sitting at the bar, leafing through a wedding album and draining the last of her G&T. She wore heavy makeup and looked — as least from this distance — to have been nipped and tucked with admirable subtlety.

"Oh, hello," she said.

At Evan's elbow Veronica said, "Janet, this is my —" She hesitated. "My son."

The word hung there, lead-heavy.

"Oh? I didn't know you had . . ." Janet trailed off.

An uncomfortable silence proceeded.

Evan cut through it. "Can you give us some privacy?"

"Oh." For Janet that seemed to be the start to every sentence. She gave a nervous chipmunk laugh, short and stuttering, a rock skipping across water. "I was just showing your . . . *mother* . . . photos from my grandson's wedding."

Evan said nothing. Veronica drifted to the bar and freshened up her own gin and tonic. "I'm sorry," she said quietly to Janet.

Her friend gathered the thick album to her chest like a shield and strode out, her head held high, a skilled practitioner of the dignified exit.

Veronica sat at a barstool, turned mostly away from Evan. "What's wrong?"

"What the hell are we doing here? You and I? Do you really care about Andre? Why did you throw me in with him?"

"I beg your pardon." She seemed to be only a few drinks in, still fresh-faced, though her cheeks were starting to flush with emotion.

"Let's call it what it is. Andre's a lost cause. Some people are just broken."

"Is that what you believe?"

"He convinced me."

The lines in her neck tensed. "Stern words from a professional assassin."

"Yes. And *you* found *me*. You asked for my help."

"And you have been helping him. In other ways, right? God, maybe I thought in saving him you could save yourself, too. It's not just about killing people."

"No. It's not. I choose to help people who deserve it, to keep them safe. I eliminate obstacles between me and that goal. Sometimes those obstacles are very dangerous people. And if that's horrifying to you, feel free to crawl back into whatever luxurious hole you've been living in these past sixty-some years."

"Sixty-*two*," she objected, with an amused purse of her lips, though it faded as quickly as it had arisen. "I'd imagine that someone with your background has kept company with a wide spectrum of people. What is it about Andre you find so personally repulsive?"

"What is it about him you find worthwhile?"

"Goddamn it." She knocked back half her drink, her words only now coming slurred. "You're so arrogant, Jacob —"

"Jacob?"

She rubbed her forehead, confused. She wore a sleeveless blouse, her arm wobbling beneath it, not toned as Evan had thought but frail, wasted. "It's easy to have empathy for something we understand. But there's a spectacular array of suffering out there." She waved her glass vaguely in his direction. "Not all of it is your flavor. That doesn't mean it's not worth your empathy."

"You don't know what I've been through. You don't know anything about me."

Her lips were trembling, an uncharacteristic show of anger, of vulnerability. "The hardest part of trying to become an adult is realizing that your suffering doesn't entitle you to anything."

"You're not the person to tell me that."

"I wasn't talking about you. I was talking about me." She breathed wetly in the pause. "You don't realize it until you're alone and there's no one there to hear you complain. Just you and, hmm, fate."

"What are you talking about?"

She set her drink down uncertainly, knocking over one of her orange pill bottles. "You struggle with Andre because he reminds you of your past."

"No."

"He reminds you that despite everything you left behind, you're still the same person you've always been."

"No."

"We all are," she said. "We don't leave anything behind, don't you understand?"

Evan felt his molars grind. "You're not hearing me. I'm done with this. I'm done with him."

"You can't be."

"Why not?"

"Because," she said quietly, "he's your brother."

She faced away from him, her hair tumbling down across one eye, the side of her face. It fluttered at intervals with her breaths.

Evan couldn't register his own breathing

or the room or the words he'd just heard. All he sensed was his heartbeat thundering in his ears, a waterfall rush of blood moving through his system, keeping him upright. His flesh felt numb.

It occurred to him that this is what full-blown denial felt like. Groping in the dark, searching for old bearings that no longer existed.

Without knowing it, he'd taken a step back.

The story beneath the words unfurled like a banner, spelling out the trauma writ large.

He relived everything now through a new lens, one that brought all the blurry edges into focus. How vividly Veronica had described the rape of Andre's mother. *She had bruises around her wrists where they'd been held down. And she was wearing the shirt still, torn at the collar where it had been . . . Broken fingernails from trying to fight back. A clump of hair missing where it had been yanked out. It was brutal. Savage.*

Not someone else.

But her.

She took those damn tests every few days, like playing a lottery you don't want to win. But sure enough, she won. And even though this was a child born of violence, it was still a child. And she decided she wanted to bring this child to term.

She'd been telling Evan her own story the only way she knew how.

She tried to raise this baby who'd done nothing wrong, who deserved so much more. But she found she didn't have the strength to look in that child's face every day and be reminded of what had been done to her. I remember her telling me that she could see in his features the face of the man who'd attacked her. Imagine living with that.

He couldn't.

So she'd put Andre up for adoption. But not right away.

She fought herself for a year. And gave this child care. But she also detested him. And it was tearing her apart. I've never seen a person so conflicted. So, yes. But by then he was a toddler, and the problem with that is . . .

Evan had finished the sentence for her: *The older a kid is, the less anyone wants him.*

He'd spoken from personal experience. But Veronica had tried to do it right the second time. With him. She'd tried to place him as a baby, where he could be loved and accepted into a real family. But the placement had fallen apart and he'd been consigned to the same fate as Andre.

His numb legs moved him cautiously across the savanna-tan carpet to the sweeping embrace of the couch. He lowered himself onto it, felt his muscles let go a bit.

His heart was still beating hard, too hard, the tuning-fork vibration from the revelation still humming in his bones.

When he lifted his gaze, Veronica was looking at him from the bar. She wasn't crying, but she was on the verge, her face altered, swollen, holding back a body full of emotion.

He looked at the gin and tonic, for once untouched at her side, and thought about Andre and his rum, himself and his vodka, the pull of their shared genes toward liquid medication, toward elusive comfort, toward forgetting.

"Sweet boy," she said, "I never wanted you to find out this way."

He had never been called a pet name. Not one single time.

It felt awful and beautiful and terribly confusing.

He said nothing. He still couldn't find his voice.

"He was searching for me, but I couldn't tell him," she said. "I didn't want him to know he was a child of . . . of . . ."

Andre had already completed his childhood quest. He'd found his mother. He just didn't know it. And now Evan was tied to him, his half brother. It felt like a burden and a violation.

Desperately, desperately, he wanted it not to be true.

"The whole time he was looking for me" — Veronica's breath hitched, but through some deep-summoned strength she suppressed the sob — "I was looking for you."

"You knew where I was," Evan said. "All that time."

"Yes, but I couldn't find my way to you. I . . . I couldn't."

"After the . . ."

"Yes. After Andre. And the circumstances surrounding him. With you — you were so pure. Those few days we had together, I never put you down. But your father, he was never going to be there. I barely knew him. I was alone again with a baby. It all felt so familiar. And I thought after Andre, I didn't . . ."

"What?"

"I didn't deserve you. After what had been done to me, after what I'd done to Andre, how was I supposed to give myself to this new baby boy? How was I supposed to ask him to give himself to *me*?"

Evan had never had a mother because of Andre.

If she'd never been raped.

If she hadn't tried to raise Andre first.

If she'd found Evan worth it.

"I'm sorry," she said, and there were tears on her cheeks, held perfectly suspended. They were clinging there in place as if they'd been painted on.

Evan rose on unsteady legs and walked out.

56
HELP ON THE GROUND

Even after he drove back to Castle Heights, Evan still felt altered, moving through a fog of anger and denial. He vaguely registered Lorilee in the lobby, bantering with Hugh Walters and the Honorable Pat Johnson over near the mail slots. Someone might have called out to him, but then he was on the elevator heading up, alone with his breath and his heartbeat.

The twenty-first-floor hallway was empty as always, a blank carpeted run to his penthouse. But his front door was ajar.

He froze as the elevator closed at his back. He had literally never come home to find it open.

The ARES unholstered with little more than a whisper. He quickly ejected the mag and pressed hard on the top cartridge with the tip of his index finger. Little play, full mag. He clicked the magazine back into place, gave a swift tug on the baseplate, reacquired his grip, and moved stealthily up the hall.

His locks undone, dead bolt retracted, four-inch gap in the frame. He collapsed his two-handed grip until the 1911's mainstream housing was against his sternum in the inside position to guard against a gun grab. Then he eased inside, elbowing the door ajar.

A glass of water on the kitchen island, set down with no coaster.

He heard noise in his master suite and jogged toward it, braced for a firefight. Bathroom light on, shower door rolled back, monitor light casting the Vault in a cool blue glow.

He exhaled and sliced the pie with the front sight as he entered the Vault.

Joey sat on the floor, Dog the dog's head in her lap as she fed him almond butter off a spoon. One of Evan's spoons. Code wallpapered the OLED screens, more programs running than he could keep track of.

The ARES was aimed directly at Joey's critical mass, the center line of her torso, six inches down at the sternum.

He exhaled angrily, lowered the gun. "The hell are you doing here, Joey?"

"This mom shit is fucking you up."

"Language."

"No." She untangled herself from the dog and stood. "What is going on with you?"

"I didn't tell you you could be here," he said. "Pick your shit off the kitchen counter. And the dog's shedding everywhere." He stormed over to the L-shaped desk, where she'd left a coffee mug steaming, and snatched it up. "Is it that hard to not mess everything up everywhere you go?"

Her voice warbled but held its anger. "You don't talk to me like that."

Not an admonishment. A wounded observation.

The hurt in her voice halted him on his feet.

"This isn't you," she said. "This isn't us. You're trying to push me away. But I *know* that drill. And I know you." Her chest jerked and her eyes welled, but she wasn't going to cry, not here, not now. "I don't care what you say. I *do* know you. So knock it off, okay?" Her mouth quaked a bit, but she firmed it angrily. "Just knock it off. Right now. Please?"

He stood there holding the coffee mug for a time. Then he set it down. He felt a week's worth of tension melt out of his shoulders, and he sank into his chair. He couldn't look at her, couldn't look at anything. He picked at the bandage over his cuticle and then picked at it some more.

When he risked a glance up, Joey was still standing there, shoulders back, spine straight, ready to fight or cry or maybe both. Dog the dog had risen to sit at her side, pressed into her leg. She rested her hand at his scruff, dug in for moral support.

Evan said quietly, "You're right."

Her shoulders lowered, almost imperceptibly. "I am?"

More words were there somewhere, but they were words for other people, the kinds of things said by people who weren't broken.

He rose quietly and headed out. Down the long hall, past the workout stations, the heavy bag hanging from its chain. Past the living wall with its breath of mint and rosemary. Into the vodka room.

Soothing coolness against his cheeks. The bottle of Guillotine rested on its glass shelf. And beyond, the rise of Century City, windows glowing into the night from the pseudo-skyscrapers. He was alone in these four walls with his alcohol and a view of the world.

It struck him just how insulated he'd kept himself.

He sensed movement outside. Joey had emerged and was watching him, Dog snugged up next to her. Evan stayed locked in the glass room, breathing his way back to some kind of sanity.

But responsibility waited out there. To Joey. To himself.

That's what people did for you, they held you to a standard you had to live up to.

He stepped out of the shell of the vodka room.

He faced Joey. "I'm . . ." The words were dry and textured, hard to dredge up. "I'm sorry."

She cleared her throat, blinked a few times. Then she bit her lip and looked away. "Shit, X. You're making me feel feelings."

It occurred to him that Joey was the only one who could get in here. Into the penthouse, into his emotions, his life. If something happened to him, it would all fall to her. The floating bed. The Vault. The vodka freezer.

The last thought was worrying. He debated putting a self-destruct mechanism on the alcohol in case the next Hellfire hit its target.

"What happened?" she asked.

Could Evan trust her with this? Could he trust himself to speak the words to someone else? That would make it real, would put it into the world where he'd have to stare it in the face. Dog the dog padded over to him and slurped his hand.

He said, "Andre is my half brother."

"Oh," Joey said. And then, "Oh."

She saw it all. He watched her get it.

He cleared his throat. Looked back at the beckoning vodka. Then gave it up. For the moment. "You said there's a heightened risk now. To him."

Joey nodded. It wasn't back to normal between them, everything still heightened, but they would reach for operational specifics and that would make it safe again.

"Molleken's putting the finishing touches on a new gen of dragonfly drones," she said.

Evan thought of those thousands of yellow-green eyes glowing at him from the darkness of the battle lab. The terror of being vastly outnumbered by a swarm of things coldly robotic and yet alive.

"They do more than seems imaginable," she said, a horrified awe touching her voice. "Once they decide to lock onto you, they're locked for life. Your face. Your thermal signature. Your electronic records. Everything. If they so much as spot you, they can store your biomarkers to find you later, once they've joined up with others. They can read your skin moisture, determine how far you live from the ocean. Assess your shirt and link to places you might have bought it —

even trace elements that might show where it was shipped from and where to. They can search for you, neighborhood by neighborhood, block by block, looking at faces on the streets, through windows into houses. They hook into whatever databases they want and don't even report back to leave a record. No oversight. No accountability. They just find you and figure out the best way to kill you, and they do it all on their own."

Evan nodded. He felt tired, so tired. He wanted to meditate, to sleep, to go back in time and refuse to answer that call from Veronica. But it was too late, and he was in now, and he owed it to himself to finish this.

"What's our time frame?"

"The swarm is due for delivery to Creech North tomorrow night. Obviously the war capabilities are, like, incredible. But I found an encrypted kill order in the system at Creech, hidden in the list of high-value targets. The rest of them are in the Middle East. But the encrypted kill order is for someone right here at home."

Evan said, "Andre."

"He's the only witness to have seen the program in action illegally on U.S. soil."

Evan said, "When they got Hargreave."

"Kill Andre, save the program," Joey said.

535

"If they launch those things, he will die."

"Tomorrow night."

"That's right. The encrypted kill order is a hack, put in place by one person at the source. Guess who?"

"Molleken."

Joey dipped her chin in a nod. "The rest of the government doesn't even know about it, obviously, since you can't kill a U.S. citizen. Or at least leave a record of it. And the thing is, I can't lift the kill order from the outside. Someone has to get in there and access the hardware directly."

Evan grimaced. "If I'm gonna get back in there, I'm gonna need help on the ground."

Joey took her phone out of her pocket, spun it on her palm, and at last broke a smile. "I was thinking the same thing."

57
SOME KIND OF THRILL

Candy McClure leaned back in the seat of the King Air plane, listening to the dipshit jumpmaster drone on.

It was an affront to her training even to be here, on a commercial skydiving jaunt in the skies above Flagstaff, Arizona. She was surrounded by overly zealous thrill seekers who were pumped up on adrenaline and their own inflated self-images. The twenty-something women next to her — Madison ("call me Maddy"!) and McKenzie ("Me and Maddy are, like, sisters but not sisters") — wore tight-fitting jumpsuits that still bore the fold marks from the store. The dude-bros wore similarly unnecessary suits with scuba-yellow sleeves, cone collars, and tight legs, patches adorning the synthetic nylon like military ribbons.

Candy wore jeans and a T-shirt, her blond hair pulled back in a ponytail. The more disinterest she showed, the more the men showed interest in her, sneaking nervous glances, eyes dropping to her not insubstantial breasts, visible between the vertical straps of the harness belt.

Her back and shoulders, covered with rippled scar tissue from a chemical burn, felt feverish against the seat. The twin propellers roared. They were nearing ten thousand feet, at least by the look of the earth below.

Over the headsets, Jumpmaster Steve kept on. "I repeat: I own the rear of the plane. Every thousand feet is six seconds. You're gonna pull at three thousand feet when you start to see ground rush." A condescending wink at Candy, Call Me Maddy, and Sister McKenzie. "Don't worry, ladies, if you pass out, an automatic activation device will make the chute deploy anyway."

One of the guys pried his gaze off Candy's superior tits to look at Jumpmaster Steve. "At what altitude is that?"

"Don't be a nervous Nellie," the jumpmaster said.

Dude-bro's friend shouldered his bud, keyed to talk over the channel. "Just remember, man. Fat chicks and fags do this all the time."

Candy set her jaw, stared out the window. Ever since she'd left the Orphan Program, she spent her time trying to find a charge. Anything to make her feel something besides the discomfort of her back, an itch that went beneath the skin all the way to the bone. At times it felt like she was composed of discomfort.

As Orphan V she'd been arguably the finest black-ops assassin at the DoD's disposal, worthy of being mentioned in a breath with Orphan X. She and X had a colorful and complex history, taking opposite paths to wind up in a version of the same place.

Out in the cold.

She'd briefly hooked up with an old associate in Frankfurt who was running skincare products in spas that surreptitiously extracted DNA from potential targets, but an Interpol raid had netted the associate, leaving Candy with too much time on her hands and little to do.

So she was here, chasing some kind of thrill, anything to throw a spark back into the dry tinder of her life.

"And make sure you're cautious jumping out," Jumpmaster Steve continued. "Fall flat, dumb, and happy, careful feet control, no backsliding. Got it, ladies? We don't want any midair tinkling."

The guys laughed, and Call Me Maddy and Sister McKenzie obliged with a titter, but Candy could see in their eyes that they felt demeaned.

Her phone hummed in her pocket. She pulled it out.

A text from *1-855-2-NOWHERE*.

It read, WANNA COME PLAY?

For the first time in a long time, she smiled. She unhooked her harness seat belt, flung the vinyl straps aside.

"Whoa, whoa, little lady," Jumpmaster Steve said, leaping up. "I haven't cleared us to —"

Candy flipped off her headset, strode over, and struck the red control button embedded in the skin of the craft. The side door started to open.

Wind whipped at them. Jumpmaster Steve was screaming at her, but mercifully his voice couldn't be heard. He moved to grab her, and she caught his arm, pronated the elbow, turned him around, and dumped him face-first back into his seat.

She stepped past the guys and young women ensconced in their designer jumpsuits and walked out the door, giving a little hop to launch her into a front flip. She corkscrewed twice for good measure and then caught the wind, rotating into a head-to-earth body position to speed her descent, arms at her sides, a rocket launched at the rising ground.

What a delightful feeling to have someplace to be.

58

A WHOLE OTHER KIND OF LONELINESS

After Evan knocked, he heard no noise inside the rented room at the top of the stairs and worried that Andre had split. Or worse. Evan had left Joey to coordinate with Orphan V for the time being while he locked down this side of the mission.

He knocked again, and then there was a shuffling noise within, the sound of a limb banging into something, a muffled expletive, and then Andre's wan face at the door, leached of human color. Charcoal-hued bags under his eyes, puffy with toxicity. His hair hangover-ruffled. His stubble had seemingly gained another full day's growth in the few hours since Evan had left him.

He had a potato chip stuck to his cheek, which he now groped for, peeled off, regarded, and then flicked away. He stank of rum and body odor, and Evan felt a vestigial flutter of repulsion, an old familiar urge to back away down the stairs and leave him to his lair.

But he ignored it.

And held steady, staring into the face of his half brother. He searched for any sign of himself in Andre's features, any hint of their shared blood, but Andre looked no more like Evan than any other boy from the Pride House Group Home. What a surreal twist of fate that bound them together in their DNA. Any thought of sharing this secret with Andre evaporated at the sight of him; some arcane rule Evan hadn't known to abide by prevented him from sharing what Veronica had not yet decided to share herself. Which was fine — it was all too much for Evan to comprehend right now, let alone convey.

"Why the hell are you back?" Andre said, snapping Evan from his trance. "I told you I —"

"You're right," Evan said. "I don't care about you like this. I care about who you could be. That's respect."

Andre's expression loosened, head lolling back on his neck, his eyes suddenly suffused with sadness. "I think I just need to sleep it off, be alone for a while."

"Your best thinking got you here," Evan said. "Time to try something else."

Andre thumbed crust from his eye. Stared

back through the doorway, leaning heavily on the knob, like it was holding him upright.

He staggered away from the door. He didn't get far before the metal bed frame hit him behind the thighs, forcing him to sit abruptly. He pinched at the bridge of his nose, literally hung his head.

When Andre spoke, his voice was cracked from dehydration. "I was good at drawing. 'Member that?" He looked up, his eyes bloodshot, weary. "Thought I could grow up, draw comics one day. Batman, right?"

"You were," Evan said. "You were good."

"I coulda been something, dunno . . . worthwhile."

"You still can be," Evan said. "Best two words in the English language: 'next time.' "

"If I figure it out. If I live that long. I been under the heel of this thing weeks now. All I feel is fear. At what it'll be like when they catch me."

"Fear needs a future," Evan said. "Let's focus on the present."

Andre spoke now in little more than a whisper. "Don't you feel it, too?"

"No," Evan said. "I just feel dread. I've been there enough times, at the point when it catches up. I've learned what it is."

"It worse than fear? Dread?"

"Not worse. But it's more awful. Because

it's my job to meet what's coming. Which means it's on me if I fail."

"How did you . . . how do you get there? Where you are?"

The question was so raw, so plaintive, that Evan took a moment to find a worthy answer. He looked down, studied the tips of his boots. "I was so goddamned scared of Van Sciver. He was so much . . . so much bigger than I was. So I covered it. And I covered it. Afraid you guys would see."

"See what?"

"Shame. At how afraid I was. How powerless. I had to prove I wasn't a coward. So I did. I faked it again and again. Until at some point I believed myself."

Andre made a thoughtful voice deep in his throat. "Maybe that's all bravery is."

"Maybe," Evan said. "And bravery comes in different guises."

"Like what?"

"Like standing up now, taking a shower, and getting to a meeting."

Andre blinked a few times quickly and shuddered off a chill. Then he rolled his head back on his neck and blew a breath at the ceiling that signaled not defeat but a different kind of giving up.

He rose.

The large church basement, toasty from an overzealous heating system, felt warm and cozy. High-set hopper windows, fogging up with a kind of holiday cheer, vibrated with the buzz of trapped flies. Cookies and coffee and a boxed cake on a table in the back. The scent of cigarettes rising from the clothes of the participants, who sat in folding chairs arrayed around a podium. A poster on the wall proclaimed DON'T PICK A FIGHT WITH REALITY, an aphorism Evan figured could make a good addition to the Commandments.

He'd driven a surveillance-detection route through the surrounding blocks before approaching the All Saints Catholic Church via an alley. He'd eased Andre to the meeting step by cautious step. The basement had stairs at both ends, providing good options for egress.

A woman in a pantsuit finished her story and said, "Would anyone else like to share?"

Andre stirred in his chair beside Evan and reluctantly rose.

He took the podium. "My name is Andre Duran, and I'm a alcoholic."

A chorus of gentle voices. "Hi, Andre."

546

"I'm about four hours sober," he said. "So I got that shit going for me."

A few chuckles. Evan looked around at the others, some of whom had shown themselves intimately over the past forty-five minutes. So much vulnerability, so little negative judgment, everyone in it together, all telling their own unique stories. Or he'd thought of them as unique, at least the first four or five, but as he'd sat here and watched person after person bare their soul, he realized that this very process of truth and sharing was the thing that made their stories not so horribly unique. Their courage bound them and allowed them to shuffle together into the light of whatever tomorrow might hold.

The flies beat themselves against the high windows, an oddly pleasing hum.

"I been under a lot of pressure," Andre said. "And I caved. Because, hey, what's better when you already got a ton of problems than adding a buncha self-inflicted ones, too?"

A lot of nods. Evan saw the wreckage in the faces around him. And some deep-seated wisdom as well.

"My first meeting, my sponsor told me, 'If God seems far away, who moved?'" Andre laughed. "I been crawlin' away for a long time. From my God, from my —" His voice caught. He pressed together his lips until they stopped trembling. "From my daughter."

He looked down at the podium as if there were notes he could refer to. "I remember two years back around this time. Sofia was . . . she was nine. I was strugglin' real bad. Paycheck going to the liquor store. Head in the bottle. All the other families around had their Christmas lights and decorations and all that shit that takes time and . . . I don't know, *care,* I guess. And there's this awful feeling at the back of your head that you're no longer just fuckin' up your own life but someone else's, someone too young to even make the choice or know what they're missing out on, but they are, and you know it, and that's a whole other kind of loneliness, and you can't help but have the sense that someone's watching you, not God really, but some other something, and that thing is never gonna forgive you even if she does. You're breakin' apart, but you try'na hold it together for the gifts, two Barbie dolls and a sweater three sizes too big, and my girl grateful for it, loving the toys that I stopped by Goodwill for the night before, that I wrapped with too much tape in leftover wrapping paper with cake and candles, and the kid is so grateful for the badly wrapped fucking Barbies you could just hate her for not knowin' she deserves better. But you don't. You hate *you.* And you see it in her eyes, how much you . . . you know, you're just *failing.* At being a adult."

Andre breathed wetly for a time.

"And instead of fighting that failure, insteada making it better, you give in to it." He caught himself. "*I* did. *I* gave in to it. I wallowed. I told myself all my pain entitled me to something. A break, right? Just a fucking break. And I haven't seen my baby in one year, five months, and sixteen days. And I don't know if I'm gonna have the chance to again."

He sobbed into the L of his thumb and forefinger for a time, and everyone let him.

They just let him.

Evan looked around in disbelief. All that patience and acceptance and quiet support on display, and Evan squirming in the face of it.

He forced himself to sit still in what he was feeling. To mirror the people around him with their prematurely lined faces, their breath heavy with coffee, clothes reeking of old cigarette smoke. He tried to see what they knew, what they'd learned.

The First Commandment: *Assume nothing.*

Including that Evan knew a damn thing about anything.

Andre saw in Evan all kinds of bravery. But sitting here in his folding chair, Evan saw only his deficits. To talk about his deepest shame and failings here in this arena was unthinkable. He'd imagined himself as a guiding light to Andre, drawing him toward some kind of wholeness. But he realized now that Andre had just as much to teach him, if he were only willing to pay attention.

And then Andre picked up his head. "But I'm gonna try 'n' do better. For myself and for her. I'm gonna try 'n' find grace again. Thank you."

Everyone clapped for him, and he nodded a few times and then caught Evan's eye, his playful smile suddenly, alarmingly familiar. "I want to invite my friend Evan up to share."

Dozens of sets of eyes lasered to Evan.

He felt all his goodwill toward Andre dissipate. In the windows the flies buzzed and buzzed. The scent of scorched coffee wafted from the rear table.

"No thanks," Evan said. "I'm good."

"Hey, man," Andre said, now warming to

a prankster's grin that Evan was simultaneously glad for and enraged by. "Denial is the first stage."

All the gazes around him were warm, accepting, which somehow made Evan feel even more exposed. The perceived threat made his training kick in, his senses revving to high. The cold metal of the chair beneath him. The dry warmth of the air. The symphony of the trapped flies.

One of the auditory notes had a vaguely jangling element to it, the faintest clink of metal against glass. Time slowed down, Andre and the others fading from consideration. Evan turned his head, looking over his shoulder at the hopper window to the side.

A fly at the window caught the ambient light from a passing car, giving off a metallic glint.

Evan's chair screeched on the tile; he'd risen abruptly.

He checked the front and back stairwells — doors still closed.

Quick strides to the window, plucking a saddlebag purse from the chair beside the pantsuited woman, everyone watching him in puzzlement. He rose on tiptoes and slammed the purse to the glass. A few flies buzzed free, but several fell against the sill.

He picked one up by a shiny glassine wing.
Carbon-fiber thorax, copper electrodes threaded through the membranous wings, tiny stamp of the Mimeticom *M* on the dorsal surface. And riding the front of the convex head, the pinpoint dot of a camera.

A surveillance drone.

Evan swung around. He had the full attention of the room. "Sorry," he said, handing the woman back her purse. "I hate flies."

Andre was on alert, all signs of joking gone.

The room, Evan imagined, had witnessed some odd displays like this. The attendees moved on without ceremony, grabbing their belongings and rising. Evan headed quickly to Andre, took him by the biceps, and pivoted to the front stairs.

Declan "the Gentleman" Gentner stood in the doorway, wearing a blue herringbone suit and a satisfied grin.

59
A BURST SEAM

As the others milled about in the wake of the meeting, they blocked Declan Gentner momentarily from view. Everyone oblivious, clustering in smaller groups, putting away the chairs or going for the exits.

Holding tight to Andre, Evan didn't want to draw his pistol and cause a stampede.

Keeping the crowd between them and Declan, Evan pivoted to the rear stairs — no sign of Queenie — and hustled Andre toward them.

Declan started forward, nodding a few hellos and slicing through the herd.

Evan reached the back stairwell, slung Andre behind him, and flung the door open hard enough to strike whoever might be lying in wait.

Empty.

Tugging Andre up the stairs, he let his other hand ride his holstered gun. Andre stumbled, caught his footing. "Is that . . .

that's them, right?"

Evan didn't answer.

They reached the top landing. Shoving Andre to the side, Evan shouldered through the door into the rear lobby.

A few after-hours workers lingered at the reception desk, Evan nearly drawing at the sight of them. Instead he turned back and beckoned Andre forward. He rushed out, panic-breathing, shallow jerks of the chest.

They jogged across to the rear door, ignoring the workers' greetings.

As they neared, the stairwell door behind them clicked open again, and Evan 180ed, expecting to see Declan emerging.

Instead an older guy with baggy eyes trickled out into sight, leading a stream of attendees.

Evan swung back around just as Andre, fueled by fear, pushed out through the back door. "No — *wait!*"

But Andre cleared the threshold into the alley before he registered Evan's voice and froze, framed for an instant just beyond the doorway.

A shape materialized at his side, an arm swinging upward at his chin, a fist topped with nine inches of carbon steel.

Evan lunged forward, the fingers of his right hand splayed, his arm supinated to guard Andre's face.

His forearm caught the fixed combat blade.

It impaled him, rising straight through the meat to the side of his radius, flesh and skin bowed off the bone like slit neoprene.

He'd stopped the tip of the blade inches from Andre's chin.

Queenie had released the knife in her surprise, and they stood there for a suspended moment, a trio just beyond the doorway.

She wore a red cold-shoulder shirt, circles of pale flesh showing at her deltoids. Aggressive scarlet lipstick, fitted jeans, red Converse shoes — like a vampire glowing in the semidarkness.

A pistol rode a holster on her right hip, but she hadn't reached for it; she'd wanted to get it done quietly in the alley.

Sound rushed back into Evan's head — Andre's screech of a gasp, the whisper of Queenie's arm against her ribs as she reached for her gun, the pounding of Evan's own heartbeat, shocked into high gear by the trauma.

His arm still extended before him, the blade improbably rising straight through his flesh. Blood hadn't flowed from the wound yet — the white connective tissue of the hypodermis peeled up like a burst seam.

He wouldn't reach his gun before she reached hers.

So he rotated his arm from the shoulder and swung the bar of his forearm at her neck, leading with the carbon steel point.

He couldn't manage much force, just a swipe of the impaled blade across the front of her throat.

It was enough.

Blood sheeted from the slit, dousing her neck, the top of her chest.

Her hands rose, fingers splayed against her breastbone as if showing off a necklace. She tried to look down, eyes straining to see the wound.

Her head rotated slowly back up, her mouth parting to release a funnel of bright arterial blood across her lips and down her chin.

She smiled languidly, mysteriously, and then her knees buckled and she slumped to the asphalt.

Evan grabbed Andre and ran.

60

THE OTHER HALF

Evan drove several exits along the freeway dripping into his lap before light-headedness caught up to him. He pulled the Ford pickup over onto the shoulder and looked at Andre, who was recoiled in his seat, still coming out of shock.

Evan spoke calmly. "I need you to get the first-aid trauma pack in the backseat."

It took a moment for the words to register, and then Andre snapped into motion, leaning into the rear of the cab. He unzipped the olive-drab backpack, laying bare the medic supplies. "Should we take the knife out?"

"No."

"What do you need?"

"Gauze, cohesive bandages."

"Cohesive . . . ?"

Evan chinned at the rolls of Coban. "There."

Andre handed them over.

The pain hadn't announced itself in full, not yet. A thin, high intensity was all Evan felt, paper-cut pain enhanced by several magnitudes, but the adrenaline was holding the deeper aching at bay. The knife had plunged in two-thirds to the hilt; the exposed edge showed the blade to be mercifully unserrated.

He laid gauze around the blade's entry and exit points and then wrapped his forearm tightly, biting off the bandage and smoothing it down so it clung to itself. The compression felt good. The bandage covered the point of union, turning blade and bone into one thing, a bound cross.

When he bent his elbow, pressure on the nerve sent a white-hot needle up through his shoulder into the side of his neck. Wincing, he reached across himself with his left hand and tried to tug the gearshift back into drive.

Before he could, his RoamZone gave its distinctive ring.

He answered to the sound of sobbing. There was a chilling quality to it, a person cracked open to the marrow, giving vent to more rage than grief. All at once it ended.

And then a voice, masculine but high-pitched, husky from crying. "I will take you apart bone by bone."

Evan said, "Okay."

"But I'll do it to Andre Duran first," Declan said. "You'll watch me every inch of the way so you'll know what's coming."

Evan said, "Okay."

"You have any idea what it's like? That kind of connection? When you have the same blood rushing through your veins?"

Evan glanced over at Andre, his thoughts flurrying. Eased out a breath through clenched teeth. "No."

"She was a part of me," Declan said. "My twin. You understand that? You killed half of me."

"Don't worry," Evan said. "I'll get to the other half soon enough."

He hung up. Sucked in a breath. Tried to relax his jaw.

His vision speckled, and he leaned his skull against the headrest and sipped a few breaths.

Andre said, "Need me to drive?"

Evan didn't want to nod, but he did.

He opened the door and half fell out onto his feet. The foreign object lodged in his arm felt like an insensate part of himself, a limb lost to anesthesia. He had to get it out as soon as possible.

He stumbled to the passenger side, passing Andre, vehicles flashing dangerously by.

He heard someone make a quiet grunt, realized it was him.

Andre took the wheel, looked over, said, "Where we going?"

Evan stared at the freeway sign ahead, realizing only now the direction he'd unknowingly steered them, his unconscious pointing the way.

He nodded through the windshield, and Andre stomped the gas, throwing gravel as they merged into traffic.

Veronica opened the door and gasped. She wore a gauzy white bathrobe over a pair of cream pajamas. The wind caught the fabric, setting her aflutter, more apparition than human.

She ushered them into the Bel Air mansion, the door's closing taking the life out of her clothing. Looking from Evan to Andre, she fastened a sash around her waist, settled into the calm of a person who'd known trauma well enough to persist lucidly in the face of it.

Evan's good arm was hooked around Andre's shoulder, but he was doing his best not to make him bear too much of his weight. Andre's gaze darted around at the water feature of the foyer floor, the high ceiling, the yippy dogs. Evan could only imagine what the house felt like to him.

Veronica stepped in to help Evan, Andre slumping his shoulder to slide him off for the transfer. The scent of lilac emanated from her. She led them back, vast rooms opening one after another like chambers in a castle. Andre kept the trauma backpack on and his eyes wide.

Veronica deposited them at a kitchen table the size of a barn door, banished the dogs up a hall, and returned. They sat around the table like a normal family were it not for the combat knife rammed through Evan's forearm.

He unwound the bandages, which peeled free with a wet crackle. When the gauze lifted from the incision, he finally felt the full measure of pain, a deep throbbing in the flesh.

Thanks to the sharpness of the combat knife, the wound was exceedingly neat, two inches on either side with minimal tearing. He set his arm on the table before him, centered like a meal. The intersecting blade looked ridiculous, a comedic prop. If it had split the radius and ulna, there'd be nerve and tendon damage aplenty, so he took a moment to be grateful for small mercies.

The surgical stapler, preloaded with thirty-five staples, came sealed in a plastic pouch.

It was office-supply white and looked like a robotic garden-hose nozzle. There was a bottle of alcohol.

This was going to suck.

Before he could brace himself, Andre stood up suddenly, wobbled a bit on his feet. "I don't . . . I'm not sure I can watch this."

"Go into the other room," Veronica said. "The last thing we need is you fainting and splitting your head open. I can help him."

Andre hesitated, taking in the sunken living room as if it frightened him. Maybe it did.

Evan looked at Veronica. "If you don't tell him, I will."

Her eyes flared, big behind her painted lashes. On the inhale the cords of her neck came clear. But she didn't flinch. She looked right back at Evan, and he could see in her face that she knew he was right, that it had to be dragged into the open.

"Tell me what?" Andre said.

But Veronica kept her eyes on Evan. For a final instant, they were sharing this, their secret, and something about that felt oddly intimate.

She tipped her head to Evan deferentially.

He cleared his throat. Blinked against the pain. "We're . . ." He couldn't say *brothers*.

"We have the same mom."

"What?" Andre said lightly. And then, "*What?* Wait, who?"

No sound but the hum of electricity feeding the oven.

"Me," Veronica said.

Andre coughed out a laugh. Eyes rolling and a touch wild. "Ms. Le— *Veronica?* Veronica is my mother?" A ragged inhalation. "And yours, too?"

Evan couldn't bring himself to say yes, so he nodded.

"Huh," Andre said. "Ain't that some shit. Ain't that some real . . ." And then it began to sink in, and he pawed at his mouth, eyes welling, and walked quietly into the next room.

Veronica and Evan sat in the silence, bound by this confusing bit of drama, a shared allegiance of some kind. It felt like closeness. Was this another facet of what it was to be family?

He felt a sudden rush of regard for Veronica. She'd calmly accepted the situation, unrattled and unflappable. She'd asked no questions, focused only on Evan's wellbeing. She'd passed no judgment on what had been brought to her door and seemed instead to be receptive, even appreciative for who Evan was in the face of what she'd launched him into. In her composure he felt a sort of acceptance that he hadn't known himself to crave. But he let her gaze warm him now.

And thought of the man in the other room, his half brother by blood.

Veronica's gaze moved to the doorway through which Andre had vanished.

He said, "Go."

"Your arm."

He looked down at the crosshatched handle scales of the knife. All he had to do was grip and extract. "I've managed worse. This is just pain. What he's feeling is something deeper."

"How do you know?"

"Because," he said, his voice threatening to crack, "I've felt it."

A half hour later, Veronica drifted back into the kitchen.

Evan's right forearm was tightly bound by cohesive bandages, triple-wrapped to form a flexible cast above the stapled incisions. He'd washed the knife and then, unsure what to do with it, placed it in the recycle bin.

The alcohol bottle sat empty on the table before him. He'd used it on the wound and then to wipe down the surface. He'd washed his hands, but still blood remained stuck in the seams of his knuckles.

"He okay?" Evan asked.

"Who the hell knows?" she said. "What a mess I've made of us all."

"Did you tell him the whole truth?"

"So help me God. I figured I owed him at least that." She adjusted her sash and kept on. "He's washing his face, and then you'll drive him back."

She moved in a daze past him to the countertop, fussed with her pill bottles, then clapped her palm to her mouth and swallowed them dry. She set her hands on the tile facing away, her shoulder blades bunched, her head lowered.

For a time she breathed, emotion seeming to move through her. It was as though Evan could see the events of the evening catch up to her and settle inside.

She finally turned back, her eyes ablaze with an inner light that he mistook for indignation.

She moved closer, and he saw it was something else, something primal, a mama-bear instinct that he'd seen a time or two in mothers he'd helped when their desperation turned to fury.

"He told me what they did," she said. "How they tracked you there. Tried to stab him in the throat. And that they want to . . . want to torture you both. There are more of them?"

Evan nodded.

"My son." She rested a hand on his cheek.

The words arrowed right through the center of him. She meant it now in full, she'd earned it, and in a manner of speaking he had, too. He couldn't find his voice, so he gave a nod.

"Are you as terrible as you say you are?"

"I can be," he said. "Yes."

Her eyes came alive, afire. She bent her head gently to kiss the back of his hand, and her lips came away faintly rouged with blood. She looked into his eyes, into the depths of who he was.

"Good," she said. "Kill every last one of them."

61
FAMILY

Evan finished duct-taping a bedsheet over the sole window in the tiny rented room. Andre sat quietly on his bed, hands folded calmly in his lap, and watched. Since that AA meeting, a peace had descended over him. None of his usual banter or fidgeting was on display, even after the news Veronica had dropped on him. In giving in he seemed to have located a kind of peace inside himself.

Evan thought about when he'd worked on Joey's shoulder, how it had been tender to the point of intolerability. It struck him that the same law of physics applied to any injury, physical or emotional. If you babied it, it stiffened even more, spreading the pain through you. But if you yielded, if you were willing to endure the white-hot agony of making vulnerable what you sought to protect, you had a shot at releasing it.

Evan turned around to face Andre. They'd

opened the window earlier to vent the stale air and tidied the place together. The groceries they'd picked up were stacked along one wall, the mini-fridge stuffed. The taped bedsheet blocked the nighttime lights of neighboring buildings, the only illumination now the sterile glow of a lamp in the corner.

"You need to stay inside," Evan said. "These next-gen drones can go window to window."

"I hear that."

"I'll come back when it's over. By Monday morning it'll be done one way or another. Promise me you won't leave this room."

"I promise."

"Promise me you won't drink."

Andre lifted his chin a touch higher. "I promise."

Evan turned for the door.

"Hey," Andre said. "We family?"

Evan paused. That sketch of Sofia stared at him from the wall, those beautifully rendered dark eyes. She was what to him? Some kind of niece? That was a question for another day.

He cleared his throat, breathed through the tension Andre's question brought up in him, tried to relax into it.

"I suppose so," he said.

"They say families are made," Andre said. "I don't know nothing about that," Evan said, realizing that the street cadence had crept once more into his voice. "But I'll be here if you need me."

"Yeah." Andre nodded. "Me, too."

62
YOUR DIRTY PARTS

Declan studied his naked image in the hotel bathroom. Each stomach muscle a distinct rectangle with four pronounced sides and something approximating right angles at the corners. His chest defined enough to catch shadow. His hair, still glistening from the shower, perfectly in place, not a single stray. Steam thickened the atmosphere of the room, fogging the edges of the mirror.

He walked into the hotel bedroom. The suits hung neatly in the wardrobe, a waterfall of luscious fabrics, some bought on Savile Row, others cut to perfection by a Hong Kong tailor. Everything outside him — flesh and muscle, cloth and leather — was as close to perfection as could be humanly managed.

And even so, all that armor barely held the chaos of his inner self in the shape of a person.

He'd cleaned out Queenie's room next

door, gathered her personals and dragged them in here. Her corpse was with the city coroner, and he would have to think long and hard about how to cut through the red tape without incriminating himself. To get to her body, his female self.

But right now only one reality mattered to him.

Killing the Nowhere Man.

On the mattress his phone rang, vibrating on the Four Seasons comforter.

He walked to it, the air cool against his bare body, and picked up. "She's dead."

His voice was low and sonorous, occupying the other space, the space of the him he hid from the world. He was embodied.

Even the doctor seemed to sense it, allowing a rare pause. "What does it feel like?" he asked.

Declan thought about it. "It's a kind of pain too deep to feel. So there's just numbness. And nothing left to care about. Which means I can do anything."

As the doctor's mouth cracked open, a faint puff of air came over the line, something well shy of a moan. "That's how I feel," he said. "All the time."

His voice was hushed, perhaps with awe. Maybe even something approaching empathy. But when he spoke again, it sounded flat once more, the humanity compressed out of it. "I'm delivering the drones tomorrow at midnight. Skeleton crew at the base means fewer eyes, fewer questions, fewer protocols. I'm using my personal team of contractors for maximum oversight."

"Because the last team did so well at the impound lot." Declan's voice, when deep, carried a different kind of authority. He wasn't afraid to let out his anger, his judgment, in full. In the fullness there was a sort of calm.

Now he could practically hear the doctor thinking about the slight to his team and deciding not to challenge it.

Instead he said, "That's why I'd like you there. Keeping an eye on the transport from afar. In case anything unexpected happens."

"I will be the only unexpected thing from here on out," Declan said, and hung up.

He got into bed, his exhaustion pasting him to the mattress. He felt all the points of his body where it touched the sheets — heels, calves, lower back, shoulder blades, base of his skull.

Before he could dread the coming darkness, he was asleep.

Three minutes or three hours later, he awoke into half consciousness.

His body locked down, tendons pulled

piano-wire taut. Even his Achilles tendon ached, his feet flexed painfully, cramps knotting the arches.

Lungs wouldn't release. Head couldn't turn. Just his eyes moving to the door.

Sure enough, there came the scrape against the wood.

Still alive, still alive.

His chest turned concave, unwilling to stretch and afford air.

The clawlike slash of fingernails flaking the paint. The door bowing inward, into his psyche itself. Then the latch released and swung inward to reveal that feminine silhouette. The long, long nails candy-apple red, the light moving through them from behind to put ten glowing points at the ends of her hands.

His heartbeat pounded out a distress signal: *Still alive, still alive.*

Now she was bedside, transported in the blink of an eye.

He'd kicked down the sheets in his sleep, the pillow cold with dried sweat beneath his neck. He wanted to scream to wake up his sister, but there was no voice.

And there was no sister.

The head cocked, that stylish bob bobbing. *I will punish your dirty parts out of you. You will learn.*

The quivering flesh of his arms, his neck, his inner thighs bare to the dead of night, bare to her to teach them what she needed to.

His mouth lurched for air, just a sip to get out the word, the tracks in his brain laid down to produce the only two syllables he'd known in his whole miserable life that could bring comfort.

Queenie.

The loss came again, fresh as a slit to the throat.

His mother leaned over his paralyzed body. Those fingernails fluttered, choosing their spot.

He had no one to help him and an eternity to morning.

63
THE MOST AWFUL THING

In the not unlikely event that he got killed, Evan hadn't made a contingency plan for Andre. So — at the end of this never-ending night — he'd reversed course to the one person who would need to step up.

He paused on the footbridge in the front yard, watching the sleeping swans bob on the placid moat. He'd spoken to Joey on the drive back to Bel Air. She was all over mission planning, interfacing with Tommy and Orphan V, laying the groundwork for the plan Evan had hatched. He could see her extraordinariness only when he considered the fullness of who she was, not just the shape of who he wanted her to be.

He wondered if that was what Veronica had arrived at with him, when she'd sat gazing across the kitchen table at his impaled arm, her face evincing total acceptance. When she'd placed her hand on his cheek, looked into him, and released him to do what it was that he did, she'd seen *him* for the first time, not the image of who she hoped him to be.

Simple as it sounded, perhaps that was what love really was.

What a lacking word, rife with clichés and misconceptions. It was so much more than what people talked about, with a depth that might accommodate even the darkness of his own soul.

There was no answer to his knock, not even from the dogs. He tried the front door and found it unlocked.

Worried, he moved inside. The dogs scampered to him but did not bark. They sniffed at his boots as he crossed the concrete stepping-stones. Seemingly contented, they bunched at his feet as he entered the kitchen, the living room.

Veronica lay on the giant white swoop of the couch, passed out, a handle of Tanqueray resting on the table before her. A crystal tumbler was tipped onto its side in a tiny puddle of melted ice.

No sign of the majordomo; perhaps he was off for the night. The dogs looked up at Evan, concerned. He crouched and petted their ratty little heads, and they licked his fingertips with rough tongues before scurrying off to curl up together in a corduroy disk of a dog bed by the bar.

He stepped down onto the lush carpet and approached Veronica. Her pajama top was hoisted slightly to show a band of her belly, which looked distended. Her face had an unhealthy pallor, jaundiced and sickly. Her breath whistled. He wondered again at her seemingly rapid deterioration. Was it because he was only now seeing her unvarnished? Or was it the haze of his own perception continuing to clear?

She blinked her eyes open lazily as he approached, and she reached for him, her fingers pale and thin. "Evan." Tears beaded at the corners of her eyes, then dotted her temples. She tried to hoist herself up but couldn't find the strength. Her words came in a slur. "What're you doin' back?"

"We have to talk about the next steps for Andre. If something happens to me —"

"I couldn't bear it," she said. "If something happened to you."

He reached for the tumbler and set it upright. "You can't keep drinking like this," he said. "It'll kill you."

She produced a tease of a grin and stretched while barely moving, an elegant twist of her spine. "I'm already dead, Evan."

"What does that mean?"

She sat up too rapidly, and her face yellowed even more with nausea. She lifted a trembling palm to her forehead, and then her pupils pulled north and she fell back against the cushions, seizing. She contorted, arched up onto the points of her shoulders, her mouth a twisted maw.

He shot around the coffee table and cradled her with his good arm, turning her head to one side to keep her windpipe clear. As quickly as it started, the seizure ended.

He held her and she breathed into his chest irregularly, one hand clawed in the fabric of his shirt.

"You okay?"

She nodded faintly, her hair rustling against him. "Happens sometimes. Just need . . . rest."

He adjusted her back into the couch, doing his best to keep pressure off his wrapped right forearm. She felt frail, light as a bird.

He laid her head gingerly on a throw pillow, and she was asleep.

He drew himself up and walked over to the kitchen counter, where she'd moved her pill bottles.

He found the rifaximin once more, the antibiotic he thought she'd taken for traveler's stomach, though it had numerous uses. Next to it the vitamin C, calcium, a bottle labeled furosemide, and several more.

With mounting dread he started tapping the names into his RoamZone, searching through medical websites, those graveyards of hope. At last he had enough overlaps to narrow the noose around a diagnosis.

"*. . . used in the treatment of chronic hepatic encephalopathy, a syndrome observed in patients with cirrhosis of the liver.*"

Scar tissue clogging her liver from excessive alcohol consumption.

And there were the symptoms. Wasted muscle in the arms, bloating in the stomach, jaundice, weight loss, fatigue, concentration and memory problems.

The prognosis was grim, the survival rate even lower in patients who continued to drink. Seizures were rare, often occurring only at the acute end stages.

I'm already dead, Evan.

Grief moved through him, pure and immediate. They had come so far to finally see each other with clear eyes. And now to lose her before anything could be built on the foundation they had imperfectly begun to lay seemed profoundly wrong, a joke from the universe itself.

He wasn't sure how long he stood there at the counter, but when he finally moved, his legs had almost fallen asleep. He found a blanket in a guest room and draped it over her.

She moved as the fringe touched her chin, opened her eyes. She stared up at him, and he stared back, and at least they had this, a few moments as fragile as the surface of a still lake.

She finally spoke, breaking the surface tension. "We all know it's near, but you never think it's right around the bend. The ski accident, the yielding cough — it's out there, sure. Your first friend dies, the end of an era. And then come your forties, the decade of breast cancer, heart attacks. Then the fifties, a few acquaintances felled by strokes. You're not ready to lose your friends yet, let alone be the one who drops, but it happens. Then the next decade . . ." She paused to catch her breath. "And now I'll be another cautionary tale, the name people lower their voices to mention when they speak over dinner tables. Veronica LeGrande, did you hear? She died a drunk."

She reached out and took his hand, her skin papery and thin. "I spent so much time trying to numb what I'd done that I lost all the time to set it right."

"Set what right?"

"What do you think, sweet boy?"

His face grew hot.

"I don't have any wailing angels or pitch-forked demons to concern myself with," she said. "No reordering of a will, no woe-is-me final trip through the south of France or the Italian Riviera or wherever the hell people spend their lifetimes wanting to go. Just this. Just you. And him."

"That's why you found me now? Because you knew . . ."

He couldn't get out the words.

"My whole life was a straight line running away from you. And Andre. We all have the story we tell, the tape that loops in our mind. Mine was that if I looked it in the face —" She stopped herself. "You. If I looked *you* in the face, I would crumble into dust from shame."

"But you didn't," he said quietly.

She shook her head, wiped her eyes. "No. But what about you? What about the waste-land I consigned you to? What did that do to you?"

He felt a pressure beneath his eyes, his voice full of gravel. "I was a small kid. Powerless. So I made a vow to do so well, to be so tough, so perfect, that I would be invulnerable. That I would no longer have to feel human. I put my mind to it second after second, year after year. And the most awful thing happened."

"What's that?"

"I succeeded."

She stared at him breathlessly. He felt breathless, too.

"But now maybe I have a chance to undo that," he said. "Because of you. Because of Andre."

And Joey.

And Mia.

And Peter.

She reached again for his cheek, and in the soft pressure of her palm and the boundless hazel of her eyes he felt something he never had before. A maternal warmth with a depth and breadth and reach like nothing he'd encountered. It was dizzying, terrifying in its scope, like staring at the night sky pinpricked with countless other worlds.

"Jacob," she whispered. "Your middle name. Evan Jacob."

He could never have anticipated the rush of emotion that brought into his chest, crowding his throat.

"One more piece," she said. "Let that be one more piece toward making you whole."

64
WEAR THE BROWN PANTS

They staged the raid from a shooting range north of Vegas at the end of a winding dirt road that led up into a seascape of moonlit dunes. Evan and Joey arrived an hour past dusk and sat on the hood of his truck in the dusty darkness, the air flavored with chaparral and sage and the allergenic scent of hay from the bales that served as backstops. The moon was thin but fierce, casting a pale glow through a cloudless sky, making the shell casings gleam like treasure. Shredded paper targets snapped in the breeze. Somewhere a coyote howled, the plaintive cry joined by another and another and another, the pack zeroing in on its prey.

Tommy was next to show his face, the piercing eyes of his headlights rumbling into view, climbing the switchbacks of the dunes. His dually truck drifted toward them and parked nose to nose with Evan's F-150.

Tommy emerged with a grunt, the earth

jogging those old warhorse joints, and he circled to sit on his own trunk, for once not offering any sage Tommyisms.

They sat in the quiet, listened to the wind. It blew invisible specks of rain across Evan's face, and for a moment the world seemed vast and peaceful and full of hope. But the awful responsibility of what was to come tightened his chest, reminded him that every breath was on borrowed time and fate could decide when she'd had enough with a snap of her fingers. Jake Hargreave had set this all in motion. One drone pilot trying to whistle-blow on a $500-million program for UAVs with their own programmed ethical adapters. A solitary man standing against a totalitarian future.

"Beautiful here," Tommy said. "Could almost make you think there's still some sense in the world."

Wasn't that how it always began? They heard the next vehicle before they saw it, an engine growling, big tires crunching over rock and mashing through mud. No head-lights.

Tommy stiffened, but Evan said, "She's with me."

A shadowy truck neared, revealing itself to be an old Jeep Wrangler. It parked with its grille to their grilles, their vehicles forming a trefoil like a three-leaf clover, a Gothic church floorplan, a hazard symbol. The door swung open.

Candy McClure slid out.

Evan heard Tommy take a sharp inhale at the sight of her.

Orphan V was something to behold. Not just her looks — which were considerable — nor her body — which was a poetic blend of curve and muscle — but the energy she conveyed with every movement, an unspoken vibe that said she was the fullest version of herself, that she was possessed with all the composure and murderous skill the world had to offer, and that her presence before you was a privilege. That she was sparing you from her terrible, terrible powers, and if you could countenance her company with grace, she might add a drop of her potency to yours.

She winked at Evan and hoisted herself onto her trunk, sat cross-legged, and stared at them. She wore slouchy boots and a fuzzy sweater off one shoulder. Her hair had grown, falling well below the firm line of her chin, and she'd tousled it out a bit in keeping with the 1980s dream-girl vibe. Her eyes had that predatory gleam that made you want to curl up in surrender just to get it over with.

"Well," Evan said, "that's all of us, then."

Candy lifted her chin, anointing him with her attention. "What happened to your arm?"

"I ran into a combat knife."

She tsk-tsked. "Careless."

Tommy couldn't take his eyes off Candy. "We gonna do this, then? Or jaw around with fancy talk?"

Joey reached behind her to her backpack and tugged out her laptop. "Transport's due to arrive at Creech North at midnight. A team of private contractors is providing security for delivery."

"Why not real army?" Candy asked.

Evan thought back to the team Molleken had dispatched to the impound lot to clean the scene. They'd been ready to kill not just their targets but any witnesses or first responders as well. "Because these guys don't have any ROEs," he said. "They're mercs ready to execute whoever gets in their way. Until these drones are delivered to the base, the hidden kill order is executed, and Andre and I are neutralized, Molleken is taking no chances."

"Will he be on site?" Tommy asked.

"Yes," Joey said. "Internal comms make clear he's overseeing it personally."

"The doctor goes down," Evan said. "And

his privately hired mercenaries. But not a single soldier."

Candy wiggled her shoulders forward in a manner that seemed flirtatious; it took Evan a moment to realize she was pulling the fabric tight across her back to soothe the itching burn scars. "What if one of them looks at me funny?" she said.

"You'll show restraint."

"Hmm." She licked her lips, considered. "Not my strong suit."

"Base is closed," Evan said. "Sunday-night crew is the leanest — essential personnel only. That's why we're doing this tonight. The timing is best for them to make a low-profile delivery, which also means it's my best shot to get inside."

"I have access to the Creech North network," Joey said, "but I can't remove the kill order for Andre Duran remotely. Altering any kill orders requires hardware-authentication tokens." Joey dug in her pocket, removed a pluglike electronic device. "This is a Yubico FIDO2 — a hardware access device I preloaded with the stolen system-authentication keys."

"We know what it is, girl," Candy said.

"I gotta teach to the lowest common denominator." Joey tilted her head at Evan. "Once this is plugged in to a networked computer, this trigger has to be tapped." Tilting the Yubico key to catch the glow from the headlights, she indicated a depressed button on top. "Once that's done, it'll perform the authentication. Then it's simple. Pop in your run-of-the-mill Hak5 USB Rubber Ducky to inject code and wipe out the kill order on Andre Duran."

"That's pretty styley," Tommy said.

Joey shrugged, her face coloring slightly. "Hacking is my love language." She continued, "The good news? Creech North is like a smart city. Tons of interconnected devices, including surveillance cameras, security access doors, even wireless smart Hue lamps. All that stuff has vulnerabilities in their wireless stack that let me deliver an infected payload via a forced over-the-air firmware update that puts control via a backdoor in my hands."

Tommy tugged at his biker mustache. "Like a video game."

"That's right." Joey hoisted the laptop. "And this is my joystick. But the next-gen drones coming in tonight? Uh-uh. Those things are lethal, walled off from anything else once they get their marching orders." She turned her gaze to Evan, and for the first time he sensed worry in her face. "If they lock onto you, you're done."

"Well, not *entirely.*" Tommy slid off his hood, walked around, and fussed in the back of his truck. He came back with a Pelican case in one hand and in the other a massive fat olive-drab gun with DRONE-WRECKER stenciled on its side. "This is a little prototype I been playing around with."

"Dronewrecker," Joey said. "Who named it *that?*"

"I did." Tommy looked affronted but managed to regain his composure. " 'Cuz it is. I brimmed it up with soft-kill countermeasures. Drones zero in on a target using electro-optical and infrared sensors. This bad boy throws off laser dazzle to overwhelm the EO sensor and blind the drones. Big ol' flare like shining a flashlight into NVGs."

Evan thought back to the impound lot when he'd done precisely that to the private military contractor wearing night-vision headgear.

"At the same time, it projects a diffuse wave of heat that'll confuse the infrared sensors, throw 'em off your thermal signature, buy you a little time. And you got smoke, too, for backup here." Tommy tilted the Dronewrecker to show off a red button, then regarded the weapon with pride. "It's also a prototype, which means it ain't in

589

any of the weapons databases, so the drones can't recognize it and identify it as a threat. Till you use it. Then you'd better hold on to your ass."

He handed the weapon to Evan. Longer than two feet, weighing less than ten pounds, it resembled a science-fiction ray gun.

"And for the lady . . ." Tommy slung the Pelican case onto his trunk and unlocked it to reveal a rugged silver device about the size of a tennis-ball can. "This is a portable electromagnetic-pulse weapon. You're gonna need to get inside the hardened concrete walls of the front guard station — according to Hacky Sue over here, that's the nerve center for perimeter security." He pointed to a switch at the base of the device. "Activate it by pulling this pin. It'll fire a burst of high-powered microwaves that'll knock out the whole goddamned perimeter, access gates, surveillance cams, and all. Everything electronic, toasted. It's got limited range and takes about ten minutes to recharge, so don't use it until you mean it. You'll just need to figure out how to get in position."

"I'm sure I'll figure something out," Candy said. "Will you be on site?"

"Hell no," Tommy said. "I ain't raiding no military base. Hell, I probably sold 'em half the gear they're gonna be looking to train on your sorry asses."

Candy's eyes found Joey. "How about you?"

"She's a minor," Evan said. "She's staying right here with her laptops. She can handle everything remotely."

"It's my fate," Joey said. "Behind every man are badass women doing all the work."

"I heard a rumor that someone's looking to retire," Candy said. "Maybe us badass women should lead the charge after this outing."

"I keep suggesting that," Joey said. "But shockingly, he doesn't listen."

Tommy stroked his biker mustache and shot a jet of tobacco juice out through the gap between his front teeth, enough to make a tapping sound when it hit the dirt. "Ain't enough bourbon in my house for me to understand the lengths you all go to to help folks who don't pay you a red cent." He side-eyed Evan. "That was a hint."

Evan pulled three tight rolls of hundreds from his cargo pocket and handed them over to Tommy. Tommy thumbed one of the edges, breathing in the scent of money. Then he started to lumber back to his driver's seat. He paused. Then swung back around, leaning on his side mirror to look at Evan.

His baggy eyes held concern, though he was never one to give voice to softer emotions. He started to say something, thought better of it, spit again, and cursed softly at the wind.

"I'll be okay," Evan said.

Beyond the dunes the coyotes were at it again, singing their death song.

"Wear the brown pants," Tommy said, turning away once more. "You're gonna need 'em."

65
DARKER DARKNESS

Evan steered the Honda Civic over the bumpy dirt road through the ruinous landscape of the Nevada National Security Site, the night sky thick enough to hide the recce drones. Joey had made clear she could manipulate the surveillance feeds through a signals intercept, erasing Evan's vehicle and heat signature. She'd yet to make a boast she'd been unable to back up; even so, as he neared the base, his back prickled with sweat when he thought about the invisible firepower drifting overhead.

At last the solid perimeter fence of Creech North came visible in the night, a seam of darker darkness.

He gave the front security gate a wide berth, peeling off down a side road. Signs at regular intervals urged EXERCISE EXTREME CAUTION. STAY ON THE ROAD. Having seen the rabbit disassembled by a land mine on his last visit, Evan minded the instructions.

He had his radio earpiece in, bone-conduction technology that sent and received audio signals through the walls of the skull, bypassing the outer ear and leaving it open to sounds in the immediate environment. He shared an encrypted channel with Joey and Candy.

Joey had used one of Creech North's own surveillance drones to watch Molleken's delivery arrive — two SUVs with tinted windows bookending a black box truck. The convoy had arrived five minutes ago, drifting into the compound easily and driving to the central lab building Evan had infiltrated yesterday. She'd zoomed in with night vision, close enough to identify their weapons, and sent the images to Evan's RoamZone. Just like the crew sent to take out Andre at the impound lot, the six contractors wore dark polo shirts and carried MP5s and Browning Hi-Power clones. But conducting semilegitimate business here, they'd forgone the black Polartec masks. Nonetheless, they'd be easy enough to differentiate from whatever base personnel remained.

Careful to hold to the road, he pulled near one of the rear gates. There was no guard station here, just a massive solid steel gate braced by concrete barriers.

He stopped in the middle of the road,

killed the engine and then his lights. He'd have a few minutes before someone spotted him and came to ask questions.

He hoped that was enough time for Candy.

The Jeep careened up to the checkpoint, windows down, country music blaring, Chely Wright singing about a single white female lookin' for that special lover.

Two MPs manned the station, one emerging swiftly, M4 carbine at the ready, giving the driver vigorous hand signals to stop. The Wrangler skidded to a halt, and Candy spilled out, a weighty tote bag swinging from her elbow. "Goddamn it, I'm all turned around. I'm supposed to meet the girls for a bachelorette party at Caesar's Palace, and my GPS says the Strip's no more than an hour from here, but it keeps glitching."

"Ma'am, please back up." He wore the navy-blue beret, sage-green combat boots, and the Airman Battle Uniform with slate-blue incorporated into the camo design. The embroidered name tape read MOORE. Shoulders pinned back in rail-straight posture, dimples in his cheeks, wide jaw. He looked good and liked looking good, and she would use that vanity to crush him.

She'd left the door open, the radio wailing, *She just might be your dream come true.*

"Goddamn it, it's hot for December." She took a wide stance, her stockinged legs shapely above the boots, hips cocked to one side, and lifted the hair from the base of her neck with both hands, a gesture that pushed her chest out and upward.

Moore's focus moved where she knew it would, and she stepped forward again, letting her hips swing, her body transformed into a hypnotist's pocket watch. The second MP came out from the guard station because — how could he not? — and said, "Ma'am, this is a classified base. You can't —"

She pretended to trip, tumbling forward into Moore, her chest pressed to his, her face in his shoulder. Surprised, he caught her under her arms, the M4 sandwiched between them.

A quick glance past him showed the guard station's door open, the monitors providing a panoramic view of the base perimeter, all that hardware safely ensconced behind the concrete-slab walls.

She giggled — "My gosh, thank you" — untangling but keeping his right arm, clutching it at the triceps so it pulled straight, the elbow locking, her forearm flexing the joint the wrong way. The second MP was stepping closer, and she brought her cheek to Moore's, whispered, "I'm sorry," and dislocated the shoulder. As he fell, she stripped the M4 from him, guiding the sling neatly over his head and torso, and wound up holding the carbine aimed directly at the other man's chest.

Her purse remained slung over her shoulder, tight against her hip.

It held a gaggle of zip ties and the portable EMP weapon.

Moore curled at her feet. To his credit he neither cried nor reached for his backup pistol, but he was breathing hard enough to stir the dirt beneath his mouth.

The MP in front of her kept his arms raised like a good little boy, gloved fingers spread.

"Well," Candy said with a wink, "aren't you gonna invite me in?"

Evan felt the movement in the ground first, a deep rumble rising through the worn tires of the Honda Civic, and then the rear access gate parted.

He drove onto the base.

Abundant testing fields lay ahead, resting for another day. They were sleek from a recent rain, moonlight shining through silver puddles, seeming to bore into the earth itself. Carving through them, he clung to a narrow dirt path worn down with Humvee tracks. No signs of life. Eventually hangars rolled past him on either side like barns rising from farmland. A trio of MQ-9 Reapers slumbered beneath a steel overhang, $50 million taking a break. Light tactical vehicles were lined like dominoes in several outdoor parking zones, waiting for war games.

The base was light on personnel as promised, ghost-town desolate. The security breach, which would present as a power-grid glitch, hadn't roused anyone yet.

He continued along the wagon-wheel spoke toward the center of the base, where the collection of buildings constituting headquarters were arrayed. Finally a few signs of life — a lone truck rattling toward the perimeter, two airmen halted on the street talking into their phones.

Evan waved. They waved back.

The disk of the lab building loomed ahead, its shiny black doors presenting a unified front. The Mimeticom box truck and dueling SUVs were parked at a slant in front, and he pulled in next to them and hopped out.

In case Joey wasn't watching, he said sotto

voce, "Now."

As he mounted the stairs, the door buzzed open. He entered.

The outside corridor was dark and desolate, but the massive lab below threw sterile light up through the interior windows. He peeked down, spotting the private contractors way below in the distant rear of the lab, mostly blocked from view by a metal contraption the size of two soccer goals but filled in with various layers. He could barely make out their movement through the slats.

He counted five forms back there — no, six. Assuming that was the full transport team, where was Molleken? Evan scanned the space, found the OpsCenter at the dead middle of the lab. That's where he'd have to insert the Yubico key and the Hak5 USB Rubber Ducky.

He pulled back to avoid being seen, walking along the curved corridor to the elevators, the wall lights turning on as Joey illuminated his way.

The sensor pad blinked green before he could touch it, summoning the elevator.

The front doors banged open behind him, two MPs moving inside. The beefy one spotted him. "Hey!"

Evan turned as they jogged toward him and waved them to hurry. "Move it! The base perimeter's been compromised. We gotta alert the transport team."

The MPs arrived as the elevator dinged open. "Who are you?"

"I'm an engineer in the microdrone division." Evan stepped onto the car. "Come on, come on."

The MPs entered and stood on either side of him, close enough that their shoulders brushed. The big guy breathed down at him from the right. "Microdrone division?"

Evan stared straight ahead, the elevator descending, taking him ever closer to a half dozen armed adversaries.

"That's right."

A third of the way down now, the lab floor drawing ever nearer. He thought about the stapled gash in his right arm, carefully wrapped beneath his long-sleeved shirt but still vulnerable. Anything he did from here on out, he'd have to be careful not to tear flesh through metal.

A radio gave with a bit of static, and the MP on Evan's left turned up the volume. "— *repeat: We have a breach. Any uncredentialed personnel should be detained and questioned. Copy, Tanner?*"

Evan sensed the men's faces swivel to him from either side.

He took a swift step back, setting his

braced ankle outside the big guy's foot, palming the side of his head, and accelerating it into the wall as he tripped him. The guy's ear slammed into metal, and he crumpled.

To Evan's left, Tanner had almost cleared leather with his SIG Sauer, but Evan grabbed it and yanked it the rest of the way out, goosenecking the wrist. He twisted the sidearm free, dropped the mag, jacked the slide to send the chambered round spinning, and emptied the rounds with fifteen quick flicks of his thumb.

Mouth gaping, Tanner stood watching the brass rain down on the tips of his boots.

The SIG spun in Evan's hands as he disassembled it, the pieces dropping, a two-second breakdown. Keeping the slide, he asked politely, "May I cuff you to the railing?"

Tanner nodded.

Evan dug a flex cuff from a cargo pocket, zipped it around the MP's wrist and the handrail. He did the same for the big guy, who was still unconscious, then plucked up his pistol. As Evan's hands took the second SIG apart in similar fashion, he looked over at Tanner, who'd recoiled against the wall.

"He's had a pretty bad concussion, but he'll be okay."

Tanner nodded, his eyes wide.

The doors opened, and Evan smacked the emergency stop button to stall the car. "I'm gonna have you guys wait here a sec," he said, dropping the SIG Sauer slides and the men's radios through the dark gap between the elevator and the lowest floor. "You're gonna want to stay quiet. I'm not the bad guy here."

Tanner nodded once more, his Adam's apple jerking in his throat.

Evan drew his ARES and stepped out onto the lab floor.

It was football-field vast, the sight lines blocked by benches, walls, and workstations. Cautiously he picked his way through a labyrinth of test gear toward the OpsCenter and the crew of mercenaries beyond.

ARES 1911 drawn, pistol tucked close to his chest in a two-handed retention position, finger indexed on the frame, not the trigger, thumb on top of the safety — precautions to avoid shooting someone who didn't need shooting, like a wayward engineer. The Tenth Commandment: *Never let an innocent die.*

Once he acquired visual on the threat and decided to deliver projectiles, he needed less than one-tenth of a second to disengage the safety and pull the trigger. He preferred a heavier press, 4.5 pounds with a little creep, which gave him more travel once he took up the mechanical slack in the trigger. So much precision training, so many minuscule adjustments to make sure he was operating as close to perfection as was humanly possible.

Voices carried back to him. The clanking of gear. He crept forward through the maze of workstations, pulse pounding, eyes darting from threat area to threat area. Jack's voice whispered in his ear, a mantra of competence: *Off target, off trigger. On target, on trigger.*

A long table strewn with disassembled motor parts. A pallet of propellers. Two soldering benches. A pony wall built of stacked electronics crates. The gasoline stink of epoxy glue.

Finally he reached the OpsCenter. Crouching to keep his head low, inching toward the nearest hardware tower.

Now the voices were louder.

"— first swarm, quick and quiet, before any oversight —"

"— cannot memorialize this launch in any way —"

"— hang on, hang on, need to fire them up —"

A rumbling filled the air, and Evan flat-

603

tened to the floor, taking a moment to realize that the sound was coming from the building itself. Way, way above, the ceiling irised open in the center, a growing spot of night sky blooming.

A flight path up and out.

Evan shouldered to the edge of a desk and peered around the corner.

Now he had a clear view of the giant contraption they'd been readying, and the sight of it stole his breath. He took it in, disbelief rolling through him.

It was wider and taller than unrolled gymnasium bleachers, but each step was as narrow as the slat of a venetian blind. A massive swarm of dragonflies perched on the slats, filling the entirety of the bleachers. These were the drones that Molleken had threatened him with in the battle lab, the glowing eyes that had risen before him in the darkness like a wall of menace.

The next-gen dragonflies were a more wicked-looking design than the one that had killed Jake Hargreave. Needlelike stilettos protruded from their faces, gleaming menacingly. In addition, each had a square box strapped to its thorax.

A bigger version of the backpack worn by the robotic bee that had blown a hole straight through the head of a mannequin.

Explosives.

At the base of the shelving unit, a jumble of empty rugged black Seahorse crates with the Mimeticom *M* emblazoned on their sides had been discarded. They were wheeled, their twist-lock latches released to show the scored charcoal foam inside.

Several of the contractors unpacked the dragonflies from the last crate, setting them equally spaced on the top slat of the shelving unit. The swarm was nearly assembled.

One of the men stared at someone out of Evan's view behind the head-high server racks. "Hey, Doctor, are you ready to set 'em loose?"

Brendan Molleken stepped into sight, palm-heeled a button on the control panel, and a thousand yellow-green eyes glowed to life on the bleachers.

66
A NIGHTMARE SYMPHONY

A menacing hum filled the air, rising in pitch, the predatory howl of the swarm. Evan ducked back behind the desk, breathing hard, digging for the gear in his pocket.

The humming intensified. The Yubico key was slippery in Evan's hand. He slid it into the port of the nearest hardware tower and tapped the trigger. The screen lit up. Authentication granted.

He already had the Hak5 USB Rubber Ducky set to go. He jammed it home.

Code whipped across the screen, a progress bar filling segment by excruciating segment as the hacked code uploaded.

Molleken's voice carried to him. "Target: Andre Duran."

A gruff voice, one of the hired guns. "Check."

Molleken said, "Set to locate and destroy."

"Should we widen target parameters to include any witnesses?"

"Yes," Molleken said. "Loosen collateral-damage restrictions on the ethical adapter. We'll need to cover our tracks on that front. Leave no trace of the temporary adjustment."

The progress bar was half filled.

Evan brought his nose within inches of the monitor, urging it to hurry.

Now two-thirds.

It reached the last bit and stalled.

Squatting at the desk to keep his head low, Evan glared at the screen.

Molleken's voice came once again. "Initiate encrypted kill-order sequence."

"Check. We are cleared hot to launch."

Evan's jaw clenched, a nerve line burning in the side of his neck.

The progress bar clicked to completion and vanished.

The humming decreased and then quieted.

Molleken said, "What the hell happened?"

Only then did Evan's muscles untense. Air eased through his teeth, his jaw letting go, like he was deflating with relief.

The gruff voice: "I don't know. Looks like the encrypted kill order has been wiped."

"Wiped?" Molleken said. "How is that possible?"

Evan braced his legs, readied his ARES.

"Looks like . . . looks like a zero-day vuln bashed the system."

"A zero-day attack? For Andre Duran? Who the fuck *is* this guy?"

Evan rose and spun around the corner into sight. All six men in view before the bleachers. Visual acquisition, safety off, finger taking the slack out of the trigger — *on target, on trigger.*

His voice came loud and clear. "He's my brother."

All six heads swiveled to take him in.

Time slowed to a virtual stop as it always did when he was locked in.

Evan sensed Molleken diving behind the server racks, the other men reaching for their sidearms, everything happening with painful slowness.

He swung the sights in a smooth ninety-degree arc right to left to encompass all five heads, not even slowing as he delivered shots at sporadic intervals. Jack's voice spoke in his ear, countless hours of coaching branded on his prefrontal cortex: *Front sight, clean press, reset trigger, front sight, clean press, reset trigger . . .*

For a moment everything remained as it was, the five mercs standing there, guns in hand, not yet aware that they had holes in their faces.

They collapsed in unison.

An instant of near-perfect silence. And then Evan heard the snick of a pistol being plucked from the floor. Molleken sliced into view around the server racks, a Browning Hi-Power gripped in both hands, and Evan jerked back.

The round hammered the slide of his ARES, ripping it from his hands with enough force that he felt both wrists wrench, the staples straining in his right forearm.

The ARES skipped across a lab bench and disappeared.

Evan ducked back into the ring of desks, rolling across his shoulders and lunging for cover behind a set of cabinets.

He could hear Molleken's shoes tapping the tile floor. "You're the one everyone's so scared of," he called out. "But you don't seem like much to me."

Evan squeezed between two desks and wormed beneath a soldering bench, putting distance between himself and where he was last sighted. He combat-crawled up an aisle between crated supplies, peering around the corner.

Twenty meters off, Molleken was stalking him, facing a half turn away. He led with the pistol, heel-toeing with extreme caution. Perspiration darkened his hair, his eyes shiny and alert, arms and hands shockingly steady. Behind him the dragonflies glowed green-yellow on the slats, a hive biding its time.

Molleken passed from view, and Evan popped soundlessly to his feet, moving swiftly up the aisle. As he eased out behind him, Molleken turned. Evan caught his arm an instant before he fired, the round lasering past Evan's knee and embedding in the floor.

As Evan knocked the pistol free, Molleken got off a cross that connected fully with his cheek. The blow staggered him, his knees buckling, and he fell against the bleachers, knocking a few dragonflies from their perch.

Fighting away nausea, blinking back to clarity.

Behind him Molleken dove for his handgun.

Evan's palm closed around a dragonfly.

He wheeled as Molleken turned, hand clutching the Browning.

Evan kicked the pistol free from his hand, lifted the dragonfly to aim its glowing eyes at Molleken's face, and compressed the wings as he'd seen Molleken do with the robotic bee.

The dragonfly drone made that same camera click, recording Molleken's facial features.

Evan dropped the drone.

Halfway to the floor, its wings batted to life.

The sound amplified, echoed hundreds of times over.

At Evan's back the hive rose from the bleachers.

Molleken's jaw trembled, the flesh beneath his right eye quivering.

The swarm kept unpacking itself from the slats, rising overhead, crowding out the view of the night sky. The rapid oscillation of the wings beat at the air, a nightmare symphony.

Molleken backed away, head cocked to take in the vast array hovering above him. His eyes flared, those double pupils drinking in what was to come.

The swarm tracked him, all those tiny components following each movement. Then it darted at him of a piece, a massive cloud of a mallet, the dagger tips tearing him to shreds. He screamed, a high-pitched note of unadulterated terror that became ragged and wet. For a moment they held his form suspended in the air like a pincushion, and then they retracted and he fell leaking to the white tile of the floor.

They rolled in waves back to the bleachers, reparking themselves on the slats. Their wings stilled, but their yellow-green eyes remained alive, waiting for the next kill order. Some gently fluttered their wings, clearing off the blood.

Evan backed away, keeping his focus on them, though if they elected to attack him, there was nothing he could do to stop them.

He kept easing away until he'd moved out of sight, and then he turned and ran. The emergency stop had held the elevator doors open. Inside, Tanner sat in the corner in precisely the same position Evan had left him in, his hand dangling from the flex cuff by his cheek. The big MP stirred on the floor, eyes trembling open.

Evan stepped in and clicked the button to rise. As the elevator doors slid shut, he realized that his legs were trembling.

He pawed sweat from his forehead, looked at the men. "Thanks for waiting."

He used the short ride to steady his breathing and jogged out, leaving the MPs behind. As he cleared the building, he jumped over the steps and then sprinted for his Honda Civic. He'd just come around the SUVs when the rolling door of the box truck rattled up.

The sixth contractor stared out at him, eyes huge, clear coil of an earpiece hanging from his left ear. Evan stared back.

The last man, left to guard the convoy. If he hadn't known who Evan was when he'd run into the building, he certainly knew now. He lifted a gun from his side, and Evan snapped his ARES up.

The sights were already lined on the guy's heart when Evan saw that he was holding not a gun but a dragonfly microdrone aimed out at Evan.

The merc's hand pulsed, and Evan fired.

The shot struck the drone, driving it back through the man's chest and knocking him flat in the cargo area. The pop of the firing gun filled Evan's ears, and when it receded, his brain finally registered the small noise he'd heard before the shot.

A tiny click.

Like a camera taking a picture.

Evan stepped back toward the Honda, his panicked stare lifting to the giant hockey puck of a building looming before him.

He heard it before he saw it.

The hum of hundreds of wings.

And then the swarm erupted from the top of the building, a volcano blowing its top.

67
MUD MONSTER

The Laser Warning Receiver alerted at the hem of Evan's shirt, the tiny three-note *Taps* bugle woefully insufficient for the threat rocketing at him.

Evan flung open the door to the Civic, snatched the Dronewrecker gun from the passenger seat, and aimed at the incoming swarm.

He fired, heat and laser dazzle erupting from the fat barrel of the weapon. A ribbon of drones fell from the right flank, their sensors blown, raining down uselessly to the earth. It felt odd to shoot a gun without recoil, whose only sound was like the flick of a pinball paddle. Stumbling backward, aiming at the sky, he shot rapidly, stripping away sheets of microdrones.

But there were so many more, kamikaze-plummeting at him, a hundred meters out, now eighty.

He pulled the trigger again and again,

initiating another burst of high-powered microwaves, disabling swaths of the dragonflies. But for every dozen he struck down, a fresh dozen filled their space.

Sixty yards out, now fifty.

All at once they parted, peeling to the sides and swooping up to regroup, protecting the swarm. He choked out a breath of relief. Their maneuver would buy him a little more time, but not much.

He realized he'd backpedaled out of the parking lot and onto the testing field. As the microdrones retreated, he kept firing, rendering as many useless as he could.

His heel caught on a mud puddle, and he went down.

Too late he saw the single dot sailing down at him, incoming.

The swarm had diverted its numbers away not just for self-protection but to draw his attention elsewhere.

And they'd send one suicide bomber directly at his head.

It zipped down.

No time to raise the Dronewrecker.

He clicked the button on the hefty gun, releasing a burst of cover smoke, flung the weapon aside, threw himself onto his feet, and dove.

A ripple of air brushed his back, and then

the night burst into light around him. The force of the explosion had him airborne, twisting over himself, a weightless cartwheel.

Somewhere beneath consciousness he registered what had happened. The solitary microdrone had chosen to take out the Dronewrecker gun first to leave him defenseless before the gathering swarm.

He landed flat on his back, the air torn from his torso at impact. For a moment he was knocked clear out of himself, floating above his sprawled, damaged body.

The siren song of surrender called to him. It was so peaceful up here, a God's-eye view of the world, impersonal and all-knowing, the omniscience of a drone.

For a moment he drifted against the constellations. And then Jack's growl came into his head. *The hell you doing here?* it said. *You got work to do.*

Evan felt himself spinning back down through the forever darkness, through the wispy claws of a few stray cirrus clouds, and he slammed back into himself with greater impact than his physical landing.

He blinked himself to alertness. He was stuck in the mud, in the earth itself, clothes and flesh weighted with mud and muck and grime. Earpiece gone, no weapon, cut off and defenseless. Forearm torn open anew. His bladder had released, his pants soggy. Smoke hovered in the air, war-zone thick, a no-man's-land miasma.

Way up above, hundreds of specks collected in the eye of the moon, the swarm gathering itself, confused. Many of them were likely still blinded from the laser dazzle, and the smoke protected him from those with intact electro-optical sensors. The haze drifted above him, shielding him from sight. The heat wave from the Dronewrecker would dissipate quickly, revealing his thermal signature.

He rolled himself through the mud in one full rotation, covering himself further, winding up again on his back. He was now encrusted in a makeshift shell scrape that camouflaged him and layered over his heat signature, protecting him from the infrared sensors.

They couldn't detect him.

As long as he didn't move.

Or blink.

Or breathe.

He lay still, cold mud plastered on his face.

The swarm churned, agitated and frenzied.

Searching.

The able communicated with the disabled, the swarm reconstituting itself with ever greater grace and menace. It flurried out across the testing fields, darted across the parking lot, swooped over the lab building.

Evan lay still. Tried not to breathe. There was no backup plan, no next step. The drones would not tire. They would search until they found him.

The smoke shifted slowly, gauzy strips floating off like clouds. Embedded in the earth, lying stock-still, he felt as if he could sense the planet's rotation moving him away, out of cover. He wondered if he'd already died; if this was what death felt like.

The mud on his arms, his neck, warmed and crusted. He felt it cracking, curling off his skin. With all the training he possessed, all the control he'd been taught over his anatomy and his mind, the one thing he could not suppress was his body temperature.

Soon enough the warmth of his flesh would become apparent.

There was almost a comfort in the inevitability. The whine of the drone heightened. They were across in the neighboring field, a flock of seagulls searching for prey. Now they dappled the edge of his peripheral vision.

The mask of mud across his face was thin enough that he felt sweat bead through it.

The swarm hesitated directly over him, trembling. He watched it re-form with a horrified awe. It pulled to a tip. Like a snout aiming down.

He'd been spotted.

Nothing left to do.

The swarm gathered itself around the point, readying for a plunge. This was it, then. It was time.

He vowed to face it on his feet.

He pulled himself up, a mud monster, the filth clinging to him, a ghillie suit made of earth. His OCD had shut down, drowned beneath the roar of incoming death, and all the disgust and judgment he carried with him like a shield to keep others at bay were inside him now. They were a part of him and not the world, and he accepted them as his own.

Up above, the dragonflies drew back like an enormous fist.

They tornadoed down at him.

He readied himself.

But all at once there was a ripple in the nosediving swarm, the front half torn away and then the back, sheeting down limply to the earth.

Behind him he heard the growl of a motor, and he swung his concrete-heavy head to see Candy commanding a joint light tactical vehicle.

She was atop the desert-tan JLTV, standing tall behind the gun turret. Bizarrely, her purse wagged from one shoulder, and she was holding something — silver, cylindrical — aloft to the sky like a wizard's staff.

It took a moment for him to put it together: She'd recharged the portable EMP weapon and used it again to fry the electronics inside the microdrones.

The vehicle was barreling at him.

There was nobody at the wheel.

Candy reared up behind the turret, readying to drop back through the roof into the driver's seat.

She was shouting at him.

His ears were blown out, and he heard the words as if through earplugs: *"Move!"*

He threw himself to the side, the massive tires ripping through the puddle where he'd stood an instant before. Peeling himself up, he stared after the JLTV as it blazed across the parking lot toward the circular building.

Just before it struck the box truck, Candy gained control, the vehicle swerving abruptly and swinging back around. Through the open window, she shouted at him from the parking lot. "Get your car and clear out!"

He gave a thumbs-up and strode back wincingly to the Civic as she powered off to her own getaway vehicle.

He fell behind the wheel, praying that the car's electronic ignition had been sufficiently out of range of Candy's EMP device. His fingers, slimy with mud, had trouble gripping the key, turning it.

Nothing.

He heard his teeth grind, felt a vein pop in the side of his neck. Tried again.

Still nothing.

He exhaled through clenched teeth and gave it one more try.

Miraculously, the engine coughed to life.

He accelerated out of the lot and up the long road to the perimeter, whipping through endless testing fields. He tried to take control of his breathing first. In through the nose. Out through the mouth. Slow, steady, keeping the heart rate low.

His earpiece was missing, and he thought to call Joey to tell her he was alive, but when he glanced at his RoamZone, the screen was slivered with countless cracks from the explosion.

Dirt and sweat stung his eyes. Steering with one hand, he wiped at them with his knuckles, but they were so dirty that he wound up just smearing the grime around.

He assessed himself for further damage. A deep throb in his right forearm. The re-opened wound had bled through his shirt, and he tore the long sleeve away and peeled back the bandage.

Groping in the backseat, he found his trauma kit, ripped out hemostatic gauze, and slapped it on. It was treated to promote rapid coagulation, which was the best he could do in the middle of a getaway.

At last he made out the rear access gate, still retracted in the distance. His exhale came as a hiss. For a moment the path was clear.

Then the gate rumbled back to life.

And started to close.

He stood on the accelerator, aiming for the gap.

His shot at freedom slowly wiping from view.

His head throbbed, his teeth ached.

Almost there. Almost closed.

The Honda hurtled forward and scraped through, the edge of the gate screeching along the side and clipping the mirror off. The car popped free, fishtailed slightly, and straightened again on the open road.

Evan choked out a breath of relief.

An instant later a red Corvette T-boned him.

68
STOP

The Civic spun a full 360 through the scrub, tilting up on its two side wheels, taking a moment to decide whether or not to roll.

It crashed back down on its chassis, rocking on the tires.

Evan tugged at the door and spilled out onto the dirt, his elbows jarring the ground. Blood-laced drool spilled from his mouth.

The Corvette stared at him. Impossibly, one headlight remained on, a cyclops eye gauging his weakness.

He coughed a few times. Rolled to his side. Pried himself off the earth.

Now a man stood before the headlight, his silhouette perfectly framed.

He shifted, the glow catching the side of him.

Declan Gentner.

He wore a gray pinstripe number, his shiny black loafers fogged slightly with dust from the impact. He held a Smith & Wesson pistol at his side, a .45 with a fancy silver-ported barrel.

"You're going to come with me," he said.

Evan coughed some more. "Just shoot me and get it over with." He sensed that he was talking too loud, his hearing still muted.

"Oh, no," Declan said, his voice deepened out with anger. "We have two hundred and six bones to get through. We're going to do this over the course of a few days."

It hurt for Evan just to hold his eyes open. He lifted his gaze. Saw a slight bulge in the ground a few steps in front of Declan.

"Well," he said. "I'm not going anywhere with you."

Declan's hand tightened around the Smith & Wesson. But he didn't move.

"When I cut your sister's throat," Evan said, "I could hear her breath leaking through the slit."

Declan's arm started to shake. His face hardened in the harsh light, a visage carved from stone, all bony points and severe lines of facial hair.

He took a step forward. A strangled noise escaped him. "Stop," he said, his voice suddenly less secure, higher-pitched.

"She knew exactly what was happening to her," Evan said. "She had time to think about it before she bled out."

Declan's lips peeled back from his teeth, the bared grimace of a wolf. He started for Evan. One more step. And then another.

His polished loafer set down once more, and a clack sounded from the earth.

He froze. Looked down.

Evan said, "Land mine."

Declan shook the gun at Evan, his neck corded with rage. "Get your ass over here."

"No thanks."

"I'll kill you. I'll fucking end you right here."

Evan realized he was stooped over in pain and with effort drew himself upright. "Naw," he said. "The recoil from the pistol will set off the charge. Can't kill me without killing yourself."

Declan was quivering now, his whole body shuddering. Evan could see him bearing down, trying to control his muscles. "If I'm gonna die anyway, might as well take you with me."

Evan said, "That would require you not being a coward."

Declan lined the sights on Evan's face. For a moment they were perfectly still, regarding each other across a moonlit stretch of scrub. Then Declan screamed, mouth stretched wide, dried spit linking his jaws. It was the purest howl of rage Evan had heard. And terror.

Evan staggered to the Civic and lowered himself painfully into the driver's seat. The car was still running, a minor miracle, though the windows were shattered, the bumper missing, and the tire screeched against the well when he turned the wheel.

He studied the ground before the headlights for more land mines, then let the car crawl forward.

He drove right past Declan, not even bothering to look over, though in his peripheral vision he could sense the gun swinging to stay aimed at his head.

The car bounced geriatrically up onto the road.

He drove away, the Civic wheezing and groaning. He just had to make the meet point and reclaim his truck.

Blinking through blood and sweat and grime, he tried to steady his hands on the wheel.

He got about a quarter mile before the boom shook what was left of the rear windshield.

69
THE LOVE YOU DESERVE

After dragging himself to the meet point, switching to his truck, and driving home, Evan slept on and off for thirty-six hours, a blissful block of hibernation in his floating bed.

Before parting ways with the others at the target range, he'd tasked Joey with contacting Andre and Veronica to inform them that they were safe so he could collapse and begin to heal. He'd tried to thank Candy, but she'd kissed him on the mouth, surprising him with her tongue. Before he could react, she'd climbed into her Jeep and vanished once more. The kiss had left him a bit breathless, but he told himself it was just from his injuries.

On Tuesday night he roused himself for good.

Cleaning and stitching himself up took longer than he would have thought, dozens of tiny injuries slowing his progress to an arthritic crawl.

He made his way downstairs, fortunately dodging any Castle Heights residents, and drove into Westwood Village. He pulled over at a drugstore and wincingly walked the aisles, finding the pet section. A dog bowl decorated with skulls and crossbones caught his eye.

He paid and exited.

En route to the truck, he passed through the scents of the college town — French roast and hookah pipes and gyro meat wafting from doorways.

Halfway up the block, he spotted a young man sitting on a park bench with a college girl lying beside him, her head resting on his thigh, blond hair spilled across his lap.

He did a double take at the kid.

Bridger Bickley, aka "Bicks."

Evan stopped, facing them, his shadow falling across Bridger's face.

Bridger started at the sight of Evan, the girl uncoiling from his lap and rising. Evan wondered if she was *Sloane* of karaoke-filibuster fame.

Evan said to her, "Can you please give us a moment?"

She looked to Bridger, who gazed back at her fearfully. That was enough for Sloane, who rose and hightailed it away, her leather saddlebag knocking against her hip.

Bridger's hands lifted, palms exposed. "You gonna threaten me?"

Evan said, "No."

"She was just young," Bridger said. "Joey. And really smart. It's hard to date a chick who's the smartest one in the room, you know. And . . . I dunno, kinda too tough."

Evan said, "Too tough for you."

Bickley looked at his hands. "I guess, yeah."

"So you disappeared. Never called."

"It's not like we were engaged."

"True," Evan said. "But you took your own insecurity and put it on her. That weakens her. And it weakens you. You treat a young woman like that with respect. If nothing else it'll teach you about yourself, teach you who you want to be whenever you're ready to be that person. Understand?"

Bridger gazed up at him, his face glowing yellow beneath the streetlight. "Yeah," he said.

Evan turned to walk off.

" 'Scuse me?" Bridger was on his feet behind Evan. "Uh . . ." He stood, one sneaker on end, grinding the toe into the sidewalk. "Thanks," he said. "No one's ever talked to me like that."

629

Evan gave him a nod and kept on.

Standing in her doorway, Joey stared down at the dog bowl in her hands. "What is this?"

"I'm trying to buy your affection," Evan said.

He waited for her to look up, those emerald eyes glowing through the sweep of her bangs. She bit her lip. "I like the skulls and crossbones."

She stepped back from her front door, leaving it ajar, as close to an invitation as he ever got.

"But I don't know what's wrong with the Red Vines bowl," Joey said. "Dog likes it."

Over on his plush bolster bed, the Rhodesian ridgeback lifted his head at the mention of his name.

She walked past him, set down the bowl, and transferred the water from the Red Vines bucket. "There."

Dog wagged his tail. Then rolled onto his side, his head flopping clear of the bed, collar tags clinking against the floor.

Evan watched her staring down at the dog, her arms crossed. She caught him looking. *"What?"*

"You don't have to pretend you don't like him."

"I *don't* like him."

"Jack had a joke he used to tell."

"Oh, great. The only thing worse than Jack telling a joke is you *retelling* a joke Jack used to tell. It's like dad humor on steroids."

"If you lock your wife and your dog in the trunk of your car for twenty-four hours, when you open it, which one's happy to see you?"

A laugh escaped Joey. She covered her mouth with her fingers. "That's awful. And, like, super sexist."

"Same holds for husbands."

"Fair enough." She stared down at Dog, her expression softening. Then she sprawled out on top of him. At a hundred-plus pounds, the ridgeback was sturdy enough to take her weight. His tail thwacked the floor a few times. Joey rose and fell with his ribs.

"If you lie on him, he growls real low," she said. "Like a purr."

Wincing against his sore muscles, Evan sat down next to them with his back to the wall and listened.

Sure enough there it was, the faintest purr accompanying each exhalation.

For a time he and Joey stayed like that, listening to the big boy growl gently with contentment.

Finally Joey flopped off Dog and rolled to

631

sit next to Evan. Side by side they stared at her little apartment.

"That's why you got him for me?" she said. "So I'll always have someone who's happy to see me when I come home?"

"Dogs are feedback loops for positive emotion," Evan said. "They're happy to see you, which makes you happy. Then you pet them and they're even happier, which makes you even happier. They . . ."

She cocked her head. "What?"

"Nothing. It's stupid."

She banged a bony elbow into his sore ribs, and he tried to act like it didn't hurt. "C'mon, X. Spill the tea."

He cleared his throat. "They teach you the love you deserve."

Her voice was open and curious now, like that of a girl or a young woman — none of the usual teenage testiness. "Why?" she asked.

"So maybe you can learn how to give that love back," Evan said. "I'd like you to learn that. I never did. Not the right way."

Joey leaned her head on his shoulder.

"You do okay," she said.

70
DARK ROAD

Evan paused on the quaint footbridge, taking a moment to gather himself.

Veronica had reached him earlier in the afternoon on his cracked-to-hell RoamZone and told him he'd better get to the Bel Air house. She'd beckoned Andre as well.

She said she wasn't sure she had much time.

Barry the movie producer didn't come home from location, but he'd had the decency to lend her the house for her final stretch. Matías didn't make the trek either, but he'd sprung for a hospice nurse, a skeletal Hispanic woman who answered the door now. She offered a warm hand, and they shook. "It's good you're here," she said. "You have to understand how it is moving forward."

"How is it moving forward?"

"Think of it this way. Every day her best day was yesterday."

Andre was already there, sitting at the kitchen table, staring at the union of his folded hands and doing his best to ignore the rat dogs sniffing at his shoes. He looked good, well rested even, color returning to his face.

He seemed relieved to see Evan.

"She's having a nap." Andre nodded at the nurse, who was jotting on a medication schedule on the fridge, and lowered his voice. "I think she thinks I'm here to fix the dishwasher."

The nurse turned to them. "I'll take you back now." She gave Evan a bright smile before turning a skeptical gaze to Andre.

Andre shook his head as they padded down the hall to the master.

The giant suite was bright and airy, with glass sliding doors that accordioned open to let onto a terrace. A garden and a swimming pool unfurled beyond, seeming to stretch to the horizon.

It was shocking how much more Veronica had deteriorated over the past few days. Oxygen tube beneath her nose, skin a sickly yellow, her collarbones and the points of her elbows pronounced.

Andre hesitated in the doorway, but Evan led him through. Her suitcase and purse rested on an upholstered bench at the foot of the bed, and it occurred to Evan that this was their final stop. A candle flickered in the bathroom, breathing sandalwood into the room. It smelled expensive. Beneath it the faintest trace of lilac.

The smell of his mother.

Veronica tried to lift her head but couldn't, so she rolled it on the pillow to take them in. "You look like hell," she said to Evan.

His swollen cheek had taken on an eggplant hue, and he'd left the stapled wound on his forearm exposed to air it out. "You should talk."

She gave a dry laugh. "Look at this. My long-lost sons beckoned to my deathbed. All that's missing is a soap-opera score. And a gin and tonic."

"I hear *that*," Andre said.

She blinked a few times, and each time Evan was unsure if her eyes would open again.

Finally she spoke. "My whole life I told myself that ducking responsibility meant I was taking care of myself." She lifted an arm trailing wires and took Andre's hand. "But it's precisely the opposite."

He dipped his head, gave a nod. They stood over her awkwardly.

"Sit down," she said. "You're making me feel like I'm already in the coffin."

Evan retrieved chairs from a bistro set on the terrace and brought them over. They sat bedside dutifully. There was so much to take in that didn't require words.

Veronica's blinks grew longer and longer. At last she said, "You spend your whole damn life proving that you're different from everyone else. What a great relief at the end to find out that you aren't."

She closed her eyes, her breath taking on a rasp.

Evan and Andre stayed with her another half hour, and then Andre rose and walked out. As Evan returned the chairs to the terrace, he accidentally knocked Veronica's purse off its perch.

He crouched to pick up the spilled contents. Her trifold leather wallet had fallen open, an edge of yellowed newsprint showing in the ID window, peeking out from behind her driver's license. He fished it out.

LOCAL RIDER CLAIMS TITLE

Freedom, OK — November 18, 1978

Jacob Baridon snared his first bull-riding title on the Professional Rodeo Cowboys Association circuit this Saturday. His 94-point effort astride El Diablo, the three-time PRCA Saddle Bronc of the Year, was sufficient for victory.

A grainy photograph showed a handsome man smiling from beneath a Stetson, the front dip of the brim shading his eyes. Jacob. His own middle name, taken from this man.

Heat found Evan's cheek, the gash in his arm, pushing its way through him, searching for exits.

So she hadn't been joking. A rodeo cowboy.

His father.

He couldn't decide whether it was an amusing cliché or just fucking absurd.

He decided on both.

Pocketing the article, he slipped out.

He was pumping gas into the pickup when he got the call. Through the cracked screen of the RoamZone, he saw the hospice nurse's number.

He answered, listened, thanked her, and hung up.

He stood beneath the overhang by the pumps, his mouth suddenly dry. He leaned against the truck, the metal warm and grounding to the touch.

The door chimed as he entered the mart and headed to the refrigerated beverages in the back. When he tugged open the glass door, a cool waft slid up his front side, and he realized he was sweating. Light-headedness came on, a reminder of his injuries, but then he sensed the twist in his chest and realized it might be something else.

Grief.

Resting a hand on the shelf, he leaned in and breathed the cool, sweet air.

A well-put-together woman in her sixties came up beside him. "You okay, hon?"

He half turned. "Yeah, yeah, I'm fine."

But she was already talking over him, and he realized she was on her Bluetooth, carrying on a conversation. She smiled kindly, embarrassed, and mouthed, *My daughter,* pointing to the phone.

Evan stepped aside. She reached past him for a Fiji water and withdrew.

Back in the penthouse, Evan paced circles around the island in the kitchen. The poured-concrete countertops looked smudged, and he wiped them down with wet paper towels. Soil had dribbled beneath the living wall, and he got a mop and worked the floor over, but when he was done, the water had dried unevenly on the island, leaving streaks, so he got more paper towels and wiped it again and again, tight circular motions that strained the staples in his forearm. He switched arms and finished and then noticed that the salt and pepper shakers were uneven, so he pushed them to the wall, but then he saw a crumb in the grouting beneath the cabinet and dug at it with his fingernail but couldn't get it, he couldn't get it perfect, and he stopped and sat down right on the floor, because nothing was working, everything was out of order, out of control, and he sensed something on his face and touched his fingertips to his cheeks and rubbed the moisture between his thumb and forefinger and stared at it.

His RoamZone chimed, alerting him to a new e-mail in the defunct account: the.nwhr.man@gmail.com. Sure enough, a fresh unsent draft had miraculously appeared, the same semi-secure comms method he used to employ to get mission directives from Jack.

No sender. No subject line.

It said, *"Request contact."*

He knew precisely what that meant.

An hour and twenty-three minutes later, Evan was buried deep in the Angeles National Forest at the western end of the San Gabriels. A recent fire had scorched a swath of earth at the base of Mount Gleason, but he'd tucked into a ribbon of luxuriant pines. The needles and sap overlaid the scent of ash with a bracing freshness that made his

639

lungs tingle. Dusk took the edge off the greens and browns of the mountains, softening the panorama into a sepia haze.

Not that he saw any of it right now.

He was zipped inside a dark nylon tent that provided no view of the flora or the topography. His recent brush with drone warfare had amped his paranoia up another notch; for the last few desolate miles, he'd pulled a length of chain-link fence behind his truck to cover his tire tracks. His battered RoamZone accommodated a virgin SIM card, and he'd moved the phone service to a company operating out of Punggol. He'd paired the phone with his laptop, hooked into a Yagi directional antenna, an SMA connector, a small omni stubby antenna, and a Blade RF stick. The makeshift GSM base station was a rogue cell site, allowing him access to the LTE network while evading any authentication between him and the nearest cell tower.

Untraceable.

He called the familiar phone number.

A switchboard operator picked up.

He said, "Dark Road."

Then he punched in Extension 32.

A click as the call was forwarded, and then the phone rang. It kept ringing. He counted to ten. Then to twenty. Told himself he'd hang up if it reached thirty.

At twenty-eight, the president of the United States answered. "I'm giving you another number enabled for video feed."

She paused, but he said nothing. She named ten digits, and he disconnected.

Pulling up an encoded videotelephony software program on his laptop, he dialed.

The feed glitched but proceeded, and a moment later President Victoria Donahue-Carr appeared.

She sat behind the Resolute desk in the Oval, flags on display at either side of her. A considered choice to show the full power of the office.

Her face was drawn. Standing by her left shoulder was Secret Service Special Agent in Charge Naomi Templeton. Templeton's blond hair had grown out a bit since Evan last laid eyes on her, but her face retained its same stubborn bearing. Though she'd played the role of his adversary in the past, he admired her greatly and sensed that she admired him, too.

Not that any of that would matter if she were tasked to come for him again.

Donahue-Carr squinted at the screen. "X? I can barely make you out."

Evan said, "That's the point."

"I've received word of an intrusion at

Creech North that seems to have your fingerprints on it."

Evan said, "You're gonna want to look into the DoD's contract with Mimeticom. They're teaching microdrones to think for themselves, make their own ethical choices."

"We wouldn't want that," Donahue-Carr said. "Someone making their own ethical choices."

She was right. He was a hypocrite, imperfect in his moral bearing, short of the mark in more ways than he could tally. But at least he built his code from lived experience, not from ones and zeros.

Evan said, "End it quietly or I'll dump the classified details online and you can deal with it in the next election."

The president's expression didn't alter, but he saw Templeton give a little nod.

"Need I remind you that you're retired?" Donahue-Carr said.

Evan remained silent.

She leaned in, set her sleeves on the desk in front of her, her shoulders squaring. "If you're *not* retired, I don't need to remind you what that means either, do I?"

Evan clicked the laptop shut.

71
READY

"I look like a dumb-ass fool," Andre said. In the passenger seat, he flipped the visor down for the fifth time and smoothed his hair into place. He wore a new button-up shirt with a clip-on tie and a clean pair of slacks, and he held a little wrapped present in his lap.

It was Christmas Eve.

"No," Evan said. "You look respectable."

"Same thing."

"You ready?"

"No, I'm not ready. Do I *look* ready?"

It had been a week and change since their mother had died, and here they were, parked outside the apartment complex a little ways up the street so Andre could muster his nerve. To the side of Evan's truck, a carport looked in danger of disintegrating, its splintering posts barely supporting the rust-eaten roof sheeting. The meth house behind them had been boarded up, the party no doubt moved to a fresh squatting location, and someone had already tagged the plywood with expletives.

But their focus remained on the ground-floor apartment up ahead. The midday sun glinted off the security screens, the window a solid sheet of gold.

Andre blew into a cupped hand, checked his breath. Fingernail rubbed a water stain off his thigh. Tossed the carefully wrapped gift onto the dashboard. He reached nervously and turned on the radio, "Desperado" coming through the speakers. He shook his head and fiddled with the control. "Damn, son. Could you *be* any whiter?"

"You're half white," Evan said.

"Yeah, my *bad* half."

Andre landed on another channel, Beth Hart singing that it was a good day to cry cry cry, and he closed his eyes, nodding with the music, and said, "Now, *that* little white girl, that little white girl's the *truth*."

Evan waited for the song to end and then asked again, "You ready?"

Andre dug for his yellow pouch, unzipped it, peered inside at the meager bills. After being cleared of wrongdoing by the cops, he'd been hired back at the impound lot and had cashed the paycheck from his first half week. A not insubstantial settlement for his destroyed house was coming, but it would take a while to work its way through the insurance bureaucracy.

He zipped the pouch back up, tapped it against his palm. "I think we should leave."

"We're not leaving."

"I don't know." Andre went back to the mirror again, adjusted the tie to center the knot. "How do I look now?"

"Distractingly handsome."

"What if she don't like me?"

"She'll like you."

"What if she don't act like it?"

"You'll take it. You'll be a man and a father, and you'll be there for her."

Andre slapped the visor shut, placed his hands on his knees, jiggled his legs. He took a deep breath. Another.

Still working up his nerve.

Evan thought about what Andre was readying to take on once more, the responsibility of a parent. Andre had never had it role-modeled for himself, and he'd failed a time or two, but here he was, showing up. Evan remembered the adage he'd mouthed to Joey a few weeks ago — *Responsibility's where you find meaning* — and thought about how Veronica had three-dimensionalized it with her dying words, her final gift to her sons, a self-portrait of regret.

The RoamZone was in his hands.

He stared down at the cracked screen. And then his thumbs were at work, applying steady pressure to the seams, the self-repairing glass piecing itself back together.

Evan took a deep breath. "Before you go," he said, "I have one thing to ask of you."

"Sure, man."

Evan kept at the phone, the cracks disappearing as he knit the polyether-thiourea screen back into a seamless whole.

From chaos, order.

"Find someone else who needs my help," he said. "Someone in as desperate a situation as you were. Give them my number: 1-855-2-NOWHERE."

Andre stared at him. A wisp of tissue stuck to his neck where he'd cut himself shaving. Evan reached over and plucked it off.

"Tell them about me," Evan said. "Tell them I'll be there on the other end of the phone."

"Okay," Andre said. "Okay."

The street darkened, the sun sliding behind a bank of clouds, and the glare lifted from the window to Brianna's apartment.

Sofia stood in the living room practicing pirouettes. Awkward at first, stumbling out of the turns. But she caught herself and tried again. And again.

Behind her the old-fashioned travel poster of Paris looked on, the promise of new worlds ahead.

Evan heard the passenger door close before he noticed that Andre had climbed out. He watched him walk into the building, pulling his shoulders back, lifting his head with an assumed air of dignity.

He disappeared into the lobby.

Evan watched Sofia spin and fail. Spin and fail.

All at once she stopped. Stared at the door.

A moment later Brianna came into sight. She walked past her daughter and opened the door. She stood a moment, blocking Evan's view, and then stepped aside.

Sofia's hand went to her mouth. Her thin shoulders rose, almost touching the gold studs in her ears. She stayed that way as her father entered.

Andre's gaze was lowered. He held the gift by his belt buckle, fussing with it in both hands. His shoulders had lost some of their steel.

Stillness claimed the living room, all the players motionless, not daring to breathe.

Then Sofia ran to him and hugged him

tightly, wrapping her arms around his waist.

He stayed frozen a moment, his lips quivering. Then he embraced his daughter. After a moment he looked up over her through the window at Evan's truck. His eyes shone with moisture, and he gave the faintest nod.

Evan dropped the truck into gear and drove off.

72
A MATTER OF TIME

The sun was uncharacteristically hot for December in Nevada, and it had blazed for a week straight after Evan's raid on Creech North. In the wake of the mayhem, a number of internal investigations had been opened, the lab floor turned into a crime scene, and hundreds of microdrones had been collected from when the swarm had rained from the sky.

A few had gone unsighted, stuck in the mud of the sprawling test field. But four days ago, as the heat dried the earth, they'd arisen, shaking loose the sheen of dirt on their wings.

Four of them.

They sought connection to the rest of the hive, but the others had been permanently fried. Until their signal reached a puddle near the parking lot. Two yellow-green eyes glitched to life in the mud. The drone's parts were loosely arrayed around it, wings shattered, the thorax twisted irreparably. However, its computer was still hardened enough to fall back to reading its NVRAM flash memory and access the last kill order it had received, the face of a man in his mid-thirties, just an ordinary guy, not too handsome.

It retrieved the image of the license plate of the Honda Civic that the target had driven away in and sent it to its four viable mates.

They lifted from the field, taking flight invisibly, unnoticed among their larger brethren.

They were programmed to carry out orders without requiring a human in the decision loop, so one of them hacked into the DMV registration database, determining that the Civic had been purchased at a used-car lot in Barstow at 11:57 A.M. on December 12.

Zipping west, the others had joined the virtual pursuit, determining that the new-owner registration had been faked. The pawnshop across the street had a Web-connected surveillance camera that partially captured the entrance to the used-car lot. The drones' computerized brains dug through the archived memory to zero in on vehicles that had entered the lot in the minutes preceding 11:57 A.M.

The images of the drivers were imprecise, but the side-angle view of shadowed torsos and arms had enough nodal points to match the buyer of the Civic to a man who'd arrived in a Ford F-150. The truck's license plate led to another dead end, but the microdrone used its Aircrack-ng Wi-Fi cracking software to perform a deauth attack on the network of the automated license-plate-recognition system that continuously recorded and stored scans of passing cars from sensors embedded in the light bars of police cruisers.

The Ford's license plate didn't record a lot of hits, indicating that it had likely been changed recently, but the preponderance of pings occurred in Greater Los Angeles, concentrating further around the Wilshire Corridor.

The four dragonflies flew across state lines in tight formation and arrived in the targeted zone on December 21, spreading out to monitor traffic. On the morning of the 22nd, they switched strategy, focusing on the residential buildings within a five-block stretch. They pulled blueprints and building permits from online city records to determine vulnerabilities in the apartments that could be exploited — load-bearing walls and water heaters and gas lines. And they started moving window to window.

Now it was only a matter of time.

73
A Little Tiny Part

The lobby of Castle Heights sported a bunch of new decorations courtesy of Peter's Crayolas: obese snowmen and misshapen reindeer proliferating across the walls. There was also what appeared to be a Buddha floating in the clouds, which at second glance proved to be baby Jesus swathed in blankets. Over the mail slots, a banner spelled out MERRY CHRISTMAS EVE with alternating red and green letters, except for the *R*'s in "Merry," which were both red, no doubt a spelling mishap set right. The "Eve" was on its own printout, ready to be removed in the morning. Peter was an amazing kid when he wasn't busy being rotten.

Since the raid on Creech North, Evan had barely left his penthouse, nursing himself back to health, eating well, stretching, meditating, and indulging more cautiously than before in the occasional jigger of vodka.

653

Lorilee entered just after Evan, shopping-bag handles riding both arms like bracelets. "Just a little retail therapy!" she proclaimed chirpily as Joaquin flashed his standard-issue smile behind the security desk and called the elevator.

She and Evan boarded together, riding up in silence. A new perfume had been applied liberally, puffing out from her with each small movement. She wore a merry red blouse in keeping with the season.

He remembered her sitting in the chair in the lobby, despondent over her non-move, how she'd delicately dabbed at her eyes so as not to ruin the made-up face she presented to the world.

Bearing down mentally, he tried to sort the logic of small talk.

He started to speak, lost his nerve, then steeled himself and tried again. "Is that a new blouse?"

She melted. "Yes. I bought it yesterday. I thought it was fun for the holidays."

They reached the third floor, the doors parting to let her out.

Evan said, "It looks nice."

She turned back, beaming, her face colored with delight. "Thank you."

In the aftermath of her departure, he breathed her lingering perfume and thought about how little it had taken to impart that much joy. She'd felt noticed. At the end of the day, maybe that was all anyone wanted.

The penthouse button was lit up, his bedroom beckoning. But he reached out and thumbed the button for the twelfth floor.

He strode down to 12B and rang the bell. When Mia opened the door, her face was flushed from cooking. A rush of warm scents drifted out at him — gravy and fresh-baked bread and a sweet citrus tinge. The prenegotiated Christmas tree rose in the corner of the living room, trimmed to exhaustion.

"Sorry I've been MIA," Evan said. "Work stuff."

He sensed her gaze snag on the bruise on his cheek, the bandage wrapping his forearm.

She said, "Is that so?"

Peter poked his head up from the kitchen table. "Evan Smoak! Come in. I'm making clove oranges."

Mia tugged at his good arm, pulling him inside. Peter was shoving cloves into an orange, his jaws mashing on chewing gum energetically enough to be heard across the room. A few oranges already studded with cloves rested by his elbow, exuding a delightful holiday scent. He wore a pale yellow dress shirt this time, cuffed sleeves dangling from his elbows.

"I'm gonna make five of 'em, and I'm gonna put 'em in a bowl for the security desk so Joaquin can have them there and the lobby'll smell all Christmassy."

Evan said, "That's —"

"And I hafta show you this video that's super gnarly. This YouTube guy? He lets himself get stung by, like, scorpions and stuff."

Mia crossed her arms. "When did you —"

"Oh! Stick your fingertip in your ear. Like this. Now wiggle it up and down. Sounds like Pac-Man, right? Right?"

Evan said, "I'm not really a video-game —"

"And wait! Watch this!" Peter swigged from a glass of Martinelli's sparkling apple cider. The bottle next to him looked mostly empty, the sugar rush no doubt accounting for his octane-powered patter. He tilted his head back and gargle-sang. It took a moment for Evan to register that he was performing "Drummer Boy."

Peter threw his arms wide for a carbonated *pa-rum-pum-pum-pum.*

"Stop that," Mia said. "Not with gum! You're going to —"

Peter choked, coughing cider all over the table, drops splattering the front of Evan's shirt.

As Evan looked down in dismay, Mia sank her face into her hands. "Apologize to Mr. Danger. And go to your room for a time-out."

"Sorry," Peter said, wiping his chin.

He scampered off, and Mia sank into a chair. After a moment Evan joined her.

"Some days I think that the main job of a parent is to keep your kids from having fun," she said.

"Or to keep them from killing themselves."

"That, too." Fanning herself with one hand, she shoved her curls up off her face. When she released them, she left streaks of flour in her hair.

"You have —"

"What?"

He reached over and brushed it off.

"You're smiling," she said. "Didn't know your face was capable of that."

"Oh, come on, I smile."

"No, you *smirk*," she said.

They looked at each other, amused.

She said, "I assume you stopped by so I could invite you to dinner tonight with my brother and his wife."

"Actually, I stopped by to talk to Peter.

But now you've excommunicated him."

"He can come out in —" She glanced past Evan through the doorway into Peter's bedroom and shouted, "Don't put your gum *there*!" Returning to Evan, who'd jerked back in his chair at her shift in tone. "Sorry. Does that mean no to dinner?"

"I'd love to join you for dinner."

"Really?" She smiled now, that full, radiant grin he felt in his spine.

"Really."

The smile vanished. She leaned past Evan and said, "You can come out now."

Peter bounded out, pounced back into his chair, blew a giant bubble, and got to work on his orange again.

Evan said to Mia, "He seems chastened."

"Hey. Evan wanted to talk to you." She snapped her fingers in front of Peter's face, and he straightened up, his charcoal eyes suddenly serious. He looked like a little man sitting there in his deceased father's shirt.

"What?" he said.

"All those decorations you do," Evan said. "Christmas. New Year's. Birthdays. Thanksgiving. Halloween."

"Kwanzaa," Peter said. "I'm working on a Kwanzaa poster with the colors of Africa for next week."

"And Kwanzaa," Evan said. "I want you

658

to know that everyone who lives here, all the old people, it cheers them up. Cheers me up, too."

"Even though you're super tough."

"Even though I'm super tough. I see how you notice people, too, when they're sad or lonely —"

"Like Lorilee Smithson."

"Like Lorilee Smithson," Evan said. "And I may not have the standing to tell you this, but I want you to know I'm proud of you. I see you, and I'm proud of you."

Peter flushed a bit and for once was silent. Next to Evan, Mia watched, too, her hand coming to rest on his knee beneath the table.

"I had someone who raised me," Evan said. "Who was a father to me. He didn't tell me he was proud of me often. And I remember that even when he did, I didn't believe it. Because I was just me, right, and even though he was honest as hell, a little tiny part of me thought he's just saying that because that's what adults say to make kids feel good about themselves. Or because they have to." He leaned forward, placed his palm on Peter's arm, looked him dead in the eyes. "I want you to know I know that little part. I know it in you. And I'm telling you, it's wrong."

Peter rose from his chair, circled the table,

and hugged Evan around the neck hard
enough to choke him.

74
NOWHERE LEFT TO GO

Fresh lemon and currant.

That's what led the nose of Guillotine Vodka. Made from white and black grapes that had been handpicked in the Champagne region, Guillotine was distilled in cognac barrels made of Limousin oak, which smoothed out the mid-palate. Velvety mouthfeel, good weighting on the finish. When Evan closed his eyes, he could pick up the faintest exclamation of Szechuan pepper.

Emerging from his vodka freezer wrapped in tendrils of mist, he set the martini glass on the kitchen counter. His RoamZone was plugged into its charging station, pinning down that yellowed newspaper clipping he'd taken from his mother's wallet.

His father.

A bronc rider.

For the love of Mary.

He figured that after the last few weeks,

he'd take some time before diving into the next familial adventure.

But he'd keep the phone near him. Someone else was out there right now in gutwrenching despair, someone who needed his help.

And it was his responsibility to be there for that call.

The events set in motion by Veronica's call had dragged him back to his past and in doing so had taught him about a different kind of future, one that integrated who he'd always been with who he wanted to be.

He needed to meditate and find how these new realities could live inside him. How he could make room for them and let them germinate.

He picked up the phone, smirked, and shot Joey a text. LUNCH AND A MOVIE TOMORROW?

The three bubbles indicated she was typing back. Then: NEW PHONE WHO DIS?

He actually laughed out loud.

Evidently she'd joined him on the other end, her next message coming through. LOL. YEAH.

He padded to his bedroom. Frost from the freezer still clouded the martini glass. It was cool in his grip, against his lips, contrasting with the warmth it spread through his belly.

Delightful.

He reached the bedroom and passed the floating bed. The Laser Warning Receiver clip rested atop his bureau with some spare change. It had served him well.

He had about an hour now to sip vodka and center himself before heading downstairs to join Mia's dinner party. Her brother would be there — and his wife — and Evan felt the old discomfort glow to life in his chest.

What should he bring? What would they talk about? What if they asked him personal questions?

He moved to the window and gazed out. The setting sun had morphed from yellow to amber, overflowing the horizon to suffuse the urban corridor of Wilshire with a royal glow.

The windows of the building across mirrored back Castle Heights. Evan could see the entirety of the building beneath him, all the floors, all those condos in which people carved out lives for themselves, lives filled with grief and joy, despair and hope.

And for the first time, he wondered if he actually might belong here.

It came so faintly he almost didn't register it.

Three notes from a bugle.

Taps.

He swung his head to face to the bureau.

Sure enough, the Laser Warning Receiver was lit up.

Panic hit his bloodstream, a mass injection of adrenaline.

He pivoted back.

Saw a metallic glint hovering twenty meters outside his bedroom window. Two yellow-green eyes staring back at him.

And ten meters behind that, three more microdrones loitered in place, a hundred meters above the boulevard below. Grouped tightly to compound their explosive effect.

The glass had already left his hand.

Vodka fountaining up, describing an arc in the air.

He was through the door into the hall by the time the martini glass shattered behind him.

He reached the big room when the first microdrone hit, penetrating the armored glass of his bedroom window.

Heat at his back, a rising hum.

The other three rocketing through the breach hole into the penthouse.

He hurdled a treadmill, shoulder glancing off a heavy bag.

Slammed into the sliding glass door of the

south-facing balcony.

Wrenched it open, ripped it shut behind him. He careened into the railing, whirling to face the drop, cars and pedestrians swimming vertiginously below. Nowhere left to go.

An instant later the penthouse exploded.

ACKNOWLEDGMENTS

Orphan X gets to live and breathe because of you, my readers. Your engagement, your energy, your passion is why I get to spend my days in a delightful reverie.

You have my gratitude.

As do:

The booksellers and librarians who have been with me from my childhood, shepherds to the world of stories.

My publishing team at Minotaur Books: Keith Kahla, Andrew Martin, Sally Richardson, Don Weisberg, Jennifer Enderlin, Alice Pfeifer, Hector DeJean, Paul Hochman, Kelley Ragland, and Martin Quinn.

My crew at Michael Joseph/Penguin Group UK: Rowland White, Louise Moore, Laura Nicol, Ariel Pakier, Jon Kennedy, and Christina Ellicott.

My representatives: Lisa Erbach Vance and Aaron Priest of the Aaron Priest Agency; Caspian Dennis at the Abner Stein

Agency; Stephen F. Breimer, Esq.; Dana Kaye, Julia Borcherts, Hailey Dezort, and Nicole Leimbach of Kaye Publicity.

The subject matter experts Evan depended on for this adventure, including:

— Geoff Baehr, expert in all matters digital

— Michael "Borski" Borohovski, hacker

— Duane Dwyer, United States Marine, co-founder of Strider Knives, professor of Gracie Barra Brasilian Jiujitsu

— Philip Eisner, narrative wizard

— Dr. Melissa Hurwitz, physician

— Jeremy Levitan, PhD, expert in microdrones

— Dr. Bret Nelson, emergency medicine (offense and defense)

— Kurata Tadashi, twenty-first-century samurai

Delinah Hurwitz, my heart; Natalie Hurwitz, my light; Simba and Cairo, my id; and Marjorie and Alfred Hurwitz, my foundation.

ABOUT THE AUTHOR

Gregg Hurwitz is the *New York Times* bestselling author of the Orphan X books, including *Into the Fire.* Critically acclaimed, his novels have graced top ten lists and have been published in 22 languages. Additionally, he's written screenplays for and sold scripts to many of the major studios, and written, developed, and produced television for various networks. Hurwitz resides in Los Angeles.

The employees of Thorndike Press hope you have enjoyed this Large Print book. All our Thorndike, Wheeler, and Kennebec Large Print titles are designed for easy reading, and all our books are made to last. Other Thorndike Press Large Print books are available at your library, through selected bookstores, or directly from us.

For information about titles, please call:
  (800) 223-1244

or visit our website at:
  gale.com/thorndike

To share your comments, please write:
  Publisher
  Thorndike Press
  10 Water St., Suite 310
  Waterville, ME 04901